DIANA PALMER

SECOND CHANCES

HQN™

ISBN 0-373-77181-9

SECOND CHANCES

Copyright © 2006 by Harlequin Books S.A.

The publisher acknowledges the copyright holder of the individual works as follows:

ENAMORED
Copyright © 1988 by Diana Palmer

MYSTERY MAN
Copyright © 1997 by Diana Palmer

www.HQNBooks.com

Printed in U.S.A.

CONTENTS

ENAMORED

PROLOGUE

THE GENTLE FACE ON THE starched white pillow was pale and very still. The man looking down at it scowled with unfamiliar concern. For so many years, his emotions had been caged. Tender feelings were a luxury no mercenary could afford, least of all a man with the reputation of Diego Laremos.

But this woman was no stranger, and the emotions he felt when he looked at her were still confused. It had been five years since he'd seen her, yet she seemed not to have aged a day. She would be twenty-six now, he thought absently. He was forty.

He hadn't expected her to be unconscious. When the hospital had contacted him, he almost hadn't come. Melissa Sterling had betrayed him years before. He wasn't anxious to renew their painful acquaintance, but out of curiosity and a sense of duty, he'd made the trip to southern Arizona. Now he was here, and it was not a subterfuge, a trap, as it had been before. She was injured and helpless; she was alive, though he'd given her up for dead all those long years ago. The cold emptiness inside him was giving way to memories, and that he couldn't allow.

He turned, tall and dark and immaculate in his charcoal-gray suit, to stare out the window at the well-kept grounds beyond the second-floor room Melissa Sterling occupied. He had a mustache now that he hadn't sported during the turbulent days she'd shared with him. He was a little more muscular, older. But age had only emphasized his elegant good looks, made him more mature. His dark eyes slid to the bed, to the slender body of this woman, this stranger, who had trapped him into marriage and then deserted him.

Melissa was tall for a woman, although he towered above her. She had long, wavy blond hair that had once curled below her waist. That had been cut, so that now it curved around her wan oval face. Her eyes were blue-shadowed, closed, her perfect mouth almost as white as her face, her straight nose barely wrinkling now and again as it protested the air tubes taped to it. She seemed surrounded by electronic equipment, by wires that led to various monitors.

An accident, the attending physician had said over a worse-than-poor telephone conversation the day before. An airplane crash that, by some miracle, she and the pilot and several other passengers on the commuter flight from Phoenix had survived. The plane had gone down in the desert outside Tucson, and she'd been brought here to the general hospital, unconscious. The emergency room staff had found a worn, carefully folded paper in her wallet that contained the only evidence of her marital status. A marriage license, written in Spanish; the fading ink stated that she was the *esposa* of one Diego Alejandro Rodriguez Ruiz Laremos of Dos Rios, Guatemala. Was Diego her husband, the physician had persisted, and if so, would he authorize emergency surgery to save her life?

He vaguely recalled asking if she had no other relatives, but the doctor had told him that her pitifully few belongings gave no evidence of any. So Diego had left his Guatemalan farm in the hands of his hired militia and flown himself all the way from Guatemala City to Tucson.

He'd had no sleep in the past twenty-four hours. He'd been smoking himself to death and reliving a tormenting past.

The woman in the bed stirred suddenly, moaning. He turned just as her eyes opened and then closed quickly again. They were gray. Big and soft, a delicate contrast to her blond fairness; her gray eyes were the only visible evidence of Melissa's Guatemalan mother, whose betrayal had brought anguish and dishonor to the Laremos family.

His black eyes ran slowly over her pale, still features and he wondered as he watched how he and Melissa had ever come to this....

CHAPTER ONE

IT WAS A MISTY RAIN, but Melissa Sterling didn't mind. Getting soaked was a small price to pay for a few precious minutes with Diego Laremos.

Diego's family had owned the *finca,* the giant Guatemalan farm that bordered her father's land, for four generations. And despite the fact that Melissa's late mother had been the cause of a bitter feud between the Laremos family and the Sterlings, that hadn't stopped Melissa from worshiping the son and heir to the Laremos name. Diego seemed not to mind her youthful adoration, or if he did, he was kind enough not to mock her for it.

There had been a storm the night before, and Melissa had ridden down to Mama Chavez's small house to make sure the old woman was all right, only to find that Diego, too, had been worried about his old nurse and had come to check on her. Melissa liked to visit her and listen to tales of Diego's youth and hear secret legends about the Maya.

Diego had brought some melons and fish for the old woman, whose family tree dated back to the very beginning of the Mayan empire, and now he was escorting Melissa back to her father's house.

Her dark eyes kept running over his lean, fit body, admiring the way he sat on his horse, the thick darkness of his hair under his panama hat. He wasn't an arrogant man, but he had a cold, quiet authority about him that bordered on it. He never had to raise his voice to his servants, and Melissa had only seen him in one fight. He was a dignified, self-contained man without an apparent weakness. But he was mysterious. He often disappeared for weeks at a time, and once he'd come home with scars on his cheek and a limp. Melissa had been curious, but she hadn't questioned him. Even at twenty, she was still shy with men, and especially with Diego. He'd rescued her once when she'd gotten lost in the rain forest searching for some old Mayan ruins, and she'd loved him secretly ever since.

"I suppose your grandmother and sister would die if they knew I was within a mile of you," she sighed, brushing back her long wavy blond hair as she glanced at him with a hesitant smile that was echoed in the soft gray of her eyes.

"They bear your family no great love, that is true," he agreed. The distant mountains were a blue haze in front of them as they rode. "It is difficult for my family to forget that Edward Sterling stole my father's *novia* on the eve of their wedding and eloped with her. My father spoke of her often, with grief. My grandmother never stopped blaming your family for his grief."

"My father loved her, and she loved him," Melissa defended. "It was only an arranged marriage that your father would have had with her, anyway, not a love match. Your father was much older than my mother, and he'd been a widower for years."

"Your father is British," he said coldly. "He has never understood our way of life. Here, honor is life itself. When he stole away my father's betrothed, he dishonored my family." Diego glanced at Melissa, not adding that his father had also been counting on her late mother's inheritance to restore the family fortunes. Diego had considered his father's attitude rather mercenary, but the old man had cared about Sheila Sterling in his cool way.

Diego reined in his mount and stared at Melissa, taking in her slender body, in jeans and a pink shirt unbuttoned to the swell of her breasts. She attracted him far more than he wanted to admit. He couldn't allow himself to become involved with the daughter of the woman who'd disgraced his family.

"Your father should not let you wander around in this manner," he said unexpectedly, although he softened the words with a faint smile. "You know there has been increased guerrilla activity here. It is not safe."

"I wasn't thinking," she replied.

"You never do, *chica*," he sighed, cocking his hat over one eye. "Your daydreaming will be your downfall one day. These are dangerous times."

"All times are dangerous," she said with a shy smile. "But I feel safe with you."

He raised a dark eyebrow. "And that is the most dangerous daydream of all," he mused. "But no doubt you have not yet realized it. Come; we must move on."

"In just a minute." She drew a camera from her pocket and pointed it toward him, smiling at his grimace. "I know, not again, you're thinking. Can I help it if I can't get the right perspective on the painting of you I'm working on? I need another shot. Just one, I promise." She clicked the shutter before he could protest.

"This famous painting is taking one long time, *niña,*" he commented. "You have been hard at it for eight months, and not one glimpse have I had of it."

"I work slow," she prevaricated. In actual fact, she couldn't draw a straight line without a ruler. The photo was to add to her collection of pictures of him, to sit and sigh over in the privacy of her room. To build dreams around. Because dreams were all she was ever likely to have of Diego, and she knew it. His family would oppose any mention of having Melissa under their roof, just as they opposed Diego's friendship with her.

"When do you go off to college?" he asked unexpectedly.

She sighed as she pocketed the camera. "Pretty soon, I guess. I begged off for a year after school, just to be with Dad, but this unrest is making him more stubborn about sending me away. I don't want to go to the States. I want to stay here."

"Your father may be wise to insist," Diego murmured, although he didn't like to think about riding

around his estate with no chance of being waylaid by
Melissa. He'd grown used to her. To a man as worldly
and experienced and cynical as Diego had become over
the years, Melissa was a breath of spring air. He loved
her innocence, her shy adoration. Given the chance, he
was all too afraid he might be tempted to appreciate her
exquisite young body, as well. She was slender, tall,
with long, tanned legs, breasts that had just the right
shape and a waist that was tiny, flaring to full, gently
curving hips. She wasn't beautiful, but her fair complexion was exquisite in its frame of long, tangled blond hair,
and her gray eyes held a kind of serenity far beyond her
years. Her nose was straight, her mouth soft and pretty.
In the right clothes and with the right training, she would
be a unique hostess, a wife of whom a man could be jus-
tifiably proud....

That thought startled Diego. He had had no intention
of thinking of Melissa in those terms. If he ever married, it would be to a Guatemalan woman of good family, not to a woman whose father had already once
disgraced the name of Laremos.

"You're always at home these days," Melissa said as
they rode along the valley, with the huge Atitlán volcano
in the distance against the green jungle. She loved Guatemala, she loved the volcanos and the lakes and rivers,
the tropical jungle, the banana and coffee plantations
and the spreading valleys. She especially loved the mysterious Mayan ruins that one found so unexpectedly. She
loved the markets in the small villages and the friendly

warmth of the Guatemalan people whose Mayan ancestors had once ruled here.

"The *finca* demands much of my time since my father's death," he replied. "Besides, *niña,* I was getting too old for the work I used to do."

She glanced at him. "You never talked about it. What did you do?"

He smiled faintly. "Ah, that would be telling. How did your father fare with the fruit company? Were they able to recompense him for his losses during the storm?"

A tropical storm had damaged the banana plantation in which her father had a substantial interest. This year's crop had been a tremendous loss. Like Diego, though, her father had other investments—such as the cattle he and Diego raised on their adjoining properties. But as a rule, fruit was the biggest money-maker.

She shook her head. "I don't know. He doesn't share business with me. I guess he thinks I'm too dumb to understand." She smiled, her mind far away on the small book she'd found recently in her mother's trunk. "You know, Dad is so different from the way he was when my mother knew him. He's so sedate and quiet these days. Mama wrote that he was always in the thick of things when they were first married, very daring and adventurous."

"I imagine her death changed him, little one," he said absently.

"Maybe it did," she murmured. She looked at him curiously. "Apollo said that you were the best there was at your job," she added quickly. "And that someday you might tell me about it."

He said something under his breath, glaring at her. "My past is something I never expect to share with anyone. Apollo had no right to say such a thing to you."

His voice chilled her when it had that icily formal note in it. She shifted restlessly. "He's a nice man. He helped Dad round up some of the stray cattle one day when there was a storm. He must be good at his job, or you wouldn't keep him on."

"He is good at his job," he said, making a mental note to have a long talk with the black American ex-military policeman who worked for him and had been part of the band of mercenaries Diego had once belonged to. "But it does not include discussing me with you."

"Don't be mad at him, please," she asked gently. "It was my fault, not his. I'm sorry I asked. I know you're very close about your private life, but it bothered me that you came home that time so badly hurt." She lowered her eyes. "I was worried."

He bit back a sharp reply. He couldn't tell her about his past. He couldn't tell her that he'd been a professional mercenary, that his job had been the destruction of places and sometimes people, that it had paid exceedingly well, or that the only thing he had put at risk was his life. He kept his clandestine operations very quiet at home; only the government officials for whom he sometimes did favors knew about him. As for friends and acquaintances, it wouldn't do for them to know how he earned the money that kept the *finca* solvent.

He shrugged indifferently. *"No importa."* He was silent for a moment, his black eyes narrow as he glanced at her. "You should marry," he said unexpectedly. "It is time your father arranged for a *novio* for you, *niña."*

She wanted to suggest Diego, but that would be courting disaster. She studied her slender hands on the reins. "I can arrange my own marriage. I don't want to be promised to some wealthy old man just for the sake of my family fortunes."

Diego smiled at her innocence. "Oh, *niña,* the idealism of youth. By the time you reach my age, you will have lost every trace of it. Infatuation does not last. It is the poorest foundation for a lasting relationship, because it can exist where there are no common interests whatsoever."

"You sound so cold," she murmured. "Don't you believe in love?"

"Love is not a word I know," he replied carelessly. "I have no interest in it."

Melissa felt sick and shaky and frightened. She'd always assumed that Diego was a romantic like herself. But he certainly didn't sound like one. And with that attitude he probably wouldn't be prejudiced against an arranged, financially beneficial marriage. His grandmother was very traditional, and she lived with him. Melissa didn't like the thought of Diego marrying anyone else, but he was thirty-five and soon he had to think of an heir. She stared at the pommel on her saddle, idly moving the reins against it. "That's a very cynical attitude."

He looked at her with raised black eyebrows. "You and I are worlds apart, do you know that? Despite your Guatemalan upbringing and your excellent Spanish, you still think like an Anglo."

"Perhaps I've got more of my mother in me than you think," she confessed sheepishly. "She was Spanish, but she eloped with the best man at her own wedding."

"It is nothing to joke about."

She brushed back her long hair. "Don't go cold on me, Diego," she chided softly. "I didn't mean it. I'm really very traditional."

His dark eyes ran over her, and the expression in them made her heart race. "Yes. Of that I am quite certain," he said. His eyes slid up to hers again, holding them until she colored. He smiled at her expression. He liked her reactions, so virginal and flattering. "Even my grandmother approves of the very firm hand your father keeps on you. Twenty, and not one evening alone with a young man out of the sight of your father."

She avoided his piercing glance. "Not that many young men come calling. I'm not an heiress and I'm not pretty."

"Beauty is transient; character endures. You suit me as you are, *pequeña*," he said gently. "And in time the young men will come with flowers and proposals of marriage. There is no rush."

She shifted in the saddle. "That's what you think," she said miserably. "I spend my whole life alone."

"Loneliness is a fire which tempers steel," he counseled. "Benefit from it. In days to come it will give you a serenity which you will value."

She gave him a searching look. "I'll bet you haven't spent your life alone," she said.

He shrugged. "Not totally, perhaps," he said, giving away nothing. "But I like my own company from time to time. I like, too, the smell of the coffee trees, the graceful sweep of the leaves on banana trees, the sultry wind in my face, the proud Maya ruins and the towering volcanoes. These things are my heritage. Your heritage," he added with a tender smile. "One day you will look back on this as the happiest time of your life. Don't waste it."

That was possible, she mused. She almost shivered with the delight of having Diego so close beside her and the solitude of the open country around them. Yes, this was the good time, full of the richness of life and love. Never would she wish herself anywhere else.

He left her at the gate that led past the small kitchen garden to the white stucco house with its red roof. He got down from his horse and lifted her from the saddle, his lean hands firm and sure at her small waist. For one small second he held her so that her gaze was level with his, and something touched his black eyes. But it was gone abruptly, and he put her down and stepped back.

She forced herself to move away from the tangy scent of leather and tobacco that clung to his white shirt. She forced herself not to look where it was unbuttoned over a tanned olive chest feathered with black hair. She wanted so desperately to reach up and kiss his hard mouth, to hold him to her, to experience all the wonder of her first passion. But Diego saw only a young girl, not a woman.

"I will leave your mare at the stable," he promised as he mounted gracefully. "Keep close to home from now on," he added firmly. "Your father will tell you, as I already have, that it is not safe to ride alone."

"If you say so, Señor Laremos," she murmured, and curtsied impudently.

Once he would have laughed at that impish gesture. But her teasing had a sudden and unexpected effect. His blood surged in his veins, his body tautened. His black eyes went to her soft breasts and lingered there before he dragged them back to her face. *"¡Hasta luego!"* he said tersely, and wheeled his mount without another word.

Melissa stared after him with her heart in her throat. Even in her innocence, she'd recognized the hot, quick flash of desire in his eyes. She felt the look all the way to her toes and burned with an urge to run after him, to make sure she hadn't misunderstood his reaction. To have Diego look at her in that way was the culmination of every dream she'd ever had about him.

She went into the house, tingling with banked-down

excitement. From now on, every day was going to be even more like a surprise package.

Estrella had outdone herself with supper. The small, plump *Ladina* woman had made steak with peppers and cheese and salsa, with seasoned rice to go with it, and cool melon for a side dish. Melissa hugged her as she sniffed the delicious aroma of the meal.

"Delicioso," she said with a grin.

"Steak is to put on a bruised eye," Estrella sniffed. "The best meat is iguana."

Melissa made a face. "I'd eat snake first," she promised.

Estrella grinned wickedly. "You did. Last night."

The younger woman's eyes widened. "That was chicken."

Estrella shook her head. "Snake." She laughed when Melissa made a threatening gesture. "No, no, no, you cannot hit me. It was your father's idea!"

"My father wouldn't do such a thing," she said.

"You do not know your father," the *Ladina* woman said with a twinkle in her eyes. "Get out now, let me work. Go and practice your piano or Señora Lopez will be incensed when she comes to hear you on Friday."

Melissa sighed. "I suppose she will, that patient soul. She never gives up on me, even when I know I'll never be able to run my cadences without slipping up on the minor keys."

"Practice!"

She nodded, then changed the subject. "Dad didn't phone, I suppose?" she asked.

"No." Estrella glanced at Melissa with one of her black eyes narrowed. "He will not like you riding with Señor Laremos."

"How did you know I was?" Melissa exclaimed. These flashes of instant knowledge still puzzled her as they had from childhood. Estrella always seemed to know things before she actually heard about them formally.

"That," the *Ladina* woman said smugly, "is my secret. Out with you. Let me cook."

Melissa went, hoping Estrella wasn't planning to share her knowledge with her father.

And apparently the *Ladina* woman didn't, but Edward Sterling knew anyway. He came back from his business trip looking preoccupied, his graying blond hair damp with rain, his elegant white suit faintly wrinkled.

"Luis Martinez saw you out riding with Diego Laremos," he said abruptly, without greeting her. Melissa sat with her hands poised over the piano in the spacious living room. "I thought we'd had this conversation already."

Melissa drew a steadying breath and put her hands in her lap. "I can't help it," she said, giving up all attempts at subterfuge. "I suppose you don't believe that."

"I believe it," he said, to her surprise. "I even understand it. But what I don't understand is why Laremos encourages you. He isn't a marrying man, Melissa, and he knows what it would do to me to see you compromised." His face hardened. "Which is what disturbs me the most. The whole Laremos family would love to see us humbled. Don't cut your leg and invite a shark to kiss it better," he added with a faint attempt at humor.

She threw up her hands. "You won't believe that Diego has no ulterior motives, will you? That he genuinely likes me?"

"I think he likes the adulation," he said sharply. He poured brandy into a snifter and sat down, crossing his long legs. "Listen, sweet, it's time you knew the truth about your hero. It's a long story, and it isn't pretty. I had hoped that you'd go away to college, and no harm done. But this hero worship has to stop. Do you have any idea what Diego Laremos did for a living until about two years ago?"

She blinked. "He traveled on business, I suppose. The Laremoses have money—"

"The Laremoses have nothing, or had nothing," he interrupted curtly. "The old man was hoping to marry Sheila and get his hands on her father's supposed millions. What Laremos didn't know was that Sheila's father had lost everything and was hoping to get *his* hands on the Laremoses' banana plantations. It was a comedy of errors, and then I found your mother and that was the end of the plotting. To this day, none of your mother's people will speak to me, and the Laremoses only do out of politeness. And the great irony of it is that none of them know the truth about each other's families. There never was any money—only pipe dreams about mergers."

"Then, if the Laremoses had nothing," Melissa ventured, "why do they have so much these days?"

"Because your precious Diego had a lot of guts and few equals with an automatic weapon," Edward Sterling said bluntly. "He was a professional soldier."

Melissa didn't move. She didn't speak. She stared blankly at her father. "Diego isn't hard enough to go around killing people."

"Don't kid yourself," came the reply. "Haven't you even realized that the men he surrounds himself with at the Casa de Luz are his old confederates? That man they call First Shirt, and the black ex-soldier, Apollo Blain, and Semson and Drago…all of them are ex-mercenaries with no country to call their own. They have no future except here, working for their old comrade."

Melissa felt her hands trembling. She sat on them. It was beginning to come together. The bits and pieces of Diego's life that she'd seen and wondered about were making sense now—a terrible kind of sense.

"I see you understand," her father said, his voice very quiet. "You know, I don't think less of him for what he's done. But a past like his would be rough for a woman to take. Because of what he's done, he's a great deal less vulnerable than an ordinary man. More than likely his feelings are locked in irons. It will take more than an innocent, worshiping girl to unlock them, Melissa. And you aren't even in the running in his mind. He'll marry a Guatemalan woman, if he ever marries. He won't marry you. Our unfortunate connection in the past will assure that, don't you see?"

Her eyes stung with tears. Of course she did, but

hearing it didn't help. She tried to smile, and the tears overflowed.

"Baby." Her father got up and pulled her gently into his arms, rocking her. "I'm sorry, but there's no future for you with Diego Laremos. It will be best if you go away, and the sooner the better."

Melissa had to agree. "You're right." She dabbed at her tears. "I didn't know. Diego never told me about his past. I suppose he was saving it for a last resort," she said, trying to bring some lightness to the moment. "Now I understand what he meant about not knowing what love was. I guess Diego couldn't afford to let himself love anyone, considering the line of work he was in."

"I don't imagine he could," her father agreed. He smoothed her hair back. "I wish your mother was still alive. She'd have known what to say."

"Oh, you're not doing too bad," Melissa told him. She wiped her eyes. "I guess I'll get over Diego one day."

"One day," Edward agreed. "But this is for the best, Melly. Your world and his would never fit together. They're too different."

She looked up. "Diego said that, too."

Edward nodded. "Then Laremos realizes it. That will be just as well. He won't put any obstacles in the way."

Melissa tried to forget that afternoon and the way Diego had held her, the way he'd looked at her. Maybe he didn't know what love was, but something inside him had reacted to her in a new and different way. And now she was going to have to leave before she could find out what he felt or if he could come to care for her.

But perhaps her father was right. If Diego felt anything, it was physical, not emotional. Desire, in its place, might be exquisite, but without love it was just a shadow. Diego's past had shocked her. A man like that—was he even capable of love?

Melissa kept her thoughts to herself. There was no sense in sharing them with her father and worrying him even more. "How did it go in Guatemala City?" she asked instead, trying to divert him.

He laughed. "Well, it's not as bad as I thought at first. Let's eat, and I'll explain it to you. If you're old enough to go to college, I suppose you're old enough to be told about the family finances."

Melissa smiled at him. It was the first time he'd offered that kind of information. In an odd way, she felt as if her father accepted the fact that she was an adult.

CHAPTER TWO

MELISSA HARDLY SLEPT. She dreamed of Diego in a confusion of gunfire and harsh words, and she woke up feeling that she'd hardly closed her eyes.

She ate breakfast with her father, who announced that he had to go back into the city to finalize a contract with the fruit company.

"See that you stay home," he cautioned her as he left. "No more tête-à-têtes with Diego Laremos."

"I've got to practice piano," she said absently, and kissed his cheek as he went out the door. "You be careful, too."

He drove away, and she went into the living room where the small console piano sat, opening her practice book to the cadences. She grimaced as she began to fumble through the notes, all thumbs.

Her heart just wasn't in it, so instead she practiced a much-simplified bit of Sibelius, letting herself go in the expression of its sweet, sad message. She was going to have to leave Guatemala, and Diego. There was no hope at all. She knew in her heart that she was never going to get over him, but it was only beginning to dawn on her that the future would be pretty bleak if she stayed. She'd wear herself out fighting his indifference, bruise her heart attempting to change his will. Why had she ever imagined that a man like Diego might come to love her? And now, knowing his background as she did, she realized that it would take a much more experienced, sophisticated woman than herself to reach such a man.

She got up from the piano, closing the lid, and sat down at her father's desk. There were sheets of white bond paper still scattered on it, along with the pencil he'd been using for his calculations. Melissa picked up the pencil and wrote several lines of breathless prose about unrequited love. Then, impulsively, she wrote a note to Diego asking him to meet her that night in the jungle so that she could show him how much she loved him until dawn came to find them....

Reading it over, she laughed at the very idea of sending such a message to the very correct, very formal Señor Diego Laremos. She crumpled it on the desk and got up, pacing restlessly. She read and went back to the piano, ate a lunch that she didn't really taste and finally decided that she'd go mad if she had to spend the rest of the afternoon just sitting around. Her father had said not to leave the house, but she couldn't bear sitting still.

She saddled her mare and, after waving to an exasperated, irritated Estrella, rode away from the house and down toward the valley. She wondered at the agitated way Estrella, with one of the vaqueros at her side, was waving, but she soon lost interest and quickened her pace. She didn't want to be called back like a delinquent child. She had to ride off some of her nervous energy.

She was galloping down the hill and across the valley when a popping sound caught her attention. Startled, her mare reared up and threw Melissa onto the hard ground.

Her shoulder and collarbone connected with some sharp rocks, and she grimaced and moaned as she tried to sit up. The mare kept going, her mane flying in the breeze, and that was when Melissa saw the approaching horseman, three armed men hot on his heels. Diego!

She couldn't believe what she was seeing. It was unreal, on this warm summer afternoon, to see such violence in the grassy meadow. So the reports about the guerrillas and the political unrest were true. Sometimes, so far away from Guatemala City, she felt out of touch with the world. But now, with armed men flying across the grassy plain, danger was alarmingly real. Her heart ran wild as she sat there, and the first touch of fear brushed along her spine. She was alone and unarmed, and the thought of what those men might do to her if Diego fell curled her hair. Why hadn't she listened to the warnings?

The popping sound came again, and she realized that the men were shooting at Diego. But he didn't look back. His attention was riveted now on Melissa, and he kept coming, his mount moving in a weaving pattern to make less of a target for the pistols of the men behind him. He circled Melissa and vaulted out of the saddle, some kind of small, chubby-looking weapon in his hands.

"Por Dios—" He dropped to his knees and fired off a volley at the approaching horsemen. The sound deafened her, bringing the taste of nausea into her throat as she realized how desperate the situation really was. "Are you wounded?"

"No, I fell. Diego—"

"Silencio!" He fired another burst at the guerrillas, who had stopped suddenly in the middle of the valley to fire back at him. He pushed Melissa to the ground with gentle violence and aimed again, deliberately this time. He didn't want her to see it, but her life depended on whether or not he could stop his pursuers. He couldn't bear the thought of those brutal hands on her soft skin.

The firing from the other side stopped abruptly. Melissa peeked up at Diego. He didn't look like the man she knew so well. His deeply tanned face was steely, rigid, his hands incredibly steady on the small weapon.

He cursed steadily in Spanish as he surveyed his handiwork, terrible curses that shocked Melissa. She tried not to cry out in fear. The smell of gunsmoke was acrid in her nostrils, her ears were deafened by the sound of the small machine gun.

Diego turned then to sweep Melissa up in his arms, holding the automatic weapon in the hand under her knees. He got her out of the meadow with quick, long strides, his powerful body absorbing her weight as if he didn't even feel it. He darted with her into the thick jungle at the edge of the meadow and kept going. Over his shoulder she saw the horses scatter, two of the riders bent over their saddles as if in pain, the third one lying still on the ground. Diego's horse was long gone, like Melissa's.

Now that they were temporarily out of danger, relief made her body limp. She'd been shot at. She'd actually been shot at! It seemed like some impossible nightmare. Thank God Diego had seen her. She shuddered to think what might have happened if those men had come upon her and she'd been alone.

"Were you hit?" Diego asked curtly as he laid her down against a tree a good way into the undergrowth. "You're bleeding."

"I fell off," she faltered, her eyes helpless on his angry face as he bent over her. "I hit…something. Diego, those men, are we far enough away…?"

"For the moment, yes," he said shortly. "Until they get reinforcements, at least. Melissa, I told you not to go riding alone, did I not?" he demanded.

His eyes were black, and she thought she'd never really seen him before. Not the real man under the lazy good humor, the patient indulgence. This man was a stranger. The mercenary her father had told her about. The unmasked man.

"Where are your men?" she asked huskily, her body becoming rigid as his lean fingers went to the front of her blouse and started to unbutton it. "Diego, no!" she burst out in embarrassment.

He glowered at her. "The bleeding has to be stopped,"

he said curtly. "This is no time for outraged modesty. Lie still."

While the wind whispered through the tall trees, she fought silently, but he moved her hands aside with growing impatience and peeled the blouse away from the flimsy bra she was wearing. His black eyes made one soft foray over the transparent material covering her firm young breasts, and then glanced at her shoulder, which was scratched and bleeding.

"We are cut off," he muttered. "I made the mistake of assuming a few rounds would frighten off a guerrilla who was scouting the area around my cattle pens. He left, but only to come back with a dozen or so of his amigos. Apollo and the rest of my men are at the casa, trying to hold them off until Semson can get the government troops to assist them. Like a fool, I allowed myself to be cut off from the others and pursued."

"I suppose you'd have made it back except for me," she murmured quietly, her pale gray eyes apologetic as she looked up at him.

"Will you never learn to listen?" he asked coldly. He had his handkerchief at the scraped places now and was soothing away the blood. He grimaced. "This will need attention. It's a miracle that your breast escaped severe damage, *niña,* although it is badly bruised."

She flushed, averting her eyes from his scrutiny. Very likely, a woman's naked body held no mysteries for Diego, but Melissa had never been seen unclad by a man.

Diego ignored her embarrassment, spreading the

handkerchief over the abrasions and refastening her blouse to hold it in place. Nothing of what he was feeling showed in his expression, but the sight of her untouched, perfect young body was making him ache unpleasantly. Until now it had been possible to think of Melissa as a child. But after tonight, he'd never be able to think of her that way again. It was going to complicate his life, he was certain of it. "We must get to higher ground, and quickly. I scattered them, but depend on it, they will be back." He helped her up. "Can you walk?"

"Of course," she said unsteadily, her eyes wide and curious as she looked at the small bulky weapon he scooped up from the ground. He had a cartridge belt around his shoulder, over his white shirt.

"An Uzi," he told her, ignoring her fascination. "An automatic weapon of Israeli design. Thank God I listened to my old instincts and carried it with me this afternoon, or I would already be dead. I am deeply sorry that you had to see what happened, little one, but if I had not fired back at them…"

"I know that," she said. She glanced at him, then away, as he led her deeper into the jungle. "Diego, my father told me what you used to do for a living."

He stopped and turned around, his black eyes intent on hers because he needed to know her reaction to the discovery. He searched her expression, but there was no contempt, no horror, no shock. "To discourage you, I presume, from any deeper relationship with me?" he asked unexpectedly.

She blushed and lowered her gaze. "I guess I've been pretty transparent all the way around," she said bitterly. "I didn't realize everybody knew what a fool I was making of myself."

"I am thirty-five years old," he said quietly. "And women have been, forgive me, a permissible vice. Your face is expressive, Melissa, and your innocence makes you all the more vulnerable. But I would hardly call you a fool for feeling an—" he hesitated over the word "—attraction. But this is not the time to discuss it. Come, *pequeña,* we must find cover. We have little time."

It was hard going. The jungle growth of vines and underbrush was thick, and Diego had only his knife, not a machete. He was careful to leave no visible trace of the path they made, but the men following them were likely to be experienced trackers. Melissa knew she should be afraid, but being with Diego made fear impossible. She knew that he'd protect her, no matter what. And despite the danger, just being with him was sheer delight.

She watched the muscles in his lean, fit body ripple as he moved aside the clinging vines for her. Once, his dark eyes caught hers as she was going under his arm, and they fell on her mouth with an expression that made her blood run wild through her veins. It was only a moment in time, but the flare of awareness made her clumsy and self-conscious. She remembered all too well the feel of his hard fingers on her soft skin as he'd removed the blood and bandaged the scrapes. She thought of the time ahead, because darkness would come soon. Would they stay in the jungle overnight? And would he hold her in the night, safe in his arms, against his warm body? She trembled at the delicious image, already feeling the muscles of his arms closing around her.

He paused to look at the compass in the handle of his knife, checking his bearings.

"There are ruins very near here," he murmured. "With luck, we should be able to get to them before dark." He looked up at the skies, which were darkening with the threat of a storm. "Rain clouds," he mused. "We shall more than likely be drenched before we reach cover. Your father is not at home, I assume?"

"No," she said miserably. "He'll be worried sick. And furious."

"Murderously so, I imagine," he said with an irritated sigh. "Oh, Melissa, what a situation your impulsive nature has created for us."

"I'm sorry," she said gently. "Really I am."

He lifted his head and stared down into her face with something like arrogance. "Are you? To be alone with me like this? Are you really sorry, *querida?*" he asked, and his voice was like velvet, deep and soft and tender.

Her lips parted as she tried to answer him, but she was trembling with nervous pleasure. Her gray eyes slid over his face like loving hands.

"An unfair question," he murmured. "When I can see the answer. Come."

He turned away from her, his body rippling with desire for her. He was too hot-blooded not to feel it when he looked at her slender body, her sweet innocence like a seductive garment around her. He wanted her as he'd never wanted another woman, but to give in to his feelings would be to place himself at the mercy of her father's retribution. He was already concerned about how it would look if they were forced to bed down in the ruins. Apollo and the others would come looking for him, but the rain would wash away the tracks and slow them down, and the guerrillas would be in hot pursuit, as well. He sighed. It was going to be difficult, whichever way they went.

The rain came before they got much further, drenching them in wet warmth. Melissa felt her hair plastered against her scalp, her clothing sticking to her like glue. Her jeans and boots were soaked, her shirt literally transparent as it dripped in the pounding rain.

Diego's black hair was like a skullcap, and his very Spanish features were more prominent now, his olive complexion and black eyes making him look faintly pagan. He had Mayan blood as well as Spanish because of the intermarriage of his Madrid-born grandparents with native Guatemalans. His high cheekbones hinted at his Indian ancestry, just as his straight nose and thin, sensual lips denoted his Spanish heritage. Watching him, Melissa wondered where he had inherited his height, because he was as tall as her British father.

"There," he said suddenly, and they came to a clearing where a Mayan temple sat like a gray sentinel in the green jungle. It was only partially standing, but at least one part of it seemed to have a roof.

Diego led her through the vined entrance, frightening away a huge snake. She shuddered, thinking of the coming darkness, but Diego was with her. He'd keep her safe.

Inside, it was musty and smelled of stone and dust, but the walls in one side of the ruin were almost intact, and there were a few timbers overhead that time hadn't completely rotted.

Melissa shivered. "We'll catch pneumonia," she whispered.

"Not in this heat, *niña*," he said with a faint smile. He moved over to a vine-covered opening in the stone wall. At least he'd be able to see the jungle from which they'd just departed. With a sigh, he stripped off his shirt and hung it over a jutting timber, stretching wearily.

Melissa watched him, her gaze caressing the darkly tanned muscles and the faint wedge of black hair that arrowed down to the belt around his lean waist. Just looking at him made her tingle, and she couldn't hide her helpless longing to touch him.

He saw her reaction, and all his good intentions melted. She looked lovely with her clothing plastered to her exquisite body, and through the wet blouse he could see the very texture of her breasts, their mauve tips firm and beautifully formed. His jaw tautened as he stared at her.

She started to lift her arms, to fold them over herself, because the way he was looking at her frightened her a little. But he turned abruptly and started out.

"I'll get some branches," he said tersely. "We'll need something to keep us from getting filthy if we have to stay here very long."

While he was gone, Melissa stripped off her blouse and wrung it out. It didn't help much, but it did remove some of the moisture. She dabbed at her hair and pushed the strands away from her face, knowing that she must look terrible.

Diego came back minutes later with some wild-banana leaves and palm branches that he spread on the ground to make a place to sit. He was wetter than ever, because the rain was still coming down in torrents.

"Our pursuers are going to find this weather difficult to track us through," he mused as he pulled a cigarette lighter from his pocket and managed to light a small cheroot. He eased back on one elbow to smoke it, studying Melissa with intent appreciation. She'd put the blouse back on, but even though it was a little drier, her breasts were still blatantly visible through it.

"I guess they will," she murmured, answering him.

"It embarrasses you, *niña,* for me to look at you so openly?" he asked quietly.

"I don't have much experience…" She faltered, blushing.

He blew out a thick cloud of smoke while his eyes made a meal of her. It was madness to allow himself that liberty, but he couldn't seem to help himself. She was untouched, and her eyes were shyly worshipful as she looked at his body. He wanted more than anything to touch her, to undress her slowly and carefully, to show her the delight of making love. His heart began to throb as he saw images of them together on the makeshift bedding, her body receptive to his, open to his possession.

Melissa was puzzled by his behavior. He'd always been so correct when they'd been together, but he wasn't bothering to disguise his interest in her body, and the look on his face was readable even to a novice.

"Why did you become a mercenary?" she asked, hoping to divert him.

He shrugged. "It was a question of finances. We were desperate, and my father was unable to face the degradation of seeking work after having had money all his life. I had a reckless nature, and I enjoyed the danger of combat. After I served in the army, I heard of a group that needed a small-arms expert for some 'interesting work.' I applied." He smiled in reminiscence. "It was an exciting time, but once or twice I had a close call. The others slowly drifted away to other occupations, other callings, but I continued. And then I began to slow down, and there was a mistake that almost cost me my life." He lifted the cheroot to his lips. "I had enough wealth by then not to mind settling down to a less demanding life-style. I came home."

"Do you miss it?" she asked softly, studying his handsome face.

"On occasion. There were good times. A special feeling of camaraderie with men who faced death with me."

"And women, I guess," she said hesitantly, her face more expressive than she realized.

His black eyes ran over her body like hands, slow and steady and frankly possessive. "And women," he said quietly. "Are you shocked?"

She swallowed, lowering her eyes. "I never imagined that you were a monk, Diego."

He felt himself tautening as he watched her, longed for her. The rain came harder, and she jumped as a streak of lightning burst near the temple and a shuddering thunderclap followed it.

"The lightning comes before the noise," he reminded her. "One never hears the fatal flash."

"How encouraging," she said through her teeth. "Do you have any more comforting thoughts to share?"

He smiled faintly as he put out the cheroot and laid it to one side. "Not for the moment."

He took her by the shoulders and laid her down against the palms and banana leaves, his lean hands on the buttons of her shirt once more. This time she didn't fight and she didn't protest, she simply watched him with eyes as big as saucers.

"I want to make sure the bleeding has stopped," he said softly. He pulled the edges of the blouse open and lifted the handkerchief that he'd placed over the cut. His black eyes narrowed, and he grimaced. "This may leave a scar," he said, tracing the wound with his forefinger. "A pity, on such exquisite skin."

Her breath rattled in her throat. The touch of his hand

made her feel reckless. All her buried longings were coming to the surface during this unexpected interlude with him, his body above her, his chest as bare and brawny as she'd dreamed it would be.

"I have no healing balm," he said softly, searching her eyes. "But perhaps *pequeña,* I could kiss it better...."

Even as he spoke, he bent, and Melissa moaned sharply as she felt the moist warmth of his mouth on her skin. Her hands clenched beside her, her back arched helplessly.

Startled by such a passionate reaction from a girl so virginal, he lifted his head to look at her. He was surprised, proud, when he saw the pleasure that made her cheeks burn, her eyes grow drowsy and bright, her lips part hungrily. It made him forget everything but the need to make her moan like that yet again, to see her eyes as she felt the first stirrings of passion in her untried body. The thought of her innocence and his resolve not to touch her vanished like the threat of danger.

He slid one hand under the nape of her neck to support it, his fingers spreading against her scalp as he bent again. His lips touched her tenderly, his tongue lacing against the abrasions, trailing over her silky skin. She smelled of flowers, and the scent of her went to his head. His free hand went under her back and found the catch of her bra, releasing it. He pulled the straps away from her shoulder and lifted her gently to ease the wispy material down her arms along with her blouse, leaving her bare and shivering under his quiet, experienced eyes.

He hadn't meant to let it happen, but his hunger for her had burst its bonds. He couldn't hold back. He didn't want to. She was his. She belonged to him.

He stopped her impulsive movement to cover herself by shaking his head. "This between us will be a secret, something for the two of us alone to share," he whispered. His dark eyes went to her breasts, adoring them. "Such lovely young breasts," he breathed, bending toward them. "So sweet, so tempting, so exquisitely formed…"

His lips touched the hard tip of her breast, and she went rigid. His arm went under her to support her back, and his free hand edged between them, raising sweet fires as it traced over her rib cage and belly before it went up to tease at the bottom swell of her breasts and make her ache for him to touch her completely. His mouth eased down onto her breast, taking it inside, savoring its warm softness as the rain pelted down overhead and the thunder drowned out the threat of the world around them. Their drenched clothing was hardly a barrier, their bodies sliding damply against each other in the dusty semidarkness of the dry ruin.

He felt her begin to move against him with helpless longing. She wasn't experienced enough to hide her desire for him or to curb her headlong response. He delighted in the shy touch of her hands on his chest, his back, in her soft cries and moans as he moved his mouth up to hers finally and covered her soft lips, pressing them open in a kiss that defied restraint.

She arched against him, glorying in the feel of skin against wet skin, her bareness under his, the hardness of his muscles gently crushing her breasts. Her nails dug helplessly into his back while she felt the hunger in the smoke-scented warmth of his open mouth on hers, and she moaned tenderly when she felt the probing of his tongue.

He was whispering something in husky Spanish, his mouth insistent, his hands suddenly equally insistent with other fastenings, hard and swift and sure.

She started to protest, but he brushed his mouth over hers. His body was shuddering with desire, and he sat up, his eyes fiercely possessive as he began to remove the rest of her clothing.

"Shhh," he whispered when she started to speak. "Let me tell you how it will be. My body and yours," he breathed, "with the rain around us, the jungle beneath us. The sweet fusion of male and female here, in the Mayan memory. Like the first man and woman on earth, with only the jungle to hear your cries and the aching pleasure of my skin against yours, my hands holding you to me as we drown in the fulfillment of our desire for each other."

The soft deepness of his voice drugged her. Yes, she wanted that. She wanted him. She arched as his hands slid down her yielding body, his lips softly touching her in ways she'd never dreamed of. The scent of the palm leaves and the musty, damp smell of the ruins in the rain combined with the excitement of Diego's feverish lovemaking.

She watched him undress, her shyness buried in the fierce need for fulfillment, her eyes worshiping his lean, fit body as he lay down beside her. He let her look at him, taking quiet pride in his maleness. He coaxed her to touch him, to explore the hard warmth of his body while he whispered to her and kissed her and traced her skin with exquisite expertise, all restraint, all reason burned away in the fires of passion.

She gave everything he asked, yielded to him completely. At the final moment, when there was no turning back, she looked up at him with absolute trust, absorbing the sudden intrusion of his powerful body with only a small gasp of pain, lost in the tender smile of pride he gave at her courage.

"Virgin," he whispered, his eyes bright and black as they held hers. He began to move, very slowly, his body trembling with his enforced restraint. "And so we join, and you are wholly mine. *Mi mujer.* My woman."

She caught her breath at the sensations he was causing, her eyes moving and then darting away, her face surprised and loving and hungry all at the same time, her eyes full of wonder as they lifted back to his.

"Hold me," he whispered. "Hold tight, because soon you will begin to feel the whip of passion and you will need my strength. Hold fast, *querida,* hold fast to me, give me all that you are, all that you have…*adorada,*" he gasped as his movements increased with shocking effect. "Melissa *mía!*"

She couldn't even look at him. Her body was climbing to incredible heights, tautening until the muscles seemed in danger of snapping. She cried out something, but he groaned and clasped her, and all too soon she was reaching for something that had disappeared even as she sought to touch it.

She wept, frustrated and aching and not even able to explain why.

He kissed her face tenderly, his hands framing it, his eyes soft, wondering. "You did not feel it?" he whispered, making her look at him.

"It was so close," she whispered back, her eyes frantic. "I almost…oh!"

He smiled with aching tenderness, his body moving slowly, his head lifting to watch her face. "Ah, yes," he whispered. "Here. And here…gently, *querida*. Come up and kiss me, and let your body match my rhythm. Yes, *querida,* yes, like that, like—" His jaw clenched. He shouldn't be able to feel it again so quickly. He watched her face, felt her body spiraling toward fulfillment. Even as she cried out with it and whispered to him he was in his own hot, black oblivion, and this time it took forever to fall back to earth in her arms.

They lay together in the soft darkness with the rain pelting around them, sated, exquisitely fatigued, her shirt and his pulled over them for a damp blanket. He bent to kiss her lazily from time to time, his lips soft and slow, his smile gentle. For just a few minutes there was no past, no future, no threat of retribution, no piper to pay.

Melissa was shocked by what had happened, so in

love with him that it had seemed the most natural thing on earth at the time to let him love her. But as her reason came back, she became afraid and apprehensive. What was he thinking, lying so quietly beside her? Was he sorry or glad, did he blame her? She started to ask him.

And then reality burst in on them in the cruelest way of all. Horses' hooves and loud voices had been drowned out by the thunder and the rain, but suddenly a small group of men was inside the ruin, and at the head of them was Melissa's father.

He stopped dead, staring at the trail of clothing and the two people, obviously lovers, so scantily covered by two shirts.

"Damn you, Laremos!" Edward Sterling burst out. "Damn you, what have you done?"

CHAPTER THREE

MELISSA KNEW THAT AS LONG as she lived there would be the humiliation of that afternoon in her memory. Her father's outrage, Diego's taut shouldering of the blame, her own tearful shame. The men quickly left the ruins at Edward Sterling's terse insistence, but Melissa knew they'd seen enough in those brief seconds to know what had happened.

Edward Sterling followed them, giving Melissa and Diego time to get decently covered. Diego didn't speak at all. He turned his back while she dressed, and then he gestured with characteristic courtesy for her to precede him out of the entrance. He wanted to speak, to say something, but his pride was lacerated at having so far forgotten himself as to seduce the daughter of his family's worst enemy. He was appalled at his own lack of control.

Melissa went out after one hopeful glance at his rigid, set features. She didn't look at him again.

Her father was waiting outside. The rain had stopped and his men were at a respectful distance.

"It wasn't all Diego's fault," Melissa began.

"Yes, I'm aware of that," her father said coldly. "I found the poems you wrote and the note asking Laremos to meet you so that you could—how did you put it?—'prove your love' for him."

Diego turned, his eyes suddenly icy, hellishly accusing. "You planned this," he said contemptuously. "*Dios mío*, and like a fool I walked into the trap…"

"How could I possibly plan a raid by guerrillas?" she asked, trying to reason with him.

"She certainly used it to her advantage," Edward Sterling said stiffly. "She was warned before she left the house that there was trouble at your estate, Estrella told her as she rode out of the yard, and she went in that general direction."

Melissa defended herself weakly. "I didn't hear Estrella. And the poems and the note were just daydreaming…."

"Costly daydreaming," her father replied. He stared at Diego. "No man with any sense of honor could refuse marriage in the circumstances."

"What would you know of honor?" Diego asked icily. "You, who seduced my father's woman away days before their wedding?"

Edward Sterling seemed to vibrate with bad temper. "That has nothing to do with the present situation. I won't defend my daughter's actions, but you must admit, Señor Laremos, that she couldn't have found herself in this predicament without some cooperation from you!"

It was a statement that turned Diego's blood molten, because it was an accusation that was undeniable. He was as much to blame as Melissa. He was trapped, and he himself had sprung the lock. He couldn't even look at her. The sweet interlude that had been the culmination of all his dreams of perfection had turned to ashes. He didn't know if he could bear to go through with it, but what choice was there? Another dishonor on the family name would be too devastating to consider, especially to his grandmother and his sister.

"I will not shirk my responsibility, *señor,*" Diego said with arrogant disdain. "You may rest assured that Melissa will be taken care of."

Melissa started to speak, to refuse, but her father and Diego gave her such venomous looks that she turned away and didn't say another word.

The guerrillas had been dealt with. Apollo Blain, tall and armed to the teeth at the head of a column led by the small, wiry man Laremos called First Shirt, was waiting in the valley as the small party approached.

"The government troops are at the house, boss," Shirt said with a grin.

Apollo chuckled, his muscular arms crossed over the pommel of his saddle. "Cleaning house, if you'll forgive the pun. Glad to see you're okay, boss man. You, too, Miss Sterling."

"Thanks," Melissa said wanly.

"With your permission, I will rejoin my men," Diego said with cool formality, directing the words to Edward.

"I will make the necessary arrangements for the service to take place with all due haste."

"We'll wait to hear from you, *señor*," Edward said tersely. He motioned to his men and urged his mount into step beside Melissa's.

"I don't suppose there's any use in trying to explain?" she asked miserably, too sick to even look back toward Diego and his retreating security force.

"None at all," her father said. "I hope you love Laremos. You'll need to, now that he's well and truly hamstrung. He'll hate both of us, but I won't let you be publicly disgraced, even if it is your own damned fault."

Tears slid down her cheeks. She stared toward the distant house with a sick feeling that her life was never going to be the same again. Her hero-worshiping and daydreaming had led to the end she'd hoped for, but she hadn't wanted to trap Diego. She'd wanted him to love her, to want to marry her. She had what she thought she desired, but now it seemed that the Fates were laughing at her. She remembered a very old saying that had never made sense before: *Be careful what you wish for, because you might get it.*

WEEKS WENT BY WHILE MELISSA was feted and given party after party with a stiff-necked Señora Laremos and Juana, Diego's sister, at her side. Their disapproval and frank dislike had been made known from the very beginning, but like Diego, they were making the most of a bad situation.

Diego himself hardly spoke to Melissa unless it was necessary, and when he looked at her she felt chilled to the bone. That he hated her was all too apparent. As the wedding approached, she wished with all her heart that she'd listened to her father and had never left the house that rainy day.

Her wedding gown was chosen, the Catholic church in Guatemala City was filled to capacity with friends and distant kin of both the bride's and groom's families. Melissa was all nerves, even though Diego seemed to be as nonchalant as if he were going to a sporting event, and even less enthusiastic.

Diego spoke his vows under Father Santiago's quiet gaze with thinly veiled sarcasm and placed the ring upon Melissa's finger. He pushed back the veil and looked at her with something less than contempt, and when he kissed her it was strictly for the sake of appearances. His lips were ice-cold. Then he bowed and led her back down the aisle, his eyes as unfeeling as the carpet under their feet.

The reception was an ordeal, and there was music and dancing that seemed to go on forever before Diego announced that he and his bride must be on their way home. He'd already told Melissa there would be no honeymoon because he had too much work and not enough free time to travel. He drove her back to the casa, where he deposited her with his cold-eyed grandmother and sister. And then he packed a bag and left for an extended business trip to Europe.

Melissa missed her father and Estrella. She missed the warmth of her home. But most of all, she missed the man she'd once loved, the Diego who'd teased her and laughed with her and seemed to enjoy having her with him for company when he'd ridden around the estate. The angry, unapproachable man she'd married was a stranger.

It was almost six weeks from the day she and Diego had been together when Melissa began to feel a stirring inside, a frightening certainty that she was pregnant. She was nauseated, not just at breakfast but all the time. She hid it from Diego's grandmother and sister, although it grew more difficult all the time.

She spent her days wandering miserably around the house, wishing she had something to occupy her. She wasn't allowed to take part in any of the housework or to sit with the rest of the family, who made this apparent by simply leaving a room the moment she entered it. She ate alone, because the *Señora* and the *Señorita* managed to change the times of meals from day to day. She was avoided, barely tolerated, actively disliked by both women, and she didn't have the worldliness or the sophistication or the maturity to cope with the situation. She spent a great deal of time crying. And still Diego stayed away.

"Is it so impossible for you to accept me?" she asked Señora Laremos one evening as Juana left the sitting room and a stiff-backed *señora* prepared to follow her.

Señora Laremos gave her a cold, black glare from

eyes so much like Diego's that Melissa shivered. "You are not welcome here. Surely you realize it?" the older woman asked. "My grandson does not want you, and neither do we. You have dishonored us yet again, like your mother before you!"

Melissa averted her face. "It wasn't my fault," she said through trembling lips. "Not completely."

"Had it not been for your father's insistence, you would have been treated like any other woman whose favors my son had enjoyed. You would have been adequately provided for—"

"How?" Melissa demanded, her illusions gone at the thought of Diego's other women, her heart broken. "With an allowance for life, a car, a mink coat?" Her chin lifted proudly. "Go ahead, *Señora*. Ignore me. Nothing will change the fact that I am Diego's wife."

The older woman seemed actually to vibrate with anger. "You impudent young cat," she snarled. "Has your family not been the cause of enough grief for mine already, without this? I despise you!"

Melissa didn't blink. She didn't flinch. "Yes, I realize that," she said with quiet pride. "God forbid that in your place I would ever be so cruel to a guest in my home. But then," she added with soft venom, "I was raised properly."

The Señora actually flushed. She went out of the room without another word, but afterward her avoidance of Melissa was total.

Melissa gave up trying to make them accept her now

that she realized the futility of it. She wanted to go home to see her father, but even that was difficult to arrange in the hostile environment where she lived. She settled for the occasional phone call and had to pretend, for his sake, that everything was all right. Perhaps when Diego had time to get used to the situation, everything would be all right. That was the last hope she had—that Diego might relent. That she might be able to persuade him to give her a chance to be the wife she knew she was capable of being.

Meanwhile, the sickness went on and on, and she knew that soon she was going to have to see a doctor. She grew paler by the day. So pale, in fact, that Juana risked her grandmother's wrath to sneak into Melissa's room one night and ask how she was.

Melissa gaped at her. "I beg your pardon?" she asked tautly.

Juana grimaced, her hands folded neatly at her waist, her dark eyes oddly kind in her thin face. "You seem so pale, Melissa. I wish it were different. Diego is—" she spread her hands "Diego. And my grandmother nurses old wounds that have been reopened by your presence here. I cannot defy her. It would break her heart if I sided with you against her."

"I understand that," Melissa said quietly, and managed a smile. "I don't blame you for being loyal to your grandmother, Juana."

Juana sighed. "Is there something, anything, I can do?"

Melissa shook her head. "But thank you."

Juana opened the door, hesitating. "My grandmother will not say so, but Diego has called. He will be home tomorrow. I thought you might like to know."

She was gone then, as quickly as she'd come. Melissa looked around the neat room she'd been given, with its dark antique furnishings. It wasn't by any means the master bedroom, and she wondered if Diego would even keep up the pretense of being married to her by sleeping in the same room. Somehow she doubted it. It would be just as well that way, because she didn't want him to know about the baby. Not until she could tell how well he was adapting to married life.

She barely slept, wondering how it would be to see him again. She overslept the next morning and for once was untroubled by nausea. She went down the hall and there he was, sitting at the head of the table. The whole family was together for breakfast for once.

Her heart jumped at just the sight of him. He was wearing a lightweight white tropical suit that suited his dark coloring, but he looked worn and tired. He glanced up as she entered the room, and she wished she hadn't worn the soft gray crepe dress. It had seemed appropriate at the time, but now she felt overdressed. Juana was wearing a simple calico skirt and a white blouse, and the *señora* had on a sedate dark dress.

Diego's eyes went from Melissa's blond hair in its neat chignon to her high-heeled shoes in one lightning-fast, not-very-interested glance. He acknowledged her with cool formality. "Señora Laremos. Are you well?"

She wanted to throw things. Nothing had changed, that was obvious. He still blamed her. Hated her. She was carrying his child, she was almost certain of it, but how could she tell him?

She went to the table and sat down gingerly, as far away from the others as she could without being too obvious. "Welcome home, *señor*," she said in a subdued tone. She hardly had any spirit left. The weeks of avoidance and cold courtesy and hostility had left their mark on her. She was pale and quiet, and something stirred in Diego as he looked at her. Then he banked down the memories. She'd trapped him. He couldn't afford to let himself forget that. First Sheila, then Melissa. The Sterlings had dealt two bitter blows to the Laremos honor. How could he even think of forgiving her?

Still, he thought, she looked unwell. Her body was thinner than he remembered, and she had a peculiar lack of interest in the world around her.

Señora Laremos also noticed these things about her unwanted houseguest but she forced herself not to bend. The girl was a curse, like her mother before her. She could never forgive Melissa for trapping Diego in such a scandalous way, so that even the servants whispered about the manner in which the two of them had been found.

"We have had our meal," the *Señora* said with forced courtesy, "but Carisa will bring something for you if you wish, Melissa."

"I don't want anything except coffee, thank you, *señora*." She reached for the silver coffeepot with a hand that trembled despite all her efforts to control it. Juana bit her lip and turned her eyes away. And Diego saw his sister's reaction with a troubled conscience. For Juana to be so affected, the weeks he'd been away must have been difficult ones. He glanced at the *señora* and wondered what Melissa had endured. His only thought had been to get away from the forced intimacy with his new wife. Now he began to wonder about the treatment she'd received from his family and was shocked to realize that it was only an echo of his own coldness.

"You are thinner," Diego said unexpectedly. "Is your appetite not good?"

She lifted dull, uninterested eyes. "It suffices, *señor,*" she replied. She sipped coffee and kept her gaze on her cup. It was easier than trying to look at him.

He hated the guilt that swept over him. The situation was her fault. She'd baited a trap that he'd fallen headlong into. So why should he feel so terrible? But he did. The laughing, shy young woman who'd adored him no longer lived in the same body with this quiet, unnaturally pale woman who wouldn't look at him.

"Perhaps you would like to lie down, Melissa," the *señora* said uneasily. "You do seem pale."

Melissa didn't argue. It was obvious that she wasn't welcome here, either, even if she had been invited to join the family. "As you wish, *señora,*" she said, her tone emotionless. She got up without looking at anyone and went down the long, carpeted hall to her room.

Diego began to brood. He hardly heard what his

grandmother said about the running of the estate in his absence. His mind was still on Melissa.

"How long has she been like this, *abuela?*" he asked unexpectedly. "Has she no interest in the house at all?"

Juana started to speak, but the *señora* silenced her. "She has been made welcome, despite the circumstances of your marriage," the *señora* said with dignity. "She prefers her own company."

"Excuse me," Juana said suddenly, and she left the table, her face rigid with distaste as she went out the door.

Diego finished his coffee and went to Melissa's room. But once outside it, he hesitated. Things were already strained. He didn't really want to make it any harder for her. He withdrew his hand from the doorknob and, with a faint sigh, went back the way he'd come. There would be time later to talk to her.

But business interceded. He was either on his way out or getting ready to leave every time Melissa saw him. He didn't come near her except to inquire after her health and to nod now and again. Melissa began to stay in her room all the time, eating her food on trays that Carisa brought and staring out the window. She wondered if her mind might be affected by her enforced solitude, but nothing really seemed to matter anymore. She had no emotion left in her. Even her pregnancy seemed quite unreal, although she knew it was only a matter of time before she was going to have to see the doctor.

It was storming the night Diego finally came to see her. He'd just come in from the cattle, and he looked weary. In dark slacks and an unbuttoned white shirt, he looked very Spanish and dangerously attractive, his black hair damp from the first sprinkling of rain.

"Will you not make even the effort to associate with the rest of us?" he asked without preamble. "My grandmother feels that your dislike for us is growing out of proportion."

"Your grandmother hates me," she said without inflection, her eyes on the darkness outside the window. "Just as you do."

Diego's face hardened. "After all that has happened, did you expect to find me a willing husband?"

She sighed, staring at her hands in her lap. "I don't know what I expected. I was living on dreams. Now they've all come true, and I've learned that reality is more than castles in the air. What we think we want isn't necessarily what we need. I should have gone to America. I should never have...I should have stopped you."

He felt blinding anger. "Stopped me?" he echoed, his deep voice ringing in the silence of her room. "When it was your damnable scheming that led to our present circumstances?"

She lifted her face to his. "And your loss of control," she said quietly, faint accusation in her voice. "You didn't have to make love to me. I didn't force you."

His temper exploded. He didn't want to think about that. He lapsed into clipped, furious Spanish as he expressed things he couldn't manage in English.

"All right," she said, rising unsteadily to her feet.

"All right, it was all my fault—all of it. I planned to trap you and I did, and now both of us are paying for my mistakes." Her pale eyes pleaded with his unyielding ones. "I can't even express my sorrow or beg you enough to forgive me. But Diego, there's no hope of divorce. We have to make the best of it."

"Do we?" he asked, lifting his chin.

She moved closer to him in one last desperate effort to reach him. Her soft eyes searched his. She looked young and very seductive, and Diego felt himself caving in when she was close enough that he could smell the sweet perfume of her body and feel her warmth. All the memories stirred suddenly, weakening him.

She sensed that he was vulnerable somehow. It gave her the courage to do what she did next. She raised her hands and rested them on his chest, against the cool skin and the soft feathering of hair over the hard muscles. He flinched, and she sighed softly as she looked up at him.

"Diego, we're married," she whispered, trying not to tremble. "Can't we…can't we forget the past and start again…tonight?"

His jaw went taut, his body stiffened. No, he told himself, he wouldn't allow her to make him vulnerable a second time. He had to gird himself against any future assaults like this.

He caught her shoulders and pushed her away from him, his face severe, his eyes cold and unwelcoming. "The very touch of you disgusts me, Señora Laremos," he said with icy fastidiousness. "I would rather sleep alone for the rest of my days than to share my bed with you. You repulse me."

The lack of heat in the words made them all the more damning. She looked at him with the eyes of a bludgeoned deer. Disgust. Repulse. She couldn't bear any more. His grandmother and sister like hostile soldiers living with her, then Diego's cold company, and now this. It was too much. She was bearing his child, and he wouldn't want it, because she disgusted him. Tears stung her eyes. Her hand went to her mouth.

"I can't bear it," she whimpered. Her face contorted and she ran out the door, which he'd left open, down the hall, her hair streaming behind her. She felt rather than saw the women of the house gaping at her from the living room as she ran wildly toward the front door with Diego only a few steps behind her.

The house was one story, but there was a long drop off the porch because of the slope on which the house had been built. The stone steps stretched out before her, but she was blinded by tears and lost her footing in the driving rain. She didn't even feel the wetness or the pain as she shot headfirst into the darkness and the first impact rocked her. Somewhere a man's voice was yelling hoarsely, but she was mercifully beyond hearing it.

She came to in the hospital, surrounded by whitecoated figures bending over her.

The resident physician was American, a blondhaired, blue-eyed young man with a pleasant smile. "There you are," he said gently when she stirred and opened her eyes. "Minor concussion and a close call for your baby, but I think you'll survive."

"I'm pregnant?" she asked drowsily.

"About two and a half months," he agreed. "Is it a pleasant surprise?"

"I wish it were so." She sighed. "Please don't tell my husband. He'll be worried enough as it is," she added, deliberately misleading the young man. She didn't want Diego to know about the baby.

"I'm sorry, but I told him there was a good chance you might lose it," he said apologetically. "You were in bad shape when they brought you in, *señora*. It's a miracle that you didn't lose the baby, and I'd still like to run some tests just to make sure."

She bit her lower lip and suddenly burst into tears. It all came out then, the forced marriage, his family's hatred of her, his own hatred of her. "I don't want him to know that I'm still pregnant," she pleaded. "Oh, please, you mustn't tell him, you mustn't! I can't stay here and let my baby be born in such hostility. They'll take him away from me and I'll never see him again. You don't know how they hate me and my family!"

He sighed heavily. "You must see that I can't lie about it."

"I'm not asking you to," she said. "If I can leave in the morning, and if you'll just not talk to him, I can tell him that there isn't going to be a baby."

"I can't lie to him," the doctor repeated.

She took a slow, steadying breath. She was in pain

now, and the bruises were beginning to nag her. "Then can you just not talk to him?"

"I might manage to be unavailable," he said. "But if he asks me, I'll tell him the truth. I must."

"Isn't a patient's confession sacred or something?" she asked with a faint trace of humor.

"That's so, but lying is something else again. I'm too honest, anyway," he said gently. "He'd see right through me."

She lay back and touched her aching head. "It's all right," she murmured. "It doesn't matter."

He hesitated for a minute. Then he bent to examine her head and she gave in to the pain. Minutes later he gave her something for it and left her to be transported to a private room and admitted for observation overnight.

She wondered if Diego would come to see her, but she was half-asleep when she saw him standing at the foot of the bed. His face was in the shadows, so she couldn't see it. But his voice was curiously husky.

"How are you?" he asked.

"They say I'll get over it," she replied, turning her head away from him. Tears rolled down her cheeks. At least she still had the baby, but she couldn't tell him. She didn't dare. She closed her eyes.

He stuck his hands deep in his pockets and looked at her, a horrible sadness in his eyes, a sadness she didn't see. "I...am sorry about the baby," he said stiffly. "One of the nurses said that your doctor mentioned the fall had done a great deal of damage." He shifted restlessly.

"The possibility of a child had simply not occurred to me," he added slowly.

As if he'd been home enough to notice, she thought miserably. "Well, you needn't worry about it anymore," she said huskily. "God forbid that you should be any more trapped than you already were. You'd have hated being tied to me by a baby."

His spine stiffened. He seemed to see her then as she was, an unhappy child who'd half worshiped him, and he wondered at the guilt he felt. That annoyed him. "Grandmother had to be tranquilized when she knew," he said curtly, averting his eyes. "*Dios mío*, you might have told me, Melissa!"

"I didn't know," she lied dully. Her poor bruised face moved restlessly against the cool pillow. "And it doesn't matter now. Nothing matters anymore." She sighed wearily. "I'm so tired. Please leave me in peace, Diego." She turned her face away. "I only want to sleep."

He stared down at her without speaking. She'd trapped him and he blamed her for it, but he was sorry about the baby, because he was responsible. He grimaced at her paleness, at the bruising on her face. She'd changed so drastically, he thought. She'd aged years.

His eyes narrowed. Well, hadn't she brought it on herself? She'd wanted to marry him, but she hadn't considered his feelings. She'd forced them into this marriage, and divorce wasn't possible. He still blamed her for that, and forgiveness was going to come hard. But for a time she had to be looked after. Well, tomorrow he'd work something out. He might send her to Barbados, where he owned land, to recover. He didn't know if he could bear having to see the evidence of his cruelty every day, because the loss of the child weighed heavily on his conscience. He hadn't even realized that he wanted a child until now, when it was too late.

He didn't sleep, wondering what to do. But when he went to see her, she'd already solved the problem. She was gone...

As past and present merged, Diego watched Melissa's eyes open suddenly and look up at him. It might have been five years ago. The pain was in those soft gray eyes, the bitter memories. She looked at him and shuddered. The eyes that once had worshiped him were filled with icy hatred. Melissa seemed no happier to see him than he was to see her. The past was still between them.

CHAPTER FOUR

MELISSA BLINKED, moving her head jerkily so she could
see him. Her gaze focused on his face, and then she shivered and closed her eyes. He pulled himself erect and
turned to go and get a nurse. As he left the room, his last
thought was that her expression had been that of a
woman awakening not from, but into, a nightmare.

When Melissa's eyes opened again, there was a shadowy form before her in crisp white, checking her over
professionally with something uncomfortably cold and
metallic.

"Good," a masculine voice murmured. "Very good.
She's coming around. I think we can dispense with
some of this paraphernalia, Miss Jackson," he told a
white-clad woman beside him, and proceeded to give
unintelligible orders.

Melissa tried to move her hand. "Pl-please." Her
voice sounded thick and alien. "I have...to go home."

"Not just yet, I'm afraid," he said kindly, smiling.

She licked her lips. They felt so very dry. "Matthew,"
she whispered. "My little boy. At a neighbor's. They
won't know..."

The doctor hesitated. "You just rest, Mrs. Laremos. You've had a bad night of it—"

"Don't...call me that!" she shuddered, closing her eyes. "I'm Melissa Sterling."

The doctor wanted to add that her husband was just outside the door, but the look on her face took the words out of his mouth. He said something to the nurse and quickly went back out into the hall.

Diego was pacing, and smoking like a furnace. He'd shed his jacket on one of the colorful seats in the nearby waiting room. His white silk shirt was open at the throat and his tie was lying neatly on his folded jacket. His rolled-up sleeves were in dramatic contrast to his very olive skin. His black eyes cut around to the doctor.

"How is she?" he asked without preamble.

"Still a bit concussed." The doctor leaned against the wall, his arms folded. He was almost as tall as Diego, but a good ten years younger. "There's a problem." He hesitated, because he knew from what Diego had told him that he and Melissa had been apart many years. He didn't know if the child was her husband's or someone else's, and situations like this could get uncomfortable. He cleared his throat. "Your wife is worried about her son. He's apparently staying at a neighbor's house."

Diego felt himself go rigid. A child. His heart seemed to stop beating, and for one wild moment he enjoyed the unbounded thought that it was his child. And then he remembered that Melissa had lost his child and that it was impossible for her to have conceived again before she'd left the *finca*. They had only slept together the one time.

That meant that Melissa had slept with another man. That she had become pregnant by another man. That the child was not his. He hated her in that instant with all his heart. Perhaps she was justified in her revenge. To be fair, he'd made her life hell during their brief marriage. And now she'd had her revenge. She'd hurt him in the most basic way of all.

He had to fight not to turn on his heel and walk away. But common sense prevailed. The child wasn't responsible for its circumstances. It would be alone and probably frightened. He couldn't ignore it. "If you can find out where he is, I will see about him," he said stiffly. "Will Melissa be all right?"

"I think so. She's through the worst of it. There was a good deal of internal bleeding. We've taken care of that. There was a badly torn ligament in her leg that will heal in a month or so. And we had to remove an ovary, but the other one was undamaged. Children are still possible."

Diego didn't look at the doctor. His eyes were on the door to Melissa's room. "The child. Do you know how old he is?"

"No. Does it matter?"

Diego shook himself. What he was thinking wasn't remotely possible. She'd lost the child he'd given her. She'd been taken to the hospital after a severe fall, and the doctor had told him there was little hope of saving it. It wasn't possible that they'd both lied. Of course not.

"I'll try to find the child's whereabouts," the doctor told Diego. "Meanwhile, you can't do much good here. By tomorrow she should be more lucid. You can see her then."

Diego wanted to tell him that if she was lucid Melissa wouldn't want to see him at all. But he only shrugged and nodded his dark head.

He left a telephone number at the nurse's station and went back to his hotel, glad to be out of Tucson's sweltering midsummer heat and in the comfort of his elegant air-conditioned room. A local joke had it that when a desperado from nearby Yuma had died and gone to hell, he'd sent back home for blankets. Diego was inclined to believe it, although the tropical heat of his native Guatemala was equally trying for Americans who settled there.

He much preferred the rain forest to the desert. Even if it was a humid heat, there was always the promise of rain. He wondered if it ever rained here. Presumably it did, eventually.

His mind wandered back to Melissa in that hospital bed and the look on her face when she'd seen him. She'd hidden well. He'd tried every particle of influence and money he'd possessed to find her, but without any success. She'd covered her tracks well, and how could he blame her? His treatment of her had been cruel, and she hadn't been much more than a child hero-worshiping him.

But Diego thought about the baby with bridled fury. They were still married, despite her unfaithfulness, and there was no question of divorce. Melissa, who was also Catholic, would have been no more amenable to that solution than he. But it was going to be unbearable, seeing that child and knowing that he was the very proof of Melissa's revenge for Diego's treatment of her.

The sudden buzz of the telephone diverted him. It was the doctor, who'd obtained the name and address of the neighbor who was caring for Melissa's son. Diego scribbled the information on a pad beside the phone, grateful for the diversion.

An hour later he was ushered into the cozy living room of Henrietta Grady's house, just down the street from the address the hospital had for Melissa's home.

Diego sat sipping coffee, listening to Mrs. Grady talk about Melissa and Matthew and their long acquaintance. She wasn't shy about enumerating Melissa's virtues. "Such a sweet girl," she said. "And Matthew's never any trouble. I don't have children of my own, you see, and Melissa and Matthew have rather adopted me."

"I'm certain your friendship has been important to Melissa," he replied, not wanting to go into any detail about their marriage. "The boy…"

"Here he is now. Hello, my baby."

Diego stopped short at the sight of the clean little boy who walked sleepily into the room in his pajamas. "All clean, Granny Grady," he said, running to her. He perched on her lap, his bare toes wiggling, eyeing the tall, dark man curiously. "Who are you?" he asked.

Diego stared at him with icy anger. Whoever Melissa's lover had been, he obviously had a little Latin blood. The boy's hair was light brown, but his skin was olive and his eyes were dark brown velvet. He was captivating, his arms around Mrs. Grady's neck, his lean, dark face full of laughter. And he looked to be just about four years old. Which meant that Melissa's fidelity had lasted scant weeks or months before she'd turned to another man.

Mrs. Grady lifted the child and cuddled him while Matthew waited for the man to answer his question.

"I'm Matthew," he told Diego, his voice uninhibited and unaccented. "My mommy went away. Are you my papa?"

Diego wasn't sure he could speak. He stared at the little boy with faint hostility. "I am your mama's husband," he said curtly, aware of Matthew's uncertainty and Mrs. Grady's surprise.

Diego ignored the looks. "Your mama is going to be all right. She is a little hurt, but not much. She will come home soon."

"Where will Matt go?" the boy asked gently.

Diego sighed heavily. He hadn't realized how much Melissa's incapacity would affect his life. She was his responsibility until she was well again, and so was this child. It was a matter of honor, and although his had taken some hard blows in years past, it was still as much a part of him as his pride. He lifted his chin. "You and your mama will stay with me," he said stiffly, and the lack of welcome in his voice made the little boy cling even closer to Mrs. Grady. "But in the meantime, I think it would be as well if you stay here." He turned to Mrs. Grady. "This can be arranged? I will need to spend a great deal of time at the hospital until I can bring Melissa home, and it seems less than sensible to uproot him any more than necessary."

"Of course it can be arranged," Mrs. Grady said without argument. "If there's anything else I can do to help, please let me know."

"I will give you the number of the phone in my hotel room and at the hospital, should you need to contact me." He pulled a checkbook from the immaculate gray suit jacket. "No arguments, please," he said when she looked hesitant about accepting money. "If you had not been available, Melissa would certainly have had to hire a sitter for him. I must insist that you let me pay you."

Mrs. Grady gave in gracefully, grateful for his thoughtfulness. "I would have done it for nothing," she said.

He smiled and wrote out a check. "Yes. I sensed that."

"Is Matt going to live with you and Mama?" Matthew asked in a quiet, subdued tone, sadness in his huge dark eyes.

Diego lifted his chin. "Yes," Diego said formally. "For the time being."

"My mommy will miss me if she's hurt. I can kiss her better. Can't I go see her?"

It was oddly touching to see those great dark eyes filled with tears. Diego had schooled himself over the years to never betray emotion. But he still felt it, even at such an unwelcome time.

Mrs. Grady had put the boy down to pour more coffee, and Diego studied him gravely. "There is a doctor who is taking very good care of your mother. Soon you may see her. I promise."

The small face lifted warily toward him. "I love Mama," he said. "She takes me places and buys me ice cream. And she lets me sleep with her when I get scared."

Diego's face became, if anything, more reserved than before, Mrs. Grady noticed. A flash of darkness in his eyes made her more nervous than before. How could Melissa have been married to such a cold man, a man who seemed unaffected even by his own son's tears? "How about a cartoon movie before bedtime?" Mrs. Grady asked Matthew, and quickly put on a Winnie the Pooh video for him to watch. The boy sprawled in an armchair, clapping his hands as the credits began to roll.

"*Gracias*," Diego said as he got gracefully to his feet. "I will tell Melissa of your kindness to her son."

Mrs. Grady tried not to choke. "Excuse me, *señor,* but Matthew is surely your son, too?"

The look in his eyes made her regret ever asking the question. She moved quickly past him to the door, making a flurry of small talk while her cheeks burned with her own forwardness.

"I hope everything goes well with Melissa," she said, flustered.

"Yes. So do I." Diego glanced back at Matthew, who was watching television. His dark eyes were quiet and faintly bitter. He didn't want Melissa's child. He wasn't sure he even wanted Melissa. He'd come out of duty and honor, but those were the only things keeping him from taking the first flight home to Guatemala. He felt betrayed all over again, and he didn't know how he was going to bear having to look at that child every day until Melissa was well enough to leave him.

He went back to the hospital, pausing outside Melissa's room while he convinced himself that upsetting her at this point would be unwise. He couldn't do that to an injured woman, despite his outrage. After a moment he knocked carelessly and walked in, tall and elegant and faintly arrogant, controlling his expression so that he seemed utterly unconcerned.

Which was quite a feat, considering that inside he felt as if part of him had died over the past five years. Melissa couldn't possibly know how it had been for him when she'd first vanished from the hospital, or how his guilt had haunted him. Despite his misgivings, he'd searched for her, and if he'd found her he'd have made sure that their marriage worked. For the sake of his family's honor, he'd have made her think that he was supremely contented. And after they'd had other children, perhaps they'd have found some measure of happiness. But that was all supposition, and now he was here and the future had to be faced.

The one thing he was certain of was that he could never trust her again. Affection might be possible after he got used to the situation, but love wasn't a word he knew. He'd come close to that with Melissa before she'd forced him into an unwanted marriage. But she'd nipped that soft feeling in the bud, and he'd steeled himself in the years since to be invulnerable to a woman's lies. Nothing she did could touch him anymore. But how was he going to hide his contempt and fury from her when Matthew would remind him of it every day they had to be together?

CHAPTER FIVE

MELISSA WATCHED DIEGO come in the door, and it was like stepping back into a past she didn't even want to remember. She was drowsy from the painkillers, but nothing could numb her reaction to her first sight of her husband in five years.

She seemed to stop breathing as her gray eyes slid drowsily over his tall elegance. Diego. So many dreams ago, she'd loved him. So many lonely years ago, she'd longed for him. But the memory of his cold indifference and his family's hatred had killed something vulnerable in her. She'd grown up. No longer was she the adoring woman-child who'd hung on his every word. Because of Matthew, she had to conceal from Diego the attraction she still felt for him. She was helpless and Diego was wealthy and powerful. She couldn't risk letting him know the truth about the little boy, because she knew all too well that Diego would toss her aside without regret. He'd already done that once.

Even now she could recall the disgust in his face when he'd pushed her away from him that last night she'd spent under his roof.

Her eyes opened again and he was closer, his face as unreadable as ever. He was older, but just as masculine and attractive. The cologne he used drifted down to her, making her fingers curl. She remembered the clean scent of him, the delicious touch of his hard mouth on her own. The mustache was unfamiliar, very black and thick, like the wavy, neatly trimmed hair above his dark face. He was older, yes, even a little more muscular. But he was still Diego.

"Melissa." He made her name a song. It was the pronunciation, she imagined, the faint accent, that gave it a foreign sound.

She lowered her eyes to his jacket. "Diego."

"How are you feeling?"

He sounded as awkward as she felt. She wondered how they'd found him, why they'd contacted him. She was still disoriented. Her slender hand touched her forehead as she struggled to remember. "There was a plane crash," she whispered, grimacing as she felt again the horrible stillness of the engine, the sudden whining as they'd descended, her own screaming.

"You must try not to think of it now." He stood over her, his hands deep in his pockets.

Then, suddenly, she remembered. "Matthew! Oh, no. Matthew!"

"*¡Cuidado!*" he said gently, pressing her back into the pillows. "Your son is doing very well. I have been to see him."

There was a flicker of movement in her eyelids that

she prayed he wouldn't see and become curious about. She stared at him, waiting. Waiting. But he made no comment about the child. Nothing.

His back straightened. "I have asked Mrs. Grady to keep him until you are well enough to be released."

She wished she felt more capable of coping. "That was kind of you," she said.

He turned to her again, his head to one side as he studied her. He decided not to pull any punches. "You will not be able to work for six weeks. And Mrs. Grady seemed to feel that you are in desperate financial straits."

Her eyes closed as a wave of nausea swept over her. "I had pneumonia, back in the spring," she said. "I got behind with the bills…"

"Are you listening to me, Señora Laremos?" he asked pointedly, emphasizing the married name he knew she hated. "You are not able to work. Until you are, you and the child will come home with me."

Her eyes opened then. "No!"

"It is decided," he said carelessly.

She went rigid under the sheet. "I won't go to Guatemala, Diego," she said with unexpected spirit. In the old days, she had never fought him. "Not under any circumstances."

He stared at her, his expression faintly puzzled. So the memories bothered her, as well, did they? He lifted his chin, staring down his straight nose at her. "Chicago, not Guatemala," he replied quietly. "Retirement has begun to bore me." He shrugged. "I hardly need the money, but Apollo Blain has offered me a consultant's position, and I already have an apartment in Chicago. I was spending a few weeks at the *finca* before beginning work when the hospital authorities called me about you."

Apollo. That name was familiar. She remembered the mercenaries with whom Diego had once associated himself. "He was in trouble with the law."

"No longer. J.D. Brettman defended him and won his case. Apollo has his own business now, and most of the others work for him. He is the last bachelor in the group. The others are married, even Shirt."

She swallowed. "Shirt is married?"

"To a wiry little widow. Unbelievable, is it not? I flew to Texas three years ago for the wedding."

She couldn't look at him. She knew somehow that he'd never told his comrades about his own marriage. He'd hated Melissa and the very thought of being tied to her. Hadn't he said so often enough?

"I'm very happy for them," she said tautly. "How nice to know that some people look upon marriage as a happy ending, not as certain death."

His gaze narrowed, his dark eyes wary on her face. "Looking into the past will accomplish nothing," he said finally. "We must both put it aside. I cannot desert you at such a time, and Mrs. Grady is hardly able to undertake your nursing as well as your son's welfare."

She didn't miss the emphasis he put on the reference to Matthew. He had to believe she'd betrayed him, and she had no choice but to let him think it. She couldn't fight him in her present condition.

Her gray eyes held his. "And you are?"

"It is a matter of honor," he said stiffly.

"Yes, of course. Honor," she said wearily, wincing as she moved and felt a twinge of pain. "I hope I can teach Matthew that honor and pride aren't quite as important as compassion and love."

The reference to her own lack of honor made his temper flare. "Who was his father, Melissa?" he asked cuttingly, his eyes hard. He hadn't meant to ask that, the words had exploded from him in quiet fury. "Whose child is he?"

She turned her head back to his. "He's my child," she said with an indignant glare. Gone were the days when she'd bowed down to him. Gone were the old adulation and the pedestal she'd put him on. She was worlds more mature now, and her skin wasn't thin anymore. "When you pushed me away, you gave up any rights you had to dictate to me. His parentage is none of your business. You didn't want me, but maybe someone else did."

He glared, but he didn't fire back at her. How could he? She'd hit on his own weakness. He'd never gotten over the guilt he'd felt, both for the loss of control that had given her a weapon to force him into marriage and for causing her miscarriage.

He stared out the window. "We cannot change what was," he said again.

Melissa hated the emotions that soft, Spanish-accented voice aroused in her, and she hated the hunger she felt for his love. But she could never let him know.

She stared at her thin hands. "Why did they contact you?"

He went back to the bed, his eyes quiet, unreadable. "You had our marriage license in your purse."

"Oh."

"It amazes me that you would carry it with you," he continued. "You hated me when you left Guatemala."

"No less than you hated me, Diego," she replied wearily.

His heart leaped at the sound of his name on her lips. She'd whispered it that rainy afternoon in the mountains, then moaned it, then screamed it. His fist clenched deep in his pocket as the memories came back, unbidden.

"It seemed so, did it not?" he replied. He turned away irritably. "Nevertheless, I did try to find you," he added stiffly. "But to no avail."

She stared at the sheet over her. "I didn't think you'd look for me," she said. "I didn't think you'd mind that I was gone, since I'd lost the child," she added, forcing out the lie, "and that was the only thing you would have valued in our marriage."

He averted his head. He didn't tell her the whole truth about the devastation her disappearance had caused him. He was uncertain of his ability to talk about it, even now, without revealing his emotions. "You were my wife," he said carelessly, glancing her way with eyes as black as night. "You were my responsibility."

"Yes," she agreed. "Only that. Just an unwelcome duty." She grimaced, fighting the pain because her shot was slowly wearing off. Her soft gray eyes searched his face. "You never wanted me, except in one way. And after we were married, not even that way."

That wasn't true. She couldn't know how he'd fought to stay out of her bedroom for fear of creating an addiction that he would never be cured of. She was in his blood even now, and as he looked at her he ached for her. But he'd forced himself to keep his distance. His remoteness, his cutting remarks, had all been part of his effort to keep her out of his heart. He'd come closer to knowing love with her than with any of the women in his past, but something in him had held back. He'd lived alone all his life, he'd been free. Loving was a kind of prison, a bond. He hadn't wanted that. Even marriage hadn't changed his mind. Not at first.

"Freedom was to me a kind of religion," he said absently. "I had never foreseen that I might one day be forced to relinquish it." He shifted restlessly. "Marriage was never a state I coveted."

"Yes, I learned that," she replied. She grimaced as she shifted against the pillow. "What did they…do to me? They won't tell me anything."

"They operated to stop some internal bleeding." He stood over her, his head at a faintly arrogant angle. "There is a torn ligament in your leg which will make you uncomfortable until it heals, and some minor bruises and abrasions. And they had to remove one of your ovaries, but the physician said that you can still bear a child."

Her face colored. "I don't want another child."

He stared down at her with faint distaste. "No doubt the one your lover left you with is adequate, is he not, *señora?*" he shot back.

She wanted to hit him. Her eyes flashed wildly and her breath caught. "Oh, God, I hate you," she breathed huskily, and her face contorted with new pain.

He ignored the outburst. "Do you need something else for the discomfort?" he asked unexpectedly.

She wanted to deny it, but she couldn't. "It...hurts." She touched her abdomen.

"I will see the nurse on my way out. I must get more clothes for Matthew."

She felt drained. "I'd forgotten. My apartment. There are clothes in the tall chest of drawers for him."

"The key?" he asked.

"In my purse." She didn't really want Diego in her apartment. There were no visible traces of anything, but he might find something she'd overlooked. But what choice did she have? Matthew had to be her first consideration.

He brought it to her, took the key she extended, then replaced the pitiful vinyl purse in her locker. The sight of her clothing was equally depressing. She had nothing. His dark eyes closed. It hurt to see her so destitute when she was entitled to his own wealth. Diego knew that Melissa's father had gone bankrupt just before his death.

The apartment she shared with Matthew was as dismal as the clothing he'd seen in her locker at the hospital. The landlady had eyed him with suspicion and curiosity until he'd produced his checkbook and asked how much his *wife* owed her. That had shaken the woman considerably, and there had been no more questions or snide remarks from her.

Diego searched through the apartment until he found a small vinyl bag, which he packed with enough clothing to get Matthew through the next few days. But he knew already that he was going to have to do some shopping. The child's few things looked as if they'd been obtained at rummage sales. Probably they had, he thought bitterly, because Melissa had so little. His fault. Even that was his fault.

He looked in another chest of drawers for more gowns and underthings for Melissa, and stopped as he lifted a gown and found a small photograph tucked there. He took it out carefully. It was one that Melissa had taken of him years before. He'd been astride one of his stallions, wearing a panama hat and dark trousers with a white shirt unbuttoned over his bronzed chest with its faint feathering of black hair. He'd been smiling at her as he'd leaned over the neck of the horse to stroke its waving mane. On the back of it was written: Diego, Near Atitlán. There was no date, but the photo was worn and wrinkled, as if she'd carried it with her for a long time. And he remembered to the day when she'd taken it—the day before they'd taken refuge in the Mayan ruins.

He slowly put it back under the gown and found something else. A small book in which were tucked flowers and bits of paper and a thin silver bookmark. He recognized some of the mementos. The flowers he'd given her from time to time or picked for her when they'd walked across the fields together. The bits of paper were from things he'd scribbled for her, Spanish words that she'd been trying to master. The bookmark was one he'd given her for her eighteenth birthday. He frowned. Why should she have kept them all these years?

He put them back, folded the gown gently over them and left the drawer as he'd found it, forcing himself not to consider the implications of those revealing mementos. After all, she might have kept them to remind her more of his cruelty than of any feeling she had had for him.

He went shopping the next morning. He knew Melissa's size, but he'd had to call Mrs. Grady to ask for Matthew's. It disturbed him to buy clothes for another man's child, but he found himself in the toy department afterward. Before he could talk himself out of it he'd filled a bag with playthings for the child, chiding himself mentally for doing something so ridiculous.

But Matthew's face when he put the packages on the sofa in Mrs. Grady's apartment was a revelation. Diego smiled helplessly at the child's unbridled delight as he took out building blocks and electronic games and a small remote-controlled robot.

"He's had so little, poor thing," Mrs. Grady sighed, smiling as she watched the boy go feverishly from one toy to another, finally settling down with a small computerized teddy bear that talked. "Not Melly's fault, of course. Money was tight. But it's nice to see him with a few new things."

"*Sí*." Diego watched the little boy and felt a sudden icy blast of regret for the child he'd caused Melissa to lose. He remembered with painful clarity what he'd said to her the night she'd run out into the rain and pitched down the steps in the wet darkness. *Dios*, would he never forget? He turned away. "I must go. Melissa needed some new gowns. I am taking them to the hospital for her."

"How is she?"

"Much better, *gracias*. The doctor says I may take her home in a few more days." He looked down at the heavyset woman. "Matthew will be going with us to Chicago. I know he will miss you, and Melissa and I are grateful for the care you have taken of him."

"It was my pleasure," she assured him.

"Thank you for my toys, mister," Matthew said, suddenly underfoot. His big dark eyes were happy. He lifted his arms to Diego to be picked up; he was used to easy affection from the adults around him. But the tall man went rigid and looked unapproachable. Matthew stepped back, the happiness in his eyes fading to wary uncertainty. He shifted and ran back to his toys without trying again.

Diego hated the emotions sifting through his pride, the strongest of which was self-contempt. How could he treat a child so coldly—it wasn't Matthew's fault, after all. But years of conditioning had made it impossible for him to bend. He turned to the door, avoiding Mrs. Grady's disapproving glance, made his goodbyes and left quickly.

Back at the hospital, while Diego went to get himself a cup of coffee, Melissa had a nurse help her into one of the three pastel gowns Diego had brought. She was delighted with the pink one. It had a low bodice and plenty of lace, and she thought how happy it would have made her years ago to have Diego buy her anything. But he'd done this out of pity, she knew, not out of love.

She thanked him when he came back. "You shouldn't have spent so much…" She faltered, because she knew the gowns were silk, not a cheap fabric.

He only shrugged. "You will be wearing gowns for a time," he said, as if that explained his generous impulse. He sat down in the armchair in the corner with a Styrofoam cup of coffee, which he proceeded to sip. "I bought a few things for your son," he added reluctantly. He crossed his long legs. "And a toy or so." He caught the look in her eyes. "He went from one to the other like a bee in search of the best nectar," he mused with stiff amusement.

Melissa almost cried. She'd wanted to give the child so many things, but there hadn't been any money for luxuries.

"Thank you for doing that for him," Melissa said

quietly. "I didn't expect that you'd do anything for him under the circumstances, much less buy him expensive toys." Her eyes fell from his cold gaze. "I haven't been able to give him very much. There's never been any money for toys."

She was propped up in bed now, and her hair had been washed. It was a pale blonde, curling softly toward her face, onto her flushed cheeks. She was lovely, he thought, watching her. There was a new maturity about her, and the curves he remembered were much more womanly now. His eyes dropped to the low bodice of the new gown he'd bought her, and they narrowed on the visible swell of her pink breasts.

She colored more and started to pull up the sheet, but his lean, dark hand prevented her.

"There is no need for that, Melissa," he said quietly. "You certainly do not expect me to make suggestive remarks to you under the circumstances?"

She shifted. "No. Of course not." She sighed. "I didn't expect you to buy me new gowns," she said, hoping to divert him. She didn't like the way it affected her when he looked at her that way. "Couldn't you find mine?" And as she asked the question, she remembered suddenly and with anguish what she'd hidden under those gowns. Had he seen— He turned away so that she couldn't see his expression. "One glance in the drawer was enough to convince me that they were unsuitable, without disturbing them," he said with practiced carelessness. "Do you not like the new ones?"

"They're very nice," she said inadequately. Silk, when she could barely afford cotton. Of course she liked them, but why had he been so extravagant?

"Has it been like this since you came to America?" he asked, glancing at her. "Have you been so hard-pressed for money?"

She didn't like the question. She stared at her folded hands. "Money isn't everything," she said.

"The lack of it can be," he replied. He straightened, his eyes narrow and thoughtful. "The child's father—could he not help you financially?"

She gritted her teeth. This was going to be intolerable. She lifted her cold gaze to his. "No, he couldn't be bothered," she said tersely. "And you needn't look so self-righteous and accusing, Diego. I don't believe for a minute that you've spent the last five years without a woman."

He didn't answer her. His expression was distant, impassive. "Has Matthew seen his father?" he persisted.

She didn't answer him. She didn't dare. "I realize that you must resent Matthew, but I do hope you don't intend taking out your grievances on him," she said.

He glared at her. "As if I could treat a child so."

"I was little more than a child," she reminded him. "You and your venomous family had no qualms about treating me in just such a way."

"Yes," he admitted, as graciously as he could. He put his hands in his pockets and studied her. "My grandmother very nearly had a breakdown when you vanished. She told me then how you had been treated. It was something of a shock. I had not considered that she might feel justified in taking her vengeance out on you. I should have realized how she'd react, but I was feeling trapped and not too fond of you when I left the Casa de Luz."

Before Melissa could respond to his unexpected confession, the door opened and a nurse's aide came in with a dinner tray. She smiled at Diego and put a tray in front of Melissa. Oh, well, Melissa thought as she was propped up and her food containers were opened for her, she could argue with him later. He didn't seem inclined to leave her anytime soon.

"You eat so little," he remarked when she only picked at her food.

She glanced at him. He sat gracefully in an upholstered armchair beside the window, his long legs crossed. He looked very Latin like that, and as immaculate as ever. She had to drag her eyes away before her expression told him how attractive she still found him.

"I'm not very hungry."

"Could you not eat a thick steak smothered in mushrooms and onions, *chiquita?*" he murmured, his black eyes twinkling gently for the first time since she'd opened her eyes and seen him in her room. "And fried potatoes and thick bread?"

"Stop," she groaned.

He smiled. "As I thought, it is the food that does not

appeal. When you are released I will see to it that you have proper meals."

"I have a job," she began.

"Which you cannot do until you are completely well again," he reminded her. "I will speak to your employer."

She sighed. "It won't help. They can't afford to hold the position open for six weeks."

"Is there someone who can replace you?"

She thought of her young, eager assistant. "Oh, yes."

"Then there should be no problem."

She glared at him over the last sip of milk. "I won't let you take me over," she said. "I'm grateful for your help, but I want no part of marriage ever again."

"I want it no more than you do, Melissa," he said carelessly, with forced indifference. "But for the time being, neither of us has any choice. As for divorce—" he shrugged "—that is not possible. But perhaps a separation or some other arrangement can be made when you are well. Naturally I will provide for you and the child."

"You will like hell," she said, shocking him not only with her unfamiliar language but with the very adult and formidable anger in her gray eyes. "This isn't Guatemala. In America women have equal rights with men. We aren't property, and I'm perfectly capable of providing for Matthew and myself."

His dark eyebrows lifted. "Indeed?" he asked lightly. "And this is why I found you living in abject poverty with a child who wears secondhand clothing and had not one new toy in his possession?"

She wanted to climb out of bed and hit him over the head with her tray. Her eyes told him so. "I won't live with you."

He shrugged. "Then what will you do, *niña?*" he asked.

She thought about that for a minute and fought back tears of helpless rage. She lay back on the pillows with a heavy sigh. "I don't know," she said honestly.

"It will only be a temporary arrangement," he reminded her. "Just until you are well again. You might like Chicago," he added. "There is a lake and a beach, and many things for a small boy to explore."

She made a face. "Matt and I will catch pneumonia and die if we have to spend a winter there," she said shortly. "Neither of us has ever been out of southern Arizona in the past f—" she corrected herself quickly "—three years."

He didn't notice the slip. He was studying her slender body under the sheets. She thought that he'd spent the past five years womanizing. Little did she know that the memory of her had destroyed any transient desire he might have felt for any other woman. Even now his dreams were filled with her, obsessed with her. So much love in Melissa, but he'd managed to kill it all. Once, he'd been sure she wanted to love him, but now he couldn't really blame her for her reticence. And his own feelings had been in turmoil ever since he'd learned about the child.

"It is spring," he murmured. "By winter, much could happen."

"I won't live in Guatemala, Diego," she repeated. "And not with your grandmother and sister under any circumstances."

He ran a restless hand through his hair. "My grandmother lives in Barbados with her sister," he said. "She still grieves for the great-grandchild she might have had if not for our intolerable coldness to you. My sister is married and lives in Mexico City."

"Did they know you were coming here?" she asked casually, though she didn't feel casual about it. The *señora* had been cruel, and so, despite her reluctance to side with her grandmother, had Juana.

"I telephoned them both last night. They wish you well. Perhaps one day there may be the opportunity for them to ask your pardon for the treatment you received."

"Juana tried to be kind," she said. She traced a thread on the sheet. "Your grandmother did not. I suppose I can understand how she felt, but it didn't make it any easier for me to stay there."

"And you blame me for leaving you at her mercy, *¿Es verdad?*"

"Yes, as a matter of fact, I do," she replied, looking up. "You never allowed me to explain. You automatically convicted me on circumstantial evidence and set out to make me pay for what you thought I did. And I paid," she added icily. "I paid in ways I won't even tell you."

"But you had your revenge, did you not?" he returned with an equally cold laugh. "You took a lover and had his child."

She forced a smile to her pale lips. "You're so good at getting at the truth, Diego," she said mildly. "I'm in awe of your ability to read minds."

"A pity I had no such ability when you left the hospital without even being discharged and vanished," he replied. "There was a military coup the same day you left, and there were several deaths."

As he spoke she saw the flash of emotion in his black eyes. She hadn't noticed before how haunted he looked. There was a deep, dark coldness about him, and there were new lines in his lean face. He looked his age for once, and the old lazy indifference she remembered seemed gone forever. This remote, polite man was nothing like the man she'd known in Guatemala. He'd changed drastically.

Then what he had said began to penetrate her tired mind. She frowned. "Several deaths?" she asked suddenly.

He laughed bitterly. "During the time the coup was accomplished there were a few isolated fatalities, and one of the bodies could not be identified." His eyes went cold at the memory. "It was a young girl with blond hair."

"You thought it was me?" she exclaimed.

He took a slow, deep breath. It was a minute before he could answer her. "Yes, I thought…it was you."

CHAPTER SIX

DIEGO'S QUIET CONFIRMATION took Melissa's breath away. She knew about the coup, of course. It was impossible not to know. But at the time her only thought had been of escape. She hadn't considered that depriving Diego of knowledge of her whereabouts might lead to the supposition that she was dead. She'd only been concerned about hiding her pregnancy from him.

"I find it very hard to believe you were concerned."

"Concerned!" He turned around, and the look in his black eyes was the old one she remembered from her teens, the one that could make even the meanest of his men back away. His eyes were like black steel in his hard face. "Shall I tell you what that young woman looked like, *niña?*"

She couldn't meet his eyes. "I can imagine how she looked," she said. "But you'll never make me believe it mattered to you. I expect you were more angry than relieved to discover that it wasn't me. How did you discover it?" she added.

"Your father told me," he said, moving restlessly to the window. "By that time you had successfully made it into the United States, and all my contacts were unable to track you down."

She wanted to ask a lot more questions, but this wasn't the time. She had other concerns. The main one was how she was going to manage living with him until she was fully recovered. And more importantly, how she was going to protect Matthew from him.

"I don't want to go with you, Diego," she said honestly. "I will, because I've no other choice. But you needn't expect me to worship the ground you walk on the way I used to. I've stopped dreaming in the past five years."

"And I have barely begun," he replied, his voice deep and soft. His gaze went over her slowly. "Perhaps it is as well that we meet again like this. Now you are old enough to deal with the man and not the illusion." He got to his feet with the easy grace Melissa remembered from the past. "I will return later. I must check on Matthew."

She turned under the sheet to keep her restless hands busy. "Tell him I love him and miss him very much, and that I'll be home soon, will you?"

"Of course." He hesitated, feeling awkward. "The child misses you, too." He smiled faintly. "He said if he could be allowed to visit you he would kiss the hurts better."

Tears sprang to her eyes and suddenly she felt terribly alone. She dabbed at the tears with the sheet, but Diego drew out a spotless white handkerchief and wiped them away. The handkerchief smelled of the cologne he favored and brought back vivid memories of him. Her eyes lifted, and she gazed at him. For one long instant, time rolled away and she was a girl with the man she loved more than her own life.

"Enamorada," he breathed huskily, his black eyes unblinking, smoldering. "If you knew how empty the years have been—"

The sudden opening of the door was like a gunshot. Melissa glanced that way as a smiling nurse's aide came into the room to check her vital signs. Diego smiled at the woman, his expression only slightly strained, and left with a brief comment about the time. Melissa clutched his handkerchief tightly in her hand, wanting nothing more than the luxury of tears. She was in pain and helpless, and she was much too vulnerable with Diego. She didn't dare let him see how she felt or make one slip that would give away Matthew's parentage. She had to bank down her hidden desire and hide it from him—now more than ever.

She was grateful Diego had left, because the look in his black eyes when he'd held that handkerchief to her eyes had brought back the most painful kind of memories. He still wanted her, if that look was anything to go by, even though he didn't love or trust her. Perhaps that might have been enough for her, but it wouldn't be for Matthew. Matthew deserved a father, not a reluctant guardian. It would be hardest for him, because of Diego's resentment. But telling Diego the truth could cost her the child, and at a time when she wasn't capable of fighting for him. She'd have to bide her time.

Meanwhile, at least she could be temporarily free of financial terrors. And that was something.

SEVERAL DAYS LATER, Melissa was released from the hospital and Diego took her to the hotel where he was staying. He had chartered a plane to take Melissa to Chicago the next day, a luxury she was reluctantly grateful for.

She pleaded to let her come along when he went to Mrs. Grady's to pick up Matthew, but he wouldn't allow it. She was too weak, he insisted. So he went to get the boy and Melissa lay smoldering quietly in one of the big double beds in the exquisite hotel suite, uncomfortable and angry.

It only took a few minutes. The door was unlocked and Matthew ran toward her like a little tornado, crying and laughing as he threw himself onto her chest and held her, mumbling and muttering through his tears.

"Oh, my baby," she cooed, smiling as she smoothed his brown hair and sighed over him. It was difficult to reach out because her stitches still pulled, but she didn't complain. She had her baby back.

Diego, watching them, glared at the sight of her blond head bent over that dark one. He was jealous of the boy, and more especially of the boy's father. He hated the very thought of Melissa's body in another man's arms, another man's bed. He hated the thought of the child she'd borne her lover.

Melissa laughed as Matt lifted his electronic bear and made it talk for her.

"Isn't he nice?" Matt asked, all eyes. "My…your… Mr. Man bought him for me."

"Diego," she prompted.

"Diego," Matthew parroted. He glanced at the tall man who'd been so quiet and distant all the way to the hotel. Matt wasn't sure if he liked Diego or not, but he was certain that the tall man didn't like him. It was going to be very hard living with a man who made him feel so unwelcome.

Melissa touched the pale little cheek. "You need sunshine, my son," she murmured. "You've spent too much time indoors."

Diego put down the cases and lit a small cheroot, pausing to open the curtains before dropping into an easy chair to smoke it at the table beside the window. "I have engaged a sitter for Matthew, since I will be away from the apartment a good deal when we get to Chicago," he told Melissa. "Perhaps the sitter will take him to the park or the beach."

Melissa felt the hair on the back of her neck bristle. Here she'd been the very model of a protective, caring mother, making sure Matt was always supervised, and now Diego came along and thought he could shift responsibility onto a total stranger about whom she knew nothing.

She clasped Matt's waist tightly. "No," she said firmly. "If he goes anywhere, it will be with me."

Diego's eyebrows lifted. She was overly protective of the child, that was obvious. Mrs. Grady had intimated something of the sort; now he could see that the older woman had been right. Something would have to be done about that, he decided. It wasn't healthy for a mother to be so sheltering. A boy who clung to his mother's apron could hardly grow into a strong man.

He crossed his legs and smoked his cheroot while his narrowed eyes surveyed woman and child. "Will you condemn him to four walls and your own company?"

She sat up, wincing as she piled pillows behind her. "I'll be able to get up and around in no time," she protested.

"Oh, yes," he agreed blandly, watching her struggle. "Already you can sit up by yourself."

She gave him her best glare. "I can walk, too."

"Not without falling over," he murmured, watching the cheroot with a faint smile as he recalled her last attempt to use her damaged leg.

"I'll hold you up, Mama," Matt assured her. "I'm very strong."

"Yes, I know you are, my darling," she said, her voice soft and loving. The man sitting in the chair felt an explosive anger that she cared so much for another man's child.

"What would you like for dinner?" he asked suddenly, getting up. "I can get room service to bring a tray."

"Steak and a salad for me, please," she said.

"Matt wants a fish." The little boy looked up, nervous and unsure, clinging to his mother's arm.

"They may not have fish, Matt," Melissa began.

"They have it," Diego said stiffly. "I had fish last night."

"Coffee for me, and milk for Matt," she said, turning away from the coldness of Diego's face as he looked at her son.

He nodded, a bare inclination of his head, and went to telephone.

"Mr. Man doesn't like Matt," Matthew said with a sad little sigh. "Doesn't he have any children?"

Melissa wanted to cry, but she knew that wouldn't solve anything. She only hoped Diego didn't hear the little boy as she shushed him and shook her head.

Diego didn't turn or flinch, but he heard, all right. It made the situation all the more difficult. He hadn't realized how perceptive children were.

Dinner was served from a pushcart by a white-coated waiter, and Matthew took his to the far side of the table, as if he wanted a buffer between himself and the tall man who didn't like him. Diego sat beside Melissa, and she tried not to smell the exotic cologne he wore or notice the strength of his powerful, slender body next to hers. He was the handsomest man she'd ever seen, and as he cut his steak she had to fight not to slide her fingers over the dark, lean hand holding the knife.

Diego finished first and went to the lobby on the pretext of getting Melissa something to read. In fact he wanted to get away from the boy's sad little face, with its big, haunting black eyes. He hated his own reactions because they were hurting that innocent little child who, under different circumstances, might have been his own.

He went to the lounge and had a whiskey sour, ignoring the blatant overtures of a slinky blonde who obviously found him more than attractive. He finished his drink and his cheroot and went back upstairs, taking a magazine for Melissa and a coloring book and crayons for Matt.

Melissa had Matt curled up beside her on the couch, and they both tensed the minute he walked in. His chin lifted.

"I brought a coloring book for the boy," he said hesitantly.

Matt didn't move. He looked up, waiting, without any expression on his face.

Diego took the book and the crayons and offered them to him, but still Matt didn't make a move.

"Don't you want the book, Matt?" Melissa asked softly.

"No. He doesn't like Matt," Matt said simply, lowering his eyes.

Diego frowned, torn between pain and his desire for vengeance. The child touched him in ways he had never dreamed of. He saw himself in the little boy, alone and frightened and sad. His own childhood had been an unhappy one, because his father had never truly loved his mother. His mother had known it, and suffered for it. She had died young, and his father had become even more withdrawn. Then, when his father had met the lovely Sheila, the older man's attitude had changed for the better. But the change had been short-lived—and that loss of hope Diego owed to Melissa's family, because his father had died loving Sheila Sterling, loving her with a hopeless passion that he was never able to indulge. The loss had warped him and Diego had seen what loving a woman could do to a man, and he had learned from it. Allowing a woman close enough to love was all too dangerous.

But the boy…it was hardly his fault. How could he blame Matt for Melissa's failings?

He put the coloring book and the crayons gently on the table by the sofa and handed Melissa the women's magazine he'd bought for her. Then he went back to his chair and sat smoking his cheroot, glancing through a sheaf of papers in a file.

"I'm going to read, Matt," Melissa said gently, nudging him to stand up. "You might as well try out your crayons. Do you remember how to color?"

Matt glanced at the man, who was oblivious to them both, and then at the crayons and coloring book. "It's all right?" he asked his mother worriedly.

"It's all right," she assured him.

He sighed and got down on the floor, sprawling with crayons everywhere, and began to color one of his favorite cartoon characters.

Diego looked up then and smiled faintly. Melissa, watching him, was surprised by his patience. She'd forgotten how gentle he could be. But then it had been a long time since she and Diego had been friends.

They had an early night. Melissa almost spoke when

Diego insisted that Matt pick up his crayons and put them away neatly. But she didn't take the child's side, because she knew Diego was right. Often she was less firm with Matt than she should be because she was usually so tired from her job.

She helped Matt into his pajamas and then looked quickly at Diego, because there were two double beds. She didn't want to be close to her estranged husband, but she didn't know how to say it in front of Matt.

Diego stole her thunder neatly by suggesting that the boy bunk down with her. It was only for the one night, because there were four bedrooms in the Chicago apartment. Matt would have his own room. Yes, Melissa thought, and that's when the trouble would really start, because she and Matt had been forced to share a room. She could only afford a tiny efficiency apartment with a sofa that folded out to make a bed. Matt wasn't used to being alone at night, and she wondered how they were going to cope.

But she didn't want to borrow trouble. She was tired and nervous and apprehensive, and there was worse to come. She closed her eyes and went to sleep. And she didn't dream.

The next morning, they left for Chicago. Despite the comfort of the chartered Lear jet, Melissa was still sore and uncomfortable. She had her medicine, and the attending physician at the hospital had referred her to a doctor in Chicago in case she had any complications. If only she could sit back and enjoy the flight the way Matthew was, she thought, watching his animated young face as he peered out the window and asked a hundred questions about airplanes and Chicago. Diego unbent enough to answer a few of them, although he did it with faint reluctance. But Matt seemed determined now to win him over, and Diego wasn't all that distant this morning.

Back in the old days in Guatemala, Melissa had never thought about the kind of father Diego would make. In her world of daydreams, romance had been her only concern, not the day-to-day life that a man and a woman had to concern themselves with after the wildness of infatuation wore off. Now, watching her son with his father, she realized that Diego really liked children. He was patient with Matthew, treating each new question as if it were of the utmost importance. He hadn't completely gotten over the shock of the child, she knew, and there was some reserve in him when he was with this boy he thought was another man's son. But he was polite to the child, and once or twice he actually seemed amused by Matt's excitement.

He was the soul of courtesy, but Melissa couldn't help thinking he'd much rather be traveling alone. Nevertheless, he carried her off the plane and to a waiting limousine for the trip to the Lincoln Park apartment he maintained, and she had to grind her teeth to keep from reaching up and kissing his hard, very masculine mouth as he held her. She hoped he didn't see how powerfully his nearness affected her. She was still vulnerable, even after all the years apart, but she didn't dare let him see it. She couldn't let him destroy her pride again as he had once before.

The apartment was a penthouse that overlooked the park and the shoreline, with the city skyline like a gray silhouette on the rainy horizon. Melissa was put to bed at once in one of the guest bedrooms and told to rest while Matthew explored the apartment and Diego introduced Melissa to Mrs. Albright, who was to do the baby-sitting as well as the cooking and cleaning. Apollo had recommended the pleasant, heavyset woman, and she'd been taking care of the apartment for Diego for over a year now.

Mrs. Albright was middle-aged and graying, with a sweet face and a personality to match. She took Melissa coffee and cake in bed and set about making her as comfortable as possible, insisting that she stay in bed to recuperate from the long flight. Then she took Matt off to the kitchen to spoil him with tiny homemade cream cakes and milk while she listened to his happy chatter about the flight from Tucson.

Once the boy and Melissa were settled, Diego picked up the phone and punched in a number.

Melissa heard him, but she couldn't make out many of the words. It sounded as though he were speaking to Apollo, and in fact he was, because Apollo showed up at the apartment an hour later with a slender, petite black woman.

Diego introduced the tall, muscular black man in the

gray suit. "This is Apollo Blain. Perhaps you remember him." Apollo smiled and nodded, and Melissa smiled back. "And this is Joyce Latham, Apollo's secretary."

"Temporarily," Apollo said with a curt nod in Joyce's direction.

"That's right, temporarily," Joyce said in a lilting West Indian accent, glaring up at the tall man. "Just until the very second I can find anybody brave enough to take my place."

Apollo glowered down at her. "Amen, sister," he bit off. "And with any luck I'll get somebody who can remember a damned telephone number long enough to dial it and who can file my clients alphabetically so I can find the files!"

"And maybe I'll get a boss who can read!" Joyce shot back.

"Enough!" Diego laughed, getting between them. "Melissa has survived one disaster. She doesn't need to be thrust into a new one, *por favor*."

Apollo grinned sheepishly. "Sorry. I got carried away." He shot a speaking glance at Joyce.

"Me, too," she muttered, shifting so that she was a little away from him. Her features weren't pretty, but her eyes were lovely, as deep and black as a bottomless pool, and her coffee-with-cream complexion was blemishless. She had a nice figure, probably, but the floppy uninspired blue dress she was wearing hid that very well.

"It's nice to meet you," Melissa told the woman, smiling. "I remember Apollo from years ago, of course. How long have you worked for him?"

"Two weeks too long," Joyce muttered.

"That's right, two weeks and one day too long," Apollo added. "Dutch and J.D. are coming over later, and Shirt says he and his missus are going to fly up to see you next week. It'll be like a reunion."

"I remember our last reunion," Diego said, smiling faintly. "We were evicted from the suite we occupied at three in the morning."

"And one of us was arrested," Apollo said smugly.

"That so?" Joyce asked him. "How long did they keep you in jail?"

He glared. "Not me. Diego."

"Diego?" Melissa stared at him in disbelief. The cool, careless man she knew wasn't hotheaded enough to land himself in jail. But perhaps she didn't really know him at all.

"He took exception to some remarks about his Latin heritage," Apollo explained with a glance at Diego, whose expression gave nothing away. "The gentleman making the remarks was very big and very mean, and to make a long story short, Diego assisted the gentleman into the hotel swimming pool through a plate-glass window."

"It was a long time ago." Diego turned as Matthew came running into the room.

"You have to come see my drawing, Mama," the boy said urgently, tugging at his mother's hand. "I drew a puppy dog and a bee! Come look!"

"*Momento*, Matthew," Diego said firmly, holding the

boy still. He introduced the visitors, who smiled down warmly at the child. "You can show your drawings to Mama in a moment, when our visitors have gone, all right, little one?"

"All right." Matthew sighed. He smiled at his mama and went shyly past the visitors and back to his crayons.

Apollo said, "He's a mirror image of you…" The last word trailed away under the black fury of Diego's eyes. He cleared his throat. "Well, we'd better get back to work. We'll be over with the others tonight. But we won't stay long. We don't want to wear out the missus, and don't lay on food. Just drinks. Okay?"

"And we'll come in separate cars next time," Joyce grumbled, darting a glance at the black man. "His idea of city driving is to aim the car and close his eyes."

"I could drive if you could stop putting your hands over your eyes and making those noises," he shot back.

"I was trying to say my prayers!"

"See you later," Apollo told Melissa and Diego. He took Joyce by the arm and half led, half dragged her out of the apartment.

"Don't they make a sweet couple?" Melissa murmured dryly when they'd gone. "I wonder if they both carry life insurance…?"

Diego smiled faintly at the mischief in her eyes. "An interesting observation, Señora Laremos. Now, if there is nothing I can do for you, you can praise your son's art while I get back to work."

Her pale gray eyes searched his face, looking for revelations, but there were none in that stony countenance. "It offended you that Apollo mentioned a resemblance."

"The boy's father obviously had some Ladino blood," he countered without expression. He put his hands in his pockets, and his black eyes narrowed. "You will not divulge your lover's identity, even now?"

"Why should it matter to you?" she asked. "I had the impression when I left Guatemala that it would be too soon if you never saw me again."

"I tried to talk to you at the time. You would not listen, so I assumed that my feelings would have no effect on you."

"Do you have any feelings?" she asked suddenly. "My father said once that if you did it would take dynamite to get to them."

He stood watching her, his slightly wavy black hair thick and clean where it shone in the light, his eyes watchful. "Considering the line of work I was in, Melissa, is that so surprising? I could not afford the luxury of giving in to my emotions. It has been both a protection and a curse in later years. Perhaps if I had not been so reticent with you the past five years would not have been wasted."

Her pulse jumped, but she kept her expression calm so he wouldn't see how his words affected her. "I understood," she replied. "Even though I was young, I wasn't stupid."

"Had you no idea what would happen when you led me into that sweet trap, Melissa?" he asked with a bitter laugh.

"It wasn't a trap," she said doggedly. "I'd written a lot of silly love poems and scribbled some brazen note to you that I meant to destroy. I'd never have had the nerve to send it to you." She colored faintly at the memory. "I tried to tell you, and my father, that it was a mistake, but neither of you would listen." Her fingers toyed with the hem of her pink blouse. "I loved you," she said under her breath. Her eyes were closed, and she missed the expression that washed over his face. "I loved you more than my own life, and Dad was on the verge of sending me away to college. I knew that I'd never see you again. Every second I had with you was precious, and that's why I gave in. It wasn't planned, and it wasn't meant to be a trap." She laughed coldly. "The irony of it all is that I was stupid enough to believe that you might come to love me if we lived together. But you left me with your family and went away, and when you came back and I tried so desperately to catch your attention—" She couldn't go on. The memory of his contemptuous rejection was too vivid. She averted her eyes. "I knew then that I'd been living in a daydream. I had what I wanted, but through force, not through choice. Leaving was the first intelligent decision I made."

He felt as if she'd hit him with a rock. "Are you telling me that you didn't have marriage in mind?"

"Of course I had marriage in mind, but I never meant you to be forced into it!" she burst out, tears threatening in her eyes. "I loved you. I was twenty and there'd never been another man, and you were my world, Diego!"

His tall, elegant body tautened. He'd never let himself think about it, about what had motivated her. Perhaps, deep inside, he'd known all along how she felt but hadn't been able to face it. He drew a thin cheroot from his pocket and lit it absently. "I went to see your father after he confirmed that you were still alive. He told me nothing, except that you despised me and that you never wanted to see me again." He lifted his gaze and stared at her. "I was determined to hear that for myself, of course, so I kept searching. But to no avail."

"I used my maiden name when I applied for United States citizenship," she explained, "and I lived in big cities. After I was settled, I contacted my father and begged him not to let you know where I was. Later, when the attorney called and told me about my father's death, I grieved. But I didn't have enough money to go to the funeral. Even then, I pleaded with the lawyer not to reveal my whereabouts. I didn't really think you'd come looking for me when you knew I'd—" she forced out the lie "—lost the baby, but I had to be sure."

"You were my responsibility," he said stiffly. "You still are. Our religion does not permit divorce."

"My memory doesn't permit reconciliation," she said shortly. "I'll stay here until I'm able to work again, but that's all. I'm responsible for myself and my son. You have no place in my life, or in my heart, anymore."

He fought back the surge of misery her statement engendered. "And Matthew?"

She pushed back her hair. "Matthew doesn't concern you. He thinks you hate him, and he's probably right. The sooner I get him away from here the better."

He turned gracefully, staring hard at her. "Did you expect that I could accept him so easily? He is the very proof that your emotions were not involved when we were together. If you had loved me, Melissa, there could never have been another man. Never!"

And that was the crux of the entire problem, she thought. He didn't realize that he was stating a fact. If he'd trusted her, he'd have known that she loved him too much to take a lover. But he didn't trust her. He didn't know her. He'd never made the effort to know her in any way except the physical.

She lay back on the pillows, exhausted. "I can't fight, Diego. I'm too tired."

He nodded. "I know. You need rest. We can talk when you are more fit."

"I hope you didn't expect me to fall in line like the little slave I used to be around you," she said, lifting cold eyes to his.

"I like very much the way you are now, *niña*," he said slowly, his accent even more pronounced than usual. His dark eyes smoldered as he drew them over her body. "A woman with fire in her veins is a more interesting proposition than a worshipful child."

"You won't start any fires with me, *señor*," she said haughtily.

"*¿Es verdad?*" He moved slowly to the bed and, leaning one long arm across her, stared into her eyes from scant inches away. "Be careful before you sling out challenges, my own," he said in the deep, soft voice she remembered so well whispering Spanish love words in the silence of the Mayan ruins. "I might take you up on them." He bent closer, and she could almost feel the hard warmth of his mouth against her parted lips, faintly smoky, teasing her mouth with the promise of the kisses she'd once starved for.

She made a sound deep in her throat, a tormented little sob, and turned her face against the pillow, closing her eyes tight. "No," she whispered. "Oh, don't!"

She felt his breath against her lips. Then, abruptly, he pushed away, shaking the bed and stood up. He turned away to light a cheroot. "There is no need for such virginal terror," he said stiffly as he began to smoke it. "Your virtue is safe with me. I meant only to tease. I lost my taste for you the day I learned just how thirsty you were for vengeance."

She was grateful for his anger. It had spared her the humiliation of begging for his kisses. Because she wasn't looking at his face, she didn't realize that her rejection had bruised his ego and convinced him that she no longer wanted his kisses.

He got control over his scattered emotions. "The man who replaced me in your affections—Matthew's father—where is he now, Melissa?"

Her eyes closed. She prayed for deliverance, and it came in the form of Matthew, who came running in to see why Mama hadn't come to look at his drawings.

Melissa got up very slowly and allowed Matt to lead her into his bedroom, her steps hesitant and without confidence. She didn't look at Diego.

That night, Mrs. Albright bathed Matthew and put him to bed so that Diego and Melissa would be free to greet their guests. Melissa's leg still made walking difficult, as did the incision where her ovary had been removed. She managed to bathe and dress alone, but she was breathless when Diego came to carry her into the living room.

He stopped in the doorway, fascinated by the picture she made in the pale blue silky dress that emphasized her wavy blond hair, gray eyes and creamy complexion. She'd lost weight, but she still had such a lovely figure that even her slenderness didn't detract from it.

Diego was wearing a dark suit, and his white shirt emphasized his very Latin complexion and his black hair and eyes. It was so sweet just to look at him, to be with him. Melissa hadn't realized how empty the years without him had been, but now the impact of his company was fierce.

She had barely a minute to savor it before the doorbell rang and the guests came in. Apollo and Joyce were together, if reluctantly, and Melissa mused that since the black man hated his secretary so much it was odd that he'd bring her along on a social call. Behind them was a slender blond man with the masculine perfection of a movie star and a mountain of a man with dark, wavy hair.

Diego introduced the blond man. "Eric 'Dutch' van

Meer. And this—" he smiled toward the big man "—is Archer, better known as J.D. Brettman. Gentlemen, my wife, Melissa."

They smiled and said all the right things, but Melissa could tell that they were surprised that Diego had never mentioned her. They apologized for not bringing their wives, Danielle and Gabby, but their children had given each other a virus and they were at home nursing them. Melissa would be introduced to them at a later time.

Melissa smiled back. "I'll look forward to that," she said politely. These men made her oddly nervous, because she didn't know them as she knew Apollo. They formed into a group and began talking about work, and Melissa felt very isolated from her husband as he spoke with his old comrades. She could see the real affection he felt for them. What a pity that he had none to give her. But what should she have expected under the circumstances? Diego was responsible for her, as he'd said. He was only her caretaker until she was well again, and she'd better remember that. There might be the occasional flare-up of the old attraction, but she couldn't allow herself to dream of a reconciliation. It was dangerous to dream—dreams could become a painful reality.

Joyce had eased away from the others to sit beside Melissa on the huge corner sofa. "I feel as out of place as a green bean in a gourmet ice-cream shop," she mumbled.

Melissa laughed in spite of herself. "So do I, so let's stick together," she whispered.

Joyce straightened the skirt of her beige dress. Her

long hair was a little unkempt, and she slumped. Melissa thought what a shame it was that the woman didn't take care with her appearance. With a little work, she could be a knockout.

"How did you wind up working for Apollo?" Melissa asked.

The other woman smiled ruefully. "I was new to the city—I moved here from Miami—and I signed up with a temporary agency." She glanced at Apollo with more warmth than she seemed to realize. "They sent me to him and he tried to send me right back, but the agency was shorthanded, so he was stuck with me."

"He doesn't seem to mind too much," Melissa murmured dryly. "After all, most bosses don't take their secretaries along on social engagements."

Joyce sighed. "Oh, that. He thought you might feel uncomfortable around all these men. Since the wives couldn't come, here I am." She grinned. "I'm kind of glad that I was invited, you know. I'm not exactly flooded with social invitations."

"I know what you mean," Melissa said, smiling. "Thanks for coming."

As Apollo had promised, they didn't stay long. But as the men said their goodbyes and left, J.D. Brettman shot an openly curious glance in Melissa's direction.

Later, when the guests had gone, Melissa asked Diego about it as he removed his jacket and tie and loosened the top buttons of his shirt.

"Why was Mr. Brettman so curious about me?" she asked gently.

He poured himself a brandy, offered her one and was refused, and dropped gracefully into the armchair across from her. "He knew there was a woman somewhere in my life," he said simply. "There was a rumor to the effect that I had hurt one very badly." He shrugged. "Servants talk, you see. It was known that you fell and were rushed to the hospital." As he lifted the brandy to his lips, his eyes had a sad, faraway look. "I imagine it was said that I pushed you."

"But you didn't!"

His dark eyes caught hers. "Did I not?" His chin lifted, and he looked very Latin, very attractive. "It was because of me that you ran into the night. I was responsible."

She lowered her gaze. "I'm sorry that people thought that about you. I was too desperate at the time to think how it might look to outsiders."

"*No importa,*" he said finally. "It was a long time ago, after all."

"I need to check on Matthew. Mrs. Albright left with the others." She started to stand, but the torn ligament was still tricky and painful, like the incision. She stood very still to catch her breath and laughed self-consciously. "I guess I'm not quite up to the hundred-yard dash."

He got up lazily and put his snifter down. His arms went under her, lifting her with ridiculous ease. "You are still weak," he murmured as he walked down the long hall. "It will take time for you to heal properly."

She had to fight not to lay her cheek against his shoulder, drinking in the scent of his cologne, savoring the warmth of his body and its lean strength as he carried her. "I like your old comrades," she remarked quietly.

"They like you." He carried her through the open door to Matthew's room and let her slide gently to her feet. The little boy was sleeping, his long lashes black against his olive skin, his dark hair disheveled on the white pillow. Diego stared down at him quietly.

Melissa saw the look on his face and almost blurted out the truth. It took every ounce of willpower in her to keep still.

"There is so little of you in him," he said, his voice deep and softly accented. "Except for his hair, which has traces of your fairness in it." He turned, his eyes challenging. "His father was Ladino, Melissa?"

She went beet red. She tried to speak, but the words wouldn't come.

"You loved me, you said," he persisted. His eyes narrowed. "If that was so, then how could you give yourself, even to avenge the wounds I caused you?"

She knew she was barely breathing. She felt and looked hunted.

"What was his name?" he asked, moving closer so that he towered over her, warming her, drowning her in the exquisite scent of the cologne he wore.

Her lips parted. "I...you don't need to know," she whispered.

He framed her face with his dark, lean hands, holding her eyes up to his. "Where did you meet him?"

She swallowed. His black eyes filled the world. In the dim light from Matthew's lamp, he seemed huge, dangerous. "Diego…"

"Yes," he breathed, bending to her soft mouth. "Yes, say it like that, *querida*. Say my name, breathe it into my mouth…."

He brushed her lips apart with the soft drugging pressure of his own, teasing, cherishing. Her nervous hands lingered at his hard waist, lost in the warmth of his body under the silky white shirt. She hadn't meant to give in so easily, but the old attraction was every bit as overwhelming as it had been years ago. She was powerless to stop what was happening.

And he knew it. He sighed gently against her mouth, tilting her head at a more accommodating angle. Then the gentleness left him. She felt his mouth growing harder, more insistent. He whispered something in Spanish, and his hands slid into her hair, dragging her mouth closer under his. He groaned and she moved against him, her body trembling with the need to be close to him, to hold him. Her arms slid around him, and suddenly his arms were around her, molding her body to his with a pressure that was painful heaven.

She gasped under his demanding mouth and he stopped at once. He lifted his head, and his eyes were fierce and dark, his breathing as quick as hers.

"I hurt you?" he asked roughly. And then he seemed

to come to his senses. He released her slowly, moving away. He turned his eyes briefly to the still-sleeping child. "I must ask your pardon for that," he said stiffly. "It was not intended."

She dropped her gaze to the opening of his white shirt, where dark olive skin and black hair peeked out. "It's all right," she said hesitantly, but she couldn't look up any farther than his chin.

He shifted restlessly, his body aching for the warm softness of hers, his mind burning with confused emotions. He raised her head. "Perhaps it would be wise for you to go to bed."

She wasn't about to argue. "No, I...you don't need to carry me," she protested when he moved toward her. "I can manage. I need to start exercising my leg. But thanks anyway."

He nodded, standing aside to let her leave. His dark eyes followed her hungrily, but when she was out of sight they turned to the sleeping child. His face was so like Melissa's, he thought quietly. But the boy's Spanish heritage was evident. He wondered if Melissa still loved the boy's father or thought about him.

The bitterness he felt drove him from the child's room and into his study. And not until he had worked himself into exhaustion did he fall into his bed to sleep.

CHAPTER SEVEN

THE ATMOSPHERE AT BREAKFAST was strained. Melissa had hardly slept, remembering with painful clarity her headlong response to Diego's ardor. If only she could have kept up the front, convinced him that she wasn't attracted to him anymore. She'd almost accomplished that, and then he'd come too close and her aching heart had given in.

She felt his eyes on her as she tried to eat scrambled eggs and bacon. Matthew, too, was unusually silent. He was much more careful of his behavior at the table than he'd ever been when he and Melissa had lived by themselves. Probably, she thought sadly, because he felt the tension and was reacting to it.

"You are quiet this morning, Señora Laremos," Diego said gently, his black eyes slow and steady on her pale face as she toyed with her toast. "Did you not sleep well?"

He was taunting her, but she was too weary to play the game. "No," she confessed, meeting his searching gaze squarely. "In fact, I hardly slept at all, if you want the truth."

He traced the rim of his coffee cup with a finger, and

his gaze held hers. "Nor did I, to be equally frank," he said quietly. "I have been alone for many years, Melissa, despite the opinion you seem to have of me as a philandering playboy."

She lifted her coffee cup to her lips for something to do. "You were never lacking in companionship in the old days."

"Before I married you, surely," he agreed. "But marriage is a sacred vow, *niña*."

"I'm not a girl," she retorted.

His chiseled lips tugged into a reluctant smile. "Ah, but you were, that long-ago summer," he recalled, his eyes softening with the memory. "Girlish and sweet and bright with the joy of life. And then, so soon, you became a sad, worn ghost who haunted my house even when you were not in it."

"I should have gone to college in America," she replied, glancing at a quiet but curious Matthew. "There was never any hope for me where you were concerned. But I was too young and foolish to realize that a sophisticated man could never care for an inexperienced, backward child."

"It was the circumstance of our marriage which turned me against you, Melissa," he said tersely. "And but for that circumstance, we might have come together naturally, with a foundation of affection and comradeship to base our marriage on."

"I would never have been able to settle for crumbs, Diego," she said simply. "Affection wouldn't have been enough."

"You seemed to feel that desire was enough, at the time," he reminded her.

Wary of Matt's sudden interest, she smiled at the child and sent him off to watch his cartoons with his breakfast only half eaten.

"He's little, but he hears very well," she told Diego curtly, her gray eyes accusing. "Arguments upset him."

"Was I arguing?" he asked with lifted eyebrows.

She finished her coffee and put the cup down. "Won't you be late for work?"

"By all means let me relieve you of my company, since you seem to find it so disturbing," he said softly. He removed a drop of coffee from his mustache with his napkin and got to his feet. *"Adiós."*

She looked up as he started to the front door, mingled emotions tearing at her.

Diego paused at the door, glaring toward Matthew, who'd just turned the television up very loud. He said something to the boy, who cut down the volume and glared accusingly at the tall man.

"If you disturb the other tenants, little one, we will all be evicted," Diego told him. "And forced to live on the street."

"Then Matt can go home with Mama," the child said stubbornly, "and go away from you."

Diego smiled faintly at that show of belligerence. Even at such a young age, the boy had spirit. It wouldn't do to break it, despite the fact that he was another man's child. Matt had promise. He was intelligent and he didn't back down. Despite himself, Diego was warming to the little boy.

Impulsively he went to the television and went down on one knee in front of the dark-eyed child. Melissa, surprised, watched from the doorway.

"On the weekend, we might go to the zoo," Diego told the boy with pursed lips and a calculating look in his black eyes. "Of course, if you really would rather leave me, little one, I can go to see the lions and tigers alone—"

Matt blinked, his eyes widening. "Lions and tigers?"

Diego nodded. "And elephants and giraffes and bears."

Matt moved a little closer to Diego. "And could I have cotton candy? Billy's dad took him to the zoo and he got cotton candy and ice cream."

Diego smiled gently. "We might manage that, as well."

"Tomorrow?"

"A few days past that," Diego told him. "I have a great deal to do during the week, and you have to take care of your Mama until she gets well."

Matt nodded. "I can read her a story."

Melissa almost giggled, because Matt's stories were like no one else's, a tangle of fairy-tale characters and cartoon characters from television in unlikely situations.

"Then if you will be good, *niño*, on Saturday you and I will go see the animals."

Matt looked at Melissa and then at Diego again, frowning. "Can't Mama come?"

"Mama cannot walk so much," Diego explained patiently. "But you and I can, *sí?*"

Matt shifted. He was still nervous with the man, but he wanted very much to go to the zoo. *"Sí,"* he echoed.

Diego smiled. "It is a deal, then." He got to his feet. "No more loud cartoons," he cautioned, shaking his finger at the boy.

Matt smiled back hesitantly. "All right."

Diego glanced at Melissa, who was standing in the doorway in her pink silk gown and her long white chenille housecoat, with no makeup and her soft blond hair curling around her pale face. Even like that, she was lovely. He noticed the faint surprise in her gray eyes, mingled with something like…hope.

His black eyes held hers until she flushed, and her gaze dropped. He laughed softly. "Do I make you shy, *querida?*" he asked under his breath. "A mature woman like you?"

She shifted. "Of course not." She flushed even more, looking anywhere but at him.

He opened the front door, his glance going from the child back to her. "Stay in bed," he said. "The sooner the leg is better, the sooner we can begin to do things as a family."

"It's too soon," she began.

"No. It is five years too late." His eyes flashed at her. "But you are my responsibility, and so is Matt. We have to come to terms."

"I've told you I can get a job—"

"No!"

She started to say something, but he held up a hand and his eyes cut her off.

"*¡Cuidado!*" he said softly. "You said yourself that arguing is not healthy for the child. *¡Hasta luego!*"

He was gone before she could say another word.

It was a hectic morning. Diego had hardly gotten to the office before he and Dutch had to go out to give a demonstration to some new clients. When they got back, voices were raised behind the closed office door. Diego hesitated, listening to Joyce and Apollo in the middle of a fiery argument over some filing.

Dutch came down the hall behind him, a lighted cigarette in his hand, looking as suave as ever. He glanced at Diego with a rueful smile.

"Somehow combat was a little easier to adjust to than that," he said, indicating the clamor behind the closed office door. "I think I'll smoke my cigarette out here until they get it settled or kill each other."

Diego lit a cheroot and puffed away. "Perhaps someday they will marry and settle their differences."

"They'd better settle them first," Dutch remarked. "I've found that marriage doesn't resolve conflicts. In fact, it intensifies them."

Diego sighed. "Yes, I suppose it does." His dark eyes narrowed thoughtfully. Last night seemed more and more like a dream as the din grew. Would he and Melissa become like that arguing couple in the office? Matthew was their unresolved conflict, and despite his growing interest in the child, he still couldn't bear the thought of the man who'd fathered him.

"Deep thoughts?" Dutch asked quietly.

The other man nodded. "Marriage is not something I ever coveted. Melissa and I were caught in a—how do you say?—compromising situation. Our marriage was a matter of honor, not choice."

"She seems to care about you," the other man ventured. "And the boy—"

"The boy is not mine," Diego said harshly, his black eyes meeting the equally dark ones of the other man.

"My God." Dutch stared at him.

"She left me after I cost her our child," Diego said, his eyes dark and bitter with the memories. "Perhaps she sought consolation, or perhaps she did it for revenge. Whatever the reason, the child is an obstacle I cannot overcome." His eyes fell to the cheroot in his hand. "It has made things difficult."

Dutch was silent for a long moment. "You're very sure that she lost your child?"

That was when Diego first began to doubt what he'd been told five years ago. When Dutch put it into words, he planted a seed. Diego stared back at him with knitted brows.

"There was a doctor at the hospital," he told Dutch. "I tried later to find him, but he had gone to South America to practice. The nurse said Melissa was badly hurt in the fall, and Melissa herself told me the child was dead."

"You got drunk at our last reunion," Dutch recalled.

"And I put you to bed. You talked a lot. I know all about Melissa."

Diego averted his eyes. "Do you?" he asked stiffly.

"And you can take the poker out of your back," Dutch said. "You and I go back a long way. We don't have many secrets from each other. Things were strained between you and her. Isn't it possible that she might have hidden her pregnancy from you for fear that you'd try to take the boy from her?"

Diego stared at him, half-blind with shock. "Melissa would not do such a thing," he said shortly. "It is not her nature to lie. Even now, she has no heart for subterfuge."

Dutch shrugged. "You could be wrong."

"Not in this. Besides, the years are wrong," he said heavily. "Matthew is not yet four."

"I see."

Diego took another draw on his cheroot. Inside the office, the voices got louder, then stopped when the telephone rang. "I had my own suspicions at first, you know," he confessed. "But I soon forgot them."

"You might take a look at his birth certificate, all the same," Dutch suggested. "Just to be sure."

Diego smiled and said something polite. In the back of his mind there were new doubts. He wasn't certain about anything anymore, least of all his feelings for Melissa and his stubborn certainty that he knew her. He was beginning to think that he'd never known her at all. He'd wanted her, but he'd never made any effort to get to know her as a person.

When Diego came home, Matthew was sprawled on the bed and Melissa was reading to him. He paused in the doorway to watch them for a few seconds, his eyes growing tender as they traced the graceful lines of Melissa's body and then went to Matt, becoming puzzled and disturbed as he really looked at the child for the first time.

Yes, it could be so. Matthew could be his child. He had to admit it now. The boy had his coloring, his eyes. Matt had his nose and chin, but he had the shape of his mother's eyes, and his hair was only a little darker than hers. Except that the years were wrong—Matt would have to be over four years old if he was truly Diego's son. Melissa had said that he was just past three. But Diego knew so little about children of any age, and there was always the possibility that she hadn't told the exact truth. Little things she'd said, slips she'd made, could reveal a monumental deception.

She didn't lie as a rule, but this was an extraordinary situation. After all, she'd had more than enough reason to want to pay him back for his cruelty. And was she the kind of woman who could go from him to another man so easily? Had she? Or had she only been afraid, as Dutch had hinted—afraid of losing her son to his real father? She might think Diego capable of taking Matt away from her and turning her out of their lives. His jaw tautened as he remembered his treatment of her and exactly why she had good reason to see him that way. If he didn't know Melissa, then she certainly didn't know him. He'd never let her close enough to know him. What if he did let her come close? He turned away from the door, tempted for the first time to think of pulling down the barriers he'd built between them. He was alone, and so was she. Was there any hope for them now?

Melissa hobbled to the supper table with Matt's help. She looked worried, and Diego wondered what had upset her.

He didn't have to wait long. Halfway through the first course, she got up enough nerve to ask him a question that had plagued her all day.

"Do you think I might get a job when the doctor gives me the all-clear?" Melissa asked cautiously.

He put down his coffee cup and stared at her. "You have a job already, do you not?" he asked, nodding toward a contented Matthew, who was obviously enjoying his chicken dish.

"Of course, and I love looking after him and having time to spend with him for a change," she confessed. "But…" She sighed heavily. "I feel as if I'm not pulling my weight," she said finally. "It doesn't seem fair to make you support us."

He looked, and was, surprised at the remark. He leaned back in his chair, looking very Latin and faintly arrogant. "Melissa, you surely remember that I was a wealthy man in Guatemala. I work because I enjoy it, not because I need to. I have more than enough in Swiss banks to support all of us into old age and beyond."

"I didn't realize that." She toyed with her fork. "Still, I don't like feeling obligated to you."

His eyes flashed. "I am your husband. It is my duty, my obligation, my responsibility, to take care of you."

"And that's an archaic attitude," Melissa muttered, her own temper roused. "In the modern world, married people are partners."

"José's mama and papa used to fight all the time," Matthew observed with a wary glance at his mother. "And José's papa went away."

Diego drew in a sharp breath. "*Niñito,*" he said gently, "your mama and I will inevitably disagree from time to time. Married people do, *comprende?*"

Matthew moved a dumpling around on his plate with his fork. "*Yo no sé,*" he murmured miserably, but in perfect Spanish.

Diego frowned. He got up gracefully to kneel beside Matthew's chair. "*¿Hablas español?*" he asked gently, using the familiar tense.

"*Sí,*" Matthew said, and burst into half a dozen incomplete fears and worries in that language before Diego interrupted him by placing a long finger over his small mouth. His voice, when he spoke, was more tender than Melissa had ever heard it.

"*Niño,*" he said, his deep voice soothing, "we are a family. It will not be easy for any of us, but if we try, we can learn to get along with each other. Would it not please you, little one, to have time to spend with Mama, and a nice place to live, and toys to play with?"

Matt looked worried. "You don't like Matt," he mumbled.

Diego took a slow breath and ran his hand gently over the small head. "I have been alone for a long time," he said hesitantly. "I have had no one to show me how to be a father. It must be taught, you see, and only a small boy can teach it."

"Oh," Matt said, nodding his head. He shifted restlessly, and his dark eyes met Diego's. "Well…I guess I could." His brows knitted. "And we can go to the zoo and to the park and see baseball games and things?"

Diego nodded. "That, too."

"You don't have a little boy?"

Diego hated the lump in his throat. It was as if the years of feeling nothing at all had caught up with him at last. He felt as if a butterfly's wings had touched his heart and brought it to life for the first time. He looked at the small face, so much like his own, and was surprised at the hunger he felt to be this child's father, his real father. The loneliness was suddenly unbearable. "No," he said huskily. "I have…no little boy."

Melissa felt tears running hot down her shocked face. It was more than she'd dared hope for that Diego might be able to accept Matt, to want him, even though he believed he was another man's child. It was the first step in a new direction for all of them.

"I guess so," Matthew said with the simple acceptance of childhood. "And Mama and I would live with you?"

"Sí."

"I always wanted a papa of my own," Matthew confessed. "Mama said my own papa was a very brave man. He went away, but Mama used to say he might come back."

That broke the spell. Diego's face tautened as it turned to Melissa, his black eyes accusing, all the tenderness gone out of him at once as he considered that his whole line of thought might have been a fabrication, created out of his own loneliness and need and guilt.

"Did she?" he asked tersely.

Melissa fought for control, dabbing at the tears. "Matt, wouldn't you like to go and play with your bear?"

"Okay." He jumped down from his chair with a shy grin at Diego and ran off to his room. Except for the first night, he'd given them no trouble about sleeping alone. He seemed to enjoy having a room of his very own.

Diego's face was without a trace of emotion when he turned to her. "His father is still alive?" he said tersely.

She dropped her eyes to the table while her heartbeat shook her. "Yes."

"Where is he?"

She shook her head, unable to speak, to tell any more lies.

He took an angry breath. "Until you can trust me, how can we have a marriage?"

She looked up. "And that works both ways. You never trusted me. How can you expect me to trust you, Diego?"

"I was not aware that he spoke such excellent Spanish," he remarked after a minute, lessening the tension.

"It seemed to come naturally to him," she said. "It

isn't bad for a child to be bilingual, especially in Tucson, where so many people speak Spanish anyway. Most of his friends did."

He leaned back in his chair, his dark eyes sliding carelessly over Melissa's body. "You grow more lovely with each passing day," he said unexpectedly.

She flushed. "I didn't think you ever looked at me long enough to form an opinion."

He lit a cheroot, puffing on it quietly. "Things are not so simple anymore, are they? The boy is insecure."

"I'm sorry I argued with you," she said sadly. "I made everything worse."

"No. You and I are both responsible for that." He shrugged. "It is not easy, is it, *pequeña,* to forget the past we share?"

"Guatemala seems very far away sometimes, though." She leaned back. "What about the *finca,* Diego?"

"I have given that more thought than you realize, Melissa," he replied. He studied his cheroot. "It is growing more dangerous by the day to try to hold the estate, to provide adequate protection for my workers. I loathe the very thought of giving it up, but it is becoming too much of a financial risk. Now that I have you and the boy to consider, I have decided that I may well have to sell it."

"But your family has lived there for three generations," she protested. "It's your heritage."

"*Niña,* it is a spread of land," he said gently. "A bit

of stone and soil. Many lives have been sacrificed for it over the years, and more will be asked. I begin to think the sacrifices are too many." He leaned forward suddenly, his black eyes narrow. "Suppose I asked you to come with me to Guatemala, to bring Matthew, to raise him there."

Her breathing stopped for an instant. She faltered, trying to reconcile herself to the fear his words had fostered.

He nodded, reading her apprehension. "You see? You could no more risk the boy's life than I could." He sat back again. "It is much more sensible to lease or sell it than to take the risk of trying to live there. I like Chicago, *niña*. Do you?"

"Why, yes," she said slowly. "I suppose I do. I don't know about the winter...."

"We can spend the winter down in the Caribbean and come back in the spring. Apollo is thinking of expanding the company, Blain Security Consultants, to include antiterrorism classes in that part of the world." He smiled. "I can combine business with pleasure."

"You haven't told me about the kind of work you do," she reminded him. She wanted to know. This was one of the few times he'd ever let down his guard and talked to her, sharing another part of his life. It was flattering and pleasant.

"I teach tactics," he said. He put out the cheroot. "Dutch and I share the duties, and I also teach defensive driving to the chauffeurs of the very rich." He looked up at her. "You remember that I raced cars for a few years."

"My father mentioned it once," she said. Her eyes ran over his dark face. "You can't live without a challenge, can you? Without some kind of risk?"

"I have grown used to surges of adrenaline over the years," he mused, smiling. "Perhaps I have become addicted." He shrugged. "It is unlikely that I will make you a rich widow in the near future, Señora Laremos," he added mockingly, thinking bitterly of the boy's father.

"Money was never one of my addictions," she said with quiet pride. She got to her feet slowly. "But think what you like. Your opinion doesn't matter a lot to me these days, Señor."

"Yet it did once," he said softly, rising to catch her gently by the waist and hold her in front of him. "There was a time when you loved me, Melissa."

"Love can die, like dreams." She sighed wistfully, watching the quick rise and fall of his chest. "It was a long time ago, and I was very young."

"You are still very young, querida," he said, his voice deep and very quiet. "How did you manage, alone and pregnant, in a strange place?"

"I had friends," she said hesitantly. "And a good job, working as an assistant buyer for a department store's clothing department. Then I got pneumonia and everything fell apart."

"Yet you have managed enough time with Matthew to teach him values and pride and honor in his heritage."

She smiled. "I wanted him to be a whole person," she

said. She looked up, searching the dark eyes so close to hers. "You blame me, don't you? For betraying you…"

Her humility hurt him. It made him feel guilty for the things he'd said to her. He sighed wearily. "Was it not I who betrayed you?" he breathed, and bent to her mouth.

He'd never kissed her in quite that way before. She felt the soft pressure of his mouth with wonder as he cherished it, savored it in a silence ablaze with shared pleasure.

"But, Matthew…" she whispered.

"Kiss me, *querida*," he whispered, and his mouth covered hers again as he drew her against his lean, hard body and his lips grew quietly insistent.

She felt the need in him. Her legs trembled against his. Her mouth followed where his led, lost in its warm, bristly pressure. She put her arms around him and moved closer until she felt him stiffen, until she felt the sudden urgency of his body and heard him groan.

"No," he whispered roughly, pushing her away. His eyes glittered. His breathing was quick and unsteady. "No half measures. I want all of you or nothing. And it is too soon, is it not?"

She wanted to say no, but of course it was too soon, and not just physically. There were too many wounds, too many questions. She lowered her eyes to his chest. "I won't stop you," she said, shocking herself as well as the man standing so still in front of her. "I won't say no."

His fingers contracted, but only for an instant. "It has been a long time," he said in a deep, soft voice. "I do not think that I could be gentle with you the first time, despite the tenderness I feel for you." He shuddered almost imperceptibly. "My possession of you would be violent, and I could not bear to hurt you. It is not wise to let this continue." He let her go and moved away, with his back to her, while he lit another cheroot.

She watched him with curious eyes. Her body trembled with frustration, her leg ached. But she wanted nothing more in life than his body over hers in the sweet darkness.

"I want you," she whispered achingly.

He turned, his black eyes steady and hot. "No less than I want you, I assure you," he said tersely. "But first there must be a lowering of all the barriers. Tell me about Matthew's father, Melissa."

She wanted to. She needed to. But she couldn't tell him. He had to come to the realization himself, he had to believe in her innocence without having proof. "I can't," she moaned.

"Then know this: I have had enough of subterfuge and pretense. Until you tell me the truth, I swear that I will never touch you again."

She exhaled unsteadily. He was placing her in an intolerable position. She couldn't tell him the truth. She didn't trust him enough, and obviously he didn't trust her enough. If he loved her, he'd trust her enough to know that Matthew was his. But that had always been the problem—she loved too much and he loved too little. He was hot-blooded, and he desired her. But desire was a poor foundation for marriage. It wouldn't be enough.

Diego watched the expressions pass over her face. When he saw her teeth clench, he knew that he'd lost the round. She wasn't going to tell him. She was afraid. Well, there was still one other way to get at the truth. As Dutch had mentioned, there would surely be a birth certificate for Matthew. He would write to the Arizona Bureau of Vital Statistics and obtain a copy of it. That would give Diego the truth about Matt's age and his parentage. Diego had to know, once and for all, who Matthew's father was. Until he did, there was no hope of a future for him and Matthew and Melissa.

"It is late," he said without giving her a chance to say anything else. "You had better get some sleep."

Melissa hesitated, but only for an instant. It was disappointing. She felt they'd been so close to an understanding. She nodded, turning toward her room without another word.

It was like sitting on top of a bomb for the next few days. Melissa was more aware of Diego than ever before, but he was polite and courteous and not much more. The nights grew longer and longer.

But if she was frustrated, her son wasn't. Diego seemed to have a new shadow, because Matthew followed him everywhere when he wasn't working. Rather than resenting it, Diego seemed to love it. He indulged the child as never before, noticed him, played with him. His efforts were hesitant at first because he'd never spent much time around children. But as time wore on he learned to play, and the child became a necessary part of his day, of his life.

They went to the zoo that weekend, leaving Melissa with the television and a new videocassette of an adventure movie for company. They stayed until almost dark, and when they came back Matthew seemed a different boy. Oddly enough, Diego was different, too. There was an expression on his face and in his black eyes that Melissa didn't understand.

"We saw a cobra!" Matt told Melissa, his young face alive with excitement. "And a giraffe, and a lion, and a monkey! And I had cotton candy, and I rode a train, and a puppy dog chased me!" He giggled gleefully.

"And Papa is worn to a nub," Diego moaned, dropping wearily onto the sofa beside Melissa with a weary grin. "*Dios mío*, I almost bought a motorcycle just to keep up with him!"

"I wore Papa out," Matt chuckled, "didn't I, Papa?"

Melissa glanced from one of them to the other, curiosity evident in her gray eyes.

"Matthew's papa isn't coming back," Diego told her. He lit a cheroot with steady hands, his black eyes daring her to challenge the statement. "So I'm going to be his papa and take care of him. And he will be my son."

"I always wanted a papa of my own," Matthew told Melissa. He leaned his chin on the arm of the sofa and stared at her. "Since my papa's gone away, I want Diego."

Melissa drew a slow breath, barely breathing as all the things she'd told Matt about his father came back with vivid clarity. She prayed that he hadn't mentioned any of them to Diego. Especially the photograph...why in heaven's name had she shown Matt that photo!

But Diego looked innocent, and Matthew was obviously unruffled, so there couldn't have been any shared secrets. No. Of course not. She was worrying over nothing.

"Did you have a good time?"

Matt grinned. "We had a really good time, and tomorrow we're going to church."

Melissa hoped she wouldn't pass out. It wouldn't be good to shock the child. But her eyes looked like saucers as they slid to Diego's face.

"A child should be raised in the church," he said tersely. "When you are able, you may come with us."

"I'm not arguing," she said absently.

"Good, because it would avail you nothing. Matt, suppose you watch television while I organize something for us to eat? Do you want a fish?"

"Yes, please," the child said with a happy laugh, and ran to turn on cartoons.

"And you, *querida?*" he asked Melissa, letting his dark eyes slide over her gray slacks and low-cut cream sweater with soft desire.

"I'd like a chef's salad," she murmured. "There's a fish dinner in the freezer that Matt can have, and the salad's already made. I prepared it while you were gone. There's a steak I can grill for you...."

"I can do it." He got up, stretching lazily, and her eyes moved over him with helpless longing, loving the powerful lines of his tall body.

"I need to move around, though," she murmured. She got up and stood for a minute before she started to walk. The limp was still pronounced, but it didn't hurt half as bad to move as it had only a week ago. She laughed at her own progress.

"How easily the young heal," Diego remarked with a smile.

"I'm not that young, Diego," she said.

He moved close to her, taking her by the waist to lazily draw her body to him, holding her gently. "You are when you laugh, *querida*," he said, smiling. "What memories you bring back of happy times we shared in Guatemala."

The smile faded. "Were there any?" she asked sadly.

He searched her soft gray eyes. "Do you not remember how it was with us, before we married? The comradeship we had, the ease of being together?"

"I was a child and you were an adult." She dropped her eyes. "I was bristling with hero-worship and buried in dreams."

"And then we took refuge in a Mayan ruin." He was whispering so that Matt, who was engrossed in a television program, wouldn't hear. "And we became lovers, with the rain blowing around us and the threat of danger everywhere. Your body under my body, *Melissa mía*, your cries in my mouth as I kissed you…"

She moved away too fast and almost fell, her face beet red and her heart beating double time. "I—" She had to try again because her voice squeaked. "I'll just fix the salad dressing, Diego."

He watched her go with a faint, secretive smile. Behind him, Matt was laughing at a cartoon, and Diego glanced his way with an expression that he was glad Melissa couldn't see. Matt had told him about the photograph of his father while they'd been looking at a poster that showed banana trees.

Those funny-looking trees, Matt exclaimed, were in the photo his Mama had of his papa. And his papa was wearing a big hat and riding a horse.

Diego had leaned against a wall for support, and he didn't remember what he'd mumbled when Matt had kept on talking. But even though he'd sent for the birth certificate, it was no longer necessary. There couldn't be another photo like the one Matt described, and it was with amused fury that he realized the man he'd been jealous of was himself.

He was Matt's father. Matt was the child Melissa had sworn she'd lost. It even made sense that she'd hidden her pregnancy from him. She'd probably been afraid that he didn't care enough about her to let her stay after the child was born. More than likely she'd thought that Diego would take her baby from her and send her away. She'd run to keep that from happening.

She was still running. She hadn't told him the truth about Matt because she didn't trust him enough. Perhaps she didn't love him enough anymore, either. He was going to have to work on that. But at least he knew the truth, and that was everything. He looked at his son with fierce pride and knew that, whatever happened, he couldn't give up Matt. He couldn't give up Melissa, either, but he was going to have to prove that to her first.

After supper, Diego and Matthew sprawled on the carpet in front of the television. Melissa's eyes softened at the two of them, so alike, so dark and delightfully Latin, laughing and wrestling in front of the television. Diego was in his stocking feet, his shirt unbuttoned in front, his hair disheveled, his eyes laughing at his son. He looked up with the laughter still in his face and saw Melissa watching him. For an instant, something flared in his eyes and left them darkly disturbing. She flushed and looked away, and she heard him laugh. Then Matthew attacked him again and the spell was broken. But it left Melissa shaken and hungry. Diego was accepting Matt, and that should have satisfied her. But it didn't. She wanted Diego to love her. When, she wondered bitterly, had she ever wanted anything else? But it seemed as impossible now as it had in the past. He wanted her, but perhaps he had nothing left to offer.

DIEGO WAS INVOLVED WITH work for the next few weeks. The atmosphere at the apartment was much less strained. Matt played with Diego, and the two of them were becoming inseparable. And Diego looked at Melissa with lazy indulgence and began to tease her gently now and again. But the tension between them was growing, and her nervousness with him didn't help. She couldn't understand his suddenly changed attitude toward Matt and herself. Because she couldn't figure out the reason behind his turnaround, she didn't trust it.

When the time came for her final checkup, Diego took time off from work to take her to the doctor.

She was pronounced cured and released from the doctor's care. He told her to progress slowly with her rapidly healing leg but said she was fit to work again.

When she told Diego that and started hinting at wanting to get a job, he felt uneasy. She'd run away from him once, and he was no longer able to hide his growing affection for the boy. What if she knew that he suspected the truth? Would she take Matt and run again, fearing that Diego might be trying to steal him away from her? His blood ran cold at the prospect, but he wasn't confident enough to put the question to her. He might force her hand if he wasn't careful. The thing was, how was he going to keep her?

He worried the question all the way back to the apartment, reserved and remote as he pondered. He went back to work immediately after dropping her off at the apartment. He didn't even speak as he went out the door. His withdrawal worried Melissa.

"You need some diversion, Mrs. Laremos," Mrs. Albright chided as she fixed lunch for them. "Staying around this apartment all the time just isn't healthy."

"You know, I do believe you're right," Melissa agreed

with a sigh. "I think I'll call Joyce and take her out to lunch tomorrow. I might even get a job."

"Your husband won't like that, if you don't mind my saying so, ma'am," Mrs. Albright murmured as she shredded carrots for a salad.

"I'm afraid he won't," Melissa said. "But that isn't going to stop me."

She dropped a kiss on Matthew's dark head as he sat engrossed in a children's program on the educational network and went into Diego's study to use the phone.

It was bad luck that she couldn't remember the name of Apollo's company. Diego surely had it written down somewhere. She didn't like going into his desk, but this was important. She opened the middle drawer and found a black book of numbers. But underneath it was an open envelope that caught her attention.

With a quick glance toward the door and a pounding heart, she drew it out and looked at it. The return address was the Arizona Bureau of Vital Statistics. Her cold, nervous hands fumbled it open, and she drew out what she'd been afraid she'd find—a copy of Matthew's birth certificate. Under father, Diego's full name and address were neatly typed.

She sighed, fighting back tears. So he knew. But he hadn't said anything. He'd questioned her and promised her that he wouldn't come near her again until she told him the truth about Matthew. Why? Did it matter so much to his pride? Or was he just buying time to gain

Matthew's affection before he forced Melissa out of their lives? Perhaps despite what he'd said about Guatemala he meant to take Matthew there and leave Melissa behind. His lack of ardor since he and Matt had gone to the zoo, his lack of attention to her, made her more uncertain than ever. And today, his remoteness when the doctor had said she could work. Was he thinking about throwing her out now that she no longer needed his support?

She was frightened, and her first thought was to pack a case and get Matthew far away, as fast as possible. But that would be irrational. She had to stop and think. She had to be logical, not make a spur-of-the-moment decision that she might come to regret.

She put the birth certificate back into the envelope and replaced it carefully, facedown under the black book, and closed the drawer. She didn't dare get a number out of it now because Diego would know that she'd been into his desk drawer.

Then she remembered that Mrs. Albright would surely have his number. She went into the kitchen and asked the woman.

"Oh, certainly, Mrs. Laremos," she smiled. "It's listed under Blain Security Consultants, Incorporated, in the telephone directory." She eyed Melissa curiously. "Are you all right? You seem very pale."

"I'm fine." Melissa forced a smile. "It's just a little hard to get around. The ligament is healed, but my leg is stiff. They wanted me to have physical therapy, but I settled for home exercises instead. I'm sure it will limber up once I start them."

"My sister had a bad back, and the doctor put her on exercises," Mrs. Albright remarked. "They helped a great deal. I'm sure you'll do fine, ma'am."

"Yes. So am I. Thank you."

She went into the living room and looked up the number, dialing it with shaky hands.

Joyce's musical voice answered after the second ring. "Blain Security Consultants. How may we help you?"

"You can come out to lunch with me tomorrow and help me save my sanity," Melissa said dryly. "It's Melissa, Diego's wife."

"Yes, I recognized your voice, Melissa," Joyce said with a laugh. "And I'd be delighted to go to lunch with you. Shall I pick you up at your apartment about 11:30? If my boss will let me—"

Apollo's deep, angry voice sounded from a distance. "Since when do I deny you a lunch hour, Miss Latham? By all means, if that's Melissa, you can take her to lunch. Stop making me out to be an ogre."

"I'd never do such a thing, Mr. Blain," Joyce assured him stiffly. "It would be an insult to the ogre."

There was a muttered curse, and a door slammed. Joyce sighed and Melissa hid a giggle.

"See you tomorrow," Joyce whispered. "I'd better get to work or I may wind up out the window on my head."

"It sounds that way, yes. Have a nice day."

"You too!"

That evening, Diego came home late. He was just in time to kiss Matthew good night. Melissa, watching them from the doorway, saw the affection and pride in his dark face as he looked at his son. How long had he known? Perhaps he'd suspected it from the beginning. She sighed, thinking how transparent she'd always been to him. She was so green, how could he help but know that she couldn't sleep with anyone except him? Probably he even knew how deeply she loved him. His cruelty in the past, his rejection, even his indifference, didn't seem to affect her feelings. She wondered where she was going to get the strength to leave him. But if he was thinking about taking Matthew away from her, she wouldn't have any choice. He'd never made any secret of his opinion about love. He didn't believe in it. She had no reason to suspect that his feelings had changed over the years.

He loved Matthew, if he loved anyone. Melissa was a complication he didn't really seem to want. When he stood up and moved to the door, Melissa hid her eyes from him. She didn't want him to see the worry in them.

"Joyce said you're taking her out to lunch tomorrow," he remarked after she'd called another good night to Matthew and closed his bedroom door.

"Yes. I thought I might try getting out of the apartment a little bit," she said. "It's…lonely here."

He stopped at her bedroom door, his eyes dark and quiet. "It will not always be like this," he said. "When time permits, now that you are able to get around, we will find some things that we can do as a family."

She smiled wistfully. "You don't need to feel obligated to include me."

He frowned. "Why?"

She'd forgotten how clever he was. She averted her eyes. "Well, boys like to be with men sometimes without women along, don't they?"

He eyed her curiously. He'd expected her to say more than that. He felt irritable at his own disappointment. What had he expected? She'd held out so long now that he didn't really expect her to give in. He was giving way slowly to a black depression. He'd left her alone, hoping she'd come to him and tell him the truth, and she hadn't. Suppose he'd misjudged her feelings? What if she didn't care? What if she left him, now that she didn't need him to take care of her?

He barely remembered that she'd asked him a question. "I suppose it is good for Matthew to spend some time with just me," he answered her wearily. His face mirrored his fatigue. There were new, harsh lines on it. He studied her slowly for a moment before he turned away. "I have had a long day. If you don't mind, Señora Laremos, I prefer sleep to conversation."

"Of course. Good night," she said, surprised by his tone as well as by the way he looked.

He nodded and went down the hall. She watched him, her eyes wistful and soft and full of regret. Love wasn't the sweet thing the movies made of it, she thought bitterly. It was painful and long-suffering for all its sweetness. He wanted Matthew, but did he want her? She wondered what she was going to do.

She turned away and went into her own bedroom, looking at herself in the mirror. She looked thinner and older, and there were new lines in her face. Did Diego ever think about the past, she wondered, about the times the two of them had gone riding in the Guatemalan valleys and talked about a distant future? She thought of it often, of the way Diego had once been.

She opened her chest of drawers and pulled out the snapshot she'd taken of Diego the day before her father had found them in the hills. Her fingers touched the face lightly and she sighed. How long ago it all seemed, how futile. She'd loved him, and pain was the only true memory she had. If only, she thought, he'd loved her a little in return. But perhaps he really wasn't capable of it. She tucked the photo away and closed the drawers. Dreams were no substitute for reality.

CHAPTER EIGHT

THE RESTAURANT THAT JOYCE and Melissa went to was small and featured French cuisine. Melissa picked her way through a delicious chicken-and-broccoli crepe and a fresh melon while Joyce frowned over her elaborate beef dish.

"You're very quiet for someone who wanted to talk," Joyce remarked fifteen minutes into the exquisite meal, her dark eyes quietly scrutinizing Melissa's face.

Melissa sighed. "I've got a problem."

Joyce smiled. "Who hasn't?"

"Yes. Well, mine is about to make me pack a bag and leave Chicago."

Joyce put down her fork. "In that case, I'm all ears."

Melissa picked up her coffee cup and sipped the sweet, dark liquid. "Matthew is Diego's son," she said. "The son I told him I lost before I ran away from him five years ago."

"That's a problem?" Joyce asked blankly.

"I didn't think he knew. He didn't seem to like Matt at first, but now they're inseparable. I thought that maybe he was beginning to accept Matt even though he thought he was another man's son. But yesterday I found a copy of Matthew's birth certificate in his desk drawer."

"If he knows, everything will be all right, won't it?" Joyce asked her.

"That's just it," Melissa said miserably. "It was important to me that he'd believe Matt was his son, without proof, that he'd believe I could never have betrayed him. But now I'll never be sure. And lately Diego acts as if he doesn't want me around. I even think I know why. He knows that Matt is his, and he hates me for letting him think I lost his child."

Joyce blinked. "Come again?"

"That's really a long story." Melissa smiled and stared into her coffee. "I thought I was justified at the time not to tell him or get in touch with him. The way he used to feel about me, I was sure he'd try to take Matt away."

"Maybe he would have," the other woman said gently. "You can't blame yourself too much. You must have had good reasons."

Melissa lifted tortured eyes. "Did I? Oh, there's been fault on both sides, you know. But now that he knows Matt is his, he has to be thinking about all the time he's missed with his son. He has to blame me for that, even though I had provocation. And now I'm afraid that he may be trying to win Matt away from me. He may take him away!"

"That is pure hysteria," Joyce said firmly. "Get hold

of yourself, girl! You can't run away this time. You've got to stay and fight for your son. Come to think of it," she added, "you might try fighting for your husband as well. He married you. He had to care about you."

Melissa grimaced as she fingered her cup. "Diego didn't really want to marry me. We were found in a compromising situation, which he thought I planned, and he was forced to marry me. He and his family made me feel like a leper, and when I discovered that I was pregnant, I couldn't bear the thought of bringing up my child in such an atmosphere of hatred. So I let him think I lost the baby and I ran away."

"There's no chance that he loves you?"

She smiled wistfully. "Diego was a mercenary for even longer than the rest of the group. He told me once that he didn't believe in love, that it was a luxury he couldn't afford. He wants me. But that's all."

Joyce studied her friend's sad expression. "You and I are unlucky in love," she said finally. "I work for a man who hates me and you live with a man who doesn't love you."

"You hate Apollo, too," Melissa pointed out.

Joyce smiled, her eyes wistful. "Do I?"

"Oh." Melissa put the cup down. "I see."

"I give him the response he expects to keep him from seeing how I really feel. Look at me," she moaned. "He's a handsome, rich, successful man. Why would he want someone as plain and unattractive as I am? I wish I were as pretty as you are."

"Me? Pretty?" Melissa was honestly astounded.

Joyce glowered at her. "Do you love Diego?"

It was a hard question to answer honestly, but in the end she had to. "I always have," she confessed. "I suppose I always will."

"Then why don't you stop running away from him and start running toward him?" Joyce suggested. "Running hasn't made you very happy, has it?"

"It's made me pretty miserable. But how can I stay with a man who doesn't want me?"

"You could make him want you." She reached out and touched Melissa's hand. "Is he worth fighting for?"

"Oh, yes!"

"Then do it. Stop letting the past create barriers."

Melissa frowned slightly. "I don't know very much about how to vamp a man."

Joyce shrugged. "Neither do I. So what? We can learn together."

This was sounding more delightful by the minute. Melissa was nervous, but she knew that Diego wanted her, and the knowledge gave her hope. "I suppose we could give it a try. If things don't work out—"

"Trust me. They'll work out."

"Then if I have to do it, so do you." Melissa pursed her lips. "Did you know that I was an assistant buyer for a clothing store? I have a passable eye for fashion, and I know what looks good on people. Suppose we go shopping together. I'll show you what to buy to make you stand out."

Joyce raised her eyebrows. "Why?"

"Because with very little work you could be a knock-out. Think of it, Apollo on his knees at your desk, sighing with adoration," she coaxed.

Joyce grimaced. "The only way he'd be on his knees at my desk would be if I kicked him in the stomach."

"Pessimist! You're the one giving the pep talk. Suppose we both listen to you and try to practice what you preach?"

The other woman sighed. "Well, what have we got to lose, after all?"

"Not much, from where I'm sitting. How about Saturday morning? You can take me to the right department stores, and I'll make suggestions."

"I do have a little in my savings account," Joyce murmured. She smiled. "All right. We'll do it."

"Great!" Melissa started on her dessert. "Amazing how good this food tastes all of a sudden. I think I feel better already."

"So do I. But if Apollo throws me out the window, you're in a lot of trouble."

"He won't. Eat up."

Melissa's head was full of ideas. Joyce had inspired her. She hadn't really tried to catch Diego's eye since they'd been back together. Even in the old days she'd never quite lived up to her potential. She wasn't any more experienced now, but she was well-traveled and she'd learned a lot from listening to other women talk and watching them in action as they attracted men. She

was going to turn the tables on her reluctant husband
and see if she couldn't make him like captivity. Whether
or not the attempt failed, she had to try. Joyce was right.
Running away had only complicated things. This time,
she had to stand and fight.

While she was out, she'd bought a memory card game
for Matthew, and when Diego came home that night she
was sprawled on the carpet with her son. She made a pretty
picture in a clinging beige sleeveless blouse and tight
jeans. Diego paused in the doorway, and when she saw him
she rolled onto her side, striking a frankly seductive pose.

"Good evening, Señor Laremos," she murmured.
"Matthew has a new game."

"I can remember where the apple is," Matthew enthused, jumping up to hug his father and babble excitedly
about the game and how he'd already beaten Mama once.

"He has a quick mind," Diego remarked as he studied the large pile of matched cards on Matthew's side
of the playing area and the small one on Melissa's.

"Very quick," she agreed, laughing at Matthew's
smug little face. "And he's modest, too."

"I know everything," Matthew said with innocent
certainty. "Will you play with us, Papa?"

"After dinner, niño," the tall man agreed. "I must
change, and there is a phone call I have to make."

"Okay!" Matthew went back to turning over cards.

"Only two," Melissa cautioned. "It's cheating if you
keep peeking under all of them."

"Yes, Mama."

She took her turn, aware that Diego's eyes were on the deep vee of her blouse, under which she was wearing nothing at all.

She sat up again, glancing at him. "Is something wrong, *señor?*"

"Of course not. Excuse me." He turned, frowning, and went off toward his bedroom. Melissa smiled secretively as she watched Matthew match two oranges.

Dinner was noisy because Mrs. Albright had taken Matthew down to the lobby to meet her daughter and grandson, who were just back from a Mexican trip, and the daughter had given Matt a small wooden toy, a ball on a string that had to be bounced into the cup it was attached to. Matt was overjoyed with both his new friend and his toy.

"Ah," Diego smiled. "Yes, these are very common in my part of the world, and your mother's," he added with a smile at Melissa. "Are they not, *querida?* I can remember playing with one as a child myself."

"Where we lived there were no toy stores," she told Matthew. "We lived far back in the country, near a volcano, and there were ancient Mayan ruins all around." She colored a little, remembering one particular ruin. She looked at Diego and found the same memory in his dark eyes as they searched hers.

"*Sí,*" he said gently. "The ruins were…potent."

Her lips parted. "Five years," she said, her eyes more eloquent than she knew. "And sometimes it seems like days."

"Not for me," he said abruptly, drawing his eyes back to his coffee cup. "It has not been easy, living through the black time that came afterward."

Matthew was trying to play with his toy, but Melissa took it and put it firmly beside his plate, indicating that he should eat his food first. He grimaced and picked up his fork.

"Did you never think of contacting me?" he asked unexpectedly, and his eyes narrowed. It disturbed him more and more, thinking about all he'd missed. Understanding the reason for Melissa's actions didn't make the lack of contact with his child any easier to bear. He'd missed so much of the boy's life, all the things that most fathers experienced and cherished in memory. Matt's first word, his first step, the early days when parents and children became bonded. He'd had none of that.

Melissa sighed sadly, remembering when Matthew had been born and how desperately she'd wanted Diego. But he hadn't wanted her. He'd made it so plain after their marriage, and even after her fall down the steps he'd been unapproachable. "I thought about it once," she said quietly, wondering if he was going to accuse her of denying him his rights. She wouldn't have had a reply. "But you'd made it clear that I had no place in your life, Diego, that you only married me to spare your family more disgrace."

He studied his cup. "You never considered that I might have had a change of heart, Melissa? That I might have regretted, bitterly, my treatment of you?"

"No," she said honestly. Her pale eyes searched his dark ones. "I didn't want to play on your guilt. It was better that I took care of myself." She dropped her gaze to the table. "And Matt."

"It must have been difficult when he was born," he probed, trying to draw her out.

She smiled faintly, remembering. "Something went wrong," she murmured. "They had to do a cesarean section."

He caught his breath. "My God. And you had no one to turn to."

She looked at Matthew warmly. "I managed very well. I had neighbors who were kind, and the company I worked for was very understanding. My boss made sure my insurance paid all my bills, and he even gave me an advance on my salary so that we had enough to eat."

His fingers contracted around the cup almost hard enough to break it. It didn't bear thinking about. Melissa must have been in severe pain, alone and with an infant to be responsible for. His eyes closed. It hurt him terribly to think that if he'd been kinder to her he could have shared that difficulty with her. He could have been there when she'd needed someone, been there to take care of her. His anguish at being denied all those years with Matt seemed a small thing by comparison.

"It wasn't so bad, Diego," she said softly, because there was pain in his face. "Really it wasn't. And he was the sweetest baby—"

Diego got up abruptly. "I have phone calls to make. Please excuse me."

Melissa watched him, aching for him. His stiff back said it all. She realized then that it wasn't so much her predicament as missing the birth of his son that had hurt him. She felt guilty about that, too, but there was nothing to be done about it now.

Diego went into the study and closed the door, leaning heavily back against it. He couldn't stand the anguish of knowing what she'd suffered because of him. If only he could talk to her. Bare his heart. Tell her what he really felt, how much she and the boy meant to him. He wondered sometimes if he was still capable of real emotion. His past had been so violent, and tenderness had no place in it. He was only now learning that he was capable of it, with his child and even with Melissa, who more and more was becoming the one beautiful thing in his life. The longer they stayed together, the harder it became for him to hide his increasing hunger for her. Not that it was completely physical now, as it had been in the very beginning in Guatemala. No. It was becoming so much more. But he was uncertain of her. She changed before his eyes, first resentful, then shy and remote, and now she seemed oddly affectionate and teasing.

That, of course, could be simply a kind of repayment, for his having taken care of her and Matt and given them a home when she'd needed time to heal. Was that it? Was it gratitude, or was it something more? He couldn't tell.

But perhaps it was too soon. She didn't trust him enough to tell him about Matthew. When she did, there might be time for such confessions.

Melissa went back into the living room with Matthew and spread the memory cards out on the floor. They were into the second round before Diego came in again. He'd taken off his jacket and tie and rolled up the sleeves of his white shirt. It was unbuttoned in front, and Melissa's eyes went helplessly to the hair-covered expanse of brown muscle.

He noticed her glance and delighted in her response to him. No woman had ever made him feel as masculine and proud as Melissa. Her soft eyes had a light in them when she looked at him that made his body sing with pleasure. Desire was the one thing he was certain of. She couldn't begin to hide it from his experienced eyes.

"Play with us, Papa!" Matthew called, inviting the tall man down onto the carpet with them.

"We'll make room for you," Melissa said, smiling softly. She moved toward Matthew, making a space beside her where she was lying on her stomach and lifting cards.

"Perhaps for a moment or two," Diego agreed. He took off his shoes and slid alongside Melissa, the warm, cologne-scented length of his body almost touching hers. "How does one play this game?"

They explained it to him and watched him turn over two cards that matched. Matthew laughed and Melissa groaned as he pulled them near him and made a neat stack.

He smiled at Melissa with a wicked twinkle in his

black eyes. "I was watching from the doorway," he confessed. "Although not so much the cards as—" his gaze went to her derriere, so nicely outlined in the tight jeans "—other things."

She flushed, but her gaze didn't falter. "Lecher," she accused in a whisper, teasing.

That surprised and delighted him. His gaze dropped to her smiling mouth, and he bent suddenly and brushed his lips over hers in a whisper of pressure.

Matthew laughed joyfully. "Bobby's mama and daddy used to kiss like that, only Bobby said his mama used to kiss his daddy all the time."

Diego chuckled. "Your mama is not up to kissing me, *niño*. She is weak from her accident."

Melissa glanced at him mischievously. "Matt, will you go to the kitchen and bring me a cold soft drink, please? And be careful not to open it, okay?"

"Okay!" He jumped up and ran from the room.

Melissa smiled at Diego wickedly. "So I'm too weak to kiss you, am I, *señor?*" she murmured with soft bravado, enjoying the dark, glittering pleasure she read in his faintly shocked eyes.

She rolled over, pushing him gently onto the carpet. He chuckled with open delight as she bent over him and kissed him with a fervor that dragged a reluctant groan from his lips before his arms reached up and gathered her against him.

"Too weak, am I?" Melissa breathed into his hard mouth.

His hand contracted in her soft, wavy blond hair, and the bristly pressure of his mouth grew rough as he turned her gently and eased her down onto the carpet. She could feel the fierce thunder of his heartbeat against her breasts as her arms curled around his neck and she sighed into his hungry mouth. Her blood sang at the sweet contact. He lifted his head abruptly, and she saw the savage desire in the black eyes that stared unblinking into hers.

"*¡Cuidado*," he murmured. "You tempt fate."

"Not fate," she whispered unsteadily. "Only you, *señor*." Her hand slid under his shirt, against his body, her fingers spearing into the dark hair that covered his warm muscles. He stiffened, and she sighed contentedly. "Well, if you don't want to be assaulted, keep your shirt buttoned."

He laughed, thrown completely off balance by the way she was acting with him. "*Dios*, what has become of my shy little jungle orchid?"

"She grew up." Her soft eyes searched his. "You don't mind...?"

He pressed her hand against his chest. "No," he said quietly. "Do what you please, little one. So long as you do not mind the inevitable consequence of such actions as this. You understand?"

"I understand," she whispered, her eyes warm with secrets.

As she spoke, she drew one of Diego's hands to her body and sat up gracefully. Holding his eyes, she pressed his palm against her blouse where there was no fabric to conceal the hard thrust of her body.

His breath sighed out as his hand caressed her. "Is this premeditated?" he asked roughly.

"Oh, yes," she confessed, leaning her head against his shoulder because his touch was so sweet. "Diego—"

He drew his hand away. "No. Not here."

She looked up at him. "Not interested?" she asked bravely.

His jaw clenched. "Sweet idiot," he breathed. "If I held you against me now, my interest would be all too apparent. But this is not the game we need to be playing at the moment."

She cleared her throat, aware of where they were. "Yes. Of course." She smiled, avoiding his eyes, and turned over again as Matt came rushing back into the room with her soft drink. She opened it after thanking the laughing little boy. Then sighing, she turned back to the game.

Diego lounged nearby, watching but not participating. The look in his dark eyes was soft and dangerous, and he hardly glanced away from Melissa for the rest of the evening. But his attitude was both curious and remote. He seemed to suspect her motives for this new ardor, and she lost her nerve because of it, withdrawing into her shell again. There were times when Diego seemed very much a stranger.

Matthew was put to bed eventually. Melissa kept her expression hidden from Diego but felt her knees knocking every time he came close. She wished she knew if her forwardness had offended him, but she was too shy to ask him. While he was bidding Matthew good night, she called her own good night and went into her room. She locked it for the first time since she'd come to the apartment, and only breathed again when she heard his footsteps going down the hall. To her secret chagrin, the steps didn't even hesitate at her door.

On Saturday, Melissa and Joyce spent the entire day buying clothes and having their hair done. The colors she pointed Joyce toward were flamboyant and colorful, bringing attention to her lovely figure and making the most of her exquisite complexion.

"These are sexy clothes," Joyce said, her misgivings evident as she tried on a dress with a halter top that clung like ivy to her slender body. The color was a swirl of reds and yellows and oranges and whites, and it suited her beautifully. "I'll never be able to pull this off."

"Of course you will," Melissa assured her. "All you really need is a little self-confidence. The clothes will give you that and improve your posture, too. You'll feel slinky, so you'll walk like a cat. Try it and see."

Joyce laughed nervously, but when she got a look at herself in one of the exclusive boutique's full-length mirrors, she blinked and drew in her breath. It was as if she suddenly felt reborn. She began to walk, hesitantly at first, then with more and more poise, until she was moving like the graceful West Indian woman she was.

"Yes!" Melissa laughed, clapping her hands. "Yes,

that's exactly what I expected. You have a natural grace of carriage, but you've been hiding it in drab, loose clothing. You have a beautiful figure. Show it off!"

Joyce could hardly believe what she was seeing. She tried on another outfit and a turban, and seemed astonished by the elegant creature who looked out of the mirror at her.

"That can't be me," she murmured.

"But it is." Melissa grinned. "Come on. You've got the clothes. Now let's get the rest of the image."

She took Joyce to a hairstylist who did her hair in a fashionable cut that took years off her age and gave her even more poise, drawing her long hair back into an elegant bun with wisps around her small ears. She looked suddenly like a painting, all smooth lines and graceful curves.

"Just one more thing," Melissa murmured, and took her friend to the cosmetics department.

Joyce was given a complete make-over, with an expert cosmetician to show her which colors of powder to have mixed especially for her and which lipsticks and eye shadows and blushers to set off her creamy, blemishless complexion.

"That is not me," Joyce assured her image when the woman was finished and smiling contentedly at her handiwork.

"Poor Apollo," Melissa said with a faint smile. "Poor, poor man. He's done for."

Joyce's heart was in her big eyes. "Is he really?"

"I would say so," Melissa assured her. "Now. Let's get my wardrobe completed and then we'll get to work on the menu for a dinner party Monday night. But you can't wear any of your new clothes or makeup until then," she cautioned. "It has to be a real surprise."

Joyce grinned back at her. "Okay. I can hardly wait!"

"That makes two of us!"

Melissa still had a little money in her own bank account, which she'd had Diego move to Chicago from Tucson. She drew on that to buy some new things of her own. She had her own hair styled, as well, and opted for the makeup job. She tingled with anticipation and fear. Diego wasn't the same easygoing man she'd known in Guatemala. He was much more mature, and his experience intimidated her. If only she could get her nerve back. She had to, because he seemed determined not to make the first move.

By the time she and Joyce finished and went back to the apartment, it was almost dark and Melissa was limping a little.

"You've overdone it," Joyce moaned. "Oh, I hope all this hasn't caused a setback!"

"I'm just sore," Melissa assured her. "And it was fun! Wait until next week, and then the fireworks begin. Don't you dare go near the office like that."

"I wouldn't dream of shocking Apollo into a nervous breakdown," the other woman promised. "I'll go home and practice slinking. Melissa, I can never thank you enough."

Melissa only smiled. "What are friends for? You gave me the pep talk. The least I could do was help you out a little. You look great, by the way. Really pretty."

Joyce beamed. "I hope that wild man at the office thinks so."

"You mark my words, he will. Good night."

"Good night."

Melissa let herself into the apartment. Mrs. Albright had the evening off, and it was a shock to find Diego and their son in the kitchen with spicy smells wafting up from the stove.

Diego was wearing Mrs. Albright's long white apron over his slacks and sports shirt, and little Matthew was busily tearing up lettuce to make a salad.

"What are you doing?" Melissa burst out after she'd deposited her packages on the living-room sofa.

"Making dinner, *querida*," Diego said with a smile. "Our son is preparing a heart-of-lettuce salad, and I am making chili and enchiladas. Did you and Joyce have a good time?"

"A wonderful time. My goodness, can't I help?"

"Of course. Set the table, if you please. And do not disturb the cooks," he added with a wicked glance.

She laughed softly, moving to his side. She reached up impulsively and brushed a kiss against his hard cheek. "You're a darling. Can I have the van Meers and the Brettmans and Apollo and Joyce to dinner Monday night?"

Diego caught his breath at her closeness and the unexpected kiss. "Little one, you can have the boy's club wrestling team over if this change in you is permanent."

"Have I changed?" she mused, her pale gray eyes searching his as she clung to his arm and smiled, encouraged by his smile and the softness in his dark eyes.

"More than you realize, perhaps. The leg, it is not painful?"

"A little stiff, that's all."

"Papa, something is burning," Matthew pointed out.

Diego jerked his attention back to the heavy iron skillet he was using, and he began to stir the beef quickly. "The cook had better return to the chili, *amada*, or we will all starve. Dessert must wait, for the moment," he added in a tone that made her toes curl.

"As you wish, *señor*. She laughed softly, moving away reluctantly to put the dishes and silverware on the table.

It was the best meal she could remember in a long time, and dinner brought with it memories of Guatemala and its spicy cuisine. She and Diego talked, but of work and shopping trips and how much Diego had enjoyed the trip to the zoo with Matthew, who enthused about seeing a real lion. For the first time, there were no arguments.

When the little boy was put to bed, Melissa curled up on the sofa to watch a movie on cable while Diego apologetically did paperwork.

"This is new to me," he murmured as he scribbled notes. "But I find that I like the involvement in Apollo's company, as well as the challenge of helping businessmen learn to combat terrorism."

"I suppose it's all very hush-hush," she ventured.

"Assuredly so." He chuckled. "Or what would be the purpose in having such a business to teach survival tactics, hmm?"

She pushed her hair away from her face. "Diego... how do you think Apollo really feels about Joyce?"

He looked up. "No, no," he cautioned, waving a lean finger at her with an indulgent smile. "Such conversations are privileged. I will not share Apollo's secrets with you."

She colored softly. "Fair enough. I won't tell you Joyce's."

"You look just as you did at sixteen," he said softly, watching her, "when I refused to take you to the bull ring with me. You remember, *querida?* You would not speak to me for days afterward."

"I'd have gone to a snake charmer's cell to be with you in those days," she confessed quietly. "I adored you."

"I knew that. It was why I was so careful to keep you at arm's length. I succeeded particularly well, in fact, until we were cut off by a band of guerrillas and forced to hide out in a Mayan ruin. And then I lost my head and satisfied a hunger that had been gnawing at me for a long, long time."

"And paid the price," she added quietly.

He sighed. "You paid more than I did. I never meant to hurt you. It was difficult knowing that my own lack of control had led me to that precipice and pushed me over. I should never have accused you of trapping me."

"But there was so much animosity in our pasts," she said. "And you didn't love me."

His dark eyes narrowed. "I told you once that my emotions were deeply buried."

"Yes. I remember. You needn't worry, Diego," she said wearily. "I know you don't have anything to offer me, and I'm not asking for anything. Only for a roof over my head and the chance to raise my son without having to go on welfare." Her pale eyes searched his hard face. "But I'll gladly get a job and pull my weight. I want you to know that."

He glared at her. "Have I asked for such a sacrifice?"

"Well, you aren't getting any other benefits, are you?" she muttered. "All I'm giving you is two more mouths to feed and memories of the past that must be bitter and uncomfortable."

He got up, holding his paperwork in one clenched fist. He stared at her angrily. "You build walls, when I seek only to remove barriers. We still have a long way to go, *querida*. But before we can make a start, you have to learn to trust me."

"Trust is difficult," she retorted, glaring at him. "And you betrayed me once."

"Yes. Did you not betray me with Matthew's father?"

She started to speak and couldn't. She turned and left the room, her new resolve forgotten in the heat of anger. They seemed to grow farther apart every day, and she couldn't get through to Diego, no matter how hard she tried.

Perhaps the dinner party would open a few doors. Meanwhile, she'd bide her time and pray. He had to care a little about her. If not, why would the past even matter to him? The thought gave her some hope, at least.

CHAPTER NINE

THE ONE CONSOLATION MELISSA had after a sleepless night was the equally bloodshot look of Diego's eyes. Apparently their difference of opinion the night before had troubled him as much as it had her. And until the argument, things had been going so well. Was Diego right? Was she building walls?

She dressed for church and helped Matthew into the handsome blue suit that Diego had insisted they buy him. She didn't knock on the door of Diego's room as they went into the living room. He was already there, dressed in a very becoming beige suit.

He turned, his dark eyes sweeping over the pale rose dress she wore, which emphasized the soft curves of her body. In the weeks of her recovery, her thinness had left her. She looked much healthier now, and her body was exquisitely appealing. He almost ground his teeth at the effect just gazing at her had on him.

"You look lovely," he said absently.

"I'd look lovelier if I got more sleep," she returned. "We argue so much lately, Diego."

He sighed, moving close to her. Matthew took advantage of their distraction to turn on an educational children's program and laugh with delight at some rhymes.

"And at a time when we should have laid the ghosts to rest, *sí?*" he asked. His lean hands rested gently on her shoulders, caressing her skin through the soft fabric. His black eyes searched hers restlessly. "A little trust, *niña,* is all that we need."

She smiled wistfully. "And what neither of us seem to have."

He bent to brush his mouth softly over her lips. "Let it come naturally," he whispered. "There is still time, is there not?"

Tears stung her eyes at the tenderness in his deep voice. She lifted her arms and twined them around his neck, her fingers caressing the thick hair at the back of his head. "I hope so," she whispered achingly. "For Matthew's sake."

"For his—and not for ours?" he asked quietly. "We lead separate lives, and that cannot continue."

"I know." She leaned her forehead against his firm chin and closed her eyes. "You never really wanted me. I suppose I should be grateful that you came when I went down in the crash. I never expected you to take care of Matt and me."

He touched her hair absently. "How could I leave you like that?" he asked.

"I thought you would when you knew about Matt," she confessed.

He tilted her chin and looked into her eyes. His were

solemn, unreadable. "Melissa, I have been alone all my life, except for family. Every day I lived as if death were at the door. I never meant to become involved with you. But I wanted you, little one," he whispered huskily. "Wanted you obsessively, until you were all I breathed. It was my own loss of control, my guilt, which drove us apart. I could not bear to be vulnerable. But I was." He shrugged. "That was what sent me from the casa. It was the reason I lied the night you ran out into the rain and had to be taken to the hospital. Repulse me?" He laughed bitterly. "If only you knew. Even now, I tremble like a boy when you touch me…."

Her heart jerked at his admission, because she could feel the soft tremor that ran through his lean body. But after all, it was only desire. And she wanted, needed, so much more.

"Would desire be enough, though?" she asked sadly, watching him.

He touched her soft cheek. "Melissa, we enjoy the same things. We like the same people. We even agree on politics. We both love the child." He smiled. "More importantly, we have known each other for oh, so long, *niña*. You know me to the soles of my feet, faults and all. Is that not a better basis for marriage than the desire you seem to think is our only common ground?"

"You might fall in love with someone—" she began.

He touched her mouth with a lean forefinger. "Why not tempt me into falling in love with you, *querida?*" he murmured. "These new clothes and the way you play lately have more effect than you realize." He bent toward her.

She met his lips without restraint, smiling against their warmth. "Could you?"

"Could I what?" he whispered.

"Fall in love with me?"

He chuckled. "Why not tempt me and see?"

She felt a surge of pure joy at the sweetness of the way he was looking at her, but before she could answer him, Matt wormed his way between them and wanted to know if they were ever going to leave to go to church.

They went to lunch after mass and then to a movie that Matt wanted to see. For the rest of the day, there was a new comradeship in the way Diego reacted to her. There were no more accusations or arguments. They played with Matt and cooked supper together for the second night in a row. And that night, when Matt was tucked up and Melissa said good night to Diego, it was with real reluctance that she went to her room.

"*Momento, niña,*" he called, and joined her at her door. Without another word, he drew her gently against him and bent to kiss her with aching tenderness. "Sleep well."

She touched his mouth with hers. "You…too." Her eyes asked a question she was too shy to put into words, but he shook his head.

"Not just yet, my own," he breathed. His black eyes searched hers. "Only when all the barriers are down will we take that last, sweet step together. For now it is enough that we begin to leave the past behind. Is it to-morrow night that our guests are expected?"

The sudden change of subject was rather like jet lag, she thought amusedly, but she adjusted to it. "Yes. Mrs. Albright and I will no doubt spend the day in the kitchen, but I've already called Gabby and Danielle and Joyce, and they've accepted. I'm looking forward to actually meeting the other wives, although we've talked on the phone quite a lot. I like them."

"I like you," he said unexpectedly, and smiled. "Dream of me," he whispered, brushing his mouth against hers one last time. Then he was gone, quietly striding down the hall to his study.

Melissa went into her room, but not to sleep. She did dream of him, though.

The next day was hectic. That evening, Melissa dressed nervously in one of her new dresses. It was a sweet confection in tones of pink, mauve and lavender with a wrapped bodice and a full skirt and cap sleeves. It took five years off her age and made her look even more blond and fair than she was.

She was trying to fasten a bracelet when she came out of her bedroom. Diego was in the living room, sipping brandy. He watched her approach with a familiar darkness in his eyes, an old softness that brought back so many memories.

"Allow me," he said, putting the brandy snifter down to fasten the bracelet for her. He didn't release her arm when he finished. He frowned, staring at the bracelet.

She knew immediately why he was staring. The bracelet was a tiny strand of white gold with inlaid emeralds, an expensive bit of nothing that Diego had given her when she'd graduated from high school. She colored delicately, and his eyes lifted to hers.

"So long ago I gave you this, *querida,*" he said softly. He lifted her wrist to his lips and kissed it. His mustache tickled her delicate skin. "It still means something to you—is that why you kept it all these years, even when you hated me?" he probed.

She closed her eyes at the sight of the raven-black head bent over her hand. "I was never able to hate you, though," she said with a bitter laugh. Tears burned her eyes. "I tried, but you haunted me. You always have."

He drew in a steadying breath as his black head lifted and his eyes searched hers. "As you haunted me," he breathed roughly. "And now *niña?* Do you still care for me, a little, despite the past?" he added, hoping against hope for mere crumbs.

"You needn't pretend that you don't know how I feel about you," she said, her chin trembling under her set lips. "You're like an addiction that I can't quite cure. I gave you everything I had to give, and still it wasn't enough…!" Tears slipped from her eyes.

"Melissa, don't!" He caught her to him in one smooth, graceful motion, his lean hand pressing her face into his dark dinner jacket. "Don't cry, little one, I can't bear it."

"You hate me!"

His fingers contracted in her hair and his eyes closed. "No! *Dios mío, amada,* how could I hate you?" His cheek moved roughly against hers as he sought her mouth and found it suddenly with his in the silence of the room. He kissed her with undisguised hunger, his hands gentle at her back, smoothing her body into his, caressing her. "Part of me died when you left. You took the very color from my life and left me with nothing but guilt and grief."

She hardly heard him. His mouth was insistent and she needed him, wanted him. She was reaching up to hold him when the doorbell sounded loudly in the silence.

He drew his head back reluctantly, and the arms that held her had a faint tremor. "No more deceptions," he said softly. "We must be honest with each other now. Tonight, when the others leave, we have to talk."

She touched his mouth, tracing the thick black mustache. "Can you bear total honesty, Diego?" she asked huskily.

"Perhaps you underestimate me."

"Didn't I always?" she sighed.

He heard voices out in the hall and released Melissa to take her hand and lead her toward the group. "When our guests leave, there will be all the time in the world to talk. Matthew has gone to bed, but you might check on him while I pass around drinks to our visitors. Mrs. Albright mentioned that his stomach was slightly uneasy."

"I'll go now." Melissa felt his fingers curl around hers with a thrill of pleasure and gazed up at him. She found his dark eyes smiling down into hers. It had been a long time since they'd been close like this, and lately it had been difficult even to talk to him. She returned the pressure of his hand as they joined a shell-shocked Apollo and a smug Joyce. The West Indian woman didn't even look like Joyce. She was wearing one of the dresses she and Melissa had found while they'd been shopping. It was a cinnamon-and-rust chiffon that clung lovingly to her slender figure, with a soft cowl neckline. Her feet were in strappy high heels. Her hair was pulled back with wisps at her ears, and she was wearing the makeup she'd bought at the boutique. She was a knockout, and Apollo's eyes were registering that fact with reluctance and pure malice.

"Now what did I tell you?" Melissa asked, gesturing at Joyce's dress. "You're just lovely!"

"Indeed she is." Diego lifted her hand to his lips and smiled at her while Apollo shifted uncomfortably and muttered, "Good evening," to his host and hostess.

"I'm just going to look in on Matthew. I'll be right back," Melissa promised, excusing herself.

The little boy was oddly quiet, his eyes drowsy. Melissa pushed back his dark hair and smiled at him.

"Feel okay?" she asked.

"My tummy doesn't," he said. "It hurts."

"Where does it hurt, baby?" she asked gently, and he indicated the middle of his stomach. She asked as many more questions as she could manage and decided it was probably either a virus or something he'd eaten. Still, it could be appendicitis. If it was, it would get worse very quickly, she imagined. She'd have to keep a careful eye on him.

"Try to sleep," she said, her voice soft and loving. "If you don't feel better by morning, we'll see the doctor, all right?"

"I don't want to see the doctor," Matthew said mutinously. "Doctors stick needles in people."

"Not all the time. And you want to get better, don't you? Papa mentioned that we might go to the zoo again next weekend," she whispered conspiratorially. "Wouldn't you like that?"

"Oh, yes," he said. "There are bears at the zoo."

"Then we'll have to get you better. Try to get some sleep, and maybe you'll feel better in the morning."

"All right, Mama."

"I'm just down the hall, and I'll leave your door open a crack. If you need me, call, okay?" She kissed his forehead and paused to smile at him before leaving. But she was almost sure it was a stomach virus. Mrs. Albright's grandson had come down with it just after Matthew had been downstairs to visit him again two days before. It was just a twenty-four-hour bug, but it could make a little boy pretty miserable all the same.

She wiped the frown off her face when she got into the living room. Gabby and J.D. Brettman had arrived by now, and Diego put a snifter of brandy into Melissa's hand and drew her to his side while they talked about Chicago and the business. His arm was possessive, and she delighted in the feel of it, in the feel of him, so close. Her love for him had grown by leaps and bounds in the past few weeks. She wondered if she could even exist apart from him now. Minutes later, Eric van Meer and his wife, a rather plain brunette with glasses and a lovely smile, joined the group. Melissa was surprised; she'd expected Dutch to show up with some beautiful socialite. But as she got to know Danielle, his interest in her was apparent. Dani was unique. So was Gabby.

"Let's let the girls talk fashion for a while. I've got something I need to kick over with you two before we eat," Apollo said suddenly, smiling at the wives and pointedly ignoring Joyce as he moved the men to the other side of the room.

"Just like men," Gabby sighed with a wistful glance at her enormous husband's back. "We're only afterthoughts."

"Someday I'll strangle him," Joyce was muttering to herself. "Someday I'll kick him out the window suspended by the telephone cord and I'll grin while I cut it."

"Now, now." Danielle chuckled. "That isn't a wholesome mental attitude."

Joyce's eyes were even blacker than usual. "I hate him!" she said venomously. "That's wholesome."

Gabby grinned. "He's running scared, haven't you noticed?" she whispered to Joyce. "He's as nervous as a schoolboy. You intimidate him. He comes from sharecroppers down South, and your parents are well-to-do. In a different way, J.D. was much the same before we married. He seemed to hate me, and nothing I did suited him. He fought to the bitter end. Apollo is even less marriage-minded than Dutch, and Dani could write you a book on reluctant husbands. Dutch hated women!"

"He thought he did," Dani corrected with a loving glance at her handsome husband. "But perhaps all they really need is the incentive to become husbands and fathers."

Melissa nodded. "Diego is very good with Matthew, and I never even knew that he liked children in the old days in Guatemala."

"It must have been exciting, growing up in Central America," Gabby remarked.

Melissa's eyes were soft with memories. "It was exciting living next door to Diego Laremos," she corrected. "He was my whole world."

Gabby's eyes narrowed as she studied the blond woman. "And yet the two of you were apart for a long time."

Melissa nodded. "It was a reluctant marriage. I left because I thought he didn't want me anymore, and now we're trying to pick up the pieces. It isn't easy," she confided.

"He's a good man," Gabby said, her green eyes quiet and friendly. "He saved my life in Guatemala when J.D. and I were there trying to rescue J.D.'s sister. Under fire he's one of the coolest characters I've ever seen. So are J.D. and Apollo."

"I suppose it's the way they had to live," Joyce remarked. Her eyes slid across the room to Apollo, and for one instant, everything she felt for the man was in her expression.

Apollo chose that moment to let his attention be diverted, and he looked at the West Indian woman. The air fairly sizzled with electricity, and Joyce's breath caught audibly before she lowered her eyes and clenched her hands in her lap.

"Excuse me, ma'am," Mrs. Albright said from the doorway in time to save Joyce from any ill-timed comments. "But dinner is served."

"Thank you, Mrs. Albright." Melissa smiled and went to Diego's side, amazed at how easy it was to slip her hand into the bend of his elbow and draw him with her. "Dinner, darling," she said softly.

His arm tautened under her gentle touch. "In all the time we have been together," he remarked as they went toward the elegant dining room, "I cannot remember hearing you say that word."

"You say it all the time," she reminded him with a pert smile. "Or the Spanish equivalent, at least, don't you?"

He shrugged. "It seems to come naturally." He pressed her hand against his sleeve, and the look he bent on her was full of affection.

She nuzzled his shoulder with her head, loving the new sense of intimacy she felt with him.

Behind them, the other husbands and wives exchanged expressive smiles. Bringing up the rear, Joyce was touching Apollo's sleeve as if it had thorns on it, and Apollo was as stiff as a man with a poker up his back.

"Relax, will you?" Apollo muttered at Joyce.

"You're a fine one to talk, iron man."

He turned and gazed down at her. They searched each other's eyes in a silence gone wild with new longings, with shared hunger.

"God, don't look at me like that," he breathed roughly. "Not here."

Her lips parted on a shaky breath. "Why not?"

He moved toward her and then abruptly moved away, jerking her along with him into the dining room. He was almost frighteningly stern.

It was a nice dinner, but the guests—two of them at least—kept the air sizzling with tension. When they'd eaten and were enjoying after-dinner coffee from a tray in the living room, the tension got even worse.

"You're standing on my foot," Joyce said suddenly, bristling at Apollo.

"With feet that size, how is that you can even feel it?" he shot back.

"That's it. That's it! You big overstuffed facsimile of a Chicago big shot, who do you think you're talking to?"

"A small overstuffed chili pepper with delusions of beauty," he retorted, his eyes blazing.

Joyce tried to speak but couldn't. She grabbed her purse and, with a terse, tear-threatening good night to the others, ran for the door.

"Damn it!" Apollo went after her out the door, slamming it behind him, while the others paused to exchange conspiratorial smiles and then continue their conversation.

When Apollo eventually came back into the apartment to say good night, he was alone. He looked drawn and a little red on one cheek, but his friends were too kind to remark on it. He left with a rather oblivious smile, and the others said their good nights shortly thereafter and left, too.

The door closed, and Melissa let Diego lead her back into the living room, where there was still half a pot of hot coffee.

"We can drink another cup together," he said, "while Mrs. Albright clears away the dishes."

She poured and watched him add cream to his coffee, her eyes soft and loving. "It went well, don't you think?"

He lifted an eyebrow and smiled. "Apollo and Joyce, you mean? I expect he has met his match there. Properly attired, she has excellent carriage and a unique kind of beauty."

"I thought so, too." She laughed. "I think she hit him. Did you notice his cheek?"

"I was also noticing the very vivid lipstick on his mouth," he mused with a soft chuckle. He leaned back in his chair with a sigh. "Poor man. He'll be married before he knows it."

She balanced her cup and saucer on her lap. "Is that how you think of marriage? As something to cause a man to be pitied?"

"Oh, yes, at one time I felt exactly that way," he admitted. He lit a cheroot and blew out a cloud of smoke. "I even told you so."

"I remember." She smiled into her coffee as she sipped it. "I was young enough and naive enough to think I could make you like it."

"Had I given you the chance, perhaps you might have," he said. His dark eyes narrowed. "I cannot remember even once in my life thinking of children and a home when I was escorting a woman, do you know? Even with you, it was your delectable body I wanted the most, not any idea of permanence. And then I lost my head and found myself bound to you in the most permanent way of all. I hated you and your father for that."

"As I found out," she said miserably.

"It was only when you lost the baby that I came to my senses, as odd as that may sound," he continued, watching her face. "It was then that I realized how much I had thrown away. I had some idea of my grandmother's resentment of you when I left you at the casa and took myself away from your influence. Perhaps I even hoped that my family's coldness would make you leave me." He dropped his dark eyes to his shoes. "I had lived alone so long, free to do as I wanted, to travel as I pleased. But the weeks grew endless without you, and always there was the memory of that afternoon in the rain on our bed of leaves." He sighed heavily. "I came home hoping to drive you away before I capitulated. And then you came to me, and because I was so hungry for you, I told you that you repulsed me. And I pushed you away." His eyes closed briefly.

She felt a stirring of compassion for what he'd gone through, even though her own path hadn't been an easy one.

"When you left, how did you manage?" he asked.

"By sheer force of will, at first." She sighed. "I had to go through a lot of red tape to get to stay in the United States, and when Matthew came along, it got rough. I made a good salary, but it took a lot of money to keep him in clothes and to provide for a baby-sitter. Without Mrs. Grady, I really don't know what I'd have done."

His chin lifted, and he studied her through narrow dark eyes. "Did you never wonder about me?"

"At first I wondered. I was afraid that you'd try to find me." She twisted her wedding band on her finger. "Then, after I got over that, I wondered if you were with some other woman, having a good time without me."

He scowled. "You thought me a shallow man, *niña*."

Her thin shoulders lifted, then fell. "You said yourself that you didn't love me or need me, that I was a nuisance you'd been saddled with. What else was I to think, Diego? That you were pining away for love of me?"

He took a draw from his cheroot and quietly put it out with slow, deliberate movements of his hand. "When I began selling my services abroad for a living, it was to help my family out of a financial bind," he began. "Because your mother had run away with your father, taking her dowry from us, the family fortunes suffered and we were in desperate need. After a while I began to enjoy the excitement of what I did, and the risk. Eventually the reason I began was lost in the need for adventure and the love of freedom and danger. I suppose I fed on adrenaline."

"There's something your family never knew about my mother's dowry, Diego," Melissa said. "She didn't have one."

He scowled. "What is this? My father said—"

"Your father didn't know. My grandfather was in financial straits himself. He was hoping for a merger between his fruit company and your family's banana plantations to help him get his head above water." She smiled ironically. "There was never any dowry. That was one reason she ran away with my father, because she felt guilty that her father was trying to use her in a dishonest way to make money. My father's father died soon afterward, and my father inherited his fortune. That's where our money came from, not from my mother's dowry."

"*Dios mío,*" he breathed, putting his face in his hands. "*Dios,* and my family blamed your father all those years for our financial problems."

"He thought it best not to tell you," she said. "The wounds were deep enough, and your father said some harsh things to him after he and my mother were married. I suppose he rubbed salt in the wounds, because my father never forgave him."

"You make me ashamed, Melissa," he said finally,

lifting his dark head. "I seem to have given you nothing but heartache."

"I wasn't blameless," she said. "The poems and the note I wrote so impulsively were genuine, you know. All I lacked was the courage to send them to you. I knew even then that a sophisticated man would never want an unworldly girl like me. I wasn't even pretty," she said wistfully.

"But you were exquisite," he said. He looked and sounded astonished at her denial of her own beauty. "A tea rose in bud, untouched by sophistication and cynicism. I adored you. And once I tasted your sweetness, *amada,* I was intoxicated."

"Yes, I noticed that." She sighed bitterly.

"I fought against marriage, that is true," he admitted. "I fought against your influence, and to some extent I won. But even as you ran from my bedroom that last night at the casa, I knew that I had lost. I was going after you, to tell you that I had meant none of what I said. I was going to ask you to try to make our marriage work, Melissa. And I would have tried. At least I was fond of you, and I wanted you. There was more than enough to build a marriage on." He didn't add how that feeling had grown over the years until now the very force of it almost winded him when he looked at her. He couldn't tell her everything just yet.

She searched his dark, unblinking eyes. "I was too young, though," she said. "I would have wanted things you couldn't have given me. You were my idol, not a flesh-and-blood man. You were larger than life, and how can a mere mortal woman live up to such a paragon? Oh, no, *señor*. I prefer you as you are now. Flesh and blood and sometimes a little flawed. I can deal with a man who is as human as I am."

He began to smile, and the warmth of his lips was echoed in his quiet, possessive gaze. "Can you, *enamorada?*" he asked. "Then come here and show me."

Her heart skipped with pure delight. "On the couch?" she asked, her eyebrows raised. "With the door wide open and Mrs. Albright in the kitchen?"

He chuckled softly. "You see the way you affect my brain, Melissa. It seems to stop working when I am in the same room with you."

"All finished, except for the coffee things," Mrs. Albright said cheerfully as she came into the room.

"Leave the coffee things until tomorrow," Diego said, smiling at her. "You have done quite enough, and your check this week will reflect our appreciation. Now go home and enjoy your own family. *¡Buenas noches!*"

"Thank you, *señor*, and *buenas noches* to you, too. Ma'am." She nodded to Melissa, got her coat from the closet and let herself out of the apartment.

Diego's eyes darkened as they slid over Melissa with an expression in them that could have melted ice. "Now," he said softly. "Come here to me, little one."

She got up, her heartbeat shaking her, and moved toward him. Diego caught her around the waist and pulled her down into his lap with her blond head in the crook of his arm and his black eyes searing down into hers.

"No more barriers," he breathed as he lowered his head, drowning her in his expensive cologne and the faint tobacco scent of his mouth. "No more subterfuge, no more games. We are husband and wife, and now we become one mind, one heart, one body...*amada!*"

His mouth moved hungrily on hers and she clung to him warmly, delighting in his possessive hold, in the need she could sense as well as feel. He was going to possess her, but she was no longer a twenty-year-old girl with stars in her eyes. She was a woman, and fully awakened to her own wants and needs.

She bit his lower lip, watching to see his expression. He chuckled softly, arrogance in every line of his dark face.

"So," he breathed. "You are old enough now for passion, is that what you are telling me with this provocative caress? Then beware, *querida,* because in this way my knowledge is far superior to yours."

Her breath quickened. "Show me," she whispered, curling her fingers into the thick hair at the nape of his neck. "Teach me."

"It will not be as tender as it was the first time, *amada,*" he said roughly, and something dark kindled in his eyes. "It will be a savage loving."

"Savage is how I feel about you, *señor,*" she whispered, lifting her mouth to tease his. "Savage and sweet and oh, so hungry!"

He allowed the caress and repeated it against her starving mouth. "Then taste me, *querida*," he whispered as he opened her lips with his and his arms contracted. "And let us feast on passion."

She moaned, because the pleasure was feverish. He bruised her against him, and she felt his hand low on her hips, gathering them against the fierce tautness of his body. She began to tremble. She'd lived on dreams of him for years, but now there was the remembered delight of his mouth, of his body. He wanted her, and she wanted him so much it was agonizing. She clung, a tiny cry whispering into his mouth as she gave in completely, loving him beyond bearing.

He rose gracefully, lifting her easily as he got up. He lifted his head only a breath away, holding her eyes as he walked down the hall with her, his gaze possessive, explosively sweet.

"No quarter, *enamorada*," he whispered huskily. "This night, I will show no mercy. I will fulfil you and you will complete me. I will love you as I never dreamed of loving a woman in the darkness."

She trembled at the emotion in his deep, softly accented voice. "You don't believe in love," she whispered shakily.

His dark eyes held her wide gray ones. "Do I not, Melissa? Wait and see what I feel. By morning you may have learned a great deal more about me than you think you know."

She buried her face in his throat and pressed closer,

shuddering with the need to give him her heart along with her body.

"Querida..." he breathed. His arms tightened bruisingly.

At the same time, a childish voice cried out in the darkness, and that sound was followed by the unmistakable sound of someone's dinner making a return appearance.

CHAPTER TEN

MATTHEW WAS SICK TWICE. Melissa mopped up after him with the ease of long practice and changed his clothes and his sheets after bathing him gently with soap and warm water.

He cried, his young pride shattered by his loss of control. "I'm sorry," he wailed.

"For what, baby?" she said gently, kissing his forehead. "Darling, we all get sick from time to time. Mrs. Albright's grandson had this virus, and I'm sure that's where you caught it, but you'll be much better in the morning. I'm going to get you some cracked ice so that you don't get dehydrated, and perhaps Papa will sit with you until I get back."

"Of course," Diego said, catching Melissa's hand to kiss it gently as she went past him. "Make a pot of coffee for us, *amada*."

"You don't need to sit up, too," she said. "I can do it."

His dark eyes searched hers. "This is what being a father is all about, is it not? Sharing the bad times as well as the good? What kind of man would I be to go merrily to my bed and leave you to care for a sick little boy?"

She could barely breathe. He was incredible. She touched his mouth with her forefinger. "I adore you," she breathed, and left before she gave way to tears.

When she came back, with the coffee dripping and its delicious aroma filling the kitchen, she was armed with a cup of cracked ice and a spoon. Diego was talking to Matthew in a low voice. It was only when Melissa was in the room that she recognized the story he was telling the boy. It was "Beauty and the Beast," one of her own favorites.

"And they lived happily ever after?" Matthew asked, looking pale but temporarily keeping everything down.

"Happiness is not an automatic thing in the real world, *mi hijo*," Diego said as Melissa perched on the side of the bed and spooned a tiny bit of cracked ice into Matthew's mouth. "It is rather a matter of compromise, communication and tolerance. Is this not so, Señora Laremos?"

She smiled at him. He was lounging in the chair beside the bed with his shirt unbuttoned and his sleeves rolled up, looking very Latin and deliciously masculine with the shirt and slacks outlining every powerful muscle in his body.

"Yes. It is so," she agreed absently, but her eyes were saying other things.

He chuckled deeply, and the message in his own eyes was more than physical.

She gave Matthew the ice and took heart when it stayed in his stomach. In a little while he dozed off, and

Melissa pushed the disheveled dark hair away from his forehead and adored him with her eyes.

"A fine young man," Diego said softly. "He has character, even at so early an age. You have done well."

She glanced at him with a smile. "He was all I had of—" She bit her tongue, because she had almost said "of you."

But he knew. He smiled, his eyes lazily caressing her. "I have waited a long time for you to tell me. Do you not think that this is the proper time, *querida?* On a night when we meant to love each other in the privacy of my bedroom and remove all the barriers that separate us? Here, where the fruit of our need for each other sleeps so peacefully in the security of our love for him?"

She drew in a steadying breath. "Did you know all the time?" she asked.

"No," he said honestly, and smiled. "I was insanely jealous of Matt's mythical father. It made me unkind to him at first, and to you. But as I grew to know him, and you, I began to have my suspicions. That was why I sent for his birth certificate."

"Yes, I saw it accidentally in your desk," she confessed, and noted the surprise in his face.

"But before I saw it," he continued softly, "Matthew described to me a photograph of his father that you had shown him." He smiled at her flush. "Yes, *niña.* The same photograph I had seen in your drawer under your gowns, and never told you. So many keepsakes. They gave me the only hope I had that you still had a little affection for me."

She laughed. "I was afraid you'd seen them." She shook her head. "I cared so much. And I was afraid, I've always been afraid, that you might want Matt more than you wanted me." She lowered her eyes. "You said that love wasn't a word you knew. But Matt was your son," she whispered, admitting it at last, "and you'd have wanted him."

"Him, and not you?" he asked softly. He leaned forward, watching her. "Melissa, I have not been kind to you. We married for the worst of reasons, and even when I found you again I was still fighting for my freedom. But now…" He smiled tenderly. "*Amada*, I awaken each morning with the thought that I will see you over the breakfast table. At night I sleep soundly, knowing that you are only a few yards away from me. My day begins and ends with you. And in these past weeks, you have come to mean a great deal to me. I care very much for my son. But Melissa, you mean more to me than anything on earth. Even more than Matthew."

She gnawed her lower lip while tears threatened. She took a slow, shuddering breath. "I wanted to tell you before I left Guatemala that I hadn't lost the baby. But I couldn't let him be born and raised in such an atmosphere of hatred." She looked down at the carpet. "He was all I had left of you, and I wanted him desperately. So I came to America, gave birth to him and raised him." Her eyes found his. "But there was never a day, or a night, or one single second, when you weren't in my thoughts and in my heart. I never stopped loving you. I never will."

"*Amada*," he breathed.

"Matthew is your son," she said simply, smiling through tears. "I'm sorry I didn't trust you enough to tell you."

"I'm sorry I made it so difficult." He leaned forward and took her hand in his, kissing the palm softly, hungrily. "We made a beautiful child together," he said, lifting his dark eyes to hers. "He combines the best of both of us."

"And we can look into his face and see generations of Sterlings and Laremoses staring back at us," she agreed. Her soft eyes held his. "Oh, Diego, what a waste the past years have been!"

He stood up, drawing her into his arms. He held her and rocked her, his voice soft at her ear, whispering endearments in Spanish while she cried away the bitterness and the loneliness and the pain.

"Now, at last, we can begin again," he said. "We can have a life together, a future together."

"I never dreamed it would happen." She wiped at her eyes. "I almost ran away again. But then Joyce reminded me that I'd done that before and solved nothing. So I stayed to fight for you."

He laughed delightedly. "So you did, in ways I never expected. I had married a child in Guatemala. I hardly expected the woman I found in Tucson."

"I couldn't believe it when I saw you there," she said. "I'd dreamed of you so much, wanted you so badly, and then there you were. But I thought you hated me, so I didn't dare let you see how I felt. And there was Matt."

"Why did you not tell me the truth at the beginning?" he asked quietly.

"Because I couldn't be sure that you wouldn't take him away from me." She sighed. "And because I wanted you to trust me, to realize all by yourself that I'd loved you far too much to betray you with another man."

"To my shame, I believed that at first," he confessed. "And blamed myself for being so cruel to you that I made you hate me enough to run away."

"I never hated you," she said, loving his face with her eyes. "I never could. I understood, even then. And it was my own fault. The note, the poems, and I gave in without even a fight…"

"The fault was mine as well, for letting my desire for you outweigh my responsibility to protect you." He sighed heavily. "So much tragedy, my own, because we abandoned ourselves to pleasure. At the time, consequences were the last thought we had, no?"

"Our particular consequence, though, is adorable, don't you think, *esposo mío?*" she smiled at their sleeping son.

He followed her glance. *"Muy adorable."* His eyes caressed her. "Like his oh-so-beautiful *madrecita*."

Touched by the tenderness in his deep voice, she reached up and kissed him, savoring the warm hunger of his embrace. Matthew stirred, and she sat back down beside him, watching his eyes open sleepily.

"Feeling better?" she asked gently.

"I'm hungry," he groaned.

"Nothing else to eat just yet, young man," she said, smiling. "You have to make sure your tummy's settled. But how about some more cracked ice?"

"Yes, please," he mumbled.

Diego got up and took the cup and the spoon from her. "I could use some coffee, *querida,*" he suggested.

"So could I. I'll get it."

She left him there after watching the tender way he fed ice to Matthew, the wonder of fatherhood and the pride of it written all over his dark face. Melissa had never felt so happy in all her life. As she left the room she heard his voice, softly accented, exquisitely loving, telling the little boy at last that he was his real papa. Tears welled up in her eyes as she left them, and she smiled secretly through them, bursting with joy.

It was a long night, but the two of them stayed with the little boy. Melissa curled up on the foot of his bed finally to catch a catnap, and Diego slept sprawled in the chair. Mrs. Albright found them like that the next morning and smiled from the doorway. But Matthew was nowhere in sight.

Frowning, she went toward the kitchen, where there was a strange smell…

"Matthew!" she gasped at the doorway.

"I'm hungry," Matthew muttered, "and mama and papa won't wake up."

He was standing in his pajamas at the stove, barefoot, cooking himself two eggs. Unfortunately, he had the heat on high and several pieces of eggshell in the pan, and the result was a smelly black mess.

Mrs. Albright got it all cleared away and picked him up to carry him back to bed. "I'll get your breakfast, my lamb. Why were you hungry?"

"My supper came back up again," he explained.

Mrs. Albright nodded wisely. "Stomach bug."

"A very bad bug," he agreed. "Papa is my real papa, you know, he said so, and we're going to live with him forever. Can I have some eggs?"

"Yes, lamb, in just a minute," she promised with a laugh as they went into the bedroom.

"Matthew?" Melissa mumbled as she looked up and saw Mrs. Albright bringing Matthew into the room.

Diego blinked and yawned as Mrs. Albright put the boy back in bed. "Where did you find him?" he asked, his face unshaven and his eyes bleary.

"In the kitchen cooking his breakfast," Mrs. Albright chuckled, registering their openly horrified expressions. "It's all right now. I've taken care of everything. I'll get him some scrambled eggs and toast if you think it's safe. I'd bet that it is, if my opinion is wanted. He looks fit to me."

"You should have seen him last night," Melissa said with a drowsy smile. "But if he thinks he's hungry, he can have some eggs."

"You two go and get some sleep," Mrs. Albright said firmly. "Matthew's fine, and I'll look out for him. I'll even call the office for you, *señor,* if you like, and tell them where you are."

"That would be most kind of you." He yawned, taking Melissa by the hand. "Come along, Señora Laremos, while I can stand up long enough to guide us to bed."

"*¡Buenas noches!*" Matthew grinned.

"*¡Buenos días!*" Melissa corrected with a laugh. "And eat only a little breakfast, okay?" She threw him a kiss. "Good night, baby chick."

She followed Diego into his bedroom and got into the bed while he locked the door. She hardly felt him removing her dress and hose and shoes and slip. Seconds later, she was asleep.

SUNSHINE STREAMED LAZILY through the windows when she stretched under the covers, frowning as she discovered that she didn't have a stitch of clothing on her body.

Diego came into the bedroom from the bathroom with a towel around his lean hips and his hair still damp.

"Awake at last," he murmured dryly. He reached down and jerked the covers off, his dark eyes appreciative of every soft, pink inch of her body as he looked at her openly for the first time in five years. The impact of it was in his eyes, his face. "*Dios mío,* what a beautiful sight," he breathed, smiling at her shy blush.

As he spoke, he unfastened his towel and threw it carelessly on the floor. "Now," he breathed, easing down beside her. "This is where we meant to begin last night, is it not, *querida?*"

She knew it was incredible to be shy with him, but it had been five years. She lowered her eyes to his mouth and looped her arms around his neck and shifted to accommodate the warm weight of his muscular body. She shivered, savoring the abrasive pleasure of his chest hair against her soft breasts, the hardness of his long legs tangling intimately with hers.

Tremors of pleasure wound through her. "Sweet," she whispered shakily, drawing him closer. Her mouth nipped at his, pleaded, danced with it. "It's so sweet, feeling you like this."

"An adequate word for something so wondrous," he whispered, smiling against her eager mouth. He touched her, watching her eyes dilate and her body stiffen. "There, *querida?*" he asked sensuously. "Softly, like this?" He did it again, and she shuddered deliciously and arched. A sensual banquet, after years of starvation.

"You...beast," she chided. Her nails dug into his shoulders as she watched the face above hers grow dark with passion, his eyes glittering as he bent to her body.

"A feast fit for a starving man," he whispered as his lips traced her soft curves, lingering to tease and nip at the firm thrust of her breasts, at her rib cage, her flat belly. And all the while he talked to her, described what he felt and what he was doing and what he was going to do.

She moved under the exploration of his hands, her eyes growing darker and wilder as he kindled the flames of passion. Once she looked directly into his eyes as he moved down, and she saw the naked hunger in them as his body penetrated hers for the first time in more than five years.

She cried, a keening, husky, breathless little sound that was echoed in her wide eyes and the stiffening of her welcoming body. She cried in passion and in pain, because at first there was the least discomfort.

"Ah, it has been a long time, has it not?" he whispered softly, delighting in the pleasure he read in her face. "Relax, my own." His body stilled, giving hers time to adjust to him, to admit him without discomfort. "Relax. Yes, *querida*, yes, yes…" His eyes closed as he felt the sudden ease of his passage, and his teeth ground together at an unexpected crest of fierce pleasure. He shuddered. "Exquisite," he groaned, opening his eyes to look at her as he moved again, his weight resting on his forearms. "Exquisite, this…with you…this sharing." His eyes closed helplessly as his movements became suddenly harsh and sharp. "Forgive me…!"

But she was with him every step of the way, her fit young body matching his passion, equaling it. She adjusted her body to the needs of his, and held him and watched him and gloried in his fulfillment just before she found her own and cried out against his shoulder in anguished completion.

He shuddered over her, his taut body relaxing slowly, damp, his arms faintly tremulous. She bit his shoulder and laughed breathlessly, feeling for the first time like a whole woman, like a wife.

"Now try to be unfaithful to me," she dared him, whispering the challenge into his ear. "Just try and I'll wear you down until you can hardly crawl away from my bed!"

He nipped her shoulder, laughing softly. "As if I could have touched another woman after you," he whispered. "*Querida,* I took my marriage vows as seriously as you took yours. Guilt and anguish over losing you made it impossible for me to sleep with anyone else." He lifted his damp head and searched her drowsy, shocked eyes. "*Amada,* I love you," he said softly. He brushed her mouth with his. "I do not want anyone else. Not since that first time with you, when I knew that your soul had joined with mine so completely that part of me died when you left."

She hid her face against him, weeping with joy and pain and pleasure. "I'm sorry."

"It is I who am sorry. But our pain is behind us, and now our pleasure begins. This is only the start, this sweet sharing of our bodies. We will share our lives, Melissa. Our sorrow and our joy. Laughter and tears. For this is what makes a marriage."

She reached up and kissed his dark cheek. "I love you so much."

"As I love you." He twined a strand of her long blond hair around his forefinger. His eyes searched hers. He bent, and his mouth opened hers. Seconds later she pulled him down to her again, and he groaned as the flare of passion burned brightly again, sending them down into a fiery oblivion that surpassed even the last one.

Mrs. Albright was putting supper on the table when they reappeared, freshly showered and rested and sharing glances that held a new depth of belonging.

Matthew was still in his room. They ate supper alone and then went to see him, delighting in the strength of their attachment to each other, delighting in their son.

"Tomorrow I will bring you a surprise when I come home from work. What would you like?" Diego asked his son.

"Only you, Papa," the little boy laughed, reaching up to be held and hugged fiercely.

"In that case, I shall bring you a battleship, complete with crew," his Papa chuckled with a delighted glance toward Melissa, who smiled and leaned against him adoringly.

Diego went to work reluctantly the next morning to find Apollo like a cat with a bad leg and Joyce as cold as if she'd spent two days in a refrigerator.

"How's Matthew?" Apollo asked when Diego entered the office.

"He's much better, thanks, but his mama and I are still trying to catch up on our sleep," Diego laughed, and told him about Matthew's attempt to make breakfast.

Joyce laughed. "I hope your fire insurance is paid up."

Apollo stared at her with unconcealed hunger. "Don't you have something to do?" he asked curtly.

"Of course, but I have to work for you instead," she said with a sweet smile. She was wearing another one of the new outfits, and she looked very pretty in a red-and-orange print that showed off her figure to its best advantage. Apollo could hardly keep his eyes off her, which made for a long and confusing workday.

When Diego went home that afternoon, Apollo was at the end of his rope. He glared at Joyce and she glared back until they both had to look away or die from the electricity in their joined gaze.

"You look nice," he said irritably.

"Thank you," she said with equal curtness.

He drew in an angry breath. "Oh, hell, we can't go on like this," he muttered, going around the desk after her. He caught her by the arms and pulled her against him, his mind registering that she barely came up to his shoulder and that she made him feel violently masculine. "Look, it's impossible to treat each other this way after what happened at the Laremoses two nights ago. I'm going crazy. Just looking at you makes my body ache."

She drew in a steadying breath, because he was affecting her, too. "What do you want to do about it?" she asked, certain that he was thinking along serious lines and wondering how she was going to bear it if he wasn't.

He tilted her mouth up to his and kissed her, long and hard and hungrily. She moaned, stepping closer, pushing against him. His arms swallowed her and he groaned.

"I won't hurt you," he promised huskily, his black eyes holding hers. "I swear to God, I won't. I'll take a long time..."

She could barely make her mind work. "What?"

"I'll get you a better apartment, in the same building as mine," he went on. "We'll spend almost every night together, and if things work out, maybe you can move in with me eventually."

She blinked. "You...want me to be your mistress?"

He scowled. "What's this mistress business? This is America. People live together all the time—"

"I come from a good home and *we* don't live together," she said proudly. "We get married and have babies and behave like a family! My mother would shoot you stone-cold dead if she thought you were trying to seduce me!"

"Who is your mama, the Lone Ranger?" he chided. "Listen, honey, I can have any woman I want. I don't have to go hungry just because my little virgin secretary has too many hang-ups to—oof!"

Joyce surveyed her handiwork detachedly, registering the extremely odd look on Apollo's face as he bent over the stomach she'd put her knee into. He was an interesting shade of purple, and it served him right.

"I quit, by the way," Joyce said with a smile he couldn't see. She turned, cleaned out her desk drawer efficiently and picked up her purse. There wasn't much to get together. She felt a twinge of regret because she loved the stupid man. But perhaps this was best, because she wasn't going to be any man's kept woman, modern social fad or not.

"Goodbye, boss," she said as she headed for the door. "I hope you have better luck with your next secretary."

"She can't...be worse...than you!" he bit off, still doubled over.

"You sweet man," she said pleasantly as she paused in the doorway. "It's been a joy working for you. I do hope you'll give me a good reference."

"I wouldn't refer you to hell!"

"Good, because I don't want to go anyplace where I'd be likely to run into you!" She slammed the door and walked away. By the time she was in the elevator going down, the numbness had worn off and she realized that she'd burned her bridges. There were tears welling up in her eyes before she got out of the building.

She wound up at Melissa's apartment, crying in great gulps. Diego took one look at her and poured her a drink, then left the women alone in the living room and went off to play the memory game with his son.

"Tell me all about it," Melissa said gently when Joyce managed to stop crying.

"He wants me to be his mistress," she wailed, and buried her face in the tissue Melissa had given her.

"Oh, you poor thing." Melissa curled her feet under her on the sofa. "What did you tell him, as if I didn't know?"

"It wasn't so much what I told him as what I did," Joyce confessed. She grinned sheepishly. "I kicked him in the stomach."

"Oops."

"Well, he deserved it. Bragging about how many women he could get if he wanted them, laughing at me for being chaste." Joyce lifted her chin pugnaciously. "My mother would die if she heard him say such a thing. She has a very religious background, and I was raised strictly and in the church."

"So was I, so don't apologize," Melissa said softly. "Let me tell you, I learned the hard way that it's best to save intimacy for marriage. I'm a dinosaur, I suppose. Where I grew up, the family had its own special place. No member of the family ever did anything to besmirch the family name. Now honor is just a word, but at what cost?"

"You really are a dinosaur," Joyce sighed.

"Purely prehistoric," Melissa agreed. "What are you going to do, my friend?"

"What most dinosaurs do, I guess. I'm going to become extinct, at least as far as Apollo Blain is concerned. I resigned before I left." Her eyes misted again. "I'll never see him again."

"I wouldn't bet on it. Stay for supper and then we'll see what we can do about helping you get another job."

"You're very kind," Joyce said, "but I think it might be best if I go back to Miami. Or even home to my mother." She shrugged. "I don't think I'll be able to fit into this sophisticated world. I might as well go back where I belong."

"I'll have no one to talk to or shop with," Melissa moaned. "You can't! Listen, we'll dig a Burmese tiger trap outside Apollo's office door..."

"You're a nice friend," Joyce said, smiling. "But it really won't do. We'll have to think of something he can't gnaw through."

"Let's have supper. Then we'll talk."

Joyce shook her head. "I can't eat. I want to go home and have a good cry and call my mother. I'll talk to you tomorrow, all right? Meanwhile, thank you for being my friend."

"Thank you for being mine. If you get too depressed, call me. Okay?"

Joyce got up, smiling. "Okay."

Melissa walked her to the door and let her out. Then she leaned back against it, sighing.

Diego came into the hall with his eyebrows raised. "Trouble?"

"She quit. After she kicked your boss in the stomach," she explained. "I think he's probably going to be in a very bad mood for the rest of the week, although I'm only guessing," she added, grinning.

He moved toward her, propping his arms at either side of her head. He smiled. "Things are heating up," he remarked.

"And not only for Joyce and Apollo," she whispered, tempting him until he bent to her mouth and kissed her softly.

She nibbled his lower lip, smiling. "Come here," she breathed, reaching around his waist to draw his weight down on hers.

He obliged her, and she could tell by his breathing as well as by the tautness of his body and his fierce heartbeat that he felt as great a need for her as she felt for him. She opened her mouth to the fierce pressure of his.

"Papa!"

Diego lifted his head reluctantly. "In a moment, *mi hijo,*" he called back. "Your mother and I are discussing plans," he murmured, brushing another kiss against Melissa's eager mouth.

"What kind of plans, Papa, for a trip to the zoo?" Matthew persisted.

"Not exactly. I will be back in a moment, all right?"

There was a long sigh. "All right."

Diego shifted his hips and smiled at Melissa's helpless response. "I think an early night is in order," he breathed. "To make up for our lack of sleep last night," he added.

"I couldn't possibly agree more," she murmured as his mouth came down again. It grew harder and more insistent by the second, but the sound of Mrs. Albright's voice calling them into the dining room broke the spell.

"I long for that ancient Mayan ruin where we first knew each other," Diego whispered as he stood up and let her go.

"With armed guerrillas hunting us, spiders crawling around, snakes slithering by, and lightning striking all around," she recalled. She shook her head. "I'll take Chicago any day, Diego!"

He chuckled. "I can hardly argue with that. Let us eat, then we will discuss this trip to the zoo that our son seems determined to make."

There was a new temporary secretary at work for the rest of the week, but Apollo didn't give her a hard time. In fact, he looked haggard and weary and miserable.

"Perhaps you need a vacation, amigo," Diego said.

"It wouldn't hurt," Dutch nodded, propped gracefully against Apollo's desk with a lighted cigarette in one lean hand.

Apollo glowered at them. "Where would I go?"

Diego studied his fingernails. "You could go to Ferris Street," he remarked. "I understand the weather there is quite nice."

Ferris Street was where Joyce's apartment was, and Apollo glowered furiously at the older man.

"You could park your car there and just relax," Dutch seconded, pursing his lips. His blond hair looked almost silver in the light. "You could read a book or take along one of those little television sets and watch soap operas with nobody to bother you."

"Ferris Street is the end of the world," Apollo said. "You don't take a vacation sitting in your damned car on a side street in Chicago! What's the matter with you people?"

"You could entice women to sit in your car with you," Dutch said. "Ferris Street could be romantic with the right companion. You were a counterterrorist. You know how to appropriate people."

"This is true," Diego agreed. "He appropriated us for several missions, at times when we preferred not to go."

"Right on," Dutch said. He studied Apollo curiously. "I was like you once. I hated women with a hell of lot more reason than you've got. But in the end I discovered that living with a woman is a hell of a lot more interesting than being shot at."

"I asked her to live with me, for your information, Mr. Social Adviser," Apollo muttered. "She kicked me in the gut!"

"What about marriage?" Dutch persisted.

"I don't want to get married," Apollo said.

"Then it is as well that she resigned," Diego said easily. "She can find another man to marry and give her children—"

"Shut up, damn you!" Apollo looked shaken. He wiped the sweat off his forehead. "Oh, God, I've got to get out of here. You guys have things to do, don't you? I'm going for a walk!"

He started out the door.

"You might walk along Ferris Street," Dutch called after him. "I hear flowers are blooming all over the place."

"You might even see a familiar face," Diego added with a grin.

Apollo threw them a fiercely angry gesture and slammed the door behind him.

Dutch got off the desk and moved toward the door with Diego. "He'll come around," the blond man mused. "I did."

"We all come to it," Diego said. He smiled at the younger man. "Bring Dani to supper Saturday. And bring the children. Matthew would enjoy playing with your eldest."

Dutch eyed him. "Everything's okay now, I gather?"

Diego sighed. "My friend, if happiness came in grains of sand, I would be living on a vast desert. I have the world."

"I figured Matthew was yours," Dutch said unexpectedly. "Melissa didn't strike me as the philandering kind."

"As in the old days, you see deeply," Diego replied. He smiled at his friend. "And your Dani, she is content to stay with the children instead of working?"

"Until they're in school, yes. After that, I keep hearing these plans for a really unique used bookstore." Dutch grinned. "Whatever she wants. I come first, you know. I always have and I always will. It's enough to make a man downright flexible."

Diego thought about that all the way home. Yes, it did. So if Melissa wanted to work when Matthew started school, why not? He told her so that night as she lay contentedly in his arms watching the city lights play on the ceiling of the darkened room. She smiled and rolled over and kissed him. And very soon afterward, he was glad he'd made the remark.

CHAPTER ELEVEN

THERE WERE BELLS RINGING. Melissa put her head under the pillow, but still they kept on. She groaned, reaching out toward the telephone and fumbled it under the pillow and against her ear.

"Hello?" she mumbled.

"Melissa? Is Diego awake?" Apollo asked.

She murmured something and put the receiver against Diego's ear. It fell off and she put it back, shaking his brown shoulder to make him aware of it.

"Hello," he said drowsily. "Who is it?"

There was a pause. All at once he sat straight up in bed, knocking off the pillow and stripping back the covers. "You what?"

Melissa lifted her head, because the note in Diego's voice sounded urgent and shocked. "What is it?" she whispered.

"You what?" Diego repeated. He launched into a wild mixture of Spanish and laughter, then reverted to English. "I wouldn't have believed it. When?"

"What is it?" Melissa demanded, punching Diego.

He put his hand over the receiver. "Apollo and Joyce

are being married two days from now. They want us to stand up with them."

Melissa laughed delightedly and clapped her hands. "We'll all come," she said. "There'll be photographers and we'll bring the press!"

"Yes, we'll be delighted," Diego was telling Apollo. "Melissa sends her love to Joyce. We'll see you there. Yes. Congratulations! *¡Hasta luego!*"

"Married!" Melissa sighed, sending an amused, joyful glance at her husband. "And he swore he never would."

"He shouldn't have," Diego grinned. He picked up the phone again and dialed. "I have to tell Dutch," he explained. "I'll tell you later about how we suggested Apollo should take his vacation in his car on Ferris Street."

Melissa giggled, because she had a pretty good idea what kind of vacation they'd had in mind....

TWO DAYS LATER, a smiling justice of the peace married Apollo and Joyce in a simple but beautiful ceremony while Melissa, Diego, the Brettmans and the van Meers, Gabby's mother and First Shirt, Semson and Drago all stood watching. It was the first time the entire group had been together in three years.

Apollo, in a dark business suit, and Joyce, in a white linen suit, clasped hands and repeated their vows with exquisite joy on their faces. They smiled at each other with wonder and a kind of shyness that touched Melissa's heart. Clinging to her husband's hand, she felt as if all of them shared in that marriage ceremony. It was like a rededication of what they all felt for their spouses, a renewal of hope for the future.

Afterward, all of them gathered at a local restaurant for the reception, and Apollo noticed for the first time the number of photographers who were enjoying hors d'oeuvres and coffee and soft drinks.

He frowned. "I don't mean to sound curious," he murmured to Diego and Dutch, "but there sure are a lot of cameras here."

"Evidence," Dutch said.

"In case you got cold feet," Diego explained, "we were going to blackmail you by sending photographs to all the news media showing that your courage had deserted you at the altar."

"You guys," Apollo muttered.

Joyce leaned against his shoulder and reached up to kiss his lean cheek warmly. "I helped pay for the photographers," she confessed. "Well, I had to have an ace in the hole, you know."

He just smiled, too much in love and too happy to argue.

Melissa and Diego left early, holding hands as they wished the happy couple the best, promised to have them over for dinner after the honeymoon and said goodbye to the rest of the gang.

Melissa sighed. "It was a nice wedding."

"As nice as our own?" he asked.

"Ours was a beautiful affair, but it lacked heart," she reminded him. "It was a reluctant marriage."

"Suppose we do it again?" he asked, studying her soft face. "Suppose we have a priest marry us all over again, so that we can repeat our vows and mean them this time?"

"My husband," she said softly, "each day with you is a rededication of our marriage and a reaffirmation of what we feel for each other. The words are meaningless without the day-to-day proving of them. And we have that."

His dark eyes smiled at her. "Yes, *querida*," he agreed quietly. "We have that in abundance."

She clung to his hand. "Diego, I had a letter yesterday. I didn't show it to you, but I think you expected it all the same."

He frowned. "Who was it from?"

"From your grandmother. There was a note from your sister enclosed with it."

He sighed. "A happy message, I hope?" he asked. He wasn't certain that his family had relented, even though they'd promised him they had.

She smiled at him, reading his uneasiness in his face. "An apology for the past and a message of friendship in the future. They want us to come and visit them in Barbados and bring Matthew. Your grandmother wants to meet her great-grandson."

"And do you want to go?" he asked.

She curled her fingers into his. "You said we might go down to the Caribbean for the summer, didn't you?" she asked. "And combine business with pleasure? I'd like to make my peace with your people. I think you'd like that, too."

"I would. But there is so much to forgive, *querida*," he said softly, his dark face quiet and still. "Can you find that generosity in your heart?"

"I love you," she said, and the words were sweet and heady in his ears. "I'd do anything for you. Forgiveness is a small thing to ask for the happiness you've given me."

"And you have no regrets?" he persisted.

She nuzzled her cheek against his jacket. "Don't be absurd. I regret all those years we spent apart. But now we have something rare and beautiful. I'm grateful for miracles, because our marriage is certainly one."

He looked down at her bright head against his arm and felt that miracle right to his toes. He brought her hand to his lips and kissed it warmly. "Suppose we get Matthew and take him on a picnic?" he suggested. "He can feed the ducks and we can sit and plan that trip to Barbados."

Melissa pressed closer against Diego, all the nightmares of the past lost in the sunshine of the present. "I'd like that," she said. She watched the sky, thinking about how many times in the past she'd looked up and wondered if Diego was watching it as she was and thinking of her. Her eyes lifted to his smiling face. She laughed. The sound startled a small group of pigeons on the sidewalk, and they flew up in a cacophony of feathery music. Like the last of her doubts, they vanished into the trees and left not a trace of themselves in sight.

MYSTERY MAN

CHAPTER ONE

"IT WAS A DARK AND STORMY NIGHT..."

A pair of green eyes glared at the twelve-year-old boy by the window who intoned the trite words in a ghostly voice.

He shrugged. "Well, everybody starts a murder mystery that way, Janie," Kurt Curtis told his older sister with a grin.

Janine ran restless fingers through her short black hair, muttering at the few words on her computer screen. "I don't," she murmured absently. "That's why I sell so many of them."

"Diane Woody," he intoned, "bestselling authoress of the famous Diane Woody Mystery series." He scowled. "Why do you use your pen name for your main character's name? Isn't that redundant?"

"It was the publisher's idea. Could you ask questions later?" she mumbled. "I'm stuck for a line."

"I just gave you one," he reminded her, grinning wider. He was redheaded and blue-eyed, so different from her in coloring that most people thought he was someone else's brother. He was, however, the image of their maternal grandfather. Recessive genes will out, their archaeologist parents were fond of saying.

Their parents were on a new dig, which was why Janine was in Cancún working, with Kurt driving her nuts. Dan and Joan Curtis, both professors at Indiana University, were in the Yucatán on a dig. There had been several other archaeologists on the team, most of whom had to return to take classes. Since this was a newly discovered, and apparently untouched, Mayan site, the Curtises had taken a temporary leave of absence from their teaching positions to pursue it. It wasn't feasible to take Kurt, who was just getting over a bad case of tonsillitis, into the jungles. Neither could they leave him in the exclusive boarding school he attended.

So they'd taken him out of his boarding school for two months—with the proviso that Janine tutor him at home. They'd rented this nice beach house for Janine, where she could meet her publisher's deadline and take care of her little brother. He was well now, but she had him for the duration, which could easily mean another month, and she had to juggle his homebound school assignments with her obligations. The dig was going extremely well, Professor Curtis had said in his last E-mail message through the computer satellite hookup at their camp, and promised to be a site of international importance.

Janine supposed it would be. The benefit of it all was that they had this gorgeous little villa in Cancún overlooking the beach. Janine could write and hear the roar of the ocean outside. It gave her inspiration, usually. When Kurt wasn't trying to "help" her, that was.

She was just slightly nervous, though, because it was September and the tail end of hurricane season, and this had been a year for hurricanes. One prognosticator called it the year of the killer winds. Poetic. And frightening. So far there hadn't been too much to worry them here. She prayed there wouldn't be any more hurricanes. After all, it was almost October.

"Did you notice the new people next door?" Kurt asked. "There's a tall, sour-looking man and a girl about my age. He's never home and she sits on their deck just staring at the ocean."

"You know I don't have time for neighbors," she murmured as she stared at the screen.

"Don't you ever stop and smell the flowers?" he asked with disgust. "You'll be an old maid if you keep this up."

"I'll be a *rich* old maid," she replied absently as she scrolled the pages up the screen. "Besides, there's Quentin."

"Quentin Hobard," he muttered, throwing up his hands. "Good Lord, Janie, he teaches ancient history!"

She glared at him. "He teaches *medieval* history, primarily the Renaissance period. If you'd listen to him once in a while, you might discover that he knows a lot about it."

"Like I can't wait to revisit the Spanish Inquisition," he scoffed.

"It wasn't as horrible as those old movies suggest," she said, sitting up to give him her undivided attention.

"I was thinking more along the lines of 'Monty Python,'" he drawled, naming his favorite classic television show. He got up and struck a pose. "Nobody escapes the Spanish Inquisition!"

She threw up her hands. "You can't learn history from a British comedy show!"

"Sure you can." He leaned forward, grinning. "Want to know the *real* story of the knights? They used coconut shells for horses—"

"I don't want to hear it," she said, and covered her ears. "Let me work or we're both going to starve."

"Not hardly," he said with confidence. "There's always royalties."

"Twelve, and you're an investment counselor."

"I learned all I know from you. I'm precocious on account of the fact that I'm the youngest child of scientists."

"You'd be precocious if you were the youngest child of Neanderthals."

"Did you know that the *h* in Neanderthals is silent and unpronounced? It was written wrong. It's a German word," he continued.

She held up a hand and her glare grew. "I don't need lessons in pronunciation. *I need peace and quiet!*"

"Okay, I get the message! I'll go out and fish for sea serpents."

She didn't even glance his way. "Great. If you catch one, yell. I'll take photos."

"It would serve you right if I did."

"Yes. With your luck, if you caught one, it would eat you, and I'd spend the rest of my life on this beach with a lantern like Heathcliff roaming the moors."

"Wrong storyline. I'm your brother, not your girlfriend."

"Picky, picky."

He made a face and opened the sliding glass door.

"Close it!" she yelled. "You're letting the cold air out!"

"God forbid!" he gasped. He turned back toward her

with bright eyes. "Hey, I just had an idea. Want to know how we could start global cooling? We could have everybody turn on their air conditioners and open all their doors and windows…"

She threw a legal pad in his general direction. Not being slow on the uptake, he quickly closed the sliding door and walked down the steps of the deck onto the sugar-white sand on the beach.

He stuck his hands into his pockets and walked toward the house next door, where a skinny young girl sat on the deck, wearing cutoffs with a tank top and an Atlanta Braves hat turned backward. Her bare feet were propped on the rail and she looked out of sorts.

"Hey!" he called.

She glared at him.

"Want to go fishing for sea serpents?" he asked.

Her eyebrows lifted. She smiled, and her whole face changed. She jumped up and bounced down the steps toward him. She was blond and blue-eyed with a fair complexion.

"You're kidding, right?" she asked.

He shrugged. "Ever seen anyone catch a sea serpent around here?"

"Not since we got off the plane," she said.

"Great!" He grinned at her, making his freckles stand out.

"Great?"

"If nobody's caught it, it's still out there!" he whispered, gesturing toward the ocean. "Just think of the residuals from it. We could sell it to one of the grocery store tabloids and clean up!"

Her eyes brightened. "What a neat idea."

"Sure it is." He sighed. "If only I knew how to make one."

"A mop," she ventured. "A dead fish. Parts of some organ meat. A few feathers. A garden hose, some shears and some gray paint."

A kindred soul. He was in heaven. "You're a genius!"

She grinned back. "My dad really is a genius. He taught me everything I know." She sighed. "But if we create a hoax, I'll be grounded for the rest of my life. So I guess I'll pass, but…"

He made a face. "I know what you mean. I'd never live it down. My parents would send me to military school."

"Would they, really?"

"They threaten me with it every time I get into trouble. I don't mind boarding school, but I hate uniforms!"

"Me, too, unless they're baseball uniforms. This year is it, this is the third time, this is the charm. This time," she assured him, "the Braves are going to go all the way!"

He gave her a long, thoughtful look. "Well, we'll see."

"You a Braves fan?" she asked.

He hadn't ever cared much for baseball, but it seemed important to her. "Sure," he said.

She chuckled. "My name is Karie."

"I'm Kurt."

"Nice to meet you."

"Same here."

They walked along the beach for a minute or two. He stopped and looked back up the deserted stretch of land. "Know where to find a mop?" he asked after a minute.

BLISSFULLY UNAWARE THAT her young brother had just doubled his potential for disaster, Janine filled her computer screen with what she hoped was going to be the bare bones of a new mystery. Some books almost wrote themselves. Others were on a par with pulling teeth. This looked like one of those. Her mind was tired. It wanted to shape clouds into white horses and ocean waves into pirate ships.

"What I need," she said with a sigh, "is a good dose of fantasy."

Sadly there wasn't anything on television that she wanted to watch. Most of it, she couldn't understand, because it was in Spanish.

She turned the set off. The one misery of this trip was missing her favorite weekly science fiction series. Not that she didn't like all the characters on it; she did. But her favorite was an arrogant, sometimes very devious alien commander. The bad guy. She seemed to be spending all her productive time lately sighing over him instead of doing the work that she got paid to do. That was one reason she'd agreed to come to Cancún with her parents and Kurt, to get away from the make-believe man who was ruining her writing career.

"Enough of this!" she muttered to herself. "Good heavens, you'd think I was back in grammar school, idolizing teachers!"

She got up and paced the room. She ate some cookies. She typed a little into the computer. Eventually the sun started going down and she noticed that she was short one twelve-year-old boy.

She looked at her watch. Surely he hadn't gotten the

time confused? It was earlier here than in Bloomington, Indiana, where Kurt lived with their parents. Had
he mistaken the time, perhaps forgotten to reset his
watch? Janine frowned, hoping that she hadn't forgotten to set her own. It would be an hour behind
Kurt's, because her apartment in Chicago was in a different time zone from Kurt and her parents' in Indiana.

He was in a foreign country and he didn't speak any
more Spanish than she did. Their parents' facility for
languages had escaped them, for the most part. Janine
spoke German with some fluency, but not much Spanish. And while English was widely spoken here in the
hotels and tourist spots, on the street it was a different story. Many of the local people in Cancún still
spoke Mayan and considered Spanish, not English, a
second language.

She turned off her computer—it was useless trying
to work when she was worried, anyway—and went
out to the beach. She found the distinctive tread of
Kurt's sneakers and followed them in the damp sand
where the tide hadn't yet reached. The sun was low
on the horizon and the wind was up. There were dark
clouds all around. She never forgot the danger of hurricanes here, and even if it was late September, that
didn't mean a hurricane was no longer a possibility.

She shaded her eyes against the glare of the sun,
because she was walking west across the beach, stopping when Kurt's sneakers were joined by another,
smaller pair, with no discernible tread. She knelt
down, scowling as she studied the track. She'd worked

as a private eye for a couple of years, but any novice would figure out that these were the footprints of a girl, she thought. The girl Kurt had mentioned, perhaps, the one who lived next door. In fact, she was almost in front of that beach house now.

The roar of the waves had muffled the sound of approaching footsteps. One minute, she was staring down at the tracks. The next, she was looking at a large and highly polished pair of black dress shoes. Tapered neatly around them were the hem of expensive slacks. The legs seemed to go up forever. Far above them, glaring down at her, were pale blue eyes under a jutting brow in a long, lean face. The lips were thin. The top one was long and narrow, the lower one had only a hint of fullness. The cheekbones were high and the nose was long and straight. The hairline was just slightly receding around straight brown hair.

Two enormous lean hands were balled into fists, resting on the hips of the newcomer.

"May I ask what you're doing on my beach?" he asked in a voice like raspy velvet.

She stood up, a little clumsy. How odd, that a total stranger should make her knees weak.

"I'm tracking my…" she began.

"Tracking?" he scoffed, as if he thought she were lying. His blue eyes narrowed. He looked oddly dangerous, as if he never smiled, as if he could move like lightning and would at the least provocation.

Her heart was racing. "His name is Kurt and he's only twelve," she said. "He's redheaded and so high." She made a mark in the air with her flat hand.

"That one," he murmured coolly. "Yes, I've seen him prowling around. Where's my daughter?"

Her eyebrows rose. "You have a daughter? Imagine that! Is she carved out of stone, too?"

His firm, square chin lifted and he looked even more threatening. "She's missing. I told her not to leave the house."

"If she's with Kurt, she's perfectly safe," she began, about to mention that he'd been stranded once in the middle of Paris by their forgetful parents, and had found his way home to their hotel on the west bank. Not only had he maneuvered around a foreign city, but he'd also sold some of the science fiction cards he always carried with him to earn cab fare, and he'd arrived with twenty dollars in his pocket. Kurt was resourceful.

But long before she could manage any of that, the man moved a step closer and cocked his head. "Do you know where they are?"

"No, but I'm sure…"

"You may let your son run loose like a delinquent, but my daughter knows better," he said contemptuously. His eyes ran over her working attire with something less than admiration. She had on torn, raveled cutoffs that came almost to her knee. With them she was wearing old, worn-out sandals and a torn shirt that didn't even hint at the lovely curves beneath it. Her short hair was windblown. She wasn't even wearing makeup. She could imagine how she looked. What had he said—her *son?*

"Now, just wait a minute here," she began.

"Where's your husband?" he demanded.

Her eyes blazed. "I'm not married!"

Those eyebrows were really expressive now.

She flushed. "My private life is none of your business," she said haughtily. His assumptions, added to his obvious contempt, made her furious. An idea flashed into her mind and, inwardly, she chuckled. She struck a pose, prepared to live right down to his image of her. "But just for the record," she added in purring tones, "my *son* was born in a commune. I'm not really sure who his father is, of course…"

The expression on his face was unforgettable. She wished with all her heart for a camera, so that she could relive the moment again and again.

"A commune? Is that where you learned to track?" he asked pointedly.

"Oh, no." She searched for other outlandish things to tell him. He was obviously anxious to learn any dreadful aspect of her past. "I learned that from a Frenchman that I lived with up in the northern stretches of Canada. He taught me how to track and make coats from the fur of animals." She smiled helpfully. "I can shoot, too."

"Wonderful news for the ammunition industry, no doubt," he said with a mocking smile.

She put her own hands on her hips and glared back. It was a long way up, although she was medium height. "It's getting dark."

"Better track fast, hadn't you?" he added. He lifted a hand and motioned to a man coming down toward the beach. *"¿Sabe donde están?"* he shot at the man in fluent Spanish.

"No, lo siento, señor. ¡Nadie los han visto!" the smaller man called back.

"Llame a la policía."

"Sí, señor!"

Police sounded the same in any language and her pulse jumped. "You said *police*. You're going to call the police?" she groaned. That was all she needed, to have to explain to a police officer that she'd forgotten the time and let her little brother get lost.

"You speak Spanish?" he asked with some disbelief.

"No, but police sounds the same in most languages, I guess."

"Have you got a better idea?"

She sighed. "No, I guess not. It's just that…"

"Dad!"

They both whirled as Karie and Kurt came running along the beach with an armload of souvenirs between them, wearing sombreros.

"Gosh, Dad, I'm sorry, we forgot the time!" Karie warbled to her father. "We went to the *mercado* in town and bought all this neat stuff. Look at my hat! It's called a sombrero, and I got it for a dollar!"

"Yeah, and look what I got, S—*mmmmffg.*" Kurt's "Sis" was cut off in midstream by Janine's hand across his mouth.

She grinned at him. "That's fine, *son,*" she emphasized, her eyes daring him to contradict her. "You know, you shouldn't really scare your poor old *mother* this way," she added, in case he hadn't gotten the point.

Kurt was intrigued. Obviously his big sister wanted this rather formidable-looking man to think he was her son. Okay. He could go along with a gag. Just in case, he stared at Karie until she got the idea, too, and nodded to let him know that she understood.

"I'm sorry...*Mom*," Kurt added with an apologetic smile. "But Karie and I were having so much fun, we just forgot the time. And then when we tried to get back, neither of us knew any Spanish, so we couldn't call a cab. We had to find someone who spoke English to get us a cab."

"All the cabdrivers speak enough English to get by," Karie's father said coldly.

"We didn't know that, Dad," Karie defended. "This is my friend Kurt. He lives next door."

Karie's dad didn't seem very impressed with Kurt, either. He stared at his daughter. "I have to stop José before he gets the police out here on a wild-goose chase. And then we have to leave," he told her. "We're having dinner with the Elligers and their daughter."

"Oh, gosh, not them again," she groaned. "Missy wants to marry you."

"Karie," he said warningly.

She sighed. "Oh, all right. Kurt, I guess I'll see you tomorrow."

"Sure thing, Karie."

"Maybe we can find that garden hose," she added in a conspiratorial tone.

He brightened. "Great idea!"

"What the hell do you want with a hose?" Karie's father asked as they walked back up the beach, totally ignoring the two people he'd just left.

"Whew!" Kurt huffed. "Gosh, he's scary!"

"No, he isn't," Janine said irritably. "He's just pompous and irritating! And he thinks he's an emperor or something. I told him we lived in a commune and you're my son and I don't know who your father is. Don't you tell him any differently," she added when he tried to speak. "I want to live down to his image of me!"

He chuckled. "Boy, are you mad," he said. "You don't have fights with anybody."

"Wait," she promised, glaring after the man.

"He reminds me of somebody," he said.

"Probably the devil," she muttered. "I hear he's got blue eyes. Somebody wrote a song about it a few years ago."

"No," he mumbled, still thinking. "Didn't he seem familiar to you?"

"Yes, he did," she admitted. "I don't know why. I've never seen him before."

"Are you kidding? You don't know who he is? Haven't you recognized him? He's famous enough as he is. But just think, Janie, think if he had gray makeup on."

"He could pass for a sand crab," she muttered absently.

"That's not what I meant," he muttered. "Listen, they call this guy Mr. Software. Good grief, don't you ever read the newspapers or watch the news?"

"No. It depresses me," she said, glowering.

He sighed. "Mr. Software just lost everything. For the past year, he's been involved in a lawsuit to prevent a merger that would have saved his empire. He just lost the suit, and a fortune with it. Now he can't merge his software company with a major computer chain. He's down here avoiding the media so he can get himself back together before he starts over again. He's already promised his stockholders that he'll recoup every penny he lost. I bet he will, too. He's a tiger."

She scowled. "He, who?"

"Him. Canton Rourke," he emphasized. "Third generation American, grandson of Irish immigrants. His mother was Spanish, can't you tell it in his bearing? He made billions designing and selling computer programs, and now he's moving into computer production. The company he was trying to acquire made the computer you use. And the software word processing program you use was one he designed himself."

"That's Canton Rourke?" she asked, turning to stare at the already dim figure in the distance. "I thought he was much older than that."

"He's old enough, I guess. He's divorced. Karie said her mother ran for the hills when it looked like he was going to risk everything in that merger attempt. She likes jewelry and real estate and high living. She found herself another rich man and remarried within a month of the divorce becoming final. She moved to Greece. Just as well, probably. Her parents were never together, anyway. He was always working on a program and her mother was at some party, living it up. What a mismatch!"

"I guess so." She shook her head. "He didn't look like a billionaire."

"He isn't, now. All he has is his savings, from what they say on TV, and that's not a whole lot."

"That sort of man will make it all back," she said thoughtfully. "Workaholics make money because they love to work. Most of them don't care much about the money, though. That's just how they keep score."

His eyes narrowed. "You still haven't guessed why he looks familiar."

She turned and scowled at him. "You said something about gray makeup?"

"Sure. Think," he added impatiently. "Those eyes. That deep, smooth voice. Where do you hear them every fourth or fifth week?"

"On the news?"

He chuckled. "Only if they had aliens doing it."

His rambling was beginning to make sense. Every fourth or fifth week, there was a guest star on her favorite science fiction show. Her heartbeat increased alarmingly. Her breath caught in her throat. She put a hand there, to make sure she was still breathing.

"Oh, no." She shook her head. She smiled nervously. "No, he doesn't look like *him!*"

"He most certainly does," Kurt said confidently. "Same height, build, eyes, bone structure, even the same deep sort of voice." He nodded contemplatively. "What a coincidence, huh? We came here to Mexico to get you away from the television so you could write without being distracted by your favorite villain. And his doppelgänger turns up here on the beach!"

CHAPTER TWO

"I DON'T LIKE HAVING YOU around that boy," Canton told his daughter when they were back in their beach house. "His mother is a flake."

Karie had to bite her tongue to keep from blurting out the truth. Obviously the Curtis duo didn't want it known that they were little brother and big sister, not son and mother. Karie would keep her new friend's secret, but it wasn't going to be easy.

Her eyes went to the new hardcover murder mystery on the coffee table. There was a neat brown leather bookmark holding Canton's place in it. On the cover in huge red block letters were the title, *"CATACOMB,"* and the author's name—Diane Woody.

There was a photo in the back of the book, on the slick jacket, but it was of a woman with long hair and dark glasses wearing a hat with a big brim. It didn't even look like their neighbor. But it was. Karie knew because Kurt had told her, with some pride, who his sister was. She was thrilled to know, even secondhand, a big-time mystery writer like Diane Woody. Her father was one of the biggest fans of the bestselling mystery author, but he wouldn't recognize her from that book jacket. Maybe it was a good thing. Apparently she didn't want to be recognized.

"Kurt's nice," she told her father. "He's twelve. He likes people. He's honest and kind. And Janine's nice, too."

His eyebrows lifted as he glanced at her over his shoulder. "Janine?" he murmured, involuntarily liking the sound of the name on his lips.

"His...mother."

"You learned all that about him in one day?"

She shrugged. "Actions speak louder than words, isn't that what you always say?"

His face softened, just a little. He loved his daughter. "Just don't go wandering off with him again, okay?"

"Okay."

"And don't go to his home," he added through his teeth. "Because even if he can't help what he's got for a mother, I don't want you associating with her. Is that clear?"

"Oh, yes, sir!"

"Good. Get dressed. We don't have much time."

IN THE DAYS THAT FOLLOWED, Kurt and Karie were inseparable. Karie, as usual, agreed with whatever her father told her to do and then did what she pleased. He was so busy trying to regroup that he usually forgot his orders five minutes after he gave them, anyway.

So Karie and Kurt concocted their "sea serpent," piece by painstaking piece, concealing it under the Rourke beach house for safety. Meanwhile, they watched World War III develop between their respective relatives.

The first salvo came suddenly and without warning.

Kurt had gone out to play baseball with Karie. This was something new for him. His parents were studious and bookwormish, not athletic. And even though Janine was more than willing to share the occasional game of ball toss, she wasn't a baseball fanatic. Kurt had grown to his present age without much tutoring in sports, except what he played at the private school where his parents sent him. And that was precious little, because the owners were too wary of lawsuits to let the children do much rough-and-tumble stuff.

Karie had no hang-ups at all about playing tackle football on the beach or smacking a hardball with her regulation bat. She gave the bat to Kurt and told him to do his best. Unfortunately, he did, on the very first try.

CANTON ROURKE CAME STORMING up onto the porch of the beach house and right onto the open patio without a knock. Janine, lost in the fifth chapter of her new book, was so foggy that she saw him without really seeing him. She was in the middle of a chase scene, locked into character and time and place, totally mindless and floating in the computer screen. She stared at him blankly.

He looked furious. The blue eyes under that jutting brow were blazing from his lean face. He had a hardball in one hand. He stuck it under her nose.

"It's a baseball," she said helpfully.

"I know what the damned thing is," he said in a tone that would have affected her if she hadn't been deep in concentration. "I just picked it up off my living-room floor. It went through the bay window."

"You shouldn't let the kids play baseball in the house," she instructed.

"They weren't playing in the damned house! Your son slammed it through the window!"

Her eyebrows rose. Things were beginning to focus in the real world. Her mind lost the last thread of connection with her plot. Before she lost her bearings too far, she saved the file before she swung her chair back to face her angry neighbor.

"Nonsense," she said. "Kurt doesn't have a baseball. Come to think of it, I don't think he knows how to use a bat, either."

He threw the ball up and caught it, deliberately.

"All right, what do you want me to do about it?" she asked wearily.

"I want you to teach him not to hit balls through people's windows," he said shortly. "It's a damned nuisance trying to find a glass company down here, especially one that can get a repair done quickly."

"Put some plastic over the hole with tape," she suggested.

"Your son did the damage," he continued with a mocking smile. "The repair is going to be up to you, not me."

"*Me?*"

"You." He put the ball down firmly on her desk, noticing the computer and printer for the first time. His eyes narrowed. "What are you doing?"

"I'm writing a bestselling novel," she said honestly.

He laughed without humor. "Sure."

"It's going to be great," she continued with building anger. "It's all about a—"

He held up a big, lean hand. "Spare me," he said. "I don't really want to hear the sordid details. No doubt you can draw plenty of material from your years in the commune."

"Why, yes, I can," she agreed with a vacant smile. "But I was going to say that this book is about a pompous businessman with delusions of grandeur."

His eyebrows lifted. "How interesting." He stuck his hands into his pockets and she fought a growing attraction to him. He really did have an extraordinary build for a man his age, which looked to be late thirties. He was lean and muscular and sensuous. He didn't have a male-model sort of look, but there was something in the very set of his head, in the way he looked at her, that made her knees go weak.

His eye had been caught by an autographed photo peering out from under her mousepad. She'd hidden it there so that Kurt wouldn't see it and tease her about her infatuation with her television hero. Sadly when she'd moved the mouse to save her file, she'd shifted the pad and revealed the photo.

His lean hand reached out and tugged at the corner. He didn't wear jewelry of any kind, she noticed, and his fingernails were neatly trimmed and immaculate. He had beautiful hands, lightly tanned and strong.

"I like to watch the television series he's in," she said defensively, because he was staring intently at the photo.

His gaze lifted and he laughed softly. "Do you?" He handed it back and in the process, leaned close to her. "It's one of my favorite shows, too," he said, his voice dropping an octave, soft and deep and sensuous. "But this is the villain, you know, not the hero."

She cleared her throat. He was close enough to make her uncomfortable. "So what?"

"He looks familiar, doesn't he?" he murmured dryly.

She glared up at him. He really was far too close. Her heart skipped. "Does he?" she asked. Her voice sounded absolutely squeaky.

He stood up again, his hands back in his pockets, his smile so damned arrogant and knowing that she could have kicked him.

"Don't you have a business empire to save or something?" she asked irritably.

"I suppose so. You can't get that show down here, at least not in English," he added.

"Yes. I know. That was the whole purpose of coming here," she murmured absently.

"Ah, I see. Drying out, are we?"

She stood up. "You listen here…!"

He chuckled. "I have things to do. You'll see to the window, of course."

She took a steadying breath. "Of course."

His eyes slid up and down her slender body with more than a little interest. "Odd."

"What?"

"Do you mind if I test a theory?"

Her eyes were wary. "What sort of theory?"

He took his hands out of his pockets and moved close, very deliberately, his eyes staring straight into hers the whole while. When he was right up against her, almost touching her, he stopped. His hands remained at his side. He never touched her. But his eyes, his beautiful blue eyes, stared right down into hers and suddenly slipped to her mouth, tracing it with such sensuality that her lips parted on a shaky breath.

He moved again. His chest was touching her breasts now. She could smell the clean, sexy scent he wore. She could feel his warm, coffee-scented breath on her mouth as he breathed.

"How old are you?" he asked in a deep, sultry tone.

"Twenty-four," she said in a strangled voice.

"Twenty-four." He bent his head, so that his mouth was poised just above hers, tantalizing but not invasive, not aggressive at all. His breath made little patterns on her parted lips. "And you've had more than a handful of lovers?"

She wasn't listening. Her eyes were on his mouth. It looked firm and hard and very capable. She wondered how it tasted. She wondered. She wished. She…wanted!

"Janine."

The sound of her voice on his lips brought her wide, curious eyes up to meet his. They looked stunned, mesmerized.

His own eyes crinkled, as if he were smiling. All she saw was the warmth in them.

"If you're the mother of a twelve-year-old," he whispered deeply, "I'm a cactus plant."

He lifted his head, gave her an amused, indulgent smile, turned and walked away without a single word or a backward glance, leaving her holding the ball. In more ways than one.

SHE GOT THE GLASS FIXED. It wasn't easy, but she managed. However, she did dare Kurt to pick up a bat again.

"You don't like him, do you?" he queried the day after the glass was repaired. "Why not? He seems to be good to Karie, and he isn't exactly Mr. Nasty to me, either."

She moved restlessly. "I'm trying to work," she said evasively. She didn't like to remember her last encounter with their neighbor. Weakness was dangerous around that tiger.

"He's gone to California," Kurt added.

Her fingers jumped on the keyboard, scattering letters across the screen. "Oh. Has he?"

"He's going to talk to some people in Silicon Valley. I'll bet he'll make it right back to where he was before he's through. His wife is going to be real sorry that she ran out on him when he lost it all."

"No foresight," she agreed. She saved the file. There was no sense working while Kurt was chattering away. She got up and stretched, moving to the patio window. She paused there, staring curiously. Karie was sitting on the beach on a towel. Nearby, a man stood watching her; a very dark man with sunglasses on and a suspicious look about him.

"Who's that? Have you seen him before?" she asked Kurt.

He glanced out. "Yes. He was out there yesterday."

"Who's watching Karie while her father's gone?"

"I think there's a housekeeper who cooks for them," he said. "He's only away for the day, though."

"That's long enough for a kidnapper," she said quietly. "He was very wealthy. Maybe someone wouldn't know that, would make a try for Karie."

"You mystery writers," Kurt scoffed, "always looking on the dark side."

"Dark side or not, he isn't hurting Karie while I'm around!" She went right out the patio door and down the steps.

She walked toward the man. He saw her coming, and stepped back, looking as if he wasn't sure what to do.

She went right up to him, aware that her two years of martial arts training might not be enough if he turned nasty. Well, she could always scream, and the beach was fairly crowded today.

"You're on my property. What do you want?" she asked the man, who was tall and well-built and foreign looking.

His eyebrows rose above his sunglasses. *"No hablo inglés,"* he said, and grinned broadly.

She knew very little Spanish, but that phrase was one she'd had to learn. "And I don't speak Spanish," she returned with a sigh. "Well, you have to go. Go away. Away! Away!" She made a flapping gesture with her hand.

"Ah. *¡Vaya!*" he said obligingly.

"That's right. *Vaya*. Right now."

He nodded, grinned again and went back down the beach in the opposite direction.

Janine watched him walk away. She had a nagging suspicion that he wasn't hanging around here for his health.

She went down the beach to where Karie was sitting, spellbound at the scene she'd just witnessed. "Karie, I want you to come and stay with Kurt and me today while your dad's gone," she said. "I don't like the way that man was watching you."

"Neither do I," Karie had to admit. She smiled rue-fully. "Dad had a bodyguard back in Chicago. I never really got used to him. Down here it's been quieter."

"You do have a bodyguard. Me."

Karie chuckled as she got up and shook out her towel. "I noticed. You weren't scared of him at all, were you?"

"Kurt and I studied martial arts for two years. I'm pretty good at it." She'd didn't add that she'd also worked as a private investigator.

"Would you teach me?"

"That might not be a bad idea," she considered. "Tell you what, Kurt and I will give you lessons on the sly. You may not want to share that with your dad right now. He's mad enough about the window at the moment."

"Dad isn't mean," Karie replied. "He's pretty cool, most of the time. He has a terrible temper, of course."

"I noticed."

Karie smiled. "You have one, too. That man started backing up the minute you went toward him. You scared him."

"Why, so I did," Janine mused. She grinned with pride. "How about that?"

"I'm starved," Karie said. "Maria went to the grocery store and she won't be back for hours."

"We'll make sandwiches. I've got cake, too, for dessert. Coconut."

"Wow! Radical!"

Janine smiled. She led the way back to the beach house, where an amused Kurt was waiting.

"Diane Woody to the rescue!" he chuckled.

She made a face at him. "I'm reading too much of

my own publicity," she conceded. "But the man left, didn't he?"

"Left a jet trail behind him," her brother agreed.

"What are you working on…oh! It's *him!*" Karie gasped, picking up the photo of the television star in makeup that Janine had left on the desk. "Isn't he cool? It's my favorite show. I like the captain best, but this guy isn't so bad. He sort of looks like Dad, you know?"

Janine didn't say a word. But inside, she groaned.

SHE WAS FEEDING THE KIDS coconut cake from a local store, and milk when a familiar threatening presence came through the patio doors without knocking. She gave him a glare that he simply ignored.

"Don't you live at home anymore?" he asked his daughter irritably.

"There's no cake at our place," Karie said matter-of-factly.

"Where's the housekeeper? I told her to stay with you."

"She went shopping and never came back," Janine said shortly. "Your daughter was on the beach being watched by a very suspicious-looking man."

"Janine scared him off," Karie offered, with a toothy grin. "She knows karate!"

The arrogant look that Canton Rourke gave her was unsettling. "Karate, hmmm?"

"I know a little," she confessed.

"She went right up to that man and told him to go away," Karie continued, unabashed. "Then she took me home with her." She glowered at him. "I could have been kidnapped!"

He looked strange for a space of seconds, as if he couldn't quite get his bearings.

"You shouldn't have been out there alone," he said finally.

"I was just lying on my beach towel."

"Well, from now on, lie on the deck," he replied curtly. "No more adventures."

"Okay," she said easily, and ate another chunk of cake.

"It's coconut cake," Kurt volunteered. "That little grocery store has them. Janie gets them all the time for us. They're great."

"I'd offer you a slice of cake, Mr. Rourke, but I'm sure you're in a terrible hurry."

"I suppose I must be. Come on, Karie."

His daughter took a big swallow of milk and got up from the table. "Thanks, Janie!"

"You're very welcome." She glanced at Canton. "Housekeepers don't make very good bodyguards."

"I never meant her to be a watchdog, only a cook and housecleaner. Apparently I'd better look elsewhere."

"It might be wise."

His eyes slid down her long legs in worn jeans, down to her bare, pretty feet. He smiled in spite of himself. "Don't like shoes, hmmm?"

"Shoes wear out. Skin doesn't."

He chuckled. "You sound like Einstein. I recall reading that he never wore socks, for the same reason."

Her eyes lifted to his face and slid over it with that same sense of stomach-rapping excitement that she experienced the first time she saw it. He did so closely resemble her favorite series TV character. It was uncanny, really.

"Are you sure you don't act?" she asked without meaning to.

He gave her a wry look. "I'm sure. And I'm not about to start, at my age."

"There go your hopes, dashed for good," Kurt murmured dryly. "He's not an illegal alien trying to fit in with humans, Janie. Tough luck."

She flushed. "Will you shut up!"

"What did you do with that autographed photo?" he asked as he passed the desk.

"Oh, she never has it out when she's working," Kurt volunteered. "If she can see it, she just sits and sighs over it and never gets a word on the screen."

He scowled, interested. "What sort of work do you do?"

"She's a secretary," Kurt said for her, gleefully improvising. "Her boss is a real slave driver, so even on vacation, she has to take the computer with her so that she can use the computer's fax modem to send her work to the office."

He made an irritated sound. "Some boss."

"He pays well," she said, warming to Kurt's improvisation. She sighed. "You know how it is, living in a commune, you get so out of touch with reality." She contrived to look dreamy-eyed. "But eventually, one has to return to the real world and earn a living. It really is so hard to get used to material things again."

His face closed up. He gave her a glare that could have stopped traffic and motioned to Karie to follow him. He stuck his hands into his pockets and walked out the door. He never looked back. It seemed to be a deep-seated characteristic.

Karie grinned and waved, following obediently.

When they were out of sight along the beach, Kurt joined her on the patio deck.

"What if that man wasn't watching Karie at all?" she wondered aloud, having had time to formulate a different theory. "What if he's a lookout for the pothunters?"

Kurt scowled. "You mean those people who steal artifacts from archaeological sites and sell them on the black market?"

"The very same." She folded her arms over her T-shirt. "This is a brand-new site, unexplored and uncharted until now. Mom and Dad even noted that it seemed to be totally undisturbed. The Maya did some exquisite work with gold and precious jewels. What if there's a king's ransom located at the dig and someone knows about it?"

Kurt leaned against the railing. "They know it can happen. It did last time they found a site deep in the jungle, over near Chichén Itzá. But they had militia guarding them and the pothunters were caught."

"Yes, but Mexico is hurting for money, and it's hard to keep militia on a site all the time to guard a few archaeologists."

"Dad has a gun."

"And he can shoot it. Sure he can. But they can't stay awake twenty-four hours a day, and even militia can be bribed."

"You're a whale of a comfort," Kurt groaned.

"I'm sorry. I just think we should be on our guard. It

could have been someone trying to kidnap Karie, but they've just as much incentive to kidnap us or at least keep a careful eye on us."

"In other words, we'd better watch our backs."

Janine smiled. "Exactly."

"Suits me." He sighed. "What a shame your alien hero can't beam down here and help us out. I'll bet he'd have the bad guys for breakfast."

"Oh, they don't eat humans," she assured him.

"They might make an exception for pothunters."

"You do have a point there. Come on. You can help me do the dishes."

"Tell you what," he said irrepressibly. "You do the dishes, and I'll write your next chapter for you!"

"Be my guest."

He gave her a wary look. "You're kidding, right?"

"Wrong. Go for it."

He was excited, elated. He took her at her word and went straight to the computer. He loaded her word processing program, pulled up the file where she'd left off, scanned the plot.

He sat and he sat and he sat. By the time she finished cleaning up the kitchen, he was still sitting.

"Nothing yet?" she asked.

He gave her a plaintive stare. "How do you *do* this?" he groaned. "I can't even think of a single word to put on paper!"

"Thinking is the one thing I don't do," she told him. "Move."

He got up and she sat down. She stared at the screen for just a minute, checked her place in the plot, put her fingers on the keyboard and just started typing. She was two pages into the new scene when Kurt let out a long sigh and walked away.

"Writers," he said, "are strange."

She chuckled to herself. "You don't know the half of it," she assured him, and kept right on typing.

CHAPTER THREE

JANINE WAS WELL INTO THE BOOK two days later when Karie came flying up the steps and in through the sliding glass doors.

"We're having a party!" she announced breathlessly. "And you're both invited."

Janine's mind was still in limbo, in the middle of a scene. She gave Karie a vacant stare.

"Oops! Sorry!" Karie said, having already learned in a space of days that writers can't withdraw immediately when they're deep into a scene. She backed out and went to find Kurt.

"What sort of party?" he asked when she joined him at the bottom of the steps at the beach.

"Just for a few of Dad's friends, but I persuaded him to invite you and Janie, too. He feels guilty since he's had to leave me alone so much for the past few years. So he lets me have my way a lot, to try and make it up to me." She grinned at Kurt. "It's sort of like having my own genie."

"You're blackmailing him."

She laughed. "Exactly!"

His thin shoulders rose and fell. "I wouldn't mind coming to the party, if you're having something nice to eat. But Janie won't," he added with certainty. "She hates parties and socializing. And she doesn't like your dad at all, can't you tell?"

"He doesn't like her much, either, but that's no reason why they can't be civil to each other at a party."

"I don't know about that."

"I do. He'll be on his best behavior. Did you know that he reads her books? He doesn't know who she really is, of course, because I haven't told him. But he's got every book she's ever written."

"Good grief, didn't he look at her picture on the book jacket?" Kurt burst out.

"I didn't recognize her from it. Neither will he. It doesn't really look like her, does it?"

He had to admit it didn't. "She doesn't like being recognized," he confided. "It embarrasses her. She likes to write books, but she's not much on publicity."

"Why?"

"She's shy, can you believe it?" he chuckled. "She runs the other way from interviews and conventions and publicity. It drove the publishing house nuts at first, but they finally found a way to capitalize on her eccentricity. They've made her into the original mystery woman. Nobody knows much about her, so she fascinates her reading public."

"I love her books."

"So do I," Kurt said, "but don't ever tell her I said so. We wouldn't want her to get conceited."

She folded her arms on her knees and stared out to sea. "Does she have a, like, boyfriend?"

He groaned. "Yes, if you could call him that. He's a

college professor. He teaches ancient history." He made a gagging gesture.

"Is he nice?"

"He's indescribable," he said after thinking about it for a minute.

"Are they going to get married?"

He shrugged. "I hope not. He's really nice, but he thinks Janie should be less flaky. I don't. I like her just the way she is, without any changes. He thinks she's not dignified enough."

"Why?"

"He's very conservative. Nice, but conservative. I don't think he really approves of our parents, either. They're eccentric, too."

She turned to look at him. "What do they do?"

"They're archaeologists," he said. "Both of them teach at Indiana University, where they got their doctorates. We live in Bloomington, Indiana, but Janie lives in Chicago."

"They're both doctors?"

He nodded and made a face. "Yes. Even Janie has a degree, although hers is in history and it's a bachelor of arts. I guess I'll be gang-pressed into going to college. I don't want to."

"What do you want to do?"

He sighed. "I want to fly," he said, looking skyward as a bird, probably a tern, dipped and swept in the wind currents, paying no attention to the odd creatures sitting on the steps below him.

"We could glue some feathers together," she suggested.

"No! I want to fly," he emphasized. "Airplanes, hel-

icopters, anything, with or without wings. It's in my
blood. I can't get enough of airplane movies. Even space
shows. Now, that's really flying, when you do it in
space!"

"So that's why you like that science fiction show
Janie's so crazy about."

"Sort of. But I like the action, too."

She smiled. "I like it because the bad guy looks like
my dad."

He burst out laughing. "He's not the bad guy. He's
the other side."

"Right. The enemy."

"He's not so bad. He saved the hero, once."

"Well, so he did. I guess maybe he isn't all bad."

"He's just misunderstood," he agreed.

She chuckled. They were quiet for a minute or two.
"Will you try to get Janie to come to our party?"

He smiled. "I'll give it my best shot. Just don't expect miracles, okay?"

She smiled back. "Okay!"

As IT TURNED OUT, Janine had to go to the Rourke party,
because for once her little brother dug in his heels and
insisted on going somewhere. He would, he told her
firmly, go alone if she didn't care to go with him.

The thought of her little brother in the sort of company the Rourkes would keep made her very nervous.
She didn't socialize enough to know much about people who lived in the fast lane, and she'd never known
any millionaires. She was aware that some drank and
used drugs. Her sheltered life hadn't prepared her for

that kind of company. Now she was going to be thrust into the very thick of it, or so she imagined. Actually she had no idea what Canton's friends were like. Maybe they were down-to-earth and nice.

She hadn't anything appropriate for a cocktail party, but she scrounged up a crinkly black sundress that, when paired with high heels, pearl earrings and a pearl necklace that her parents had given her, didn't look too bad. She brushed her flyaway hair, sprayed it down and went to get her black leather purse.

"I didn't even have enough warning to go and buy a new dress. I hate you," she told Kurt with a sweet smile.

"You'll forgive me. I'll bet when he's dressed up, he's really something to look at," he replied.

"I've seen him dressed up."

"Oh. Well, he's supposed to be the stuff dreams are made of. Karie says half the women in Chicago have thrown themselves at him over the years, especially since his wife remarried."

"They live in Chicago?" She tried to sound disinterested.

"Part of the time," he affirmed. "They have an apartment in New York, too, in downtown Manhattan."

"He may not ever be super rich again," she reminded him.

"That doesn't seem to discourage them," he assured her. "They're all sure that any man who could make it in the first place will be able to get it back."

There was a sort of logic to the assumption, she had to admit. Most men who made that sort of money were workaholics who didn't spare themselves or any of their

employees. Given a stake, there was every reason to believe Canton Rourke could rebuild his empire. But she
felt sorry for him. He wouldn't ever know who liked him
for himself and who liked him for what he had.

"I'm glad I'm not rich," she said aloud.

"What?"

"Oh, I just meant that I know people like me for myself and not for what I've got."

He folded his arms across his neat shirt. "Do go
on," he invited. "Tell me about it. What was that in-
vitation you got back home to come to a cocktail party
and explain how to get published to the hostess's guest
of honor, who just happened to have written a
book…?"

She sighed.

"Or the rich lady with the stretch limo who wanted
you to get her best friend's book published. Or the mystery writer wannabe who asked for the name of your
agent and a recommendation?"

"I quit," she said. "You're right. Everybody has
problems."

"So does Mr. Rourke. If you get to know him, you
might like him. And there's a fringe benefit."

"There is?"

"Sure. If you nab him, you can buy him a plastic appliance like the one your favorite alien wears and make
him over to suit you!"

The thought of Canton Rourke sitting still for that
doubled her over with laughter. He'd more than likely
give her the appliance face first and tell her where she
could go with it.

"I don't really think that would be a good idea," she replied. "Think how his board of directors might react!"

"I suppose so. We should go," he prompted, nodding toward the clock on the side table.

She grimaced. "All right. But I don't want to," she said firmly.

"You'll enjoy yourself," he promised her. "Nobody knows who you are."

She brightened. "I didn't think of that."

"Now you can."

He opened the door for her with a flourish and they walked down the beach through the sand to the Rourke's house. It was ablaze with light and soft music came wafting out the open door of the patio. Several people holding glasses were talking. They all looked exquisitely dressed and Janine already felt self-conscious about her own appearance.

Kurt, oblivious, darted up the steps to his friend Karie, wearing a cute little dress with a dropped waistline and a short skirt that probably had cost more than Janine's summer wardrobe put together. As she went up the steps, she paused to shake the sand out of her high heels, holding on to the banister for support.

"Need a hand?" a familiar velvety voice asked. A long, lean arm went around her and supported her while she fumbled nervously with her shoe, almost dropping it in the process.

"Here." He knelt and emptied the sand out of the shoe before he eased it back onto her small foot with a sensuality that made her heart race.

He stood up slowly, his eyes meeting hers when they

were on the same level, and holding as he rose to his towering height. He didn't smile. For endless seconds, they simply looked at each other.

"This was Kurt's idea," she blurted breathlessly. "I didn't even have time to buy a new dress…"

"What's wrong with this one?" he asked. His lean hand traced the rounded neckline, barely touching her skin, but she shivered at the contact.

"You, uh, seem to have quite a crowd," she faltered, moving a breath away from him.

"Right now, I wish they were all five hundred miles away," he said deeply, and with an inflection that made her tingle.

She laughed nervously. "Is that a line? If it is, it's probably very effective, but I'm immune. I've got a son and I've lived in a com…"

He held up a hand and chuckled. "Give it up," he advised. "Kurt is twelve and you're twenty-four. I really doubt that you conceived at the age of eleven. As for the commune bit," he added, moving close enough to threaten, "not in your wildest dreams, honey."

Honey. She recalled dumping a glass of milk on a pushy acquaintance who'd used that term in a demeaning way to her. This man made it sound like a verbal caress. Her toes curled.

"Please." Was that her voice, that thin tremulous tone?

His fingers touched her cheek gently. "I'm a new experience, is that it?"

She shivered. "You're a multimillionaire. I'm working for wages." Not quite the truth, but a good enough comparison, she thought frantically.

He leaned closer with a smile that was fascinating. "I gave up seducing girls years ago. You're safe."

Her wide eyes met his. "Could I have that in writing, notarized, please?"

"If you like. But my word is usually considered equally binding," he replied. His hand fell and caught hers. "As for the multimillionaire bit, that's past history. I'm just an ordinary guy working his way up the corporate ladder right now. Come in and meet my guests."

His fingers were warm and strong and she felt a rush of emotion that burst like tangible joy inside her. What was happening to her? As if he sensed her confusion and uncertainty, his fingers linked into hers and pressed reassuringly. Involuntarily her own returned the pressure.

As they gained the top of the steps, a vivacious brunette about Janine's age came up to them with a champagne glass in her hand. She beamed at Canton until she saw him holding hands with the other woman. Her smile became catty.

"There you are, Canton. I don't believe I know your friend, do I?" she asked pointedly, glancing at Janine.

"Probably not. Janine Curtis, this is Missy Elliger. She's the daughter of one of my oldest friends."

"You're not that old, darling," she drawled, moving closer to him. She glared at Janine. "Do you live here?"

"Oh, no," Janine said pleasantly. "I live in a commune in California with several men."

The other woman gaped at her.

"Behave," Canton said shortly, increasing the pressure of his fingers. "This is Janine Curtis. She's here on vacation with her little brother. That's him, over there with Karie. His name's Kurt."

"Oh." Missy cleared her throat. "What a very odd thing to say, Miss...Curtsy?"

"Curtis." Janine corrected her easily. "Why do you say it's odd?"

"Well, living in a commune. Really!"

Janine shrugged. "Actually it wasn't so much a commune as it was a sort of, well, labor camp. You know, where they send political prisoners? I voiced unpopular thoughts about the government..."

"In America?!" Missy burst out.

"Heavens, no! In one of the Balkan countries. I seem to forget which one. Anyway, there I was, with my trusty rifle, shooting snipers with my platoon when the lights went out..."

"Platoon?"

"Not in this life, of course," Janine went on, unabashed. "I believe it was when I was a private in the Czech army."

Missy swallowed her champagne in one gulp. "I must speak to Harvey Winthrop over there. Do excuse me." She gave Canton a speaking look and escaped.

Canton was trying not to laugh.

Janine wiggled her eyebrows at him. "Not bad for a spur-of-the-moment story, huh?"

"You idiot!"

She smiled. He wasn't bad at all. His eyes twinkled even when he didn't smile back.

"I'm sorry," she said belatedly. "She's really got a case on you, you know."

"Yes, I do," he replied. He brought up their linked hands. "That's why I'm doing this."

All her illusions fell, shattered, at her feet. "Oh."

"Surely you didn't think there was any other reason?" he mused. "After all, we're almost a generation apart. In fact, you're only a year older than Missy is."

"So I'm a visual aid."

He chuckled, pressing her fingers. "In a sense. I didn't think you'd mind. Enemies do help one another on occasion. I'll do the same for you, one day."

"I'm not that much in demand," she said, feeling stiff and uncomfortable now that she understood his odd behavior. "But you can have anyone you like. I read it in a magazine article."

"Was that the story they ran next to the one about space aliens attending the latest White House dinner?" he asked politely.

She glowered up at him. "You know what I mean."

He shrugged. "I'm off women temporarily. My wife wrote me off as a failure and found someone richer," he added, with a lack of inflection that was more revealing than the cold emptiness in his eyes.

"More fool, her," she said with genuine feeling. "You'll make it all back and she'll be sorry."

He smiled, surprised. "No, she won't. The magic left during the second year of our marriage. We stayed together for Karie, but eventually we didn't even see each other for months at a time. It was a marriage on paper. She's happier with her new husband, and I'm happier alone." He stared out to sea. "The sticking point is Karie. We ended up with joint custody, and that doesn't suit her. She thinks Karie belongs with her."

"How does Karie feel?"

"Oh, she likes tagging along with me and going on business trips," he said. "She's learning things that she wouldn't in the exclusive girls' school Marie wants her in. I pulled her out of school and brought her here with me for a couple of weeks, mainly to get her out of reach of Marie. She's made some veiled threats lately about wanting more alimony or full custody."

"Education is important."

He glared at her. "And Karie will get the necessary education. She's only missing a few weeks of school and she's so intelligent that she'll catch up in no time. But I want her to have more than a degree and a swelled head when she grows up."

She felt insulted. "You don't like academics?"

He shrugged. "I've been put down by too damned many of them, while they tried to copy my software," he countered. "I like to design it. But in the past, I spent too much time at a computer and too little with my daughter. Even if I hadn't lost everything, taking a break was long overdue."

"You went to Silicon Valley, Karie said."

"Yes. Among other reasons, I was looking for guinea pigs." He glanced down at her with a faint scowl. "Come to think of it, there's you."

"Me?"

"I need someone to test a new program for me," he continued surprisingly. "It's a variation on one of my first word processors, but this one has a new configuration that's more efficient. It's still in the development stages, but it's usable. What do you think?"

She wasn't sure. She'd lost whole chapters before to new software and she was working on a deadline.

"Don't worry about it right now," he said. "Think it over and let me know."

"Okay. It's just that… Well, my boss wants this project sent up within a month. I can't really afford to change software in the middle of it."

"No, you can't. And I didn't mean I wanted you to download the program within the next ten minutes," he added dryly.

"Oh. Well, in that case, yes, I'll think about it."

His hand tightened over hers. "Good."

He led her through his guests, making introductions. Surprisingly his friends came from all walks of life and most of them were ordinary people. A few were very wealthy, but they didn't act superior or out of order at all. However, Missy Elliger watched Janine with narrow, angry eyes and faint contempt.

"Your guest over there looks as if she'd like to plant that glass she's holding in the middle of my forehead," she commented as they were briefly alone.

"Missy likes a challenge. She's too young for me."

She glanced at him. "So you said."

His eyes searched hers. "And I'm not in the market for a second Mrs. Rourke."

"Point taken," she said.

His eyebrow jerked. "No argument?"

Her eyes sparkled. "I wasn't aware that I'd proposed

to you," she replied with a grin. "We're temporary neighbors and frequent sparring partners. That's all."

"What if I'd like to be more than your neighbor?" he asked with deliberate sensuality.

Her grin didn't waver. That was amusement in his face, not real interest. He was mocking her, and he wasn't going to get away with it. "Quentin might get upset about that."

"Quentin? Is there a real husband somewhere in the background?" he probed.

She hesitated. He hadn't bought the commune story, so there was no way he was going to buy a secret husband. This man was a little too savvy for her usual ways of dissuading pursuers.

"A male friend," she countered with a totally straight face.

The hand holding hers let go, gently and unobtrusively, but definitely. "You didn't mention him before."

"There wasn't really an opportunity to," she countered. She smiled up at him. "He's a college professor. He teaches medieval history at the University of Indiana on the Chicago campus, where my parents teach anthropology."

His stance seemed to change imperceptibly. "Your parents are college professors?"

"Yes. They're on a dig in some Mayan ruins in Quintana Roo. Kurt's been ill with tonsillitis and complications. They took him out of school to get completely well and I'm tutoring him with his lessons until he goes back. We're near our parents, here in this villa, and I can get some work done and take care of Kurt as well."

He was wary, now, and not at all amused. "I suppose you have a degree, too?" he continued.

She wondered about the way he was looking at her, at the antagonistic set of his head, but she let it go by and took the question at face value. "Well, yes. I have an honors baccalaureate degree in history with a minor in German."

He seemed to withdraw without even moving. He set his glass on an empty tray and his lean hands slid into his pockets. His eyes moved restlessly around the room.

"What sort of degree do you have?" she asked.

It was the wrong question. He closed up completely. "Let me introduce you to the Moores," he said, taking her elbow. "They're interesting people."

She felt the new coolness in his manner with a sense of loss. She'd either offended him or alienated him. Perhaps he had some deep-seated prejudices about archaeology, which was the branch of anthropology in which both her parents specialized. She was about to tell him that they were both active in helping to enact legislation to help protect burial sites and insure that human skeletal remains were treated with dignity and respect.

But he was already making the introductions, to a nice young couple in real estate. A minute later, he excused himself and went pointedly to join his friend Missy Elliger, whom he'd said was too young for him. Judging by the way he latched on to her hand, and held it, he'd already forgotten that she was too young for him. Or, she mused humorously, he'd decided that Missy was less dangerous than Janine. How very flattering!

But the rest of the evening was a dead loss as far as Janine was concerned. She felt ill at ease and somewhat contagious, because he made a point of keeping out of her way. He was very polite, and courteous, but he might as well have been on another planet. It was such a radical and abrupt shift that it puzzled her.

Even Karie and Kurt noticed, from their vantage point beside a large potted palm near the patio.

"They looked pretty good together for a few minutes," Kurt said.

"Yes," she agreed, balancing a plate of cake on her knee. "Then they seemed to explode apart, didn't they?"

"Janie doesn't like men to get too close," Kurt told her with a grimace. "The only reason her boyfriend, Quentin, has lasted so long is because he forgets her for weeks at a time when he's translating old manuscripts."

"He what?" Karie asked, her fork poised in midair.

"He forgets her," he replied patiently. "And since he isn't pushy and doesn't try to get her to marry him, they get along just fine. Janine likes her independence," he added. "She doesn't want to get married."

"I guess my dad feels that way right now, too," Karie had to admit. "But he and my mom were never together much. Mom hates him now because she couldn't get exclusive custody of me. She swore she'd get me away from him eventually, but we haven't heard from her in several weeks. I suppose she's forgotten. He's forgetful, too, sometimes, when he's working on some new program. I guess that's hard on moms."

"He and Janie would make the perfect couple," Kurt ventured. "They'd both be working on something new all the time."

"But it doesn't look like they'll be thinking about

it now," Karie said sadly. "See how he's holding Missy's hand?"

"He was holding Janie's earlier," Kurt reminded her.

"Yes, but now they're all dignified and avoiding each other." She sighed. "Grown-ups! Why do they have to make everything so complicated?"

"Beats me. Here. Have some more cake."

"Thanks!" She took a big bite. "Maybe they could use a helping hand. You know. About getting comfortable with each other."

"I was just thinking that myself," Kurt said. He grinned at his partner in crime. "Got any ideas?"

"I'm working on some."

Meanwhile, oblivious to the fact that she was soon going to become a guinea pig in quite another way than software testing, Janine sat in a corner with a couple whose passion was deep-sea fishing and spent the next hour being bored out of her mind.

CHAPTER FOUR

"NEVER, NEVER GET ME ROPED into another party at the Rourkes'," Janine told her brother the next morning. "I'd rather be shot than go back there."

"Karie said she went home with her parents, after the party," Kurt said cautiously.

She pretended oblivion. "She, who?"

"Missy Elliger," he prompted. "You know, the lady who had Mr. Rourke by the hand all night?"

"She could have had him by the nose, for all I care," she said haughtily, and without meaning a word of it.

He glanced at her, and smiled secretively, but he didn't say anything.

"I think I'll invite Quentin down for the weekend," she said after a minute.

His eyebrows were vocal. "Why?"

She didn't want to admit why. "Why not?" she countered belligerently.

He shrugged. "Suit yourself."

"I know you don't like him, but he's really very nice when you get to know him."

"He's okay. I just hate ancient history. We have to study that stuff in school."

"What they're required to teach you usually is bor-

ing," she said. "And notice that I said 'required to.'
Teachers have to abide by rules and use the textbooks
they're assigned. In college, it's different. You get to
hear about the *real* people. That includes all the naughty
bits." She grinned. "You'll love it."

He sighed irritably. "No, I won't."

"Give Quentin a chance," she pleaded.

"If you like him, I guess he's okay. It just seems like
he's always trying to change you into somebody else."
He studied her through narrowed eyes. "Are you sure
you don't like Karie's dad?"

She cringed inside, remembering how receptive
she'd been last night to his pretended advances, before
she knew they were pretend. She'd tingled at the touch
of his hand, and he probably knew it, too. She felt like
an idiot for letting her emotions go like that, for letting
them show, when he was only using her to keep Missy
at bay. And why had he bothered, when he spent the rest
of the night holding the awful woman's hand?

"Yes, I'm sure," she lied glibly. "Now let me get
to work."

"Will Quentin stay here?" he asked before he left her.

"Why not?" she asked. "You can be our chaperon."

He sighed. "Mom and Dad won't like it."

"I'm old enough, and Quentin probably wants to
marry me," she said. "He just doesn't know it yet."

"You wouldn't marry him!" he exclaimed.

She shifted. "Why not? I'm going on twenty-five. I
should get married. I want to get married. Quentin is
steady and loyal and intelligent."

Also the wrong sort of man for Janine to get serious

about, Kurt thought, but he held his tongue. This wasn't a good idea to get his sister more upset than she already was. Besides, he was thinking, having Quentin here just might make Karie's dad a little jealous. There were all sorts of possibilities that became more exciting by the minute. He smiled secretively and waved as he left her to her computer.

"JANIE'S BOYFRIEND IS coming to stay," he told Karie later, making sure he spoke loudly enough that her father, who was sitting just down the beach, heard him.

"Her boyfriend?" Karie asked, shocked. "You mean, she has a boyfriend?"

"Oh, yes, she does," he said irritably, plopping down beside her in the sand. "He teaches ancient history. He's brainy and sophisticated and crazy about her."

Karie made a face. "I thought you said she wasn't interested in getting married."

"She said this morning that she was," he replied. "It would be just my luck to end up with him as my brother-in-law."

Karie giggled at the concept. "Is he old?"

"Sure," he said gloomily. "At least thirty-five."

"That's old," she agreed.

Down the beach, a young-thinking man of thirty-eight glared in their general direction. Thirty-five wasn't old. And what the hell was Janine thinking to saddle herself with an academic? He wanted to throw something. She had a degree, he reminded himself. Her parents were academics; even her boyfriend was.

But Canton Rourke was a high-school dropout with

a certificate that said he'd passed a course giving him the equivalent of a high-school diploma. He'd been far too busy making money to go to college. Now, it was too late. He couldn't compete with an educated woman on her level.

But he was attracted to her. That was the hell of it. He didn't want to be. Freshly divorced, awash in a sea of financial troubles, he had no room in his life for a new woman. Especially a young and pretty and very intelligent woman like Janine. He'd been smitten before, but never this fast or this furiously. He didn't know what he was going to do.

Except that he was sure he didn't want the college professor to walk away with his neighbor.

JANINE CALLED QUENTIN later that day. "Why don't you fly down here for a couple of days," she suggested.

"I can't leave in the middle of the summer semester, with classes every day," he replied. "I've got students who have makeup exams to take, too."

She sighed. "Quentin, you could leave early Friday and fly back Sunday."

"That's a rather large expense for two days' holiday," he replied thoughtfully.

She felt her temper oozing over its dam. "Well, you're right about that," she agreed hotly, "my company is hardly worth the price of an airline ticket."

"Wh...what?"

"Never mind. Have a nice summer, Quentin." She hung up.

Kurt stuck his head around the door. "Is he coming?"

She glared at him and threw a sofa pillow in his general direction.

Kurt went out the patio door, whistling to himself.

JANINE SANK INTO THE DEPTHS of depression for the next hour. She and Quentin were good friends, and in the past few months, they'd gone out a lot together socially. But to give him credit, he'd never mentioned marriage or even a serious relationship. A few light, careless kisses didn't add up to a proposal of marriage. She was living in pipe dreams again, and she had to stop.

But this was the worst possible time to discover that she didn't have a steady boyfriend, when she wanted to prove to Canton Rourke that he had no place at all in her life. As if she'd want a washed-up ex-millionaire, right?

Wrong. She found him so attractive that her toes curled every time she thought about him. He was the stuff of which dreams were made, and not because he'd been fabulously wealthy, either. It was the man himself, not his empire, that appealed to Janine. She wondered if he'd believe that? He was probably so used to people trying to get close to his wallet that he never knew if they liked him for himself.

But she didn't want him to know that she did. If only Quentin hadn't been so unreasonable! Why couldn't he simply walk out on his classes, risk being fired and spend his savings to rush down here to Cancún and save Janine's pride from the rejection of a man she coveted?

She burst out laughing. Putting things back into perspective did have an effect, all right.

The phone rang. She picked up the receiver.

"Janie?" Quentin murmured. "I've reconsidered. I think I'd like to come down for the weekend. I can get Professor Mills to take my Friday classes. I need a break."

She grinned into the telephone. "That would be lovely, Quentin!"

"But I'll have to leave on Sunday," he added firmly. "I've got to prepare for an exam."

"A few days will be nice. You'll like it here."

"I'll pack plenty of bottled water."

"You won't need to," she told him. "We have plenty. And at the restaurants, we've never had a problem."

"All right then. I'll phone you from the airport when I get in. I'll try to leave early in the morning, if there's a flight. I'll phone you."

"Bring your bathing trunks."

There was a pause. "Janine, I don't swim."

She sighed. "I forgot."

"Where are your parents?"

"Still out at the dig."

"You'd better book me in at a nearby hotel," he said.

"You could stay with Kurt and me…"

"Not wise, Janine," he murmured indulgently. "We aren't that sort of people, and I have a position to consider. You really must think more conventionally, if we're to have any sort of future together."

It was the first time he'd mentioned having a future with her. And suddenly, she didn't want to think about it.

"I understand that the Spaniards landed near Cancún, on Cozumel," he said. "I'd love to take the time to search through the local library, if they're open on Saturday. I read Spanish, you know."

She did know. He never missed an opportunity to remind her. Of course, he also spoke Latin, French, German and a little Russian. He was brilliant. That was
what had attracted her to him at first. Now, she wondered what in the world had possessed her to ask him
down here. He'd go off on an exploration of Spanish history in the New World and she wouldn't see him until
he was ready to fly out. On the other hand, that might
not be so bad.

"I'll meet you at the airport."

"Good! See you Friday. And Janine, this time, try not
to forget to take the car keys out of the ignition before
you lock the door, hmmm?"

She broke the connection and stared out the window.
What in heaven's name had she done? Quentin's favorite pastime was putting her down. In the time since
she'd seen him, she'd forgotten. But now she remembered with painful clarity why she'd been happy to leave
Bloomington, Indiana, behind just a few months ago
and move to a small apartment in Chicago. How could
she have forgotten?

Later in the day, she noticed again the dark man
who'd been watching Karie on the beach. He was downtown when she took the kids in a cab to visit one of the
old cathedrals there, for research on the book she was
writing.

He didn't come close or speak to them, but he
watched their movements very carefully. He had a cel-
lular phone, too, which he tried to conceal before Janine
spotted it. She went toward a nearby policeman, intent
on asking him to question the man. About that time, her

intentions were telegraphed to the watchful dark man, and he immediately got into a car and left the area. It disturbed Janine, and she wondered whether or not she should tell Canton about it. She didn't mention it to Karie or Kurt. After all, it could have been perfectly innocent. There was no sense in upsetting everyone without good reason.

They arrived back at the beach house tired and sweaty. The heat was making everyone miserable. Here, at least, there was a constant wind coming off the ocean. She made lemonade for the three of them and they were sitting on the patio, drinking it, when Canton came strolling along the beach below them.

He was wearing dark glasses and an angry expression. He came up onto the deck two steps at a time. When he reached the top, he whipped off the dark glasses and glared at his daughter.

"When I got back from Tulsa, the house was empty and there was no note," he said. "Your lack of consideration is wearing a little thin. Do I have to forbid you to leave the house to get some cooperation?"

Karie groaned. "Dad, I'm sorry!" she exclaimed, jumping up out of her chair. "Kurt and Janie asked me to go to town with them on a re—"

"Recreational trip," Janine added at once, to forestall her young guest from using "research trip" and spilling the beans about her alter ego.

"Recreational trip," Karie parroted obediently. "I was so excited that I just forgot about the note. Don't be mad."

"I've lost half a day worrying where you were," he

said shortly. "I've phoned everyone we know here, including the police."

"You can take away my allowance for three years. Six," she added helpfully. "I'll give up chocolate cake forever."

"You hate chocolate," he murmured irritably.

"Yes, but for you, I'll stop eating it."

He chuckled reluctantly. "Go home. And next time you don't leave me a note, you're grounded for life."

"Yes, sir! See you, Janie and Kurt. Thanks for the trip!"

"I have to wash my pet eel," Kurt said at once with a grin at Janie, and got out of the line of fire.

"Craven coward," she muttered after him.

"Strategic retreat," Canton observed with narrowed eyes. He looked down at her. "You're corrupting my daughter."

"I'm what?"

"Corrupting her. She never used to be this irresponsible." His eyes grew cold. "And if you're going to have your boyfriend living here with you, without a chaperon, she isn't coming near the place until he leaves!"

She actually gaped at him. "Exactly what century are you living in?" she exclaimed.

"That's your boyfriend's specialty, I believe, ancient history," he continued. "I've seen too many permissive lifestyles to have any respect for them. I won't have my daughter exposed to yours!"

"Permissive...exposed..." She was opening and closing her mouth like a fish. "You're one to talk, with your hot and cold running women and your... your cover girl lovers!"

"Escorts," he said shortly. "I was never unfaithful to my wife. Which is a statement she damned sure couldn't make! I'm not raising Karie to be like her."

She felt pale and wondered if she looked it. Her hands were curled painfully into the arms of her chair. She'd never been verbally attacked with such menace. "My boyfriend is a respected college professor with a sterling moral character," she said finally. "And for your information, he insists on staying in a hotel, not here!"

He stood there, towering over her, hands deep in his pockets, barely breathing as his blue eyes went over her light cotton dress down to the splayed edges of her skirt that revealed too much of her lovely, tanned long legs.

She tossed the skirt back over them and sat up, furious. "But even if he did decide to stay here, it would be none of your business!" She got to her feet, glaring up at him. "You can keep Karie at home if you're afraid of my corrupting influence. And you can stay away, too, damn you!"

The speed with which his lean hands came out of his pockets to catch her bare arms was staggering. He whipped her against the length of him and stared down into shocked, wide green eyes.

"Damn you, too," he said under his breath, searching her face with an intensity that almost hurt. "You're too young, too flighty, too emotional, too everything! I'm sorry I ever brought Karie down here!"

"So am I!" she raged. "Let me go!" She kicked out at his leg with her bare foot.

The action, far too violent to be controlled, caused her to lose her balance, and brought her into a position so intimate that she trembled helplessly at the contact.

His hands were on her back now, preventing a fall, slowly moving, sensuous. "Careful," he said, and his voice was so sensual that she lost all will to fight.

Her fingers clenched into the front of his knit shirt. She couldn't make herself look up. The feel of his body was overpowering enough, without the electric pull of those blue, blue eyes to make her even worse. She didn't move at all. She wasn't sure that she could. He smelled of spice and soap. She liked the clean scent of his body. In the opening of his shirt there was a thick mat of hair showing, and she wondered helplessly if it went all the way down to his slacks. She wondered how it would feel under her hands, her cheek, her mouth. Her thoughts shocked her.

His big hands splayed on her back, moving her closer. His breath at her temple stirred her short hair warmly.

His nose moved against her forehead, against her own nose, her cheek. His thin lips brushed her cheek and the corner of her mouth, pausing there as they had once before, teasing, taunting.

She felt her breath shaking out of her body against his lips, but she couldn't help it. His mouth was the only thing in the world. She stared at it with such hunger that nothing else existed.

His hand came up. His thumb brushed lightly against her lower lip, and then slightly harder, tugging. As her lips parted, his head bent. She felt the whispery pressure with a sense of trembling anticipation, with hungry curiosity.

"Close your eyes, for God's sake," he breathed as his mouth opened. "Not your mouth, though..."

She imagined the kiss. She could already feel it. It would be as unexpected as the sudden surge of the wind around them. She felt her body stiffen with the shock of desire it kindled in her. She'd never had such an immediate reaction to any man. He would be experienced, of course. His very demeanor told her that he knew everything there was to know about kissing. She was lost from the very first touch. Her eyes closed, as he'd told them to, and her mouth opened helplessly. She heard someone moan as she anticipated the heat and passion of his embrace...

"Do you know who I am?" he asked.

Her eyes opened. He hadn't moved. He hadn't kissed her. His mouth was still poised, waiting. She'd...imagined the kiss. Her eyes shot up, struggling to cope with steamy emotions that had her knees shaking.

His eyes held hers. "I'm not your college professor," he murmured. "Are you missing him so much that even I can stand in for him?" he added with a mocking smile.

She tore out of his arms with pure rage, her face red, her eyes and hair wild.

"Yes!" she cried at him. "I'm missing him just that much! That's why I invited him to come down to Cancún!"

His hands went back into his pockets, and he didn't even look ruffled. She was enraged.

His eyebrow jerked as he looked at her with kindling amusement, and something much darker. "You're still too young," he remarked. "But whatever effect your boyfriend has had on you is minimal at best."

"He has a wonderful effect on me!"

His eyelids dropped over twinkling eyes. "Like I just did?"

"That was...it was..."

He moved a little closer, his stance sensually threatening. "Sensuous," he breathed, watching her mouth. "Explosive. Passionate. And I didn't even kiss you."

Her hand came up in a flash, but he caught it in his and brought the damp palm to his mouth in a gesture that made her catch her breath. His eyes were intent, dangerous.

"We come from different worlds," he said quietly. "But something inside each of us knows the other. Don't deny it," he continued when she started to protest. "It's no use. You knew me the minute we met, and I knew you."

"Oh, sure, when I was a soldier in the Czech army in some other life...!"

The back of his fingers stopped the words, gently. "I'm not a great believer in reincarnation," he continued. "But we know each other at some level. All the arguments in the world can't disguise it."

"I don't want you!" she sputtered.

His fingers caught hers and held them almost comfortingly. "Well, I want you," he said shortly. "But you're perfectly safe with me. Even if you didn't have a boyfriend, you'd be safe. I don't want involvement."

"You said that already."

"I'm saying it again, just to make the point. We're neighbors. That's all."

"I know," she snapped. She moved away, and his hand let go. "Stop touching me."

"I'm trying to," he replied with an odd smile. "It's like giving up smoking."

"I don't like you to touch me," she lied.

He didn't even bother with a reply. "I wouldn't dare kiss you," he said. "Addictions are dangerous."

She expelled a shaky breath. "Exactly."

His pale eyes searched hers for a long moment, and the world around them vanished for that space of seconds.

"When you've had a couple of serious affairs and I've remade my fortune, I'll come back around."

She glared at him. "I don't like rich people."

His eyebrows shot up. "I'm not rich and you don't like me."

"You're still rich inside," she muttered.

"And you're just a little college girl with a heartless boss," he murmured. He smiled. "You could come to work for me. I'd give you paid holidays."

"You don't have a business."

"Yet," he replied, smiling with such confidence that she believed in that instant that he could do anything he liked.

"But you will have," she added.

He nodded. "And I'll need good and loyal employees."

"How do you know I'd be one?"

"You're working on your vacation. How much more loyal could you be?"

She averted her eyes. "Maybe I'm not exactly what I seem."

"Yes, you are. You're the most refreshing female I've met in years," he confessed reluctantly. "You're honest and loyal and unassuming. God, I'm so tired of socialites and actresses and authoresses who attract attention with every move and can't live out of the limelight! It's a relief to meet a woman who's satisfied just to be a cog instead of the whole damned wheel!"

She felt a blush coming on. He had no idea what her normal life was like. She was a very famous authoress indeed, and on her way to a large bankroll. She wasn't a cog, she was a whole wheel, in her niche, and even reviewers liked her. But this man, if he knew the truth, would be very disillusioned. He'd lost so much because he'd trusted the wrong people. How would he feel if he knew that Janine had lied to him?

But that wouldn't really matter, because he didn't want an intimate relationship and neither did she.

"Well, as one neighbor to another, you're fairly refreshing yourself. I've never met a down-on-his-luck millionaire before."

He smiled faintly. "New experiences are good for us. Short of kissing you, that is. I'm not that brave."

"Good thing," she replied, tongue-in-cheek. "I don't know where you've been."

He smiled. He laughed. He chuckled. "Good God!"

"I don't," she emphasized. "You are who you kiss."

"Bull. Your mouth doesn't know one damned thing about kissing."

"Oh, yes, it does."

His chin lifted. "I might consider letting you prove that one day. Not today," he added. "I'm getting old. It isn't safe to have my blood pressure tried too much in one afternoon."

"Is it high?" she asked with real concern.

He shrugged. "It tends to be. But not dangerously so." He searched her eyes. "Don't care about me. You're the last complication I need."

"I was about to say the same thing. Besides, I have a boyfriend."

"Good luck to him," he replied with a short laugh. "If you're pristine at twenty-four, he's lacking something."

Her mouth opened without words, but he was already leaving the deck before the right sort of words presented themselves. And of all the foul names she could think of to call him, only "scoundrel" came immediately to mind.

"Schurke!" she yelled in German.

He didn't break stride. But he turned, smiled and winked at her. His smile took the wind right out of her sails.

While she was still trying to think up a comeback, he walked on down the beach and out of earshot. The man was a mystery—and what she felt when he was around her was a puzzle she was unsure she'd ever solve.

CHAPTER FIVE

FOR THE NEXT HOUR, Janine did her best to look forward to Quentin's forthcoming visit. She and Quentin were good friends, and in the past, while she was still living at home, they'd gone out a lot together socially. But to give him credit, he'd never mentioned marriage or even a serious relationship. A few light, careless kisses didn't add up to a proposal of marriage.

On the other hand, what she experienced with Canton Rourke was so explosive that all she could think about was the fact that one day soon, she'd have to go back to Chicago and never see him again. In a very short time, she'd come to know their down-on-his-luck neighbor in ways she never should have. She wanted him just as much as he wanted her, despite the fact that he infuriated her most of the time. But she was living in dreams again, and she had to stop. Having Quentin here even for a weekend might snap her out of her growing infatuation with Canton Rourke.

Quentin came down three days later. He got off the plane in Cancún, looking sweaty and rumpled and thoroughly out of humor. He sent a dark glare at a young woman with red hair who smiled at him sweetly and then sent a kiss his way.

Quentin glared after the woman as he joined Janie, carry-on bag in hand. He wiped his sweaty light brown hair with his handkerchief, and his dark eyes weren't happy.

"English majors," he spat contemptuously. "They think they know everything!"

"Some of them do," Janine remarked. "One of my English professors spoke five languages and had a photographic memory."

"I had old Professor Blake, who couldn't remember where his car was parked from hour to hour."

"I know how he felt," she murmured absently as she scanned the airport for the rental car she was driving.

He groaned. "Janie, you didn't lock the keys in it?"

She produced them from her pocket and jangled them. "No, I didn't. I just can't remember where I put it. But it will come to me. Let's go. Did you have a nice flight?"

"No. The English professor sat beside me on the plane and contradicted every remark I made. What a boor!"

She bit her tongue trying not to remind him that he did the same thing to her, constantly.

"God, it's hot here! Is it any cooler at the hotel?"

"Not much," she said. "There's air-conditioning inside. It helps. And there's always a breeze on the beach."

"I want to find the library first thing," he said. "And then the local historical society. I speak Spanish, so I'll be able to converse with them quite well."

"Do you speak Mayan?" she asked with a smile. "I do hope so, because quite a few people here speak Mayan instead of Spanish."

He looked so uncomfortable that she felt guilty.

"But most everyone knows some English," she added quickly. "You'll do fine."

"I hope that redheaded pit viper isn't staying at my hotel. Where is my hotel, by the way?" he demanded.

"It's about three miles from my beach house, in the hotel zone. I can drive you to and from, though. I rented the car for a month."

"Isn't it dangerous to drive here?"

"Not any more dangerous than it is to drive in Chicago," she replied. "Ah. There it is!"

"I thought your brother was with you," he remarked.

"He is. He has a playmate, and he's staying with her family today." She didn't add that he'd refused to go to meet Quentin, who wasn't one of his favorite people.

"I see. Is he still as outspoken and ill-mannered as ever?"

She hated that smug smile of his. This was going to be a fiasco of a vacation, she could see it right now.

KURT WAS POLITE TO QUENTIN; just polite and no more. He spent the weekend tagging after Karie and avoiding the beach house where Quentin was poring over copies of old manuscripts he'd found in some archives. They were all in Spanish. Old Spanish.

"This is sixteenth century," he murmured absently, with pages spread all over the sofa and the floor while he sat cross-legged on the small rug going from one to another. "Some of these verbs I don't even recognize. They may be archaic, of course…"

He was talking to himself. Across from him, Janine was poring over a volume on forensic medicine, searching for new methods of bumping off her villains.

Into the middle of their studious afternoon, Karie and Kurt came back from a walk on the beach, with Karie's father looming menacingly behind them. Both children were flushed and guilty-looking.

Janine laid her volume aside and sighed. "What have you done, now?" she asked Kurt with resignation.

"Remember the garden hose I bought them?" Canton asked her with barely a glance for the disorderly papers and man on the floor.

"Yes," Janine said slowly.

"They were hacking it up with a very sharp machete under the porch at our place."

"A machete? Where did you get a machete?" Janine exclaimed to Kurt.

Before he could answer, Quentin got to his feet, his gold-rimmed glasses pushed down on his nose for reading. "I told you that you'd never be able to handle Kurt by yourself," Quentin said helpfully.

Janine glared at him. "I don't 'handle' Kurt. He's not an object, Quentin."

Canton had his hands deep in his pockets. He was looking at Quentin with curiosity and faint contempt.

"This is our neighbor, Mr. Rourke," Janine introduced. "And this is Quentin Hobard, a colleague of my parents' from Bloomington, Indiana. He teaches ancient history at Indiana University."

"How ancient?" Canton asked.

"Renaissance," came the reply. He held up a photocopied page of spidery Spanish script. "I'm researching—"

Midsentence, Canton took the page from him and gave it a cursory, scowling scrutiny. "It's from a diary. Much like the one Bernal Díaz kept when he first came from Spain to the New World with Cortés and began protesting the *encomienda*."

Quentin was impressed. "Why, yes!"

"But this writing deals with the Mayan, not the Aztec, people." Canton read the page aloud, effortlessly translating the words into English.

Rourke finally looked up. "Who wrote this?" he asked.

Quentin blinked. He, like the others, had been listening spellbound to the ancient words spoken so eloquently by their visitor.

"No one knows," the scholar replied. "They're recorded as anonymous, but he writes as if he were a priest, doesn't he? How did you read it?" he added. "Some of those verbs are obsolete."

"My mother was Spanish," Rourke replied. "She came from Valladolid and spoke a dialect that passed down almost unchanged from the Reconquista."

"Yes, when Isabella and Ferdinand united their kingdoms through marriage and drove the Moors from Spain, in 1492. They were married in Valladolid," Quentin added. "Have you been there?"

"Yes," Rourke replied. "I still have cousins in Valladolid."

This was fascinating. Janine stared at him with open curiosity, met his glittery gaze and blushed.

"Well, thank you for the translation," Quentin said.

"I'd be very interested to have you do some of the other pages if you have time."

"Sorry," Rourke replied, "but I have to fly to New York in the morning. I should be back by midnight. I wanted to ask Janie if she'd keep my daughter while I'm away."

It was the first time he'd abbreviated her name. She felt all thumbs, and was practically tongue-tied. "Why...of course," she stammered. "I'd be glad to."

"I'll send her over before I leave. It'll be early."

"Good luck getting a flight out," Quentin murmured.

Canton chuckled. "No problem there. I have a Lear-jet. See you in the morning, then." He glanced down at the book lying on the sofa and his eyebrows went up. "Forensic medicine? I thought history was your field."

"It is," Janine said.

"Oh, she does that for her books," Quentin said offhandedly.

"The ones I'm trying to sell," she added quickly, with a glare at Quentin.

He didn't understand. He started to speak, but Janine got to her feet and walked Canton to the door.

"I took the machete away from them, by the way, and hid it." He glanced past her at the kids, who were on the patio by now. "Don't let them out of your sight. Good God, I don't know what's gotten into them. Why would they hack up a perfectly good garden hose?"

"Fishing bait to catch gardeners?" she suggested.

He made a gruff sound. Behind her, Quentin was already reading again, apparently having forgotten that he wasn't alone.

"Dedicated, isn't he?" he murmured.

"He loves his subject. I love it, too, but my period is Victorian America. I don't really care much for earlier stuff."

He searched her eyes. "Do tell?"

"You're very well educated," she remarked. "You read Spanish like a native."

"I am a native, as near as not, even if I don't look it," he replied. He lifted his chin. "As for the education part, I was a little too busy in my youth to get past the tenth grade. I have a certificate that gives me the equivalent of a high-school diploma. That's all."

She went scarlet. She'd had no idea that he wasn't college educated. He'd been a millionaire, and had all the advantages. Or had he?

The blush fascinated him. He touched it. "So you see, I'm not an academic at all. Far from it, in fact. I got my education on the streets."

Her eyes met his. "No one who could invent the software you've come up with is ignorant. You're a genius in your own right."

His intake of breath was audible. He looked odd for a moment, as if her remark had taken him off guard.

"Weren't your parents well-off?" she asked.

"You mean, did I inherit the money that got me started? No, I didn't," he replied. "I made every penny myself. Actually, Miss Enigma, my father was a laborer. I had to drop out of school to support my sister when he died of cancer. I was seventeen. My mother had already died when I was fourteen."

She did gasp, this time. "And you got that far, alone?"

"Not completely alone, but I made every penny honestly." He chuckled. "I'm a workaholic. Doesn't it show?"

She nodded. "The intelligence shows, too."

He cocked an eyebrow and there was an unpleasant smile on his firm mouth. "Buttering me up, in case I make it all back?"

She glowered. "Do I look as if money matters to me?"

"Women are devious," he replied. "You could look like an angel and still be mercenary."

Her pride was stung. "Thanks for the compliment." She turned to go back in.

He caught her arm, pulled her outside and shut the door. "Your pet scholar in there is an academic," he said through his teeth. "That's why you keep him around, isn't it? And I don't even have a high-school diploma."

"What does that matter?" she said with equal venom. "Who cares if you've got a degree? I don't! We're just neighbors for the summer," she added mockingly. "Just good friends."

His eyes fell to her mouth. "I'd like to be more," he said quietly.

The wind was blowing off the ocean. She felt it ruffle her hair. Sand whipped around her legs. She had no sense of time as she looked at his face and wondered about the man hidden behind it, the private one that he kept secret from the world.

Suddenly, with a muffled curse, he bent and brushed his lips lightly over hers, so softly that she wasn't sure he'd really done it.

"Thanks for looking after Karie," he said. "I'll pay you back."

"It's no hardship."

"Like children, don't you?" he murmured.

She smiled. "A lot."

"I love my daughter. I'd like a son, too." His gaze lifted to meet hers and he saw the pupils dilate suddenly. His jaw tautened. "Don't sleep with him," he said harshly, jerking his head toward the door.

Her jaw fell. "Sleep…!"

"Not with him, or anyone else." He bent again. This time the kiss was hard, brief, demanding, possessive. His eyes were glittering. "God, I wish I'd never met you," he said under his breath. And without another word, he turned and left her at the door, windblown and stunned, wondering what she'd done to make him kiss her—and then suddenly get angry all over again. She could still feel the pressure of his mouth long after she went back into the living room and tried to act normally.

KARIE WAS A JOY TO HAVE AROUND, but she and Kurt seemed to find new ways to irritate Quentin all the time. From playing loud music when he was studying his manuscripts to refusing to leave Janine alone with him, they were utter pests.

And there was one more silent complication. The man was back again. He didn't come near the house, but Janine spotted his car along the highway most mornings. He just sat there, watching, the sun glinting off his binoculars. Once again, she started toward the road, and the car sped away. She was really getting nervous. And she hadn't heard from her parents.

She tried to explain her worries to Quentin, but he'd found a reference to Chichén Itzá in the manuscript and was dying to go there.

"There's a bus trip out to the ruins, but it takes all day, and you'll be very late getting back."

"That doesn't matter!" he exclaimed. "I have Saturday free. Come on, we'll both go."

"I can't take Kurt on a trip like that. He's still recovering."

He glared at her. "I can't miss this. It's the opportunity of a lifetime. There are glyphs on the temple that I really want to see."

She smiled. "Then go ahead. You'll have a good time."

He pursed his lips and nodded. "Yes, I will. You don't mind, do you?"

"Oh, of course not," she said. "Go ahead."

He smiled. "Thanks, Janine, I knew you'd be understanding about it."

When was she ever anything else, she wondered. He didn't mind leaving her behind, when they were supposed to be spending their vacation together. But, then, that was Quentin, thoughtless and determined to have his own way. She thought that she'd never forget the sound of Canton Rourke's deep voice as he translated that elegant Spanish into English. Quentin had been impressed, which was also unusual.

"Your neighbor looked very familiar, didn't he?" Quentin asked suddenly.

She had to fight down a thrill at just the mention of him. "He should. Haven't you looked at a newspaper recently? Canton Rourke? Founder of Chipgrafix software?"

"Good Lord!"

"That was him," she said.

"Imagine, a mind like that," Quentin mused. "He

doesn't look all that important, does he? I would have passed him on the street without a second glance. But he still reminds me of somebody… Aha! I've got it! The alien on that science fiction series…"

"No," she said, shaking her head. "He doesn't really look much like him at all, once you've been around him for a while."

"Sounds like him, though," he countered. "Nice voice."

He wasn't supposed to like Canton Rourke. He was supposed to be jealous and icy and contemptuous of the man. She sighed. Nothing was going according to plan. Nothing at all.

KARIE SPENT THE NEXT DAY with Janine while Quentin boarded a tour bus at his hotel and was gone all day and most of the night. He came over the next afternoon by cab, on his way to the airport.

"I had a great time at Chichén Itzá," he told Janine. "Of course, the English whiz was on the tour, too," he added sourly. "She's from Indianapolis and is going back on the same flight I am. I hope they seat her on the wing. She knows all about the Maya culture. Speaks Spanish fluently," he added with pure disgust. "Has a double major in English and archaeology. Show-off."

She didn't quite look at him. "Is she married?"

"Who'd have her?" he spat. "She's so smug. Read the stelae to me before the tour guide could."

She smothered a grin. "Imagine that."

"Yes." He still looked disgusted. "Well, it's been a wonderful trip, Janine. I'm glad you talked me into it.

I've got some great things to take back to my classes, including several rolls of film at Chichén Itzá that I'll share with the archaeology department. Think your parents might like some shots?"

She hesitated to mention that they'd taken more slides of the site than most tourists ever would. "You might mention it to them," she said tactfully.

"I'll do that. Well, I'll see you when you come home to visit your parents, I suppose. Any word on how your parents are coming along at that new site?"

She shook her head. "I'm getting a little worried. I haven't heard anything in a couple of weeks, not even one piece of E-mail."

"Hard to find electrical outlets in the jungle, I imagine," he said and then grinned at his joke.

She didn't smile. "They have an emergency generator and a satellite hookup for their computers."

"Well, they'll turn up," he said airily, ignoring her obvious concern. "I have to rush or I'll miss my flight. Good to have seen you. You were right, Janine. I did need a break."

He brushed a careless kiss against her cheek and went back out to his waiting cab.

And that was that.

JANINE WAS HALFHEARTEDLY READING a tome on forensics while Kurt and Karie had gone out to the beach to watch a boy go up on a parasail, which she'd forbidden them to go near. The abrupt knock at the patio wall caught her attention. Her heart jumped when she found Karie's dad standing there, dressed in lightweight white slacks and a tan knit shirt that showed anyone who cared to look just how powerful the muscles in his chest and arms were. For a man his age, he was really tremendously fit.

"I'm looking for Karie," he said without greeting.

She was still stung from his cold words while Quentin had been poring over his photocopies. "They're down the beach watching a parasail go up. Don't worry, I told them not to go near the thing."

He went to the railing, shaded his eyes and stared down the beach. "Okay, I see them. They're wading in the surf, watching."

"Oh."

He turned back to her and searched her flushed face quietly. "Where's the boyfriend?"

"Gone back to Indiana. You just missed him."

"Pity," he said languidly.

She laughed mirthlessly. "Right."

He glanced at her computer screen. A word processor had been pulled up, but no files were open. "That's obsolete," he stated. "Why aren't you using the new one?"

"Because it takes me forever to learn one." She smiled at him. "I guess they're all child's play to you. I couldn't write a computer program if my life depended on it!"

That was interesting. "Why not?"

"Because I can't do math," she said simply. "And I don't understand machines, either. You must have a natural gift for computer science."

He felt less inferior. "Something like that, maybe."

"You didn't go to school at all to learn how to write programs?"

He shook his head. "I worked with two men who were old NASA employees. They learned about computing in the space program. I suppose I picked up a lot from them. We started the company together. I bought them out eventually and kept going on my own."

"Then you must have known how to get the best and brightest people to work for you, and keep them."

He smiled faintly. "You aren't quite what I expected," he said unexpectedly.

"Excuse me?"

"Some academics use their education to make people who don't have one feel insignificant," he explained.

She smiled ruefully. "Oh, that would be a good trick, making a millionaire feel insignificant because I have a degree in history."

"What do you do with it?" he asked unexpectedly.

She stared at him. "Do with it?"

"Yes. Do you teach, like your parents?"

"No."

"Why not? Are you happy being a secretary and working for a slave driver?"

She remembered, belatedly, the fictional life she'd concocted. "Oh. Well, no, I don't, really. But degrees are a dime a dozen these days. I know a man with a doctorate in philosophy who's working at a fast-food joint back home. It was the only job he could get."

He leaned against the wall, with his hands in his pockets. "How fast do you type?"

"A little over a hundred words a minute."

He whistled. "Pretty good."

"Thanks."

"If I can get the refinancing I need, you can come to work for me," he suggested.

Was he trying to make up for his behavior when he'd said he was sorry he'd ever met her? She wondered. "That's a nice offer," she said.

"Think about it, then." He shouldered away from the wall. "I'll go get Karie and tell her I'm back."

"They won't have gone far. Have you found out anything about that man who was watching her?" she added, concerned.

He scowled. "No."

"I guess that's good."

"I wouldn't say that," he said absently. His eyes met hers. "Has he turned up again?"

She sighed. "He's been around. He bothers me."

"I know. I'll keep digging and see what I discover."

She was staring at the computer, sitting there like a one-eyed predator, staring at her with its word processing program open and waiting.

"Busy?" he asked.

"I should be."

He held out a hand. "Come along with me to get Karie. Your work will still be there when you get back."

She smiled, tempted. This was going to be disastrous, but why not? It was just a walk, after all.

She turned off the computer and, hesitantly, took the hand he offered. It closed, warm and firm, around hers.

"I'm safe," he said when she flushed a little. "We'll hold hands, like two old friends, and pretend that we've known each other for twenty years."

"I'd have been four years old…"

His hand contracted. "I'm thirty-eight," he said. "You don't have to emphasize that fourteen-year jump I've got on you. I'm already aware of it."

"I was kidding."

"I'm not laughing." He didn't look at her. His eyes were on the beach as they descended the steps and walked along, above the damp sand.

Kurt gave them a curious look when he saw them holding hands. He waved, grinned and went back to chasing down sand crabs and shells, the parasail already forgotten. Karie was much further down the beach, talking to some girls who were about her age. She hadn't looked their way yet.

"When are your parents due back?" he asked.

"God knows," she replied wearily. "They get involved and forget time altogether. They're like two children sometimes. Kurt and I have to keep a close eye on them, to keep them out of trouble. This time, we're a little worried about pothunters, too."

"Pothunters? Collectors, you mean?"

"Actually I mean the go-betweens, the people who steal archaeological treasures to sell on the black market. Sometimes they already have a buyer lined up. This is a brand-new site and my parents think it's going to be a major one in the Mayan category. If it's a rich dig, you can bet that they'll be in trouble. The government can't afford the sort of protection they'll need, either. I just hope they're watching their backs."

"They should be here, watching the two of you," he murmured.

"Not them," she said on a chuckle. "It's been an interesting upbringing. When I was twelve, I sort of became the oldest person in my family. I've taken care of Kurt, and them, since then."

His fingers eased between hers sensuously. "You should marry and have children of your own."

Her heart leapt. She'd never thought of that in any real sense until right now. She felt the strength and attraction of the man beside her and thought how wonderful it would be to have a child with him.

Her thoughts shocked her. Her hand jerked in his.

He stopped walking and looked down at her. His eyes searched hers in the silence of the beach, unbroken except for the watery crash of the surf just a few feet away.

The sensations that ripped through her body were of a sort she'd never felt with anyone. It was electric, fascinating, complex and disturbing. They seemed to talk to each other in that space of seconds without saying a word.

Involuntarily she moved a step closer to him, so that she could feel the heat of his body and inhale the clean scent of it.

He let go of her hand and caught her gently by the shoulders. "Fourteen years," he reminded her gently. "And I'm a poor man right now."

She smiled gently. "I've always been on the cutting edge of poor," she said simply. "Money is how you keep score. It isn't why you do a job."

"Amazing."

"What is?"

"That's how I've always thought of it."

Her eyes traced his strong face quietly. "This isn't a good idea, is it?"

"No," he agreed honestly. "I'm vulnerable, and so are you. We're both out of our natural element, two strangers thrown together by circumstances." He sighed deeply and his lean hands tightened on her shoulders. "I find you damnable attractive, but I've got cold feet."

"You, too?" she mused.

He smiled. "Me, too."

"So, what do we do?"

He let go of her shoulders and took her hand again. "We're two old friends taking a stroll together," he said simply. "We like each other. Period. Nothing heavy. Nothing permanent. Just friends."

"Okay. That suits me."

They walked on down the beach. And if she was disturbed by his closeness, she didn't let it show.

Karie was now talking to an old woman holding four serapes, about a fourth of a mile down the beach from the house.

"Dad!" she cried, running to catch his hand and drag him to the old woman. "I'm glad you're back, did you have a good trip? Listen, you know I can't speak Spanish, and I've got to have this blanket, will you tell her?" she asked in a rush, pointing to an exquisite serape in shades of red and blue.

He chuckled and translated. He spoke the language so beautifully that Janine just drank it in, listening with pleasure.

He pulled out his wallet and paid for the serape, handing it to Karie as the old woman gave them a toothy grin and went back along the beach.

"Don't do that again!" he chided his daughter. "It

isn't safe to wander off without letting anyone know where you are."

"Okay, I won't. I spotted her and this blanket was so pretty that I just had to have it. But I couldn't make her understand."

"I'll have to tutor you," he mused.

"Yes, you will, and Kurt, too. I've got to show this to him! Glad you're home, Dad!" she called over her shoulder.

She tore off back down the beach toward Kurt, the serape trailing in the wind.

"You speak Spanish beautifully," Janine said. "How did you learn it so fluently?"

"At my mother's knee," he replied. "I told you that she was from Valladolid, in Spain." He smiled. "I went there when I finally had enough money to travel, and found some cousins I'd never met."

"Were your parents happy together?"

He nodded. "I think so. But my father worked long hours and he wasn't very well. My mother was a cleaning lady for a firm of investment brokers, until she died. I'm sorry Karie had to be torn between two parents. She still loves her mother, as she should. But now there's a stepfather in the picture. And he's a little too 'affectionate' to suit me or Karie. So we find excuses to make sure she has time alone with just her mother."

She lifted her eyes to his. "What happens if he shows up while she's there?"

"Oh, I had a long talk with him," he said easily, and one corner of his mouth curved. "He knows now that I have a nasty temper, and he doesn't want to spend the rest of his life as a soprano. Consequently he'll keep his hands off my daughter. But Marie wants custody, and she's been unpleasant about it in recent months. I've told her how I felt, and she knows what I'll do if she pushes too hard. I may not have money, but I've got a hot temper and plenty of influence in the right places."

She smiled. "Is it really true, that men with Latin blood are hot-tempered and passionate?"

He pursed his thin lips and glanced at her. "If we weren't just old friends, I'd show you."

"But we are, of course. Old friends, that is."

"Of course!"

They walked on down the beach, content in each other's company. Janine thought absently that she'd never been quite so happy in her life.

They reached the beach house and she started to go up the steps.

"I have to fly to Miami in the morning on business."

"You just got back from New York!" she exclaimed.

"I'm trying to regroup. It's wearing," he explained. "I'm meeting a group of potential investors in Miami. I'm going to take Karie along with me in the Learjet this time. Would you and Kurt like to come?"

Her heart leapt. She could refuse, but her brother would never speak to her again if she turned down a flight in a real baby jet.

"Will the plane hold us all?" she asked with honest curiosity.

"It seats more than four people," he said dryly.

"You'll have to have a pilot and a copilot..."

"I fly myself," he replied. "Don't look so perplexed,

I'm instrument rated and I've been flying for many years. I won't crash."

She flushed. "I didn't mean to imply...!"

"Of course you didn't. Want to come?"

She shrugged. "Kurt loves airplanes and flying. If I say no, he'll stake me out on the beach tonight and let the sand crabs eat me."

He chuckled. "Good. I'll come by for you in the morning."

"Thanks."

"De nada," he murmured. His eyes narrowed as he studied her. He glanced down the beach, where Karie and Kurt were now oblivious to the world, building a huge sand castle near the discarded serape that Karie seemed to find uninteresting now that she owned it.

"What is it?" she asked when he hesitated.

"Nothing much," he replied, moving closer. "I just wanted to answer that question for you. You know, the one you asked earlier, about men with Latin blood?"

"What quest...!"

His mouth cut the word in half. His arm caught her close against the side of his body, so that she was riveted to him from thigh to breast. His mouth was warm and hard and so insistent that her heart tried to jump right out of her chest. The light kisses that had come before were nothing compared to this one.

Against his mouth, she breathed in the taste of him, felt his teeth nibble sensuously at her upper lip to separate it from the lower one. Then his tongue shot into her mouth, right past her teeth, in an intimacy that corded her body like stretched twine. She stiffened, shivering, frightened by the unexpected rush of pure feeling.

"Easy," he breathed. His slitted eyes looked right into hers. "Don't fight it."

His mouth moved onto hers again, and this time there was nothing preliminary at all about the way he kissed her. She felt the world spinning around her wildly. She held on for dear life, her mouth swelling, burning, aching for his as the kiss went on and on and on.

When his head finally lifted, her nails were biting into the muscles of his shoulders. Her hair was touseled, her eyes misty and wild, all at once, as they met his.

Her mouth trembled from the pressure and passion of his kiss. He looked down at it with quiet satisfaction.

"Yes," he whispered.

His head bent again, and he kissed her less passionately, tenderly this time, but with a sense of possession.

He let her go, easing her upright again.

She couldn't seem to find words. Her eyes sought reassurance in his, and found only a wall behind which he seemed hidden, remote, uninvolved. Her heart was beating her to death, and he looked unruffled.

"You're young for a woman your age," he remarked quietly.

She couldn't get words out. She was too busy trying to catch her breath.

He touched her swollen lips gently. "I won't do that again," he promised solemnly. "I didn't realize...quite how vulnerable you were." He sighed, brushing back her wild hair. "Forgive me?"

She nodded.

He smiled and dropped his hand. "I'll see you and Kurt in the morning."

"Okay."

He winked and walked back down the beach, totally unconcerned, at least on the surface. Inside he was seething with new emotions, with a turmoil that he didn't dare show to her. Innocence like that couldn't be faked. She wasn't in his league, and he'd better remember it. That sort of woman would expect marriage before intimacy, he knew it as surely as if she'd said it aloud. She wasn't modern or sophisticated. Like her academic parents, she lived in another world from the one he inhabited.

Of course, he was thinking to himself, marriage wouldn't be so bad if it was with a woman he liked and understood. He laughed at his own folly. Sure. Hadn't he made that very mistake with his first wife? He'd better concentrate on his business empire and leave love to people who could handle it.

All the same, he thought as he entered his house, Janine was heaven to kiss.

CHAPTER SIX

THE NEWS THAT HE WAS GOING to get to fly in a Lear-jet made Kurt's head spin. He didn't even sleep that night. The next morning, he was awake at daybreak, waiting for his sister to wake up and get dressed so they could leave.

"He won't be here yet," she grumbled. "It's not even light!"

"All the more reason why we should be ready to go when he does get here," he said excitedly. "A *real* Lear-jet. My gosh, I still can't believe it!"

"You and airplanes," she mumbled as she made coffee. "Why don't you like bones and things?"

"Why do you like old books?"

"Beats me."

"See?"

She didn't see anything. She was wearing shorts with a white T-shirt, her usual night gear, and neither of her eyes seemed to work. A cup of coffee would fix that, she thought as she made it.

"Do I hear footsteps?" he asked suddenly, jumping up from the table in the kitchenette. "I'll go see if someone's at the door."

Unbelievably it was Canton. "Why don't you go

over and keep Karie company while your sister gets ready?" he invited. "She's got cheese danishes and doughnuts."

"Great! Hurry up, sis!" he called over his shoulder.

Janine, still drowsy, turned as Canton came into the small kitchenette area, stifling a yawn. "Sorry. I didn't expect you this early."

"Kurt did," he chuckled.

She smiled. "He barely slept. Want some coffee?"

His eyes slid down to the white T-shirt. Under it, the darkness of her nipples was visible and enticing. As he looked at them, they suddenly reacted with equal visibility.

Janine, shocked, started to cross her arms, but he was too quick for her.

As her arms started to lift, his hands slid under the T-shirt. His head bent. He kissed her as his thumbs slid gently over her soft breasts and up onto the hard tips.

She made a harsh sound. His mouth hardened. He backed her into the wall and held her there with his hips while his hands explored her soft body. All the while, his mouth played havoc with her self-control, with her inhibitions.

"The hell with this," he growled.

While her whirling mind tried to deal with the words, his hands were peeling her right out of the T-shirt. Seconds later, his shirt was unbuttoned and they were together, nude from the waist up, her soft breasts buried in the thick pelt that covered his hard muscles.

She whimpered at the heat of the embrace, at the unexpected surge of passion she'd never experienced before. Her arms locked around his neck and she lifted herself to him, feeling the muscles of his thighs tighten and swell at her soft pressure.

He lifted his mouth a breath away and looked into her eyes from so close that she could see the faint specks of green there in the ocean blue of his eyes.

"What the hell are we doing?" he whispered harshly.

Her eyes fell to his swollen mouth. "At your age, you ought to know," she chided with dry humor.

His hips ground into hers. "Feel that?" he snapped. "If you don't pull back right now, I'll show you a few more things I ought to know at my age."

She was tempted. She never had been so tempted before. Her eyes told him so.

That vulnerability surprised him. He'd expected her to jerk back, to be flustered, to demand an apology. But she wasn't doing any of those things. She was waiting. Thinking. Wondering.

"Curious?" he asked gently.

She nodded, smiling self-consciously.

"So am I," he confessed. He eased away from her, holding her arms at her sides when he moved back so that he could see the exquisite curves of her body. She was firm and her breasts had tilted tips. He smiled, loving their beauty.

"I like looking at you," he said, but after a second, he let her go.

She moved back, picking up her T-shirt. She pulled it on and brushed back her hair, her eyes still curious and disturbed when she looked at him.

He was buttoning his shirt with amused indulgence. "Now you know."

"Know...what?"

"That I'm easy," he murmured, provoking a smile on her lips. "That I can be had for a kiss. I have no self-control, no willpower. You can do whatever you like with me. I'm so ashamed."

She burst out laughing. He was impossible. "I'll just bet you are," she murmured.

He held up a hand. "Don't embarrass me."

"Ha!"

"No kidding. I'm going to start blushing any minute. You just keep that shirt on, if you please, and stop tormenting me with your perfect body."

She searched his eyes, fascinated. She'd never dreamed that intimacy could be fun.

He rested his hands on his hips. "Well, we've established one thing. I know too much and you don't know a damned thing."

"I do now," she replied.

He chuckled. "Not much."

She studied her bare feet. "Care to further my education?"

His heart seemed to stop beating. He hesitated, choosing his words. "Yes."

She lifted her gaze back to his face and searched it quietly. "So?"

"We're flying to Miami," he reminded her.

"I didn't mean right now."

"Good thing. I'm hopeless before I've had two cups of coffee."

She grinned at the obvious humor.

He moved close and took her by the waist. "Listen,

we're explosive together. It feels good, but we could get in over our heads pretty quickly. You're not a party girl."

She frowned. "What do you mean?"

"If you had a modern outlook on life, you wouldn't be a virgin at your age," he said simply. "You're looking for marriage, not a good time. Right?"

"I never thought about it like that."

"You'd better start," he replied. "I want you, but all I have to offer is a holiday affair. I've been married. I didn't like it. I'm free now and I want to stay that way."

"I see."

"This isn't something I haven't said before, Janie," he reminded her. "If you want me, with no strings attached, fine. We'll make love as often as you like. But afterward, I'll go home and never look back. It will be a casual physical fling. Nothing more. Not to me."

She felt confusion all the way to the soles of her feet. She was hungry for him. But was it only physical? Was it misplaced hero worship? And did she want more than a few nights in his arms?

He made her feel uncomfortable. All her adult life she'd spent her days and nights at a computer or with her nose stuck in books. She'd never had the sort of night life that most of her friends had. Intimacy was too solemn a thing for her to consider it casually. But with this man, here, now, she could think of nothing else.

He touched her cheek gently. "Do you want the truth? You're a repressed virgin in the first throes of sexual need, and you're curious. I'm flattered. But after you've spent a night in my arms, no matter how good it is, you're going to have doubts and you're not going to be too happy with yourself for throwing control to the winds. You need to think this through before you do something you might regret. What about the man back in Indiana? Where does he fit in? And if you have an affair with me, how will he feel about you, afterward? Is he the sort of man who'd overlook it?"

"No," she said without thinking.

He nodded. "So don't jump in headfirst."

She sighed. He made it sound so complicated. Imagine, a man who wanted her that much taking time to talk her out of it. Maybe he did care a little, after all. Otherwise, wouldn't he just take what was blatantly offered and go on with his life?

"Just friends," she said with a grin, looking up at him. "Very old friends."

"That's right."

"Okay. But you have to stop kissing me, because it makes me crazy."

"That makes two of us." He stuck his hands into his pockets to keep them off her. "And you have to stop going braless."

"I didn't know you'd be here this early, or I wouldn't be."

He smiled. "Just as well," he confessed. "I wouldn't have missed that for the world."

She chuckled. "Thanks."

"Get dressed, then, would you? Before all this bravado wears off."

She gave him a wicked grin and went to get dressed for the trip.

IT WAS A WONDERFUL, joyful trip. Canton let Kurt sit in the cockpit with him and they talked about airplanes and jets all the way to Miami.

When they got to town, a big white stretch limousine met them at the airport. To Kurt, who was used to traveling in old taxis and beat-up cars, it was an incredible treat. He explored everything, under Canton's amused eyes.

"It's just a long car," he informed the boy. "After a while, they all look alike."

"It's my first time in a limo, and I'm going to enjoy it," he assured him, continuing the search.

Janine, who frequently went on tour and rode around in limos like this, watched her brother with equal amusement. She'd wanted to take him with her on the last trip, but he couldn't lose the time from school. Only illness had gotten him this break.

"Aren't you curious?" Canton asked her. "You seem very much at home in here."

Her eyebrows lifted. "Do I? Actually I'm very excited."

"Are you?"

She smiled sweetly, and turned her attention back to Kurt.

Later, while Canton was in his meeting, Karie and Kurt went to a big mall with Janine, where they peeked and poked through some of the most expensive shops in town. By the time they ended up at an exclusive chocolatier shop and bought truffles, they were all ready to go home.

Canton accepted a chocolate on the way back to the airport, smiling as he tasted it. "My one weakness," he explained. "I love chocolate."

"He's a chocoholic," Karie added. "Once, he went rushing out in the middle of the night for a chocolate bar."

"Sounds just like Janie," Kurt replied with a smile. "She keeps chocolate hidden all over the house."

"Hidden?" Canton probed.

"We stop her from eating it if we find any in her hiding places. She gets terrible migraines when she eats it," he explained. "Not that it ever stopped her. So we have to."

"She's just eaten two enormous truffles," Karie said worriedly.

Janine glared at the kids. "I'm perfectly all right," she informed them. "Anyway, it doesn't *always* give me migraines," she told her brother firmly.

THAT NIGHT, LYING IN THE bed and almost screaming with pain, she remembered vividly what she said to Kurt.

She lost her lunch, and then her supper. The pain was so bad that she wished for a quick and merciful death.

She didn't even realize that Kurt had gone to get Canton until she felt his hand holding hers.

"You don't have anything to take?" he prompted.

"No," she squeaked.

He let go of her hand and called a doctor. Scant minutes later, a dark gentleman in a suit administered a whopping injection. And only a little later, pain gave way to blessed oblivion.

SHE WOKE WITH A WEIGHT on her arm. Her eyes opened. Her whole head felt sore, but the headache was so subdued that it was almost a memory.

She looked toward the side of the bed, and there was

Canton Rourke, in a burgundy robe, with his face lying on her arm. He was sound asleep, half in a chair and half against her side of the bed.

"Good heavens, what are you doing here?" she croaked.

He heard her, blinking to sudden alertness. He sat up. He needed a shave and his hair was tousled. His eyes were bloodshot. He looked tired to death, but he was smiling.

"Feel better?" he asked.

"Much." She put a hand to her head. "It's very sore and it still hurts a little."

"He left a vial of pills and a prescription for some more. I'm sorry," he added. "I had no idea that Karie would take you to the chocolate shop."

"She couldn't have stopped me," she replied with a pained smile. "They have the best, the most exquisite chocolates on earth. It's my favorite place in the world. And it was worth the headache. Where did you find a doctor in the middle of the night?"

"Karie had appendicitis when we were down here a couple of years ago," he replied. "Dr. Valdez is one of the best, and he has a kind heart."

"Yes, he does. And so do you. Thanks," she said sincerely.

He shrugged. "You'd have done it for me."

She thought about that. "Yes, I would have," she said after a minute.

He smiled.

He stretched largely, wincing as his sore muscles protested.

"Come to bed," she offered with a wan smile, patting the space beside her. "It's too late to go home now."

"I was just thinking the same thing."

He went around to the other side of the bed, but he kept his robe on when he slid under the covers.

"Prude," she accused weakly.

He chuckled drowsily. "I can't sleep normally with Karie anywhere around. Usually I wear pajama bottoms, but they're in the wash, hence the robe."

"That's considerate of you."

"Not really," he confessed. "Actually, I *am* a prude. I don't even like undressing in front of other men." His head turned toward hers. "I was in the Marine Corps. You can't imagine how that attitude went down with my D.I."

She chuckled and then grabbed her head. "Modesty shouldn't be a cardinal sin, even in the armed services."

"That's what I told him."

She took a slow breath. Her head was still uncomfortable.

"Go back to sleep," he instructed, drawing her into his arms. "If it starts up again, wake me and I'll get the pills."

"You're a nice man," she murmured into his shoulder.

"Yes, I am," he agreed. "And don't you forget it. Now go to sleep."

She didn't think she could, with him so close. But the heavy, regular beat of his heart was comforting, as was the warmth of his long, muscular body against her. She let her eyelids fall and seconds later, she slept.

There was a lot of noise. She heard rustling and footsteps and the clanking of metal pans. It all went over her head until something fell with an awful clatter, bringing her eyes open.

"Where the hell are the frying pans? Don't you have a frying pan?" he asked belligerently.

She sat up gingerly, holding her head. "I don't think so," she told him.

"How do you scramble eggs?"

She blinked. "I don't. Nobody here eats them."

"I eat them. And you're going to, as soon as I find a—" he expressed several adjectives "—frying pan!"

"Don't you use that sort of language in my house," she said haughtily.

"I've heard all about your own vocabulary from Kurt, Miss Prim and Proper," he chided. "Don't throw stones."

"I almost never use words like that unless my computer spits out a program or loses a file."

"Computers do neither, programmers do."

"I don't want to understand how a computer works, thank you, I only want it to perform."

He chuckled. "Okay. Now what about pots and pans?"

"It won't do you any good to find one, because I don't have any eggs."

He presented her with a bowl of them. "Our housekeeper came back this morning laden with raw breakfast materials. I even have bacon and freshly baked bread."

"I hope you don't expect me to eat it, because I can't," she murmured weakly. "And I'm going to need some of those pills."

He produced them, along with a small container of bottled water. "Here. Swallow."

She took the pills and lay back down, her eyes bloodshot and swollen. "I feel terrible," she whispered.

"Is it coming back?"

"Yes. It's not so bad as it was yesterday, but it still throbs."

"Stop eating chocolate."

She sighed. "I forget how bad the headaches are when I don't actually have one."

"So Kurt says."

"There are pans in the drawer under the stove," she said helpfully.

He opened it and retrieved a tiny frying pan. He held it up with a sigh. "Well, I guess it'll hold one egg, at least. I have to have an egg. I can't live without an egg every morning, and damn the cholesterol."

"Addictions are hell," she murmured.

He glared at her. "You have to have your coffee, I notice. And we won't mention chocolate…"

"*Please* don't," she groaned.

He shook the frying pan at her. "Next time, I'll go along when you shop. You'll have to get through me to get at any chocolate."

She stared at him with blank eyes. "That sounds very possessive."

He returned her quiet scrutiny. His eyes began to warm. "Yes, it does, doesn't it?" The smile faded. "Just remember. I'm not a marrying man. Not anymore."

"Okay. I promise not to ask you to marry me," she agreed, groaning when movement set her headache off again. She rolled over and held her head with both hands.

"The pills should take effect soon," he said sympathetically. "Have you had coffee yet?"

"No," she whispered.

"That might be making it even worse. Here, I'll get you a cup."

"Excuse me?"

He poured black coffee into a cup, added a little cold water to temper the heat and sat down beside her.

"If you drink coffee all the time, you can get a headache from leaving it off. Caffeine is a drug," he reminded her.

"I know. I remember reading about withdrawal, but I was too sick when I first woke up to want even water."

"Just the same, you'd better have some of the hair of the dog."

"Chocolate has caffeine," she remarked as she sipped the strong coffee. He made it just as she did—strong enough to melt spoons.

"So it does. Want a chocolate truffle?"

She glared at him and sipped another swallow of coffee.

"Sorry," he murmured. "Low blow."

"Wasn't it?" She laid back down with a long sigh. "Why are you being so nice to me?"

"I have a soft spot for problem chocoholics," he gibed. He smiled at her as he got up. "Besides, we're old friends."

"So we are," she mused, wincing with pain.

He tossed the empty eggshells into the garbage can. He searched through drawers until he found a fork. "No wire whip," he muttered.

"I don't torture my food."

He glanced at her. "A wire whip isn't torture. It's an absolute necessity for scrambled eggs and any number of exquisite French cream sauces."

"Listen to the gourmet chef," she exclaimed.

"I can cook. I've done my share of it over the years. I wasn't born rich."

She rolled over on her side to stare at him. "How did you grow up?"

He chuckled. "On the lower east side of Manhattan," he told her. "In a lower middle class home. My father worked long hours to support us."

"Your mother?"

"She died when my younger sister was born," he explained. "I was fourteen. Dad had a boy and an infant girl to raise and provide for. He did the best he could, but he wore out when I was seventeen, and I had to take over. He died of lung cancer." He glanced at her. "And, no, he didn't smoke. He worked in a factory brimming over with carcinogens. He wasn't literate or educated, so he did the work he could get."

"I'm sorry. That must have been rough on all of you."

"It was." He stirred the eggs absently. "I took care of him myself for as long as I could. We couldn't afford nursing care. Hell, we couldn't afford a doctor, except at the free clinic." He drew in a long breath. "I was holding down two jobs at the time, one full-time at a printing shop and the other part-time at an investment house, as a janitor." He gave her a long look. "Yes, that's where I learned the ropes. One of the older executives lost his son in a traffic accident in New Jersey about the same time my father died. He worked late and we ran into each other occasionally and talked. Eventually, when he found out how hard it was for me, he started teaching me about money. By God, he made an investment wizard out of me, long before I started designing software and linked up with the ex-NASA guys. And I never even got to thank him. He dropped dead of a heart attack before I made my first million." He shook his head. "Ironic, how things work out."

"Yes." She watched him move. He had an elegance of carriage, a sensuous arrogance that made him a pleasure to watch. Muscles rippled in his arms and chest under the close fitting knit shirt and slacks he wore. "Are you still close to your sister?"

He didn't answer for a minute. "My sister died of a drug overdose when she was sixteen. It was my fault."

CHAPTER SEVEN

"WHAT DO YOU MEAN, it was your fault?" she asked, curious.

"She got in with a bad crowd. I didn't even know," he said. "I was just too damned busy—working, trying to stay afloat with Marie, being a new dad, all those things. I tried to keep an eye on her. But I didn't know who she was dating. It turned out that she was in a relationship with our neighborhood drug dealer. He was her supplier. One night, she took too much. They called me from the emergency room. The rat took off the minute she went into cardiac arrest."

"He got clean away, I gather?"

Canton stirred eggs until they cooked, and then took them off the stove before he answered. "No, he didn't," he said deliberately, "although it took me a few years to get rich enough to go looking for him. He's doing ten years on a dealing charge. I hired private detectives to watch him. It didn't take long to catch him with enough evidence to send him up. But it didn't bring her back."

She could sense his pain. She sat up in bed, grimacing as the movement hurt her head. "I know. But there's only so much you can do to keep people out of trouble. If they really want to hurt themselves, you can't stop them, no matter how much you love them."

He glanced at her over the eggs he'd just spooned onto a plate. "You see deeper than most people. Much deeper."

She shrugged. "That can make life pretty hard sometimes."

"It can make it worth living, as well."

She smiled back. "I suppose so."

"I don't suppose you have a toaster?"

"Waste of money," she said. "The toast never comes out warm enough to butter. I make it in the oven broiler."

"That's what I was afraid of."

All the same, he accomplished cinnamon toast with a minimum of fuss, though, and then spoon-fed her delicious scrambled eggs and a bite of toast with some strong black coffee.

She smiled as he put the empty plate aside. "You're a nice man," she said.

"You needn't sound so surprised," he replied. "I'm just a man."

"A man who built an empire all alone," she elaborated.

"I had plenty of help. The problem is that when people get famous, they stop being people to the public. I'm no different than when I used to get my little sister up and ready for school. I'm just older and better dressed."

"People get lost in the glamour, I guess," she agreed.

"All too often, they do. Making money is mostly just plain hard work and sacrifice. No sane person would do anything to excess just to make money."

"Then why did you?" she asked.

"For fun," he replied. "I love creating computer software. It's a challenge to combine numbers and logic and make a new program from scratch that does exactly what you want it to. I never thought about making money."

She chuckled softly. "But you did."

"A hell of a lot of it," he said, nodding. "And it was nice, while it lasted. But you know what?" he added, leaning closer. "I'm just as happy now, with the challenge of making it all back again."

She understood that. It was the same with her, when she wrote a book. She wondered what he'd say if he knew what she did for a living, that she'd deceived him into thinking she was just a secretary on holiday. His opinion of famous women wasn't very high. Of course, she wasn't all that famous. And he wasn't in love with her, either. Perhaps she was making a problem of it.

"You look pale," he remarked. He smoothed back her hair, concern in his blue eyes as he studied her wan, drawn face. "You've had a hard night. Why don't you try and get some sleep? I'll watch Kurt for you."

"Thanks. I think it might help."

He drew the sheet over her. "I'll lock up on my way out. Has Kurt got a key?"

"Yes. But he won't remember where he put it. It's in his windbreaker pocket that zips up. It's on the couch."

"I'll take it with me." He bent and kissed her forehead gently. "Will you be all right alone, or do you want me to stay?"

"I'll be fine now," she promised. She smiled drowsily, because the pills were starting to take effect. "Thanks."

He shrugged. "Old friends help each other out," he reminded her.

"I'll remember that if you're ever in trouble."

He looked funny for a minute. She reached up and touched his dark hair. "Doesn't anyone look after you?"

"Karie tries to, I guess."

"No one else?"

He thought about that. "Actually no," he said finally.

She traced his high cheekbone. "Then I will, when I'm better."

He gave her an inscrutable look and got to his feet, frowning. "I'll check on you later. Need anything else?"

"No. And thanks for breakfast. You're not a bad cook."

"Anyone can scramble eggs."

"Not me."

"I'll teach you one of these days. Sleep tight."

She lay back and closed her eyes. He cleaned up the kitchen quickly and efficiently, and then went out and locked the door behind him.

BY EARLY AFTERNOON, Janine was improved enough to get up and dress, which she did, in jeans and a white tank top.

"God, you're young," he remarked when she joined him in the living room.

Her eyebrows lifted. She was still pale, and wore only a little pink lipstick. "I beg your pardon?"

"You're young," he muttered, hands deep in the pockets of his loose-fitting slacks. His blue eyes had narrowed as he studied her lithe figure and her blemishless complexion.

"Twenty-four isn't exactly nursery-school age," she said pointedly. "And you aren't over the hill."

He chuckled. "I feel it, sometimes. But, thanks, anyway."

She averted her eyes. "You must know that you're devastating physically."

There was a silence that eventually made her look at him. His face had tautened, his eyes had gone glittery. Their intent stare made her pulse leap.

His chin lifted almost imperceptibly. "Come here," he said in a deep, velvety tone.

Her legs obeyed him at once, even though her mind was protesting what amounted to nothing less than an order.

But when he reached for her, it didn't matter. Nothing mattered, except the pressure of his arms around her and the insistent, devouring hunger of the hard mouth on hers.

She leaned into him with a sigh, all hope of self-protection gone. It could have led anywhere, except that young, excited voices floated in through the patio door, warning of the imminent arrival of the kids.

He let her go with obvious reluctance. "I could get addicted to your mouth," he said huskily.

"I was thinking the same thing," she agreed with a breathless laugh.

"Don't get your hopes up," he mused, glancing toward the door where footsteps grew louder. "We'd have better luck on the floor of Grand Central Station."

"I noticed."

Before she could add anything else, Kurt and Karie came running into the beach house carrying some huge feathers.

"Where did you get those?" Janine asked.

"A guy was selling them on the beach. Do you know where we can get a skeleton?"

She blinked. "A what?"

"Not a real one." Kurt cleared his throat. "Karie and I are sort of studying anatomy. We need a skull. Or something."

"They sell cow skulls at the *mercado* in town." Canton reached into his pocket and produced two twenty-dollar bills. "That ought to do it."

"Okay. Thanks, Dad!" Karie exclaimed. "How about cab fare to town?"

He produced more bills. "Come right back," he said firmly. "And if you get lost, find a policeman and have him call me."

"Will do. Thanks!"

They were off at a dead run again. Janine and Canton stood on the deck and watched them head toward the front of the house. A movement caught Janine's attention.

There he was again.

The dark man was standing near the front of the house, beside a sedan. The kids hailed a taxi that had just come from one of the big hotels on a nearby spit of land. They climbed in and as Janine watched in barely contained horror, the dark man climbed into his vehicle and proceeded to follow the cab.

"Did you see that?" she asked her companion worriedly.

"See what?" he asked.

"A man got into a car and followed the cab."

He frowned. "I didn't notice the man. What was he driving?"

"Some old beat-up sedan. I've seen it before." She grimaced. "It probably wasn't a good idea to let them go off alone. If my parents have found something major, who knows what a determined pothunter might do? What if someone's after Kurt?" she suggested.

He took in a deep breath and rammed his hands deep into his pockets. "I was just thinking the same thing, but too late. I'll go after them. Don't worry. Even a pothunter would think twice about abducting an American child right off the streets of Cancún."

"I'm not so sure."

SHE PACED THE FLOOR until Canton returned with the children in tow. They had their skull and were content to stay on the beach and study it. Janine was worried, though, and not only about the mysterious dark man. She was worried because Canton seemed to deliberately downplay the incident, as if it didn't really concern him very much. She wondered why, because he looked much more preoccupied than she'd seen him before.

"I was too sick to ask before. How did it go in Miami with your investors?" she asked after she'd fixed them a pot of coffee.

"I did better than I expected to," he replied. "Apparently they think I can pull it off."

"I agree with them."

He searched her eyes and smiled. "Nice of you."

She shrugged. "You're that sort of man. I'll bet your employees are crazy about you."

"I offered you a job, I seem to recall," he mused. "Come work for me. I'll make you rich."

"I'm not sure I want to be." She glanced up. "Money isn't everything, but it must be a help when you have death-defying parents." She drew in a long breath. "And I still haven't heard from them. I phoned the university this morning. They haven't heard anything, either."

"How do they contact you?"

"There's a small satellite link they use in the field," she explained. "They can send me E-mail anytime they like. But even the local guide service hasn't been able to contact them. I haven't told Kurt. I thought it best not to. This is a big deal, this new site. I couldn't bear it if anything's happened to them."

"Why didn't you say something before?" he muttered. "I may not have millions, but I have influence. Give me that phone."

It was impossible to follow what he was saying, but one of the names he mentioned in his conversation was very recognizable.

"You know the president of Mexico?" she exclaimed when he hung up.

"You don't speak Spanish," he reminded her, "so how did you know that?"

"I recognized his name," she returned. "Do you know him?"

"Yes, I know him. They're going to send someone right out in an aircraft to look for your parents. I'd go myself, but the Learjet isn't ideal for this sort of search."

"How will they know where to look?"

"They had to contact the appropriate government agency to get permission to excavate, didn't they?"

She smiled her relief. "Of course they did. Thank you," she added belatedly.

"Don't mention it. Now drink your coffee."

BY THE END OF THE DAY, there was a telephone call. It was brief and to the point, but welcome.

"They're fine," Canton told a nervous Janine when he put down the receiver. "Their communications equipment had a glitch, and they had to send a runner to the nearest town to fetch an electronics man. He only arrived today. No problems."

"Oh, thank God," she said fervently.

He smiled at her rakishly. "Don't I get anything?"

She moved toward him. "What would you like?" she asked, aware that the kids were close by, sitting on the darkened deck, watching some people down the beach play music and dance in the sand. "A reward?"

"That would be nice," he murmured when she reached him.

"A gift certificate?" she suggested.

His hands framed her face and lifted it. "I had something a little more…physical…in mind."

She felt as breathless as she sounded when she spoke. "How physical?" she whispered.

"Nothing dire." His mouth covered hers and he kissed her softly, sweetly, deeply. His arms enveloped her gently and the kiss grew to a shattering intensity in the soft silence of the room.

He let her go by breaths. "You're a drug," he breathed shakily.

"I know. So are you." She moved closer, only to find herself firmly put away.

"You're the marrying kind," he reminded her. "I'm not."

"It might not matter."

"It would," he said.

She sighed heavily. "Prude."

He chuckled. "Count on it. Your lipstick is smudged."

"I don't doubt it." She ran a finger around her mouth and fixed the smear. "I'll bet you make love like a pagan."

He smiled slowly, confidently. He leaned toward her slightly, and his voice lowered to a deep purr. "I do."

Her eyes lowered demurely. "Show me," she whispered.

He was barely breathing at all, now. His fists clenched by his side. "This isn't a game. Don't tease."

She looked up again, saw his eyes glitter, his jaw clenched as tightly as the lean hands in fists on his thighs.

"I'm not teasing," she said quietly. "I mean it. Every word."

"So do I," he replied. "I am not, repeat *not*, taking you to bed."

She threw up her hands. "Are you always so cautious? Is that how you made those millions?"

"I don't mind a calculated risk, with money. I mind one with human bodies. Mistakes happen in the heat of passion. I'm not taking chances with you, ever. You're going to marry some normal, steady man like your professor boyfriend and live happily ever after."

"Is that an order?"

"You bet!"

She searched his face with sad eyes. "I'd only spend the rest of my life dreaming about you."

"It's the glamour," he said flatly. "If I were a poor man, or a wage earner, you'd feel differently. Hell, I can look in a mirror! I know what women see, without the glitter. You're a working girl and I've been a multimillionaire. A little hero worship is inevitable."

"You think I'm attracted to your wallet?" she exclaimed on a hushed laugh. Only a working girl! She was world famous. He didn't know that, though.

"No, I don't think you're a gold digger," he said emphatically. "But I do think that you're attracted to an image that doesn't really exist."

"Images don't kiss like you do."

"I'm leaving. I don't like losing arguments."

"Neither do I. Stay and finish this one."

He shook his head. "Not a chance. Get some sleep. I'll see you tomorrow. Karie!" He raised his voice. "Time to go!"

"Coming, Dad!"

He walked out the front door, joined immediately by Karie. They called good-nights over their shoulders, leaving Janine and Kurt by themselves. The room seemed to close in around them.

"Mom and Dad are fine," she told her young brother, putting an affectionate arm around his shoulders as they watched the Rourkes stroll down the beach toward their own house. "Canton called the president's office and they sent out a search party."

He whistled. "Nice to have influence, huh?"

"Nice for us," she agreed. "It's a relief to know they haven't been kidnapped or something."

"You bet!" He glanced up at her. "He reads your books, did you know?"

Her heart jumped. *"Canton Rourke?"*

"Karie says he's got everything you've ever written, including *Catacomb.* Good thing he hasn't looked at the photo."

"He wouldn't recognize me if he did," she said. "I hope."

"Why don't you tell him?" he asked curiously.

She grimaced. "It's too late for me to tell him now. He'd want to know why I didn't before." She shifted. "He doesn't like famous women."

"He likes you. It won't matter."

"Think not? I wonder," she said thoughtfully.

"He's a great guy."

"So Karie says." She remembered the car following them, then, at the mention of his friend. She glanced down at him. "Have you seen that dark man again, the one I attacked on the beach?"

"Why, yes, I have. He was in town when we were at the *mercado,*" Kurt said. "He saw us watching him and took off when I walked toward a policeman."

"I don't like it."

"Neither do I. He's after something. Reckon it's us or Mom and Dad?" he queried.

"I don't know. I'm going to pay more attention to what's going on around us, though, you can count on that."

She went to bed, but the memory of Canton's kisses

kept her awake far too long. She got up, dressed in her long white embroidered gown and strolled out onto the deck.

In the moonlight, she saw a figure on the beach, turned toward the Rourke house. Something glinted in the moonlight, something like metal. Could it be a telescope? There was a light on in Canton's living room. There was a figure silhouetted against the curtains. The glint flashed again. Her heart jumped. What if it was a gun, trained on Canton?

She never thought of consequences. Without a thought for her own safety, she darted up to the front of the Rourke home and then rushed out from the side of it toward the man, yelling as she went.

The man was surprised, as she expected, but he reacted much too quickly. He raised an arm and motioned. Before Janine could slow her steps, before she even realized what was coming, two men shot out of the darkness with a sheet. It went over her head and around her. There was a sharp blow to her head, and after the pain came oblivion.

SHE WOKE UP WITH A SPLITTING headache and nausea. The floor rocked under her, and her bed was unusually hard. She opened her eyes and rolled over, right onto the hard floor. As she righted herself, she saw where she was. This wasn't her house. It was a boat, a big cabin cruiser, and the dark man who'd been stalking the children was suddenly there, yelling furiously at his two shorter, darker companions. They seemed to be pleading with him, their hands raised in supplication. He wasn't responding. He shouted at them even more.

She groaned involuntarily and they looked toward her menacingly. She knew then, at once, that if she didn't keep her head, she was going to die, right here. The tall, dark man had a pistol tucked into his belt, and his hand suddenly rested on it.

She closed her eyes and pretended to be unconscious. If he knew that she saw and recognized him, she had little doubt that she'd be a goner. A minute later, she was tossed onto the bunk and rolled over. Her hands were tied firmly behind her.

"No es la muchacha Rourke, ¡idiotas! Es una mujer—es el otra, la vecina," the tall man raged at them.

She didn't understand Spanish, but the words "Rourke girl" and "not" were fairly familiar after two weeks in Mexico. They thought she was Karie! They'd meant to kidnap Karie, and because she'd run out from the Rourke house, in the darkness they'd mistaken her for Karie. They'd got the wrong person. God in heaven, they were after Karie!

The child's life might depend on her now. If they were willing to go to these lengths, to kidnapping at gunpoint, to get Karie, they were deadly serious about what they meant to do. A potential witness, Janine might become expendable any minute. She had to get away, she had to warn Canton and Karie. The reason behind the kidnapping wasn't important right now, but warning them was.

She pretended to sleep. The men stood over her, talking quickly. The tall one muttered something that sounded ominous and his companions agreed with whatever he'd said and followed him up on deck.

The noise of a motor sounded, but not loudly enough to be that of the cabin cruiser itself. This was a big, expensive ship. Obviously there was a small launch used for getting to and from shore. There was money behind this attempted kidnapping. The question was, whose, and what did they stand to profit by it? Canton had no money, at least, not yet. Perhaps he had a trust or a Swiss bank account about which no one knew anything.

Her heart raced madly as she relaxed her arms and wrists. She'd deliberately tensed them while she was being bound, an old trick her karate teacher had taught her. Now the bonds were much looser than they would have been. It would take time and concentration to get them off, but she had a chance. God willing, she'd get free. Then she could worry about how to escape. If the boat was close to shore, she could probably swim it. If there was no riptide, that was. A riptide might carry her miles off course. And if it were possible to swim to shore, why was a launch needed by her captors?

She couldn't waste time worrying about that, she decided. First things first. She'd get loose. Then she'd figure out how to get off the ship.

All she needed now was luck and a little time.

CHAPTER EIGHT

THE ROPES WERE TIED SECURELY. After several minutes of twisting and turning and contorting, she couldn't manage to loosen them even enough to get a finger free, much less an entire hand.

It was like one of her books, she thought with dark humor, but by this point, her heroine would be free and giving her captors hell.

Janine hated reality.

There was the sound of the launch returning, and suddenly she knew real fear. The man had a gun. He was impatient, and angry that the kidnapping had gone awry. He might shoot her. It might be the only way for him.

She thought about her parents and Kurt. She thought about Canton. Death had never been a preoccupation of hers, but now she couldn't escape it. She might die here, in her nightgown, without ever having the chance to say goodbye to the people she loved most. And almost that bad was the realization that the sequel to *Catacomb* was barely one third of the way finished. They'd give it to another writer to finish. Oh, the horror of it!

As she gave renewed effort to her attempt to get away, she heard voices again, and suddenly the door of the cabin opened. The tall man was back, wearing a ski mask and gloves. Obviously he didn't think she'd been conscious enough to recognize him before, so he was disguised. That was hopeful. If he meant to kill her, he wouldn't need a disguise. But there was a pistol in his hand. He moved toward her, noting that she was wide-awake and watching him.

With a rasp in his voice, he ordered her, in thickly accented English, to stand up. He marched her ahead of him to the starboard side of the big cabin cruiser, and prodded her toward the rail.

"Jump," he commanded.

There was no launch below. It looked a frightfully long way to the water, and her hands were still tied.

"I'm not going to jump like this, with my hands tied!" she raged at him.

The gun was prodded firmly into her back. She felt a pressure on her bound wrists, and they were suddenly free, a knife having parted them.

"Get off the boat or die," the voice said harshly. "This is the only chance you'll get."

She didn't wait around to argue. She was a strong swimmer and there was a moon. It wasn't that far to shore. She could see the lights of the beach houses from here. Odd, lights at this hour of the morning...

The pistol punched her spine. She said a quick prayer, stood on the rail with her arms positioned and dived into the water.

It was cooler than she expected, but not so bad once she accustomed herself to the water. She struck out for shore, her heart throbbing as she waited to see if the man would shoot her in the back once she was on her way.

If he was willing to kidnap a child, what would stop him from murdering a potential witness? He was wearing a ski mask now, though; he must have thought that she hadn't had a good look at him. She'd never opened her eyes fully just after she'd regained consciousness. That might save her life.

She swam, counting each stroke, not even pausing for breath as she went steadily toward shore.

There was one bad place where she felt the surge of the waves, but she managed to get through it by relaxing her body and letting the waves sweep her on toward the beach.

She was getting tired. The blow to her head, the disorientation, the lack of sleep all combined dangerously to make her vulnerable to the effort she was expending. She rolled onto her back, floating, while above her the moon made a halo through the clouds. It looked unreal, all gossamer. She was trying to recall some lines about moons and silver apples when she heard a splashing sound close by. All at once, an arm snaked around her head, under her jaw, and she cried out.

"I've got you," Canton's deep voice rasped at her ear. "I'm going to tow you to shore. Are you all right?"

"Head hurts," she whispered. "They hit me."

"Good God!" He turned and struck out for the shore. He was a much more powerful swimmer than she was, each stroke more forceful than the last as he made his way through the waves to the shallows where he could finally stand up.

He tugged her along with him, fighting the powerful undertow. When he was through it, he bent and lifted her sopping wet form in the gown and started toward her beach house.

"The lights...are on," she managed to say weakly.

"I heard you yell," he said curtly. "You weren't in your bed or anywhere else. I've been searching for almost an hour. It only just occurred to me that the cabin cruiser was sitting out there anchored. It's gone now, but I've got the police after it. I thought you were on it. I was watching it with binoculars when I saw you come on deck with someone and jump off."

"I didn't jump. He pushed me off," she said. Every step he took jarred her poor head. She touched her temple. "Oh, dear God, I'm so tired of headaches! That animal hit me over the head!"

His arms contracted. He didn't speak, but his silence was eloquent.

"It's a miracle you didn't drown," he said through his teeth. "By God, someone's going to pay for this!"

"They're after Karie," she whispered, clutching at his soaked shirt. "I heard the tall man mention her name. It's the same man, the one who was...following the kids."

His face went even harder. "Marie," he muttered. "I couldn't meet her financial demands, so she's stooped to kidnapping to make me fork up the money she wants. Damn her!"

"She wouldn't hurt Karie," she mumbled.

"Not intentionally. But they hit you thinking you were Karie, didn't they?"

"I'm afraid so."

He muttered something else and carried her up into her darkened beach house.

"Kurt isn't awake?" she asked worriedly.

"No." He went through to her bedroom, stood her by the bed, stripped her quite forcefully and deftly and stuck her under the covers without a word. "Stay right there until I change clothes. I'm taking you in to the hospital."

"But Karie…" she moaned.

"We'll all go. I'll wake Kurt on my way out. No nausea?" he asked, hesitating in the doorway. For the first time, she saw that he had on trousers and a shirt, but no shoes. "No confusion?"

"Not yet…"

"I'll be right back."

She heard him bang on Kurt's door, heard her brother's thready reply. Her head throbbed so that she couldn't think at all. Kurt came into the room, worried and nervous when he saw her white face.

"What happened?" he exclaimed.

"Some men kidnapped me and took me out to a cabin cruiser," she rasped. "Kurt, put that wet gown in the bathtub and get me a nightgown out of my drawer, please."

"Kidnapped you?"

"They thought…I was Karie, you see," she muttered. She held her head. "Boy, am I going to have a headache now."

"How did they get you?" he persisted.

"I went out when I saw moonlight glinting on a gun barrel. I thought they were going to shoot Canton."

"And you rushed in to the rescue." He shook his head. "I wish I could convince you that you aren't Diane Woody," he groaned, "before you die trying to act like her."

"I got the point, just now," she assured him. "The gown?"

"Sure."

He carried the gown off to the bathtub and didn't come back. Canton did, dressed and impatient. "Where are your clothes?" he demanded, and started looking for them before she could answer him. "These will do."

He closed the door, tossed her underwear to her and jerked the covers off. "No time for a bath right now," he said. "You'll have to go as you are. Here." He helped her into her underthings as if he'd done it all his life. He slid a cool cotton sundress over her head, slid sandals onto her bare feet, then picked her up and strode out of the room with her. It was all too quick for her to feel embarrassment, but she was certain that she would, later.

"I want my purse and my makeup," she said weakly.

"You don't need either. I'm not flat broke and you're too sick for makeup."

"I look awful without it," she whispered weakly.

"That's a matter of perspective." He called to Kurt. The boy had just finished wringing out her gown. He came running, and locked the door behind them before they all went to Canton's waiting rental car. Karie was already in the front seat, wide-awake and concerned when she saw Janine.

"Is she going to be all right?" she asked quickly.

"Of course she is." Canton helped her into the back seat and motioned Kurt in beside her.

He drove like a madman to the hospital, ignoring traffic signs and other motorists. His set expression kept the children from asking any more questions.

He strode right into the emergency room with Janine in his arms and started shooting orders in Spanish right and left the minute he got through the doorway.

In no time at all, Janine was tested for everything from blood loss to concussion and placed in a private room.

"Slight concussion without complications," Canton said a minute later, dropping into a chair beside her bed.

"The kids?" she murmured drowsily.

"Down the hall. They have a guest room."

"What about you?" she persisted.

He took her cool hand in his and leaned back, still holding it. "I'm not leaving you for a second," he murmured, closing his eyes.

She felt warm all over, protected and cherished. Her fingers curled trustingly into his and clung. They must have given her something in that shot, she thought as the world began to recede. She was certainly sleepy.

It was daylight when she woke. Canton was standing by the window, his back to it, staring at her in the bed. Her eyes opened and she looked across at him with slowly returning consciousness.

She felt as if she'd known him all her life. The odd feeling brought a smile to her face.

He didn't return it. His eyes were wary now, watchful. "How are you feeling?" he asked, and even the tone of his voice was different.

"Better. I think," she qualified.

His hands were in his pockets. He didn't move any closer to the bed. His face was drawn, his jaw taut.

While she pondered his sudden change of attitude, the door opened and a nurse came in.

"I'm just going off duty," she said. She had a book under her arm and she approached the bed a little shyly. "I won't bother you right now, I know you're still feeling under the weather. But I bought *Catacomb* as soon as it came out and it's just the most wonderful mystery I've ever read. I recognized you the minute I saw you, even though the photo in the back is pretty vague. I know your real name, you see, as well as your pen name. I have all your books." She moved closer, smiling shyly at Canton. "I was telling Mr. Rourke what a thrill it was to get to see you in person. I don't want to intrude or anything. I just wondered if I left my book, if you'd sign it? I put a slip of paper with my name inside the cover. If you don't mind."

"I don't mind," Janine said with a wan smile. "I'll be glad to."

"Thank you!" The young nurse laid the book on the bedside table, flushing. "It's a pleasure. I mean it. I just think you're wonderful! I hope you get better very soon. Thank you again. I really appreciate it. Gosh, you look just like I pictured you!"

She rushed out the door, going off duty, with stars in her eyes. Janine looked toward the door with painful realization.

"So you know," she said without looking at him.

"You could have told me. You knew I read your books. I had *Catacomb* on the side table at my party."

"I knew. Karie told Kurt that you read my books." She studied her hands. "You'd said that you hated famous women, authoresses and actresses." She shrugged, still not meeting his eyes. "I didn't know how to tell you after that."

He didn't speak. His eyes were stormy.

"Did the nurse tell you?"

"No," he said, surprising her into looking up. "Kurt spilled the beans. He was upset. He said that you got into the worst scrapes because you thought you were your own heroine. I asked what he meant, and Karie said you were acting like Diane Woody." He took a slow breath. "It wasn't much of a jump after that. The nurse had brought your book with her to read on her breaks. She saw you and recognized you at once when they brought you onto her ward."

"A conspiracy."

He laughed without humor. "Of a sort. Fate."

She didn't know what to say. The man who'd taken such exquisite, tender care of her now seemed to want nothing more to do with her. She was sorry that he'd had to find it out the hard way. But they had more immediate problems than her discovered identity.

"What about the men who kidnapped me?" she asked, changing the subject.

"They're being hunted" was all he had to say.

"They weren't after my parents at all," she remarked after a long silence. "But I'm sorry they're trying to take Karie."

"I've put on some extra security."

"Good idea."

He was still glaring in her direction. "Kurt told me what you did."

"I have a bad habit of rushing in headfirst," she said.

"You thought the man had a gun aimed at me," he continued relentlessly.

She cleared her throat. "It looked like it. It was probably a pair of binoculars, but I couldn't be sure."

"So instead of yelling for help, you rushed him. Brilliant!"

She blushed. "You could be dead instead of yelling at me!"

"So could you!" he raged, losing his temper. "Are you a complete loon?"

"Don't you call me names!"

He went toward her and she picked up the nearest thing to hand, a plastic jug full of ice, ready to heave.

He stopped and her hand steadied.

Into the standoff came Kurt and Karie, stopping in the doorway at once when they realized what was going on.

"He's the good guy," Kurt said pointedly.

"That's what you think!" she retorted, wide-eyed and furious.

"Put the jug down," Kurt entreated, moving to her side. "You're in no condition to fight."

He took the jug away from her.

"The voice of reason," she muttered as she gave it to him.

"The still, small voice of reason," he agreed with a grin. "Feeling better?"

"I was," she said darkly, glaring toward Canton.

His expression wasn't readable at all. "I have some things to do," he said. "I'll leave Kurt here with you for the time being."

"When can I go home?" she asked stiffly.

"Later today, if there are no complications."

"I have to have someone translate for me, about insurance and so forth."

"The nurses speak English," he stated. "So do the people in the front office."

"Fine."

He gave her one last, long look and motioned to his daughter. He didn't say goodbye, get well, so long, or anything conventional. He just left with Karie.

"It's my fault," Kurt said miserably. "I spilled the beans."

"It was inevitable that someone would," she reassured him. "No harm done. A millionaire and a writer are a poor combination at best."

"He isn't a millionaire."

"He will be, again. I don't move in those circles. I never did."

"He stayed in here all night," he said.

She shrugged. "He felt responsible for me, I suppose. That was kind of him." She squared her shoulders. "But I can take care of myself now." She glanced at him. "You didn't try to contact Mom and Dad about this?" she asked with concern.

He shook his head. "We thought we'd wait."

"Thank God!" She sat up. Her head still throbbed. She lay back down against the pillow with a rough sigh. "I wonder what he hit me with," she said. "It must have been something heavy."

"The doctor said it was a light concussion and you were lucky. From now on, let the police do hero stuff, okay?"

She chuckled. "I suppose I'd better."

SHE STAYED ONE MORE night in the hospital, this time with Kurt for company. The next morning, she did all the necessary paperwork and checked herself out early.

They went back to the beach house in a cab, arriving just as Canton Rourke and his daughter were getting into their rental car.

She paid the cabdriver, being careful not to look at Canton. It did no good. He came storming across the sandy expanse with fierce anger in his lean face.

"Just what the hell are you doing home?" he demanded. "I was on my way to the hospital to get you."

"How was I to know that?" she asked belligerently. She was still pale and wobbly, despite her determination to come home. "You left with no apparent intention of returning. I can take care of myself."

He looked vaguely guilty. His eyes went to Karie. He motioned her back into the house. She waved and obeyed.

"I'll go talk to Karie while you two argue," Kurt said helpfully, grinning irrepressibly as he ambled toward Karie's house.

"Everybody's deserting me," she muttered, turning toward the house, purse in hand. Kurt had asked Canton to bring it to the hospital the morning after Janine had regained consciousness, and he had. The money had been a godsend, because she had to get a cab to the house.

"I wouldn't have, if you'd leveled with me from the beginning. I hate being lied to."

She turned on him. "You have no right to ask questions about me. You're not a member of my family or even a close friend. What makes you think I owe you the story of my life?"

He looked taken aback. His shoulders moved under the thin fabric of his gray jacket. "I don't know. But you do. I want to know everything about you," he said surprisingly.

"Why bother to find out?" she asked. "I'll be gone in less than a month, and we're not likely to run into each other again. I don't move in your circles. I may be slightly famous, but I'm not a millionaire, nor likely to be. I keep to myself. I'm not a social animal."

"I know." He smiled gently. "You don't like crowds, or life in the fast lane. Marie did. She felt dead without noise and parties. She liked to go out, I liked to stay home." He shrugged. "We were exact opposites." His blue eyes narrowed. "On the other hand, you and I have almost too much in common."

"I've already told you, I'm not going to propose to you," she said solemnly. "I like being independent. You need to find a nice, quiet, loving woman to cook you scrambled eggs while you're fighting your way back up the corporate ladder. Someone who likes being yelled at," she added helpfully.

"I didn't yell."

"Yes, you did," she countered.

"If I did, you deserved it," he returned shortly. "Running after armed felons, for God's sake! What were you thinking?"

"That I was going to make a citizen's arrest, for one thing." She searched his lean face. "You say you've read my books. Didn't you read the book jackets?"

"Of course," he muttered.

"Then tell me what I did for a living before I started writing novels."

He had to think for a minute. He frowned. His eyes widened and dilated. "For God's sake! I thought that was hype."

"It was not," she replied. "I was a card-carrying private detective. I'm still licensed to carry a weapon, although I don't, and I haven't forgotten one single thing I know about law enforcement."

"That's how you learned the martial arts."

She nodded. "And how to approach a felon, and how to track a suspect. I was doing just fine until the would-be kidnapper pointed a gun at you and I did something stupid. I rushed right in without thinking."

"And it almost got you killed," he added.

"A miss is as good as a mile. Thank God I have a hard head."

He nodded. He touched her hair gently. "I'm sorry I yelled."

She shrugged.

"I mean it," he stated with a smile.

She sighed. "Okay."

She was a world away from him now. He wasn't sure that he could breach the distance, but he had thought of a way to try. "Are you still a licensed private investigator?"

She nodded.

"Then why don't you come to work for me and help me crack this case?"

She pursed her lips. "I'm on a deadline," she said pointedly.

"You can't work all the time."

She considered it. It was exciting to chase a perpetrator. But more important than the thrill of the chase was to prevent someone from taking Karie away. Just thinking about that blow on the head made her furious. They'd thought she was Karie and they had no qualms about hurting her physically. They needed to be stopped, before they did something to harm the child.

"I'll do it," she said.

He grinned. "I can't pay you just yet. But I'll give you a pocketful of I.O.U.s. I promise they'll be redeemable one day."

She chuckled. "I believe it. Okay. That's a deal, then. But I'll need a couple of days to rest up." She touched the back of her head. "I've still got a huge bump."

"No wonder," he muttered, glowering at her. "You are a nut."

"Hiring me doesn't entitle you to call me names," she declared.

He held up both hands. "Okay, I'll reform."

HE DIDN'T. HE KEPT MUTTERING all the while several days later while they were lying in wait for the perpetrators to try again, her deadlines forgotten in the excitement of the chase.

"This is so damned boring," he grumbled after they'd been lying behind a sand dune, watching the kids build sand castles for over two hours.

"Welcome to the real live world of detective work," she replied. "You watch too much television."

His head turned and his lips pursed as he studied her. "So do you. Particularly of the science fiction variety."

She glared at him. "That's hitting below the belt."

"Is that any way to talk to a man of my rank and station?" he asked. His lips pursed. "I could have you interrogated, you know," he said in the same mocking tone her favorite series TV character used. He cocked one eyebrow to enhance the effect. "I could do it myself. I have a yen for brunettes."

She cleared her throat. "Stop that."

"Hitting you in your weak spot, hmmm?" he taunted.

"I don't have any weak spots," she replied.

He moved closer, rolling her over onto her back. "That's what you think." He bit off the words against her shocked mouth.

CHAPTER NINE

FOR JUST AN INSTANT SHE GAVE in to her longing for him and lay back, floating on waves of pure bliss as his mouth demanded everything she had to give. His lean body fit itself to hers and delicious thrills ran down her spine. She moaned, pulling him closer, the danger forgotten as she gave in to her hunger for him.

But her sense of self-preservation was too well developed not to assert itself eventually. When his thigh began to ease her long legs apart, she stiffened and wriggled away quickly, with a nervous laugh.

"Cut that out," she murmured. "We're on a case here."

He was breathing roughly, his eyes glittery with amusement and something deeper. "Spoilsport," he said huskily. "Besides, you were the one trying to seduce me a few days ago."

She put her hand over her wildly beating heart. "Scout's honor, I won't try it again," she promised.

His eyes narrowed. "I didn't ask for any promises," he said. "Take off that blouse and lie back down here—" he patted the sand beside him "—and let's discuss it."

She shook her head, still smiling. "We have to catch a kidnapper," she reminded him. "So don't distract me."

"I told you, this is boring," he said. "I'm not used to inactivity."

"Neither am I, but this goes with the job description." She peered up over the dune. The kids were still working on that sand castle, making it more elaborate by the minute. But there was no one in sight, no one at all. The kids had been kept close while Janine got over her concussion and was recovering. Perhaps the kidnappers had given up.

She murmured the thought aloud. Canton lay on his back with his arm shading his eyes from the sun. "Fat chance," he said curtly. "Marie wants her cut of the money and she'll go to any lengths to get it. Karie knows how she is. Poor kid. The last time I went off on business, before the divorce, Marie had one of her lovers upstairs and she was screaming like a banshee with him. When I got home, Karie was sitting on the steps out front in the snow."

She was shocked. "What did you do?"

He sat up, glancing at her. "What would you have done?" he countered.

She shrugged. "I'd have thrown him out the front door as naked as a jaybird and left him to get home the best way he could," she said.

He chuckled. "You and I think alike."

"You didn't!" she exclaimed.

He nodded. "Yes, I did. But I have a more charitable heart than you do. I threw his clothes out after him."

"And your wife?"

"I think she knew it was all over. She packed and left with a few veiled threats, and something to the effect that she needed other men because I couldn't satisfy her in bed."

She rolled over and looked up at him. Men were vulnerable there, in their egos, she thought. His eyes were evading hers, but there was pain in the taut lines of his face.

"They say that—"

He cut her off. "Don't start spouting platitudes, for God's sake," he muttered. "I don't want any reassurances from a woman who's never had a man in the first place."

"I was only going to say that I don't think sex matters much unless people love each other. And if they do, it won't really make any difference how good or bad they are at it."

He shifted, lying on one elbow in the sand. "I wouldn't know. I married Marie because she was outgoing and beautiful, one of the sexiest women I'd ever known. I had money and she wanted it. I thought she wanted me. Life teaches hard lessons. Glitter can blind a man."

"It can blind anyone. I'm sorry it didn't work out for you."

"We had ten years together," he said. "But only the first few months counted. I had my head stuck in computer programs and she was traveling all over the world to every new fashionable resort for the next nine years. Karie had no family life at all."

She made an awkward movement and peered over the dune. The kids were still fine, and nobody was in sight.

"Karie seems happy with you," she said.

"I think she is. I haven't been much of a father in the

past. I'm trying to make up for it." He studied her face
and smiled gently. "What about you and Kurt? Do your
parents care about you?"

She chuckled. "In their way. They're flighty and unworldly and naive. But we take care of them."

He sighed and shook his head. "Parenting is not for
the weakhearted."

"I guess not. But kids are sweet. I've always loved
having Kurt around."

He pursed his lips and narrowed his eyes and
watched her. "Do you want kids of your own?"

"Yes."

He didn't say anything else. He just went on watching her, looking at her with intent curiosity.

"Is my face on crooked?" she murmured, blushing.

He reached up and touched her cheek, very gently.
"It's a sweet face," he said solemnly. "Full of concern
and mischief and love. I've never known anyone like
you. You aren't at all what I thought successful writers
were. You're not conceited or condescending. You don't
even act like a successful writer."

"I wouldn't have a clue," she replied. "And I'll tell
you something. I know a lot of successful writers.
They're all nice people."

"Not all of them."

She shrugged. "There are always one or two bad apples in every bunch. But my friends are nice."

"Do they all write mysteries?"

She shook her head. "Some are romance authors,
some write science fiction, some write thrillers. We talk
over the Internet." She cleared her throat. "Actually a

number of us talk about the villain on that science fiction series. We think he's just awesome."

He chuckled. "Lucky for me I look like him, huh?"

She laughed and pushed him. He caught her and rolled over, poised just above her with his face suddenly serious. "That isn't why you're attracted to me, is it?" he asked worriedly.

"I think maybe it was, at first," she admitted.

"And now?"

She bit her lower lip. "Now..."

His thumb moved softly over her mouth, her chin. "Now?"

Her eyes met his and the impact went right through her. Her lips parted. "Oh, glory," she whispered unsteadily.

"Oh, glory," he agreed, bending.

He kissed her in a way he never had before, his mouth barely touching hers, cherishing instead of demanding. His arms were warm but tender, the pressure of his long, powerful body not at all threatening. When he lifted his mouth, hers followed it, her dazed eyes lingering on his lips.

His breathing was as ragged as hers. He touched her face with quiet wonder. It was in his eyes, too, the newness of what he was feeling. He looked odd, hesitant, uncertain.

"I don't have a dime," he said slowly. "Maybe I'll make my fortune back, maybe I won't. You could end up with a computer programmer working for wages."

Her heart jumped. "That sounds like you're talking about something permanent."

He nodded. "Yes."

"You mean...as in living together."

"No."

She blushed. "Sorry, I guess I jumped the gun…"

His fingers pressed against her lips. He struggled for the right words. "It's too soon for big decisions," he said, "but you might start thinking about marriage."

She gasped.

Her reaction hit him right in his pride. Obviously she hadn't even considered a permanent life with him. He cursed and rolled away from her, getting to his feet. He stared out toward the kids, toward the sea, his hands stuck deep in his pockets.

She didn't understand his odd behavior. She got up, too, hesitating.

He glanced at her uneasily. "I'm thirty-eight," he said.

"Yes, I…I know."

"You're twenty-four," he continued. "I suppose your professor is closer to the right age. He's got a degree, too, and he fits in with your family." His eyes went back to the ocean.

She felt a vulnerability in him that made her move closer. "But I don't love him, Canton."

He turned slowly. "I like the way you say my name," he said softly.

She smiled hesitantly. "I like the way you say mine," she replied shyly. Her eyes fell. "Are you sorry you mentioned marriage?"

He moved a step closer. "I thought you were."

Her eyes came up.

"You gasped," he said curtly. "As if it were unthinkable."

"You'd only just said a few days ago that you never wanted to get married again," she explained.

"A man says a lot of things he doesn't mean when a woman's got him tied up in knots," he murmured. "God in heaven, can't you see how it is with me? I want you. But I'm not in your league educational-wise, and I'm flat busted. My wife left me for someone who was better in bed. I'm pushing forty…what are you doing?"

Her hands were busy on the front of his shirt, working at buttons. "Taking your clothes off," she said simply. She looked up with wide green eyes. "Do you mind?"

He didn't seem to be able to speak. His mouth was open.

She pushed the shirt aside, over the expanse of thick hair and hard muscle. He wasn't darkly tanned, but he was sexy. He smelled of spices. She smiled and buried her face in his chest, pressing her lips to it.

He shivered.

She looked up, still caressing him slowly. "You've seen me without any clothes at all, although my head was hurting too much at the time for me to enjoy it. Turnabout is fair play."

"It's a public beach," he noted, barely able to speak.

"You proposed."

"I didn't," he protested huskily. "I said I wanted you to think about it."

Her eyes went back to his chest. He was moving helplessly against the slow caress of her fingers. "I've thought about it."

"And?"

"I like kids." She looked up. "I'd like several. I make

a good living writing books. I can take care of the bills until you settle on what you want to do, or while you make your fortune back. I'm good at budgeting, and Karie likes me. I like her, too."

He couldn't get his breath. "You're driving me mad," he said through his teeth.

Her eyebrows lifted. Her eyes darted to the movement of her hands on his bare chest and back up again to his stormy eyes. "With this?" she asked, fascinated.

His chest rose and fell heavily. His hands covered hers and stilled them. "I've been more concerned with a failing empire and my employees' futures lately to pay much attention to women. It's been a long dry spell," he added. "You understand?"

"Sort of."

"I suppose I'm not the only one who spends too much time at the computer," he mused.

She shifted a little. "I've never found men very attractive physically."

"Oh?"

"Well, until now," she amended. Her searching eyes met his. "I used to dream about traveling. Now I have the most embarrassing dreams about you."

He grinned. "Do tell."

"I wouldn't dare."

"If you'll marry me, we can do something about them."

"I have to marry you first?"

He smiled gently. "My mother was Spanish. She raised me very strictly, in an old-world sort of way. I never messed around with virgins. I'm much too old to start now."

"In other words, good girls get married before they get…"

"I'll wash your mouth out with soap if you say it," he promised.

She wrinkled her nose at him. "I'll bet you'd say it."

"And more," he agreed. "I have a nasty temper."

"I noticed."

"So you know the worst already. And since you aren't experienced, and you have no one to compare me with in bed," he added, tongue-in-cheek, "I'll seem worldly and wise to you." He pursed his lips. "Now, that's an encouraging thought."

She looped her arms around his neck. "I love you," she said softly. "You'll seem like Don Juan to me."

He actually blushed.

"Shouldn't I say that I love you?" she asked.

His arms tightened. "Say it a lot," he instructed. "Karie says it sometimes, but Marie never did. Funny, I never noticed, either." He smiled. "I like the way it sounds."

"You could say it back," she pointed out.

He cleared his throat. "I don't know."

"It's easy." She looked briefly worried. "If you mean it."

"Oh, I mean it, all right," he said, and realized with a start that he did. He hadn't given much thought to the emotional side of his turbulent relationship with her, but the feeling was definitely there. He wanted her, he liked her, he enjoyed being with her. And he most certainly did…love her.

Her eyes had brightened. "You do?"

He nodded. He searched her face quietly. "It's risky, marriage."

"No, it isn't. We'll love each other and take care of Karie, and Kurt when we need to. We'll have kids and love them and I'll never leave you."

His jaw tautened. His arms closed around her bruisingly, and he held her for a long time without speaking. His tall body shuddered as he felt the full impact of commitment.

She closed her eyes and sighed, moving her soft cheek against the thick hair on his chest. "I like hairy men," she whispered. "It's like holding a teddy bear."

He chuckled, his voice deep at her ear. "Thank God. I'd hate to have to shave my chest every day."

Her arms tightened. "When?" she asked dreamily.

He made the transition without trouble. "Whenever you like," he said. "We have to get rings and arrange a ceremony. It should be easy in Mexico." He lifted his head. "I have a town house in Lincoln Park. I've divided my time between Chicago and New York, but I only have an apartment in New York. I'll try to hold on to it. You might want to go shopping in Manhattan from time to time, or visit your publishers."

She grinned. "You're a prince."

"I'm a pauper," he insisted.

She sighed. "That's okay. I like you better poor. You'll always know that I married you for what you didn't have."

He burst out laughing and lifted her high in his arms. "So I will."

The kids, hearing the commotion, came up the beach to see what all the laughter was about.

"We're going to get married," Canton told them, totally forgetting that he'd only asked Janine to think about marriage. He wasn't about to let her get away. He watched his daughter's face, and was relieved when he saw it light up.

"You're going to marry Janine? She'll be my step-mom? Cool!" She rushed up and hugged Janine with all her might. "Oh, Janine, that's just the best present I ever got for my birthday!"

"Today's your birthday?" Janine exclaimed. "I didn't know!"

"I got her a cake and a present. We were going to have you both over tonight to celebrate," Canton explained. He grimaced. "I got so wrapped up in what we were talking about, I forgot to mention it."

"I have a neat game program for you," Janine told the girl. "A CD-ROM of Mars. It's a mystery."

"Cool! I love space stuff."

"Yes, I noticed," Janine chuckled. She sighed. "I'm going to love having you for a stepdaughter. But let's leave the step off of it, okay?" she added. "How about Mom and daughter?"

"That suits me," Karie said warmly.

"What about me?" Kurt wailed. "Won't I get to stay with you anymore? I'll be stuck with…*them?*" His voice trailed off as he looked past Janine. "What in the world are they doing here?"

Janine turned, and there were her parents, sweaty and stained with dirt, both wearing khakis and wide-brimmed hats, waving from the deck of the beach house.

"Something must have happened," she said. "Come

on." She took Canton by the hand and they all went back down the beach, the stakeout for the would-be kidnappers forgotten for the moment.

THE INTRODUCTIONS WERE MADE quickly. Professors Dan and Joan Curtis were fascinated by Canton Rourke, whom they'd certainly heard of. To learn that he was marrying their daughter caused them both to be momentarily tongue-tied.

"You don't know each other very well," Joan cautioned worriedly.

"We have so much in common that discovering each other will be a lifelong pleasure," Canton said, and won her over on the spot.

She grinned at him, looking just like Janine, with her dark hair and green eyes. Dan was tall and thin with graying hair and blue eyes. He looked older than ever as he sat sprawled in a chair sipping cold bottled water.

In the middle of the living room was a huge crate. Dan nodded toward it. "That's why we're back."

Janine's eyebrows rose. "Something special?"

"A few good pieces," Dan replied. "We've tried to contact our man in the Mexican government, but our satellite link was sabotaged."

"It was what?" Janine exclaimed. "I knew there had been problems, but I hadn't realized the extent."

"We've had a pothunter on our tails," Dan replied. "A very determined one. He shot at us."

Janine sat down, with Canton right behind her, his hand on her shoulder.

"We're all right," Joan said. "But we thought it would

be wise to get back to civilization as quickly as possible. We jumped into the Land Rover, with that—" he indicated the crate "—and drove back at top speed. We lost our guide on the way. He was behind us in his truck, but we didn't see him again. We phoned the police the minute we got in. They should be along momentarily."

"If there's anything I can do, I'll be glad to help," Canton volunteered.

"He got us in touch with you," Janine added helpfully. "He knows the president of the country personally."

The Curtises were impressed. They both stared at Canton with renewed interest.

"Would the pothunters try anything here in Cancún?" Janine asked worriedly.

"For what's in that box, they would," Dan said mournfully. "In a way, I'm sorry we found such a brilliant site. We've mapped everything, taken photos, documented every step of the excavation so that nothing was overlooked. That will help future expeditions in their excavations."

"Won't the government send someone to take possession of these pieces?" Janine asked.

"Certainly," Joan replied with a smile. "It's just a matter of getting them down here. And keeping the pothunters away until they can."

Dan Curtis took a pistol from his pocket and put it on the table. "This business is getting to be very dangerous."

"Archaeology always was," Janine said pointedly. "Even in the early days. But it's worthwhile."

"We always thought so, didn't we, dear?" Joan asked her husband, with a loving hand on his shoulder.

His hand went up to take hers. "We still do. But we're getting old for this."

Dan stared at the crate again. "I hope that isn't going to get any of us hurt. We almost checked into a hotel instead of coming here, but this seemed wiser."

"It is," Canton said firmly. "I've got a man watching my beach house. He can get another man to help him and watch this one, too."

Joan frowned. "Why do you have someone watching it?"

"Because my mom tried to have me kidnapped," Karie explained. "Janine got kidnapped instead and hit on the head and was in the hospital..."

"*What?*" Joan and Dan exclaimed together.

"I'm fine," Janine said gently, holding up a hand. "I haven't forgotten any of my training."

"You and detective work," Joan moaned. "Darling, archaeology would have been so much safer!"

"Ha! You're the ones who got shot at, remember?" Janine replied. "Anyway, we saved Karie from kidnappers, but we're not sure that they've given up. It's been sort of hectic around here for the past week."

"And here we come with more trouble," Dan groaned.

Janine patted him on the shoulder. "It's okay, Dad. There are enough of us to guard the crate and Karie. We'll be fine."

"Of course we will," Canton agreed.

Dan and Joan exchanged wan smiles, but they didn't look convinced.

"Just out of idle curiosity, what have you got in the box?" Janine asked.

"Several Mayan funerary statues, some pottery, a few tablets with glyphs on them and some gold jewelry with precious stones inlaid. Oh, and a jeweled funeral mask."

Janine's eyes widened. "A king's ransom," she said.

"And all the property of the Mexican government, as soon as we can turn it over," Dan added. "We're hoping to keep at least one or two of the pots for our own collection at the university, but that's up to the powers-that-be."

"Considering what you've gone through to get it, I imagine they won't begrudge you a piece or two," Canton said. He moved forward. "It's been nice to meet you. I have to get Karie home and make a couple of business calls. We'll see you later."

"I'll walk out with you," Janine said after the Curtises had made their goodbyes.

Karie went ahead of them. Canton slid his arm around Janine's shoulders and held her close. "Complications," he murmured.

"More and more. Maybe the kidnappers will back off, with so many people around."

"Maybe they'll join forces with the pothunters," he murmured.

She poked him in the side with her elbow. "Stop being pessimistic. This is all going to work out. It has to, and soon. I want to get married."

"What a coincidence, so do I!" he murmured facetiously.

She laughed, turning her face up to his. "The sooner the better," she added.

He nodded. "The sooner, the better." He bent and kissed her gently. "Go home."

"Be careful."

"You, too. I'll phone you later. Lock your doors. I'm going to make a few telephone calls and see what I can do to help things along."

"Have your ex-wife arrested," she suggested.

"Nice sentiment, but not practical." He chuckled. "All the same, there may be some way to discourage her. I'll find one." He winked. "Stay out of trouble."

"You do the same."

CHAPTER TEN

"I CAN'T BELIEVE THIS," Joan Curtis said heavily. "My daughter is marrying Mr. Software. Do you have any idea how famous he is, how much money he's made in his life?"

"He's broke right now," Janine stated.

"He'll never be broke, not with a mind like his," Dan said with a grin. "He's one smart guy. He'll make it all back, with interest."

"Even if he doesn't, it won't matter. I'm crazy about him," Janine confessed.

"It seems to be mutual. And here I thought you were going to wait around forever for Quentin to propose," Joan teased. "I'm glad that never happened, Janine," she added. "Quentin was never the man for you."

"I know that, now. I just drifted along until I met Canton."

"Listen," Joan called suddenly, her eyes on the television. "They're tracking a hurricane. They say it's coming this way!"

"A hurricane?" Dan groaned. "Just what we need!" He glanced at his daughter. "You didn't mention this."

"I didn't know," she said. "I don't speak Spanish!"

"It's in English now," Joan observed.

Janine looked sheepish. "Well, I've been rather out of things for several days, and I haven't been watching television."

"No wonder," Dan mused.

"You must have noticed the wind picking up, and the clouds," Joan said, sighing. "They've just said that they may have to evacuate the coast if it comes any closer. And it looks as if it's going to."

"I had hoped to get a plane back to the States," Dan said, glancing worriedly at the crate. "Now what do we do?"

"We go further inland," Janine said at once. "Canton has a rental car. We need a van, so that we can take your cargo with us."

"With pothunters and potential kidnappers two steps behind." Dan Curtis sighed. "Remember the old days in graduate school, when the most dangerous thing we did was set off a cherry bomb in the dean's car?"

"You what?" Janine exclaimed, grinning.

Dan grinned and exchanged a look with his wife. "We weren't always old," he murmured.

"No time for reminiscing," Joan said, and she was picking up things as she went. "Get cracking. We have to pack up and get out of here, quick."

Before she had a case packed, Canton and the kids were back.

"Hurricane Opal is headed our way," he began, noticing the disorder in the living room.

"We know," Janine said. "We're packing up to go inland. We need to rent a van."

"Leave that to me. There's safety in numbers. We'll go together. I have a friend who owns an estate halfway between here and Chichén Itzá. He'll be able to have us stay. And he has armed security," he added with a chuckle.

"Armed security?" Janine was intrigued.

"He was a mercenary in his younger days. Now he's a married man with two kids. They moved down here from Chicago because of the tough winters. Not much snow in Quintana Roo," he added merrily.

"What interesting people you know, Mr. Rourke," Dan remarked.

"Call me Canton. Yes, I do have some unique acquaintances. I'll see about that van. Karie, you stay here with Kurt and Janine."

"Oh, Dad, does he have a TV?" she asked worriedly. "I have to watch the Braves game. It's the playoffs!"

"They're never going to win the series," he began.

She stuck out her lower lip. "Yes, they are! I believe in them!"

He just shook his head.

Two hours later, they were fighting headwinds and rain as they plowed down the long narrow paved road toward the estate of Canton's friends.

The jungle was on either side of them. They saw small *pueblos* nestled among the trees, many with satellite dishes and electricity. Advertising signs were nailed to trees and even the sides of small wooden buildings here and there. There were huge speedbreakers at the beginning and end of each little town they passed.

Down the dusty streets, children played in the rain and dogs barked playfully. As they went past the small, neat houses, they could see hammocks nestled against the walls, ready to be slung again each night. The floors of the whitewashed houses, though earthen, were unlittered and smooth. Tiny stores sat among unfamiliar trees, and in several places, religious shrines were placed just off the road.

Two tour buses went by them. The buses were probably bound for ancient Mayan cities like Chichén Itzá. Janine and Kurt had been on one during their first week in Cancún. The large vehicles were surprisingly comfortable, and the tour guides were walking encyclopedias of facts about present and past in the Yucatán.

"You're very quiet," Joan remarked from the front seat of the van. "Would you rather have gone with the Rourkes?"

"They've got Kurt," she said. "I thought I might need to stay with you."

Dan chuckled. "Protecting us, is that it?"

She only smiled. "Well, neither of you know any martial arts."

"That's true, darling." Joan touched her hand gently. "Whatever would we do without you?"

"I have no idea," Janine said dryly, and meant it, although they didn't suspect that.

THE ESTATE OF CANTON'S FRIEND had two men with rifles at the black wrought-iron gates. Whatever Canton said to them produced big smiles. The gate opened, and Canton's arm out the window motioned the van to follow.

The house had arches. It was snowy white with a red

tile roof, and blooming flowers everywhere. It looked Spanish, and right at home in the jungle.

As they reached the front porch, wide and elegant with a few chairs scattered about and a huge hammock, the front door opened and two people came out.

The man was tall, dark, very elegant. He had a mustache and looked very Latin. The woman was smaller, with long blond hair and a baby in her arms. A little boy of about nine came out the door behind them.

When the vehicles stopped, the Curtises got out and joined the Rourkes and Kurt.

The dark man came forward. "You made good time," he told Canton, and they shook hands warmly. "These are the Curtises of whom you spoke? *Bienvenidos a mi casa,*" he said. "Welcome to my home. I am Diego Laremos. This is my wife, Melissa, our son Matt, and our baby daughter, Carmina." He turned and spoke softly to the blond woman. "*Enamorada,* this is Canton Rourke, of whom you have heard me speak."

"I'm delighted to meet you," the woman spoke with a smile and a faint British accent. "Diego and I are happy to have you stay with us. Believe me, you're all quite safe here."

"Many thanks for putting us up," Dan Curtis said, extending a hand. "We have some priceless things that pothunters have been trying their best to steal. We had hoped to fly to the States today, but they were evacuating Cancún."

"So Canton told me," Diego replied solemnly. "Pothunters are ever a problem. So it was in Guatemala, where Melissa and I lived."

"We tried to live in Chicago, but the winters were too harsh," Melissa said with a rueful smile. "We were nervous about taking Matt to Guatemala, so we eventually moved here. Isn't it beautiful?"

"Absolutely," Janine said. "It must be wonderful to live year-round in such a paradise."

Canton put an arm around her. "Think so?" he asked gently. "Then I'll see about buying some land nearby, if you like it."

"Could we?" Janine exclaimed. "How wonderful. We could visit Melissa."

Melissa beamed. "Yes, you could. I have all your books," she added sheepishly.

"Now that really makes me feel welcome. May I hold him?" she asked, moving toward the baby with bright, intrigued eyes.

"Her." Melissa corrected her with a chuckle. "Indeed you may." Melissa handed the baby over, and Janine cradled her warmly, her whole face radiant as the tiny little girl looked at her with dark blue eyes and began to coo.

"Oh, what a darling!" she exclaimed, breathless.

Canton, watching her, had an incredible mental picture of how Janine would look holding their own baby, and he caught his breath.

She looked up, into his eyes, smiling shyly. "Can we have several of these?"

"As many as you like," he replied huskily.

"I'll take you up on that," she promised.

The Laremoses were the most interesting people Janine had met, and she'd met a lot. Diego had two other ex-mercenary friends in Chicago, one who'd practiced law there for years and was now an appellate court judge, and another who ran a top secret security school of some sort. Both were married and had families.

"There's another member of the old group in Texas," he added. "He's married, too, and they have a ranch. And then there's one who lives in Montana. He got fed up with the city and took his wife and kids out there. They have a ranch, too. We have reunions every year, but with all the kids involved, we have to have them in the summer."

"They're a unique bunch," Canton said musingly. "And all ex-mercenaries. I'm amazed that you all lived to marry and have families in the first place."

Laremos leaned forward. "So were we."

Canton smiled at Janine over the huge dinner table, where they were eating salads and drinking fine, rich coffee. "I met this bunch at a time in my life when I was having some extreme problems with a small hardware enterprise I'd set up in a Third World country. Mine was ecologically friendly, but there was a rival company tearing up the rain forest and killing off the natives. When the government said that it didn't have the money or manpower to do anything about the situation, I sent Laremos and his group over and they arranged a few unpleasant, but nonlethal, surprises for them. They packed up and left."

"Good for you," Janine said with admiration.

"We also set up a trust and bought land for the tribe, which is theirs forever. I don't like profit with a bedrock of destruction," Canton said simply. "I never did."

"I hope you get it all back, *amigo*," Laremos said sincerely. "We need more industrialists like you, men who balance profit with compassion for the environment."

"Profit is the last thing on my mind right now," Canton said, leaning back. "I hope that we can discourage the people who are after us. I think we were followed coming down here."

"No doubt you were. But," Laremos said with a grin, "your pursuers are in for a great surprise if they attempt to come here. My men are dedicated and antisocial. And armed."

"We noticed," Janine said. Her eyes twinkled. "I'm already getting ideas for another book."

"Are you going to put us in it?" Melissa asked, bright-eyed. "I want to be a blond, sexy siren who entices this big, strong Latino and makes him wild."

"You do that every day of my life, *enamorada*," Diego said, bringing her soft hand to his mouth. "No need to tell the world about it."

She only smiled. A look passed between them that made Janine smile, too. It must be wonderful to be married so long, and still be in love. Her gaze went to Canton, and found him watching her.

He didn't say a word. But his eyes told her that she and he would be that happy, for that long. In fact, his smile promised it.

THEY HAD TO STAY for two days at the estate before the storm was on its way. Before it finally became disorganized, it left major damage along its path.

There had been no sign of the would-be kidnappers or the pothunters, but when the Curtises and the Rourkes left the elegant Laremos estate, it was to find themselves once again being trailed. And this time, there were two vehicles in pursuit and they didn't bother to hang back.

The Rourke car and the van in which the Curtises were riding raced past small villages, only slowing for the speedbreakers. Still the two cars gained on them. They came to a crossroads, and Canton suddenly motioned to Dan Curtis to follow him. He took the right fork at speed and then suddenly whipped the car off onto a little dirt trail into some trees, motioning out the window for Dan to follow.

The tree cover was thick and the rain had removed the problem of telltale dust rising to give away their positions.

He cut off his engine. Dan did likewise. Then they sat and waited. Only seconds later, the two pursuing cars slowed, stopped, looked around. They pulled up beside each other on the narrow little paved road and spoke rapidly, after which each car took a fork and raced away.

Canton reversed the car until it was even with the van. "We can return to the last village and cut through there back to the Cancún road. Don't lose your nerve."

"Not me," Dan said with a grin. "Lead on."

"Are you okay?" he asked Janine, who was once again with her parents.

She nodded. "I'm fine. Take care of Kurt and Karie."

"You know I will."

He waved and raced away, with the van right behind. They managed to get enough of a head start to lose the pursuing vehicles, but they were not out of danger. The occupants of the car would soon realize that they'd been outfoxed and turn around.

By the time the pursuers got back into the village, though, the people they were chasing were long gone. Of course, there was only one road, and they'd surely know to backtrack on it. But at the last *pueblo* there had been a turnoff to Cancún that had two forks. One of them led north, the other east. The pursuers would be obliged to split up. And even if one car took the right fork, there wouldn't be any way they could catch up in time. Janine thought admiringly that her future husband would make a dandy detective.

THEY ARRIVED IN CANCÚN after dark and checked into a hotel, having decided that the beach house would be much too dangerous. They unloaded the car and the van, which were then returned to the rental agencies and another, different van was rented from still another agency. Janine thought it might be possible to throw the pursuers off the track this way.

And it might have been; except that the would-be kidnappers spotted Canton with Janine at the car rental lot and immediately realized what was going on. They didn't follow the van back to the hotel. One of the local men had a cousin who was friendly with an employee at the car rental agency. All she had to do was flirt a little with the agent. Within an hour, they knew not only which hotel, but which rooms, contained their prey.

To make matters worse, the pothunter, also a local man, had family connections to one of the people who were after Karie. They decided to pool their resources and split the profits.

With no suspicion of all this, Canton and Janine and the others settled into adjoining rooms of the hotel while they waited to get on the next flight to Chicago. Karie had discovered that there was no way she was going to get any telecast of a Braves game now, with communications affected by the hurricane. Power lines and communications cables had been downed and service was interrupted. As she told her dad, they might not have a tropical beach in Chicago, but they did have cable.

The Curtises were ready to go home as well. Their weeks of grubbing in the outer reaches of Quintana Roo had paid great dividends. They not only had plenty to show the Mexican government, but they also had enough research material for a book and several years of lectures.

A representative of the government was going to meet them early in the morning in the hotel and go over the crated artifacts with them.

Little did they know, however, that the representative had been waylaid and replaced by a henchman of the pothunters....

"IT'S GOING TO BE A GREAT relief to have these treasures off our hands," Dan Curtis remarked over dinner that evening. "Not that I'm sorry we found them, but they're quite a responsibility."

"Did you know that in the early part of this century, archaeologists went to Chichén Itzá to look for artifacts and were murdered there?" Joan added.

"I was watching a program on that on the Discovery Channel," Janine remarked. "It was really interesting. After the first archaeologists went there, the Peabody Museum of Harvard had an agent in Mexico gathering material for them in the early part of the century. It's in drawers in the museum and isn't on display to the public. But it belongs to Mexico. So why doesn't the Mexican government ask them to give it back? In fact, there are human skeletal remains in that collection as well, aren't there? Certainly with all the new laws governing such remains, they should be reinterred, shouldn't they?"

"Those laws don't apply universally," Dan Curtis ventured. "And there probably would be something like a grandfather clause even if they did. That particular collection dates to the time before the Mexican Revolution, long before there were such laws." He smiled gently. "It's more complicated than it seems to a lay person. But believe me, archaeology has come a long way in the past few decades."

"Just the same, it's a pity, isn't it?" Janine added. "I mean, nobody gets to see the exquisite Maya artwork in the collection, least of all the descendants of the Mayan people in Quintana Roo."

"But they're also preserved for future generations," Dan explained. "Artifacts left in situ are very often looted and sold on the black market, ending up with collectors who don't dare show them to anyone." He smiled at his daughter. "I know it's not a perfect system," he mused, "but right now, it's the best we can do."

"Yes, I know. There are two sides to every story. You both take your work seriously. And you do it very well,"

Janine said with a smile, because she was proud of her parents. They cared about their work. They were never slipshod in their excavations or disrespectful of the human skeletal remains they frequently unearthed.

"I do wish we'd had a little more time," Dan said ruefully. "I think we were onto something. We found an unusual ceremonial site, unlike anything we've discovered before. We were just beginning to unearth it when the trouble started."

"A superstitious mind would immediately think of curses," Janine said wickedly.

Dan chuckled, winking at his wife. "Trust a writer to come up with something like that. No, there's no curse, just bad luck. Señor Perez has been following us ever since we got off the plane. He tried bribery at first, and when that didn't work he began making veiled threats about intervention by the Mexican government. We had all the necessary permits and permissions, so the threats didn't work, either. Then he set up camp nearby and began harassing us."

"Harassing? How?" Janine asked, noting that Canton was listening attentively.

"Sudden noises in the middle of the night. Missing supplies. Stolen tools. There wasn't anything we could specifically charge him with. We couldn't even prove he was at the site, although we knew it was him." Dan shook his head. "Finally it was too much for us, especially after we lost the satellite link. We took what we had and left."

"But what about the site now?" Canton asked somberly. "Won't he loot it?"

"He thinks we have everything that was there, that's the funny part," Joan said. "We were so cautious about the newest find that we didn't even let the workers near it. We concealed it and marked the location on our personal maps. We'll make sure those get into the right hands. Meanwhile," she added heavily, "we've got to get the artifacts we recovered into the right hands, before Señor Perez can trace us here and do something drastic."

"Would he?" Janine asked worriedly.

Dan nodded. "An expedition lost a member along with some priceless gold and jeweled artifacts some years ago. Perez was implicated but there wasn't enough evidence for him to be prosecuted. He always hires henchmen to do his dirty work."

Janine felt chilled. She wrapped her arms around herself, glad that Kurt and Karie were on the patio and not listening to this.

"I have my man and another watching the hotel," Canton said. "We'll be safe enough here until we can get a plane out."

Karie and Kurt had left the balcony and had gone into Kurt's room. They came out with a rather large bag.

"Could we go down to the beach for just a minute?" Karie asked, with her camera slung around her neck. "We want to snap some photographs."

"I don't think that's a good idea," Canton said.

"Aw, please, Dad," Karie moaned. "It's safe here, you said so. There are people looking out for us. Mom won't try again."

Karie took off her Atlanta Braves baseball cap and wiped her sweaty blond hair. "Please?"

They looked desperate. It was hard for kids to be cooped up all day.

"All right. Let me make a phone call first," Canton said. "And make sure Kurt's parents don't mind."

"It's okay, if they'll be watched," Dan agreed.

They exchanged conspiratorial glances. "Thanks, Dad!" Karie said enthusiastically.

Canton made his phone call. The kids took their bag and went down the steps to the ground floor, and out toward the white beach.

"Stay out of the ocean!" Canton called after them.

"Sure, Dad!" Karie agreed.

"What have they got in that bag?" Janine asked curiously.

"They're probably going to collect seashells in it," Canton murmured, sliding an arm around her. He smiled. "Don't worry. I'll make sure they don't bring anything alive back with them."

Janine shuddered delicately. "You're sure your man will watch them?"

He nodded. "He's one of the best in the business. When he isn't working for me, he works for the federal government."

"Oh? As what?"

He chuckled. "I don't know. He says it's classified. He travels a lot." He glanced down at her and smiled. "But he's good. Very good. The kids will be safe."

"Okay."

KURT GLANCED OVER HIS shoulder as he and Karie rushed down to the sand near the water. "Whew," he said, wiping his brow. "I never thought they'd let us out of the room! And we've gone to all this trouble to get things together, too!"

"I know," Karie said, equally relieved. "And they didn't even ask about the bag, thank goodness."

"We'd better get busy," he said. "We don't have much time."

"Stupid kidnappers and pothunters," she muttered as she unzipped the bag. "They sure know how to make life hard on enterprising preteens, don't they?"

CHAPTER ELEVEN

THE KIDS PLAYED ON THE BEACH. Dan and Joan Curtis rummaged through their crate of artifacts, double-checking everything in preparation for the arrival of the government antiquities representative.

Meanwhile, Canton and Janine sat on the balcony, holding hands. They were too nervous to let Kurt and Karie completely out of sight.

"What are they doing?" Janine asked, frowning as she watched the bag being slowly unpacked.

"Maybe they've got some cups and glasses to use in sand castle sculpting," he suggested. "Karie always empties the china cupboard when she's planning one."

"Could be," she murmured. But that didn't look like cups and glasses. It looked like pieces of hose, a cow skull, some pieces of rubber, a bag of feathers, several small balloons and a little fur. "Look at all that stuff," she exclaimed. "Could they be making a sand castle with it?"

He let go of her hand and moved closer to the balcony. His eyebrows lifted. "Strange sort of a sand castle…"

The sudden shrill of the telephone caught their attention. Inside the room, Dan Curtis picked up the receiver and began conversing with someone.

"Yes, I could," Dan said slowly, and Janine knew

from the past that he was deliberating when he spoke like that. "But why?"

There was a pause.

"I see. But it's a lot of work to pack it all up again," Dan explained. "Why can't you come to the hotel?"

Canton, interested now, got up and went into the room. "Who is it?" he mouthed at Dan.

Dan put his hand over the receiver. "The man from the ministry of antiquities."

"What's his name?" he asked shortly.

"What's your name?" Dan asked the man.

"Carlos Ramirez" came the reply.

Dan relayed it to Canton.

Canton nodded. His eyes narrowed. "Now ask him how Lupe likes her eggs cooked."

It was an odd request, but Dan passed it on. Seconds passed and suddenly the connection was cut.

"Ha!" Canton burst out with a satisfied smile.

"You sound just like him," Janine sighed dreamily.

He scowled. "Just like whom?"

She flushed. "Never mind."

Canton threw up his hands. "I am not an alien," he said. "Neither am I an actor!"

"Sorry," she said, wincing.

He glared at her. "Later, we have to talk." He turned back to Dan. "What did he want you to do?"

"He wanted me to crate up all the artifacts and drive them into town, to a government warehouse, he said."

"More likely into a trap," Canton replied angrily. "They must realize that we have this place staked out. They tried to trick you. It didn't work. They won't stop there."

"What will they do now?" Joan asked worriedly.

"I don't know" came the quiet reply. "But the first step would be to put a call through to the real minister of antiquities," he added. "And I can do that for you, right now."

He picked up the telephone and made a long-distance call to Mexico City and asked for the official by name when he was connected with the governmental offices.

There was a greeting and a rapid-fire exchange of greetings and questions. Janine heard the name Lupe mentioned.

"Lupe is the minister's wife," Joan translated. She chuckled as she listened to the conversation. "And she doesn't eat eggs—she's allergic to them."

Another question and a pause and still another, then a quick thank you and Canton hung up.

"He's sending some men right down," Canton said. "And they'll not only have proper identification, they'll have guns. If the pothunter has tapped into this telephone line, he got an earful."

Janine listened interestedly, and then suddenly realized that they'd left Karie and Kurt on the beach and weren't watching them.

She turned and ran out onto the balcony, scanned the beach, and her heart stopped. The kids were nowhere in sight. There was a long, odd mound of sand where they'd been, but no kids.

"They're gone!" she cried.

Canton and Dan were halfway out the door before she finished, leaving her to follow and Joan to stay behind and watch the crate.

They took the stairs to the ground floor instead of the elevator and ran toward the beach, automatically splitting up as they reached the back of the hotel. Dan went one way, Canton and Janine the other.

A loud cry alerted them. It came from the shadowy confines of the unoccupied wooden scuba rental station.

Two men had Karie and Kurt and two others were rushing toward them. One had a gun.

"Oh, my God, it's him!" Janine blurted out when she got a good look at the man with the gun. "It's the kidnapper and his cohorts!"

"That's Perez, the pothunter, who has Kurt," Dan Curtis said furiously. "For God's sake, they've joined forces," he groaned. His voice carried as he glared toward them. "Let go of those kids, you slimy cowards!" he raged at the men.

The two men holding Karie and Kurt moved out into the sunlight, the man with the exposed pistol by their side. Janine sank a little lower into the sand, thinking. She didn't dare rush the man with the gun, but if there was any opening at all she was going to take it.

"Don't," Canton said under his breath as he saw her tense and sensed what she was thinking. "For God's sake, you have to trust me, this once. I have an ace in the hole. Give me a chance to play it!"

Dan, standing beside his daughter, didn't understand. Neither did Janine. But Canton's deep voice held such conviction, such certainty, that they hesitated. He wouldn't risk Karie. He must have a trade in mind, a bargain of some sort. Wheeling and dealing was his stock in trade. If there was an angle, he'd know it.

Janine waited with bated breath, hardly daring to look at the frightened faces of the children as they were held securely by the two men.

"We want the Mayan treasure, Señor Curtis," the man, Perez, demanded. "We want it now. If you give it to us, we will let the children go. Otherwise, we will take them with us until you comply with our... request."

"Joined forces, have you?" Canton drawled. "How convenient."

"There is an advantage in superior numbers," Perez said smoothly. "I required assistance and these men only want to be paid off. They have no further wish to work for Señor Rourke's former wife, who has not even paid them for their services to date."

"Typical of Marie," Canton replied. "They should have known better. And so should you. You crossed the line this time. And you'll pay with a very long prison sentence."

"We have the gun, *señor*," Perez said with a mocking smile.

"Do you really?" Canton nodded toward the familiar tall, dark man with the gun, who turned with an action so smooth and quick that Janine barely saw him move as he freed Karie and Kurt from the grasps of their captors, leaving both men groaning and shivering on the sand. Perez backed away with his hands in a supplicating position. The gun was trained on him now, and the attacker hardly looked mussed.

Janine's gasp was audible as Dan held out his arms to Kurt and Canton did the same to a frightened, weeping Karie.

"For scaring the children so, I really should finish them off," the tall, dark man said without expression as he looked from Perez to the still writhing men on the ground. The pistol hadn't wavered once. Perez swallowed audibly.

"It is a misunderstanding," he faltered.

"Yours," the dark man agreed. His eyes cut back to Canton. "Well?"

"The Mexican authorities can deal with them," Canton said coldly. "And the more harshly, the better. Kidnapping is a cowardly act. If he'd hurt my daughter, I'd have killed him."

"I was close by," the dark man replied. "And so was my colleague." He waved to a man down the beach, who turned and went away. "There was never a minute when the children were in any real danger, I assure you." His black eyes slid over Perez's pale face. "I could have dropped him at any time."

"I think he realizes that. Thanks for your help, Rodrigo."

He shrugged. "*De nada.* I owed you a favor." He nodded, motioning for Perez and the other two men, who were on their feet if shaken, to go ahead of him.

"But he pushed me off the boat," Janine said insistently. "Didn't you hear what I told you about him?"

"He infiltrated the kidnapping gang," Canton told her. "I didn't dare tell you who he was. One slip could have cost him his life. Not that he's ever been shy about risking it for a good cause," he added. He looked down at Karie. "Are you okay, pumpkin?"

"Yes, Dad. *Wasn't it exciting?*" she burst out.

"It sure was! He had a gun, too! Where's Mom?" Kurt added, looking around. "I've got to go tell her!"

"Make her sit down first," Dan called.

Karie took off with him, and Janine wondered all over again at the resilience of the very young. She just shook her head.

"No wonder he was always hanging around," she said. "I should have my detective's license pulled for being so blind."

"He's good at his job."

"Tell me about it." She glanced at him. "Is he CIA?"

He smiled. "I don't know. I told you, I've never been clear about the agency he works for. When I knew him, he, like Laremos and the others, was a mercenary. He was with them in Africa."

She pursed her lips. "A book is forming in my mind…" she began.

"Have Señor Perez eaten by giant alligators," Dan suggested to her. "On second thought, quicksand is a nice touch."

"Prison sounds much better, don't you think?" she countered. "Don't worry, I'll take care of that little detail." She looked up at Canton. "Will she try again?" she asked worriedly.

"Who, Marie?" He shrugged. "I doubt it. She's basically lazy, and when she realizes that she may be implicated in the gutter press in an international kidnapping story, that will probably be enough to stifle any future ambitions. She'll have to wait for her alimony."

"How can she get alimony when she's remarried?" Janine wanted to know.

"She calls it child support."

"You have the child," she said pointedly.

He chuckled. "True."

"You need a good attorney."

"I suppose so." He caught her hand warmly in his. "And a minister."

She smiled gently. "Oh, yes. And a minister."

Dan slipped away while they were staring at each other, thinking privately that they were going to be a good match. Canton and Janine had a lot in common, not the least of which was their penchant for surprises. He was overwhelmed that the pothunter was finally going to be out of circulation.

He went back into the hotel room to find a pale Joan being regaled with gory summations of the incident by the two children.

"Don't believe anything they told you," Dan told her comfortingly. "It's all lies."

"Aw, Dad," Kurt groaned. "We were building her up."

"Let her down," he suggested. "It's all over now."

"Or it will be," Joan said, sighing, "when the government official gets here to take the artifacts back to Mexico City."

"The guy that Janine attacked was a spy, and he was working for Karie's dad," Kurt told his mother. "You should have seen him deck those guys. Gosh, it was like watching that spy movie we just saw—"

"Except that it was real," Karie added. She glanced at her watch. "The game's already started," she groaned. "I won't even get to see if my team makes it to the World Series!"

"The airport will be back on schedule by tomorrow, I'm sure, and we can all go home," Dan Curtis said with relief. "I can't say I'll be sorry, this time."

"Nor I," Joan agreed. She hugged Kurt. "One way or another, it's been a hard few weeks. Where are the other two?" she asked suddenly, looking around.

"Down on the beach staring at each other."

"They'll get over that in about thirty years," Dan mused.

Joan grinned at him. "Think so? Then we have ten to go."

"At least."

CANTON WAS WALKING BACK toward the hotel with Janine's hand in his, but he looked preoccupied and aloof. She knew that something was worrying him, but she didn't know what.

"Are you absolutely sure that it isn't my resemblance to your science fiction hero that made you agree to marry me?" he asked.

So that was it. She was relieved. Her fingers curled into his big ones. "Yes, I'm sure," she told him. "I've already said so."

"So you have. But you keep coming up with these little comparisons. It's worrying."

"I'm sorry," she said genuinely, stopping to look up at him. "I won't do it again."

He sighed, searching her eyes quietly. "I've been thinking about getting married."

She could see it coming, as if she sensed a hesitation in him. "You don't want to?"

His eyes were troubled. "I want to. But not yet."

Her heart felt as if it were breaking. She smiled in spite of it. "Okay."

"Just like that?"

"Never let it be said that I trapped a man into marriage," she said airily, turning her pained eyes away, so that he couldn't see them. "I've got a deadline that I have to meet right now, so it would be more convenient for me, too, if we put our plans on the back burner and let them simmer for a while."

He shoved his hands into his pockets. "Then let's do that. I'll give you a call in a month or so and we'll see where we stand."

"Fine," she agreed.

They parted company at the front door, all the excitement over for the moment. Janine put on a brave face for her family all evening and then cried herself to sleep. The one kind thing was that nobody had asked any questions. She couldn't know that her pinched, white face told them all they needed to know. The next day, the government official arrived and took charge of the artifacts. Shortly thereafter, the Curtises boarded a plane for Indiana and Janine flew to Chicago. Canton and Karie had elected to stay another few days in Cancún, so they'd said their goodbyes at the beach house. It had wounded Janine that Canton didn't even shake hands. He smiled very pleasantly and wished them a good trip home, promising to be in touch. And that was it.

IT TURNED OUT NOT to be one month, but two, before she heard from Canton again. In that length of time, the Atlanta Braves won the World Series in an incredible game that went all the way to the eighth inning with no score until a home run by the Braves ended the deadlock. The other team couldn't catch up, although they tried valiantly. Kurt had a call from an almost hysterically happy Karie, who sent him a Braves cap and a World Series victory T-shirt by overnight mail. From Canton, there was no word. Even Karie didn't mention him in her telephone call. Apparently her mother had stopped pursuing either her or her father, and that was good news.

Janine, meanwhile, finished her book and started on a new one, set in Cancún. She went back to watching her favorite television program, groaning at the continued absence of her alien villain until news of his reappearance surfaced through the Internet fan club to give her a reason for celebration. She watched him in one rerun and on tape, and it occurred to her that even though he resembled Canton, the resemblance wasn't strong enough to account for her ongoing attraction to the missing tycoon. She wondered what he was doing and where he was. His movements lately seemed a mystery to everyone, including the media, which was now joyfully following him again.

The only tidbit of news came through a tabloid, which pictured him with a ravishing brunette at some elegant party. She was looking up at him with bright eyes, and he was smiling down at her. So much for hope, Janine thought as she shredded the picture in the paper and smushed it into the trash can. The heartless philanderer!

She went back to work with a sore heart, not even roused by the forthcoming holiday season. Christmas decorations were up now in Chicago, the television

schedule was scattered with reruns of regular programs
and holiday specials. Janine worked right through them.

Her parents and Kurt had put up a Christmas tree.
Quentin called to say hello and mentioned that he was
having the occasional date with the English major he'd
met on his trip. He spoke of her with such warmth that
Janine was certain that education was not the only
thing the two of them discussed. She was happy for
him. She and Quentin could never have lived together.

"Hey, isn't this one for the books!" Kurt exclaimed.
"Take a look!"

He handed Janine a financial magazine. Inside there
was a story about a successful merger of a software company with a hardware computer firm, and there was a
photo of Canton Rourke shaking hands with a well-
known Texan who owned a line of expensive computers.

"They say he'll make back every penny he's lost, and
more," Kurt read. He glanced wickedly at Janine. "I
told you he would."

She looked away. "So you did. More power to him."

"Doesn't it matter to you?"

She turned back with a poker face. "Why should it?"
she asked. "He hasn't even phoned in two months. I'm
sure he wrote me off as a holiday flirtation, and why
not? He can have the most beautiful women in the
world. What would he want with me?"

Kurt was taken aback. Janine was a dish. She didn't
seem aware of it, but Kurt was certain that Canton
Rourke had found her irresistible. Karie had said as
much, when they were in Cancún. Of course, Janine was
right, he hadn't even called since their return to Chic-

ago. That really was too bad. He'd have thought they were made for each other.

He wanted to say something to comfort her, but Janine was already buried in her book again. With a sigh, he went on about his business.

Idly he wondered what Karie had done with the photographs they'd taken in Cancún. Every day, he'd expected to hear something momentous from her about them. She had contacts, she'd said, and she was bound to find someone who'd be ecstatic about them. But to date, he hadn't heard a word. Perhaps she'd given up on the idea in the fervor of having the Braves win the pennant. Or maybe her dad had gotten wind of their secret project and confiscated the photos. Either way, he thought he'd heard the last of it….

TWO DAYS LATER, a tabloid's front page showed a "sea monster" washed up on the beach at Cancún, of all places! It had fur and feathers and gruesome green skin. Its skull resembled most closely that of a bovine. Scientists said it was a new form of life.

Kurt bought three copies and ran back from the corner newsstand to the house he shared with his parents. Janine was visiting over the weekend. Kurt waved the headline under Janine's nose, disrupting one of her best new scenes on her laptop computer. "Look!" he exclaimed. "Just look! It was found right on the beach where we were!"

She looked at the creature with a frown. Something was nagging at the back of her mind when she saw the blown-up photo of the "creature."

Before she could really have time to think about it, there was a knock at the front door.

"See who that is while I save my file, could you?" she asked Kurt, putting the tabloid aside. "Look through the peephole first."

"I remember." He went to the door, peered out and suddenly opened it with a laugh. "Hello!" he greeted.

Canton Rourke smiled at him. Karie was with him, grinning from ear to ear in her Braves cap and shirt.

"Where's Janine?" Canton asked.

"In Dad's study," he said. "Right through there."

Canton's deep voice had already announced his presence, but Janine felt a jolt somewhere near her heart when she saw him. Two months was so long, she thought. She'd missed him unbearably. Her eyes told him that for her, nothing had changed. She felt the same.

He didn't seem to need words. He smiled tenderly and held out his arms. She got up quickly and ran right into them and lifted her face for a kiss that seemed to have no end at all.

Hectic seconds later, she pressed close, trembling.

"No need to ask if you missed me," he said huskily. "We can get a license in three days, or we can fly down to Mexico and be married in one. Your choice."

"Here," she said immediately. "So that my parents and Kurt can come."

He nodded. "I'd like that, too. I don't have many friends, but the ones I have are the best in the world."

"Mine, too." She reached up and touched his lean cheek. "You look worn."

"I am. It's been a hectic two months. I have my financing and my merger, and Marie is now history."

"What?"

"I flew to Greece with my attorney and had it out with her about Karie," he explained. "Kidnapping is a very serious offense. If I pushed it, the Mexican authorities might find a way to extradite her for trial. She knew it, too. She capitulated without a groan and was willing to settle for what I offered her. She'll have visiting rights, but just between us, I don't think she'll be using them. Karie isn't thrilled at the idea of visiting her at all."

"I remember." She searched his face. "You couldn't have called once?"

He smiled ruefully. "I wanted to be sure you knew who I was."

"I already did," she assured him. "The more I watch the series, the more differences I find between you and my screen hero. I still think he's tops. But I love you," she added shyly, dropping her eyes.

He took a slow breath. "And I love you. Never like this," he added huskily, his eyes brilliant. "Never in my life."

"Me, neither," she agreed breathlessly.

He kissed her again, hungrily, only pausing for breath when young voices came closer.

"Don't tell me," Kurt said dryly when he saw the two of them standing in each other's arms. "The marriage is on again, right?"

"Right," Janine said dreamily.

"Whoopee!" Karie enthused. "Now maybe you'll stop being so grouchy, Dad."

He glared at her.

"Same for you, Janine," Kurt agreed with a grin.

Canton glanced from the children's smug faces to Janine's. "Have you seen the tabloid this week?" he asked, naming one of the biggest ones.

"Yes. Kurt showed it to me," she explained. "It had a sea creature that had washed up on a Mexican beach."

"You didn't recognize it?" He reached into his pocket and unfolded the front page of one, that he'd been carrying around with him. Kurt and Karie looked suddenly restless.

Janine stared at the color photo with a frown. "Well, I thought it was rather familiar…"

"The cow skull?" he prompted. "The hacked-up garden hose? The feathers? The fur?"

She gasped and looked at Kurt with wide eyes. "It can't be!"

Karie cleared her throat. "Now, Dad," she began when his eyes narrowed.

"We covered it up the minute we took the photo," Kurt said helpfully. "The tide would have washed it all out to sea, we made sure of it."

"Why?" he demanded.

Karie pursed her lips, glanced at Kurt and produced a check. "Well, this is why," she explained.

He unfolded the check, made out to his daughter, and almost choked. "You're kidding."

She shook her head. "I wasn't sure you were going to make back all that money you lost," she said. "So I hit on this keen idea. I have to split it with Kurt, of course, but it should get me through college. Gosh, it should get us both through college!"

He was torn between being touched and committing homicide. "This is a hoax! It's all going back, and there will be a retraction printed."

"And I told them so in my letter," she assured him. "I kept a copy of it. They said it didn't matter, it was a super hoax." She put her hand on her hip and struck a pose. "Get real, Dad, do you honestly think Elvis is living on Mars, like they said last week?"

She sounded so old and sophisticated that both of the adults broke up, though Canton was still determined to set things right.

"She's your daughter," Janine said through tears of laughter.

"And yours," he reminded her, "as soon as the ring is on your finger."

"Lucky you," Karie said with an irrepressible grin.

"Lucky me," Kurt agreed. "Just think of all the wonderful times we're going to have together."

Canton and Janine looked at the picture in the tabloid, and then at the children.

"Private schools," Canton said.

"In different states," Janine agreed.

The kids only looked at one another with knowing smiles. Canton took Janine by the hand and led her out of the room, into the office and closed the door behind them.

"Now," he murmured as he took her in his arms. "I believe we were discussing our forthcoming marriage? I think I stopped just about…here."

He bent and kissed her with slow, steady warmth, and she smiled with pure joy under his mouth. And it was no mystery at all that he loved her. Or vice versa.

If you enjoyed what you just read,
then we've got an offer you can't resist!

Take 2 bestselling love stories FREE!
Plus get a FREE surprise gift!

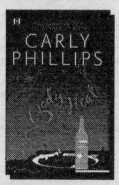